LIES

the

MUSHROOM
PICKERS
TOLD

Also by Tom Phelan

In the Season of the Daisies
Iscariot
Derrycloney
The Canal Bridge
Nailer

LIES
the
MUSHROOM
PICKERS
TOLD

a novel

TOM PHELAN

Arcade Publishing • New York

First Edition

This is a work of fiction. Names, places, characters, and incidents are either the products of the author's imagination or are used fictitiously.

Arcade Publishing books may be purchased in bulk at special discounts for sales promotion, corporate gifts, fund-raising, or educational purposes. Special editions can also be created to specifications. For details, contact the Special Sales Department, Arcade Publishing, 307 West 36th Street, 11th Floor, New York, NY 10018 or arcade@ skyhorsepublishing.com.

Arcade Publishing® is a registered trademark of Skyhorse Publishing, Inc.®, a Delaware corporation.

Visit our website at www.arcadepub.com.
Visit the author's website at www.tomphelan.net.

10 9 8 7 6 5 4 3 2 1

Library of Congress Cataloging-in-Publication Data

Phelan, Tom, 1940–
  Lies the mushroom pickers told : a novel / Tom Phelan. — First edition.
     pages ; cm
  ISBN 978-1-62872-428-8 (hardcover)
  1. Cold cases (Criminal investigation)—Fiction. 2. Murder—Investigation—Fiction. 3. Ireland—Fiction. I. Title.
  PR6066.H37L54 2015
  823'.914—dc23   2014038866

Cover design by Brian Peterson
Cover art: *Turning Back 2*, 2005, by Keith Wilson

Ebook ISBN: 978-1-62872-470-7

Printed in the United States of America

*To Patricia and Joseph and Mica
with love*

*In memory of
my elementary school teacher E. J. Breen*

Contents

Author's Note

For readers unfamiliar with the Irish vernacular, a glossary appears at the back of the book on page 313.

Cast of Characters

Annie Lamb: farmer's wife; wife of Simon Peter, mother of Mikey, Molly and Fintan

Bridie Coughlin: farmer, Eddie's and Jarlath's sister

David Samuel "Sam" Howard: retired solicitor, husband of Elsie

Deirdre Hyland: a civil servant, object of the Civil Servant's desire

Eddie "Eddie-the-cap" Coughlin: farmer, Bridie's and Jarlath's brother

Elsie "Else" Howard: wife of Sam

Estelle Butler: best friend of Peggy Mulhall

Fintan Lamb: youngest child of Annie and Simon Peter

Jarlath Coughlin: missionary priest, brother of Bridie and Eddie

Joseph Aloysius Morrissey: garda sergeant

Kevin "the Civil Servant" Lalor: son of Pascal Lalor

Lawrence "Doul Yank" Gorman: aspiring gentleman farmer, uncle of Mattie Mulhall

Mattie "Matt-the-thatcher" Mulhall: nephew of Doul Yank

Mikey Lamb: oldest child of Annie and Simon Peter

Molly Lamb: middle child of Annie and Simon Peter

Pascal Lalor: postman, father of Kevin

Patrick "Barlow" Bracken: newspaper correspondent

Peggy Mulhall: homemaker, Mattie's wife

Simon Peter Lamb: farmer; husband of Annie, father of Mikey, Molly and Fintan

"The Martyr" Madden: laborer for Bridie and Eddie Coughlin

LIES

the

MUSHROOM
PICKERS
TOLD

1

Waiting to Be Let In

In which Patrick Bracken, a sixty-six-year-old retired newspaper reporter from Muker in Yorkshire, visits a lawyer in the Irish village of Gohen where he spent part of his childhood.

To EVERYONE WATCHING—and Patrick Bracken knew that many eyes were on him—the man standing at the edge of the broad footpath looking at the entrance to Mister Howard's house was spare and tall. All the curious watchers knew that Mister Howard was a solicitor, and they knew that the stranger was one, too, because he was dressed in a fawn camel hair overcoat, a brown trilby hat and gleaming brown shoes. He was wearing brown gloves. But Patrick Bracken was not a solicitor.

Black iron handrails set into four limestone steps led up to Mister Howard's house. Although Patrick Bracken had passed the doorway thousands of times in his younger life, he had never admired it before. The door was a showcase for the polished brass letterbox, knob, keyhole and lion's head knocker. As he stepped forward he saw the Masonic square and compasses carved into the keystone of the limestone arch framing the door.

While he waited for an answer to his clattering of the lion's nose ring, Bracken turned and surveyed the street. Many things had changed in fifty-five years: the drab, gray, cracked pavement where the farmers once rested the shafts of their piglet carts on fair days had been replaced with red bricks set in geometric designs; the house from whence the parish priest had reigned was now a hardware shop with green-headed rakes and red metal wheelbarrows displayed along its front wall; the once dignified Bank of Ireland building had been transmogrified into an electronics shop, its blaring advertisements flapping in the wind along its walls like loud, plastic shopping bags trapped in windy trees; Gormans' Pub—renamed "1014" and with a fake thatched roof, plastic battle-axes and horned Norse war helmets—might have been purposefully aged to replicate a shebeen. The Irish flag displayed high on the wall of John Conroy's drapery shop seemed to have faded, but then Patrick saw the new signage over the door: ENZO'S PIZZERIA; and where Tom Bennet's sweet shop used to be, a large golden dragon hung out over the footpath.

"Jesus! How did the Chinese find Gohen?"

Up and down the street, cars were parked willy-nilly, half up on the footpaths' red bricks. Near the cinema two tyrannous lorries, one loaded with new cars, the other piled high with bales of straw, were squeezing past each other. A short, black-haired man came out of Enzo's and, gesticulating wildly, assumed the role of traffic director.

The sixteenth-century town had been overrun in this early year of the twenty-first, its narrow streets defeating the traffic. But with more Continental money, the town would soon have its own personal bypass, an amulet of cement magically returning Gohen to the natives.

Without Patrick hearing it, the black door behind him swung open on its silent hinges. "Mister Bracken, I presume," a self-possessed voice asked, and as Patrick turned he removed his hat at the same time. His thick gray hair, parted on the left side, touched the tips of his ears.

"Yes, Patrick Bracken."

She had shrunk with age, but even a half century later, Bracken could have picked out her face on a crowded London sidewalk.

"Missus Howard," he said. "I hope you are keeping well."

The years had transformed her, but the underlying foundation that had once made her the rival of a certain Protestant minister's wife was still there. She could have been a young woman disguised as an older one. Patrick saw she was still wearing the ivory cameo at her throat, a girl-child with ringlets in profile.

"Even after fifty-five years," Patrick thought.

"The mind is quick but the body is slow," Missus Howard said. "Better that than the other way around. You are very welcome, Mister Bracken. Step inside so I can shake your hand. It's unfriendly to shake hands over a doorstep."

Her fingers felt like bits of sticks in a glove, but her grasp was strong. "I didn't know your family, but Sam says your father did some work for him—puttied and painted windows."

"Yes, indeed. My father turned his hand to anything that would earn him a few pounds."

"Shillings, more likely. Those were bad times, the forties: war just over, the Depression still here and the country trying to struggle to its feet after the English left. . . . Give me your coat and hat, Mister Bracken." As he slipped off his coat, Missus Howard stepped behind him, took it and draped it across a hallway chair.

"Please call me Patrick. How is Mister Howard?"

"You can call me Else, for Elsie. . . . Sam is an old blackthorn on a hill—he can still stand up to gale-force winds. He'll last forever, become petrified like one of those old trees in America. He's out in the back in the sunroom. At our age we're like reptiles—need a bit of sun to get the body moving."

She turned and Bracken followed her. As he walked through the old house, Patrick realized that the shellacked front door with its brilliant brass was an extension of a fastidiously maintained interior. The walls were hung with engravings of classical Roman scenes, and as he passed an open door he saw polished black furniture, a black, iron fireplace with a clock and vases on its mantel, ancient family portraits and an embroidered fire screen within a brass-railed fender.

The kitchen was a surprise with its brightness, Formica counters, hanging cabinets and modern appliances. Bracken felt he had stepped through half a century in the blink of an eye. "Gosh," he said.

"What's that, Patrick?" Missus Howard asked.

"Your kitchen . . . it's so bright and airy."

"Yes, it is nice, isn't it? It's a strong contrast to the rest of the house. I wish my mother had had the same one—the labor it would have saved her. Sam made me have it installed." She depressed the button on the electric kettle as she walked by.

Bracken followed Else into the sunroom where several pots of soft-fronded ferns hung from the ceiling. Mister Howard was levering himself out of a cushioned wicker chair. He had shrunk too, his head as bald and freckled as a turkey's egg. He wore an open-necked, dark green shirt and an Aran cardigan with imitation chestnut buttons. Holding out his hand, Mister Howard said, "Don't believe her, Mister Bracken. I never made that woman do anything in my life, even though she promised to obey me when we got married."

"Hah," Else said, dismissively. "And you can call him Patrick, and he can call you Sam."

"You are very welcome, Patrick," the old man said. "I remember your father well. . . . Ned, wasn't it?"

"Yes indeed, it was Ned. My mother called him Edward when she was being tender toward him."

"Here it's usually the other way around. Else calls me David Samuel when she's impatient with me. The rest of the time it's plain Sam. If she's trying to get on my good side, she calls me Sammy. When she calls me that, I know there's something coming, like planting bulbs or zapping a spraying cat in the garden with the pellet gun."

"Sam rattles like a pebble in a bucket sometimes," Else said. "There's the kettle singing. You're not to begin talking about anything important till I get back. I want to hear everything." She went back to the kitchen.

Mister Howard indicated a chair with its back to the window wall. "Sit, Patrick," he said, and he lowered himself to a soft landing onto the roses embroidered in high relief on the cushion in his own chair. Patrick now saw several plants on the floor in Roman urns cast in bronze-tinted plastic. In the six paintings on the walls, birds in bare-leafed, berried bushes displayed the art of the painter. On the wicker table next to Mister Howard lay a thick book, *The Raj* by Lawrence James, with the tip of a pewter bookmark showing it was about three-quarters read. On the other side of the table, beside Missus Howard's chair, sat a battered dictionary and a newspaper page folded open at a crossword puzzle, a biro clipped onto its crease. Beside the dictionary lay a red-covered book, but Patrick could not see its title. A lamp, its china base strewn with ceramic roses, sat in the table's center.

"Did your wife come over with you, Patrick?" Sam Howard asked.

"She did. We're visiting her brother's family, the Lambs, in Clunnyboe. We try to come every year, but sometimes life interferes with the plans."

"The best-laid plans . . ." Sam said. "How is Fintan Lamb? Still as busy as ever?"

"Fintan will die with his boots on. He's as fit as a snipe."

"Lamb!" Mister Howard said with a smile. "It's an amusing name for a vet."

"We call him the Lamb of God. His wife's name is Mary, and of course Mary has had a little Lamb many times. They can joke about it: they named their house Lamb's Quarters."

"After the weed," the older man said, smiling. "Names can be touchy things. It helps if you have a sense of humor if you're saddled with something awful. Have you heard about the man named Jack Shite who got tired of people laughing at him and changed his name by deed to Jim Shite?"

Bracken laughed not so much at the joke as at the incongruity of the vulgarity and his memory of David Samuel Howard as the proper and remote Protestant esquire of his childhood.

Missus Howard came into the room with a tray. "Tell the truth, Patrick. Had you heard that joke before?" Her husband moved the red book to make room on the table.

"I had," Bracken admitted.

"If I had a penny for every—"

"Oh, Else, a good joke can be enjoyed many times," Sam said.

Bracken could now see the spine of Missus Howard's book—*A Social History of Ancient Ireland,* Vol. 2 by P. W. Joyce—and he knew that even if their bodies were old, he was talking with two cerebral gymnasts.

As the tea and biscuits were dispensed, more small talk revealed that Patrick Bracken was presently living in Muker in the Yorkshire Dales.

"Famous for the Farmers Arms and the Literary Institute," he said, with a facetious smile.

"Surely the Yorkshire Dales are far off the beaten path for a reporter?" Missus Howard asked.

"Old reporters become special correspondents, and that's what I am now, Missus Howard . . . Elsie. I'm sixty-six, and reporting is for young lads who can run. Computers and the Internet allow me to do most of my work from home."

"We see your pieces in the *Irish Times* every so often," Elsie said. "We always keep an eye out for them."

As everyone sipped their tea, silence momentarily descended, and Patrick decided now was the time to get down to business.

"I want to thank you for agreeing to talk to me about—"

"*Listen* is the word, Patrick," Mister Howard said. "First I will listen, and then I will decide if I will talk." Bracken noticed a slight shake in Sam's hands.

"Oh, for God's sake, Sam, stop your word splitting," Else said. "You're worse than a Jesuit." She turned to Patrick. "Sam takes the seal of confession more seriously than the pope. I've heard stuff at funerals and weddings and in shops years ago that Sam still won't talk about because he heard it as privileged information."

"I understand about privileged information, Mister . . . Sam," Patrick said, "but all I may need is your recollection of what was said at the inquest. I tried to get a copy of the inquest in Portlaoise but—"

"You spoke to Harrigan—Alphonsus A., Esquire?" Elsie interrupted, and Patrick nodded. "And he told you it wouldn't be fair to the Coughlin family even though inquests are public affairs. He's worse than Saint Peter stopping people at the Pearly Gates for gossiping. All the Coughlins are dead. Alphonsus A. Harrigan, Esquire, is as tight as a crab's backside. . . . He's as bad as Sam."

"Clam," Sam said, completely unruffled.

"What?" she asked.

"It's a clam," he said, and impatiently waved his own words into significance.

"What's a clam?" she persisted.

"The saying is, as tight as a clam's arse, not a crab's. And please let me get a word in edgeways, Else." Sam looked at Patrick. "You said in your letter that this enquiry of yours is a personal thing, that you've no intention of writing about it. Even so, I am wary of you as a reporter. I'm eighty-nine, and you're what? Mid-sixties? You'll outlive—"

"Sam," Bracken interrupted, "I take the seal of confession as seriously as you. I've made many promises about secrecy, and I've never broken one. Many of my sources have died, and I have never betrayed them. I will not betray you. As you said, this is purely personal."

"It's no secret that you've been digging into this thing in Gohen and Clunnyboe and Drumsally for several years. I suspected you would eventually come here to our house. But why is it so important to you? We're talking about something that happened, what? Fifty-five years ago, for Christ's sake."

"As a child I did not realize there were contradictions in what I saw and heard about the deaths of Father Coughlin and Lawrence Gorman, things that were never spoken about by the adults. For my own satisfaction I want to know what really happened. And yes, over the years I have been collecting bits and pieces of the story. The people who were involved or who know the details are dying off and—"

"And that's why you're here now, Patrick," Else said. "You're afraid Sam and I will fall off the perch soon." She was smiling.

"Sam is the only one left who—"

"I had my own part to play in the drama," Elsie said, determined not to be sidelined.

"Else, for God's sake! You had nothing to do with anything," her husband growled.

"I did, too, Sam. For one thing, I spilled tea on Deirdre Hyland's skirt."

"Be serious, Else. The man doesn't want to hear your asides."

Elsie was not intimidated. "Patrick, I know as much as Sam, probably more."

Patrick tried to break up this back-and-forth. "When I spoke to the others, I promised I would not write about what I discovered. I told them that I simply wanted to find out what happened for my own satisfaction. I quickly realized that what I knew was only the glimpse of an outsider—and an outsider child at that. Of them all, Peggy Mulhall was the most suspicious. Before she told me anything, she accused me of trying to disassociate myself from my poor beginnings because I now call myself Patrick instead of Barlow."

"I didn't know you were called Barlow," Missus Howard said. "Why *did* you change your name?"

"My first editor thought Patrick was more dignified, that Bartholomew was archaic and Barlow undignified."

"He must have been an—"

"Else, can you hang on for one minute?" Mister Howard said. He turned to Patrick. "You must have some reason besides curiosity for dragging up the past about Coughlin and Gorman."

"I'm curious about how and why an entire village covered up the murder of two men."

Missus Howard clapped her hands and sat up straight. She was beaming. "Sam! Sam! I always told you." She looked at Bracken. "I always told him, Patrick. I always said it—the two of them *were* murdered. But Sam will only admit to the official finding that both deaths were accidental."

"You will stop this, Else. You are in the realm of gossip and calumny." Sam's voice was stern. "This is a very serious matter. The Coughlin inquest determined the priest's death was accidental, and Inspector Larkin from Dublin concluded that Doul Yank Gorman unintentionally killed himself."

"Sam. Sam," Patrick said, his hands out as if trying to calm the impatience that had crept into Sam's tone. "What about this approach: if I tell you everything I know, will you tell me everything you know?"

"No, I can't make a sweeping promise. But I will consider individual questions you may have."

"Oh, for God's sake, Sam," Else said, and she shifted in her chair like a fussy hatching hen. She addressed Patrick. "I know as much as he does about the two deaths. I'll fill in the gaps for you."

"But only if it is not privileged information," her husband reminded her.

"David Samuel Howard! You have *never* shared privileged information with me. My information comes from the grapevine."

"*Gossip*, Else."

"You call it gossip when *I* hear something on the grapevine." She turned to Patrick again. "What Sam hears on the grapevine he calls community news."

"It's a matter of discernment."

"You're saying again that I'm gullible."

"No, Else. I simply believe that I have had more training and experience at weeding the fiction out of what is presented as fact."

"God! The delusions of the man!"

"But she loves me, Patrick, and I love her," Mister Howard said. "We've had a good life together. We were lucky."

"People make their own luck," Patrick said by way of compliment.

The three of them sat in silence for a few moments to absorb the little pleasantnesses. Then Patrick said, "All right! Should I start?"

"Go ahead," Sam said. "And Else . . ."

"I know, Sam. I know. You don't have to say it."

Patrick began. "Mikey Lamb—"

Elsie immediately interrupted. "That young man who died in Amsterdam? How many years ago was it?"

"Yes, that was Mikey. Thirty-two years ago, and he was thirty-four when he died."

"He was murdered, wasn't he? Was anyone ever caught for that?"

"Mikey Lamb?" Mister Howard asked. "Oh, of course. He was your wife's brother."

"The family believes Mikey worked for the C.I.A."

"The Americans?" Elsie said, as distastefully as if she were talking about tapeworm.

"Yes. He was good with languages and was probably recruited in Trinity. He was tortured and shot in the heart and thrown in a canal."

"Jesus Christ tonight!" Sam whispered.

"I'm sorry, Patrick," Else said. "That must have been terrible on everyone."

"It was. The family didn't tell anyone about the torture or the shooting. They let everyone believe he'd been robbed and drowned. Anyhow . . ." The Howards' eyes wandered out into the garden.

"How terribly sad," Sam eventually said.

Patrick sighed, expelling the painful memories. Then he broke the somber mood. "Mikey Lamb and I became friends when we were eleven, and only for him I would not have known anything about the Coughlin and Gorman deaths, nor would I have married Molly. The Lambs lived in Clunnyboe and the father's name was Simon Peter, and like all . . ."

2

The Birthday Present

1951

In which eleven-year-old Mikey Lamb, eldest son
of Simon Peter and Annie Lamb, is disappointed
in the birthday present he receives from his aunt
in England.

L IKE ALL THE FARMERS in Clunnyboe, Simon Peter Lamb worked six
days a week, from seven in the morning to evening's last light.
On Sundays he only worked four hours. Every year he ran up bills
in the shops in Gohen, and even though he settled some accounts
when he sold an animal on a fair day or his barley at harvesttime, he
was never out of debt. His animals seldom brought in top price, and
his barley was never of the superior quality to interest the Guinness
buyers. It was Simon Peter's belief that good fortune only happened
to other people.

Simon Peter Lamb was secure in his belief that, if he accepted
his lot in this life without whining, he would be rewarded in the next
life. He wallowed in his many miseries, miseries he saw as trials sent
by a testing God. To enumerate these divine whims in a list inures
the mind to their immediacy and their irritancy; the quality of the
miseries is appreciated all the better when savored one at a time.

Simon Peter existed in a perpetual state of unkemptness, looking
as if he had just climbed out of a boghole. Every day since he was a

child, the bodily waste of some farm animal had stuck to his clothing and his boots. On most days his feet were wet, the wetness seeping in from the water lying in his fields or running down the legs of his trousers into his footwear when it rained. Sometimes, the water from a urinating animal splashed warmly over his boots' hard leather rims.

Simon Peter Lamb smelled more like the back end of cow than a newborn calf, more like stinkweed than roses. But the only person in the townland of Clunnyboe who appreciated Simon Peter's odors was the Civil Servant—Kevin Lalor—the one person in Clunnyboe who not only washed himself every day, but who put on a clean shirt and clean socks every Monday morning.

When his oldest son was born, Simon Peter Lamb insisted that the boy be named Simon Peter. To distinguish between the two, Missus Lamb had taken to calling the baby Mikey.

By the age of eleven, Mikey Lamb had begun to molt out of the cuteness of childhood and had taken his first steps into the disconnectedness of adolescence. There were times when he looked like a disheveled chicken. His hair was black spikes sticking up like metal shavings on a magnet, and his nose was growing faster than the rest of his face. The legs of his knee-length trousers hung unevenly, and one of his gartered knee stockings was often crumpled at an ankle. Always, as if he were wearing the family coat of arms, some kind of animal dung clung to his boots. From the bottom of his nostrils to his right ear there was evidence that when Mikey had a runny nose he used his sleeve instead of a handkerchief. When he became excited he passed a gas which pierced surprised nostrils like needles dipped in rotten eggs. Dirt was so embedded in his hands and knees that it would take caustic soap, scalding water and a wire brush to remove it.

Mikey Lamb was a sitting duck for every boy in the National School in Gohen. But he never complained to his parents, and he always had an excuse when his bruises were obvious. If Mikey himself wasn't attacked, it was his bike that bore the brunt of hard boots. The sound of a wheel rubbing against a dented mudguard often accompanied him home along the road over the Esker into Drumsally and down into Clunnyboe.

On the day of his eleventh birthday, Mikey came home from school with Indian-torture burns smarting on each of his wrists, but his expectation of a package from England took the edge off the pain. And when he ran into the kitchen after putting his bike away, the package was on the kitchen table.

"Maybe there's English comics," he thought, seeing himself in the schoolyard, the envy of all the Townies. *Valiant, The Hotspur, Eagle.* He farted. *Commando, Victor.* And because he was hoping for comics, he would have been disappointed if the parcel contained a thousand pounds sterling.

"Will you stop wondering what's in it and open it?" Annie, his mother, said. She was curious to see what her daft sister in Leeds had sent this time. Last year it had been a rubber duck for a bathtub, and the sister knowing damn well there wasn't one bathtub in all of Clunnyboe. Another time she had sent the makings of a kite with no instructions. The Lambs had asked the Civil Servant for help, but even he couldn't figure it out. For two months everyone tripped over the pieces of kite until Simon Peter angrily threw them into the fire one morning after discovering a weasel had killed six hens during the night. "I wouldn't mind so much if he et the hens. But he just cut their necks for the blood. Bastard!"

Careful not to damage the stamps, which Molly would bring into the nuns for the African missions, Mikey cut off the wrapping. Inside was a box. He took off the lid, and he saw a layer of tissue paper. When he took out the paper, he didn't know what he was looking at, but he knew it wasn't comics.

"What is it?" Annie demanded from the high, open fireplace, where she stood stirring a pot of calfshare. The heat and steam had unfurled her hair, and she pushed an annoying tress off her face.

"It's a yoke."

"What kind of a yoke? Bring it over here so I can keep an eye on the calfshare."

Mikey carried the box to the fireplace.

"Hold it in the light of the chimney," his mother said. Without missing a stroke with her stirring stick, she leaned over and looked into the box. "It's a brass yoke," she said, "a bit of a shiny brass. What will that aunt of yours think of next?"

"How can I play with it?"

"I don't know. Take it out and give us a look at it."

Mikey brought the box back to the table. He took out the birthday gift and examined it, turned it around several times.

"Well?" his mother asked. She pushed a strand of black hair out of her mouth.

"It's just a bit of a pipe with a bit of glass in one end."

"Well, isn't that one a terrible cod," the mother said to herself, and she thought of her sister Maggie living in her house in Leeds, a house with a stairs, no less. To Annie Lamb there was something secret and exciting at the top of a stairs. Things went on in the upstairs rooms that the children in the downstairs rooms couldn't hear—running around with no clothes on, sinful things that Protestants in England did. The English were terrible pagans.

"There's a lump of glass at the other end, too," Mikey said.

"A bit of brass with a bit of glass at each end," Annie Lamb said. "Look inside, Mikey. Maybe there's sweets or something."

The boy held the brass up to one eye and scrunched the other shut; his top lip, pulled into a snarl, exposed his teeth. "There's nothing," he said.

"Look at the other end."

Mikey turned the present around. "There's nothing."

"Well!" Annie declared, and with that one word she expressed her annoyance at that Maggie. She thought of the two-storied, red-bricked house in Leeds with a fireplace in every room and a flushing lavatory outside the back door, and the sinful savages running around naked upstairs. No matter how careful they were, Irish Catholic emigrants in England were always in danger of losing their souls, what with black Protestants around them the whole time. Annie Lamb stirred the calfshare with a new vigor. It would have been as good if Maggie had sent nothing, she thought.

"Well, birthday or no birthday," Annie finally said to her son, "you'll have to change your clothes and do your jobs, and then we'll have the lemonade and the biscuits and sweet cake in the parlor. Put that yoke away before Molly comes home from school or Fintan wakes up. If you see the Civil Servant going by, you might show it to him. Maybe he'll know what it is."

3

The Gift from Leeds

1951

In which Kevin Lalor, the Civil Servant, admires Mikey Lamb's birthday present and they both discover what distant neighbors are doing in their garden.

Two hours after opening his birthday present, Mikey Lamb was standing in the fresh weeds growing between the gable end of the thatched barn and the edge of the lane. He had done all his jobs. Besides bedding the animals with straw, he had pulped six baskets of turnips in the Mash House. After mixing a scoopful of beet pulp and a handful of bonemeal in the bottoms of eleven buckets, he filled them off with the sliced turnips and carried them to the cattle's troughs. Lastly, he filled the plywood tea chest in the kitchen with two baskets of turf. It was now the precious time between the last job done and his father's arrival in the farmyard from the fields when more orders would have to be carried out. He should have been doing his homework.

With his back against the whitewashed mud wall, Mikey waited for the Civil Servant to come by on his way home from work in Gohen. Mikey regarded the Civil Servant as a tender version of his father. People said about the Civil Servant, "That lad has a great job," "That lad's terrible brainy," "That lad's terrible lucky," "That lad's so clean he must be always washing himself," "I'd feel quare being as clean as the Civil Servant."

In the clump of knee-high weeds Mikey used his fingers in his pockets to count the number of days left until the first of May. "Bastille Day," his father called it. That was the day the cattle were driven to the fields for the summer after their long sequester in the sheds. In thirteen days' time Mikey would be freed from the winter drudgery. The anticipated joy of being released from the farmyard work left no room in Mikey's head for the grind of summer in the fields that would ineluctably replace the grind of winter. At least during the summer the yard would not have to be swept as often with the heavy yard brush; what the two cows casually dropped in the farmyard as they came and went at milking time dried up quicker in the sunshine.

When he saw Kevin Lalor coming in the distance, the boy stepped out into the middle of the lane. Lalor had no choice but to slow down and throw his leg over the saddle of his bike.

Mikey's father once said that when Kevin Lalor was being born he was pulled out of his mother so quickly that he'd been made unnaturally long and had never regained his proper shape. Everyone in Clunnyboe repeated this story to show how daft Simon Peter Lamb was and how smart they were.

Beside his bike, Lalor was asymmetrically long and lean. There always seemed to be too many knees and elbows in his immediate vicinity. He wore a peaked cap, a brown tie on his white shirt and a brown suit under his khaki gabardine overcoat. Without a word of greeting, Mikey handed the brass pipe to Lalor and said, "What's this oul yoke, Kevin?"

"Where did you get it?"

"From dant in Leeds, but I wanted English comics to bring to school," Mikey said.

"Why would you want English comics?" Kevin Lalor asked and then answered his own question. "So the Tilers could kick the bejazus out of you entirely?"

Mikey always felt better about himself when the Civil Servant used grown-up language in front of him. But the child knew if he ever said "bejazus" back to the Civil Servant he would get a warning in the form of the question, "Do you want me to knock your block off?"

"If you brought English comics to school, the Tilers would attack you and the bike at the same time." It was the Civil Servant who repaired Mikey's bike every time it was damaged in Gohen.

With the saddle of his bike lying against his hip, Kevin Lalor pulled the ends of the brass pipe and elongated it to its full length.

"Aw, Janey!" Mikey said. "I could have done that myself."

"Why didn't you?"

"I didn't know it was a spyglass. Here, give it back to me."

"Hold your horses, Mikey. And since when did the word 'please' fall out of your vocabulary?" Lalor said. "This is a good spyglass. Will you look at that brass?" He took off his glasses and his face was different, his eyes smaller. He pointed the telescope toward Drumsally high on the slope of the Esker. "It's not just a good spyglass," he said. "It's a great spyglass. Will you look at that! I can see the whiskers on Sally Coughlin. She's lying down at the front door. Be jakers! Isn't that great? This is better than any comics. Here, put that to your eye and you'll think you're in the Coughlins' yard."

Mikey couldn't stop the world whizzing past in the spyglass. Lalor had to tell him three times to lower it onto the bike saddle to steady it.

With his body adjusted to the distance between his feet and the spyglass, with one eye clamped shut and with his teeth bared in a snarl, Mikey finally slowed down the picture at the end of the barrel.

"I can't see Sally," he said. "But there's a big pile of straw moving around in the front garden."

"You mustn't be looking at the Coughlins' house," the Civil Servant said.

"It's the Coughlins' all right. I just saw Eddie's cap flashing by. He's leading the horse by the winkers and there's the biggest load of straw I ever saw. He's backing up the horse and cart. Bridie's behind the cart telling him where to go with her hand."

"I don't think you're looking at the Coughlins' front garden at all," the Civil Servant said. "That's where Bridie has her geraniums and her sweet peas. Can you see the dog at the door?"

"She's not there. She must have moved."

"Give me a look," Kevin demanded.

"Wait. There's Bridie still waving at Eddie."

"They can't be in the flower garden."

"Amen't I looking at them? They're in the flower garden, Kevin."

"You're cracked, Mikey. What would they be doing with the horse's cart in the flower garden? Give me a look."

"Wait. They're opening the ropes on the shafts."

"Give me a look," Lalor demanded again. "You can look through the spyglass all day after I've gone home." He held out his hand.

Mikey ignored Lalor. "Eddie tried to heel up the cart by himself," he said dramatically, "but Bridie had to help him. There it goes . . . there it goes, and the horse is moving up, and Eddie had to jump away. The straw's all over the place."

"Mind yourself, Mikey," Kevin Lalor said with impatience. "I'm going to move the bike. I have to go home." He gently swayed the bike and shook the spyglass.

"Aw, Kevin, don't move the bike. I just saw Sally for a second near Eddie."

Kevin Lalor blocked the end of the spyglass with his hand. "Mikey Lamb!" he said. "Mikey! Take your eye away from that spyglass and look at me."

Holding the spyglass on the saddle with both hands, with one eye still closed and his face still distorted, Mikey bent his head back until he was squinting up into the Civil Servant's face. "What?" he asked.

"Stand up straight, take the spyglass off the saddle and let me go home." Mikey finally heard the impatience in Lalor's voice.

The boy straightened up. Afraid he had upset the only person outside his family who treated him better than a dog, he held out the spyglass. "Take a look, Kevin. The straw's all over the place."

Kevin's curiosity about the straw in Bridie Coughlin's flower garden was stronger than his annoyance at Mikey Lamb. He took the proffered spyglass out of the dirty hand.

Sure enough, the eternally becapped Eddie Coughlin had just pulled down the shafts of the cart, was putting the backband into the wooden bridge on the straddle. Bridie was at the far side of the horse, and from the way she was moving and bending, Lalor knew she was helping with the yoking. A pile of yellow straw behind the cart stood out against the dark green of the Esker as bright as a solitary votive candle in an evening church. "They're hardly going to thatch their house again," the Civil Servant said, the spyglass still at his eye. Then he muttered, "They only thatched that roof a few years ago."

Kevin Lalor handed the spyglass back to Mikey. "Don't bring that to school or the Townies will take it from you."

"But I want to show it off."

"Show it off to everyone in Clunnyboe, but don't take it to school. Do you hear me, Mikey? Look at me. Do you hear me?"

"What use is it if I can't show it off to the lads?"

"Did you hear what I said about not taking it to school?"

"I did."

As he rode the last half mile home, Kevin Lalor made a bet with himself that Mikey would bring the spyglass to school, that one of the Townies would talk it out of him for a few dated and torn English comics. Then he wondered if Bridie and Eddie Coughlin were going to patch a leak in their roof. A full load of straw would not be needed for a small repair. Maybe they didn't want a few feet of new thatch to stand out like a beacon against the old faded straw, so they were going to do the whole roof. That was it! Bridie was fastidious about the appearance of her house. Besides that, people like the Coughlins who had a priest in the family were inclined to improve the setting from which one of their members had rocketed to the top of the social heap by way of a religious rite. A repaired thatched roof was as socially indelicate as a missing front tooth. Bridie Coughlin would no more have a repair on her roof than she would ride her bike to town with a patch in her good blue coat.

4

The Peeper

1951

In which Simon Peter Lamb mourns his dead
father, uses Mikey's spyglass to peer into the
distant garden of Eddie-the-cap, bachelor, and
Bridie Coughlin, spinster, and speculates on
what he sees.

EVEN THOUGH THE FARMYARD was behind their house, the Coughlins did not have a back door. And so it was that on the morning
after Mikey Lamb's birthday, when Bridie Coughlin hesitated for a
moment before stepping out through her front door at seven o'clock,
Simon Peter Lamb trapped her in Mikey's spyglass. When Bridie
appeared to stare straight at him, Simon Peter snatched the spyglass
away from his eye and quickly dodged behind the door jamb of the
turf shed.

"Janey Mack!" he said. Then he glanced around fiercely to see if
anyone had heard him. But it was only a red hen, busy giving herself
a dust bath in the turf mull, that had heard him.

Cautiously, Simon Peter moved his body until one eye was
exposed to the Esker. He could barely see Bridie's house in the
distance. He took in a deep breath and held it. "Amen't I a terrible
eegit? Bridie couldn't see me unless she had a spyglass, too." He put
the telescope back to his eye and held it against the jamb to steady it.

Bridie was still standing in the doorway. She was holding something in her right hand, but she kept it out of sight while she stuck out her head and peeped to her left. Then she stepped forward and walked quickly to her right with her head down. Just as she disappeared around the corner of the house, Simon Peter moved the spyglass and there, not an arm's length away, was Bridie Coughlin's white porcelain chamber pot with a bunch of red flowers painted on its side, its rim gold-leafed.

"Janey Mack! Flowers on her pisspot! And she carries it with her thumb on the inside." Simon Peter lowered the spyglass and looked at it. "This is a great yoke altogether." He turned it over in his hand. "So smooth and nice to feel." He put the wide end to his eye and looked over at the Esker again. "Janey, everything's miles away."

He looked around for something to sit on. There was nothing but the x-framed sawhorse for holding tree branches steady when the two-handled crosscut saw was used. Carefully, he placed the spyglass in the turf mull and pulled the sawhorse over to the open doorway. The bathing hen muttered and Simon Peter absentmindedly kicked it in the arse, sending it into the air in a flutter of wings and dust and squawkings.

Simon Peter should have been milking one of his cows, his forehead against a warm, bovine belly, the squish-squish of the milk into the bucket lulling him back to sleep. But Mikey's announcement last night about what he saw in the Coughlins' flower garden was too much for Simon Peter to be wondering about all day. Mikey wouldn't be up for school till eight o'clock. By then the spyglass would be in its place at the back of the knife-and-fork drawer in the kitchen dresser.

It took Simon Peter some time to find the Coughlin house again. When he did, the front door was closed. Blue chimney smoke was rising straight into the sky. The stillness of the air, and the possibility that the Coughlins were getting ready to thatch reminded him of the Irish proverb Mikey had learned during the winter. Over and over the child had chanted it while staring into the red flames of the turf fire, driving everyone in the house half-mad. *Ní hé lá na gaoithe lá na scoilb.* The day of the wind is not the day of the scollop. Don't try to thatch on a windy day. Don't piss into the wind. Don't fart in the confession box.

In the eyepiece Simon Peter found the heap of yellow straw in the Coughlins' garden, and there, too, was Eddie-the-cap. "So that's why Bridie was waiting; for Eddie to turn his back before she'd take her pisspot out to the dunghill at the back of the house."

Eddie's shirtsleeves were rolled up past his elbows. He was teasing the straw, going through it looking for bits of grass and weeds and briars, removing them with a flick of the two-pronged fork, cleaning the oaten straw as carefully as a woman preparing wool for spinning.

"So, they *are* going to thatch. And I was talking to Mattie Mulhall on the road yesterday and he never said a word. Cagey Mattie! Maybe it's a rushed job, just patching a leak."

In the end of the spyglass Eddie Coughlin gathered the straw he had cleaned and carried it to where he had already started the bed convenient to the house. He swung the forkful of thatching back over his shoulder and then flipped it forward, the whipping action taking the tangle out of the straw and straightening it to some extent. "Not bad for a Sloper," Simon Peter grudgingly allowed inside his own head.

He kept Coughlin in the glass, and as he intimately studied his unsuspecting neighbor, a feeling of perverse delight glowed in Simon Peter's belly. "Wouldn't it be great if Eddie took off the cap? I'd be the first person ever to see his third ear. But, shag, I wouldn't be able to let anyone in on the secret because I'd have to tell how I saw it. Still, I'd be the only one who'd know what's wrong with his head."

As he watched Coughlin picking his way through another forkful of straw, Simon Peter wondered if Eddie had cut and cleaned the scollops yet, wondered if he was going to buy them from your man Dunphy over near Gohen. If it was a rush job, then Eddie would be buying, but of course the Slopers could afford to spend money on things that the Boggers had to scrounge out of the hedges.

It was fifteen years since Simon Peter had cut and cleaned scollops for the thatching of his own house. It was also fifteen years since he had last felt that terrible anger at his father. It had been his father's thick-headed reaction to the son's adolescence that had placed the seed of anger inside Simon Peter. The seed festered over the years because neither father nor son had the tools to talk about the poison and draw it out.

When Simon Peter had emerged from his teenage years, his father had continued to relate to his son as an adolescent. As well as remaining angry at each other, they grew to loathe being in each other's company. Like two people caught in a balancing act on the edge of a cliff, neither could let go of the other. For the son, it was either the farm or emigration; the father needed the son to work on the farm, but he was unable to loosen his possessive grasp and graciously hand it over to the son.

Over the years, communication between Simon Peter and his father had evolved back to the grunts of the first two communicating apes. It was the woman in their lives, the wife and mother, who bridged the gap for them. "Your father wants to know . . ." she'd say to Simon Peter. "Simon Peter wants to know . . ." she'd say to her husband. When she died, the apelike grunting evolved upward again to the point where a bare paucity was spoken. Both had become such adept wielders of Occam's razor that they had honed their use of the language to the point where one word was sufficient to carry a day.

Fifteen years ago, when Simon Peter was thirty-six, he and his father had set out in silence to look for scollops, each dressed in raingear of old cap, tattered topcoat and flopping Wellingtons. It was the last job they worked together. It was the last time the father treated the son like a child: picking up scollops Simon Peter had cut and cleaned and, with a grunt, pointing to a missed protrusion even though it wouldn't have interfered with the thatching at all; handing the offending scollop back to Simon Peter for correction instead of nicking off the small imperfection with his own knife.

Together in the drizzling rain, they plundered the clumps of slender shoots. They measured each scollop from armhole to tip of index finger, pointed each end with one swipe of the knife, and dressed each piece by nicking off every growth and bump. They placed the pliant rods in bundles across two pieces of old binder twine and finally tied them together, leaving them in the soaking grass to be picked up later in the pony and cart.

They would need two thousand scollops, and it was the father who kept a running tally of the number gathered. The inside-out cigarette box, picked up off a street in Gohen, and the stub of pencil which his shaky fingers fumbled out of his waistcoat pocket before each bundle was tied up, were two more symbols of the father's autocracy and the son's subservience.

Around the edges of the wet fields they went, ravaging stands of hazel, black sally and eggbush shoots. After each plundering, they set out for the next clump without reference to each other. Even if there had been a narrow channel of communication open between them, there would have been no need to discuss where to go next—each knew every bush, tree and briar in the hedges of the farm.

As side by side they cut, measured, pointed and dressed, Simon Peter noticed his father straining to match him scollop for scollop. He became aware of his father's breathing, saw that he hesitated each time he dropped a fresh scollop on the bundle. But in his heart, Simon Peter was not sympathetic to the older man's distress. There was no reason why his father should be out in the rain working like this. But the old man was stubborn, and he would show the world he could keep up with his son. And by keeping up with him he would retain the right to make all the decisions that affected their lives.

With the father leading the way, the two men were trudging to the far side of the Beech Field when the father stopped walking. He put his hand to his chest. Simon Peter quickened his step.

"Are you all right?" he asked. Then, as he stepped over to the old man's side, he realized his father was about to die. The son dropped his scollop knife and caught his father as he fell into him. Simon Peter eased the lifeless body down onto the wet earth. Then, as if reacting to some old instinct, he knelt down on the sopping ground, and with his arms around the shoulders he hadn't touched since he was a child, he laid the side of his face on his father's chest. From the depths of his belly, jagged sobs clawed their way up his throat and spread themselves over his father's body like blankets of remorse and sorrow.

When the sobs had worn themselves out, Simon Peter spoke in the gulping voice that can only be managed after a long cry. "I always thought we'd have time to talk to each other. I always thought there would be a time." Then he whispered, "I'm so fucking sorry, so fucking sorry."

Twenty minutes after his father died, Simon Peter stood up, took off his raggedy topcoat and covered the cooling body. Across the soaking April fields he slogged, the chocolate-colored water from old hoof-holes squirting up in the air when he inattentively stepped into them. When he reached the farmyard, he wheeled his bike out of the shed and set off to get the priest and the doctor in Gohen.

On the uncomfortable sawhorse in his turf shed, Simon Peter Lamb came to himself, his head bent and the spyglass dangling from his hands between his legs. "May God have mercy on him and on Mam, too. I hope Mikey and myself never get to the point where Pops and myself got."

He brought the spyglass to his eye and searched until he caught Eddie Coughlin still working the straw.

"They won't be ready for Mattie Mulhall for a couple of days." Simon Peter folded the spyglass into itself. "I wonder are they expecting visitors. If they start whitewashing after the thatching, it'll be a sure sign someone's on the way. The only one they have is the brother in India. 'Course the pope could be coming to see them, and Bridie and Eddie wouldn't tell anyone."

Simon Peter pulled the sawhorse back out of the doorway and went into the kitchen to the knife-and-fork drawer.

5

In the Sunroom

In which David Samuel Howard, Esq., speculates that the ancient community of Gohen and adjacent townlands may have been unsettled by the occurrence of two new people in their midst.

MISTER HOWARD HELD UP his hand like a child about to ask permission to go to the bathroom. "Hold on, Patrick," he said. "The old prostate is encroaching on the urethra."

"Gosh, Sam, you could be a little more delicate," his wife said. "We *do* have company."

Mister Howard levered himself onto his feet. "You know I *am* being delicate, Else."

A smile twitched at Elsie's mouth, but she would not give in to it.

"It's nice to be at the age where one can live without fear of the reprimand," Sam said as he went out.

"Patrick," Missus Howard said immediately, "Sam told me your entire family emigrated to England together."

"Yes, two girls, three boys and my parents."

"That must have been terrible for everyone."

"Yes, it was."

Missus Howard noticed twinges of pain in Patrick's eyes, and she quickly veered off onto a different scent. "How did you manage to make a success of yourself in a new country in such a short time?"

"It was luck to a large extent," Patrick said.

"We make our own luck, like you said yourself. What did you do to make it happen?"

"I was an avid reader, and it showed in my school essays. A teacher took me under his wing."

"Ah!" Missus Howard almost purred the word, sighed the sound as if she could already see many pieces floating down out of the air to take their places in a grand design.

"Mister Charrot was his name—Jules Charrot. After I took the O Levels he made sure I continued on into sixth form and took the advanced level in the General Certificate. He set my sights on the University of Birmingham and tutored me to win an exhibition to read English."

Missus Howard silently clapped her hands together. "There are saints all around us, even though I don't believe in God. They make up for the rest of us."

"Mister Charrot was a good man, a saint if you like," Patrick said. "On alternate Mondays during my years in Birmingham, I received a brown envelope with a red ten-shilling note inside. Even when I told him I had a secret benefactor straight out of Dickens, he never admitted his assistance. 'Abel Magwitch is still alive,' I'd tell him to assure him the money was reaching me."

"A story like that gives me a warm feeling all over and at the same time makes me feel so inadequate. I haven't given back near as much as I've taken."

"Like you said, Else, the saints make up for the rest of us. And I do know that you ran a thrift shop here in Gohen for many years."

With her left hand, Missus Howard waved away Patrick's reference to her care of the poor of the town.

"Mister Charrot would have shrugged off any reference to his goodness just like you did now, Else."

"Is he still alive—Mister Charrot?" she asked quickly, as if embarrassed that her own saintliness had entered the conversation.

"No, he died sixteen years ago. When he retired he moved to Muker, and we—Molly and I—got to know the Dales from visiting him. He always insisted that we climb to the top step of the Literary Institute in Muker when we went for a walk. 'So we can sit and look down on the pheasants,' he'd say."

"He must have been very proud of you, must have had a wonderful sense of fulfillment through you."

"He did. He was a widower, had no children, so I became his son and then Molly became his daughter. One day when we were walking around the cemetery surrounding the village church, he showed me the place where he would be buried beside his wife. A few months later we were sitting at the institute and I told him Molly and I had bought the plot beside his. He put his arm across my shoulders and pulled me into himself—not bad for an Englishman."

"Not bad for an Englishman, indeed," Missus Howard echoed, "and very touching for a man with no children of his own."

"Who had no children?" Mister Howard asked as he approached the door to the sunroom.

"Sam! You know I hate it when you do that—walk into the middle of a conversation and say 'what?'"

"I didn't say what. I said who."

Patrick wondered if the Howards kept their relationship lively and healthy by knocking sparks off each other at every opportunity. At first, he'd been uncomfortable with their sniping, but now he thought they weren't sniping at all. They were like two pieces of old field-flint keeping each other sharp and showing their love with their gentle whacking off each other. They were like two children who slap and smack and push each other at every passing to show their affection.

Mister Howard stood beside his chair. "A man often has great thoughts when he's relieving himself," he announced. "There must be some chemical infusion into the brain with the exfusion of urine from the body."

"It must be a male thing," his wife said. "And there's no such word."

"Maybe it *is* a man thing," her husband said absently. "Patrick, you have surely read *The Valley of the Squinting Windows*? I finally read it ten years ago after hearing about it all my life. I think it's a hateful book, and so does Else. MacNamara revealed himself as the most scrofulous old yenta in the village, even though he didn't write a word about himself. He must have been a miserable old bollicks, a genuine gobshite. There was only one observation in the whole book that had some validity for me: 'they,' the village people, 'hate the occurrence of new people in their midst.' I don't agree with the word 'hate'; I would agree, though, that the occurrence of new people in any group can give rise to a general anxiety." Sam looked at his wife and Patrick.

"And . . . ?" Else asked.

"And . . . and Father Coughlin and Doul Yank Gorman, for all practical purposes, were new people even though they were born here."

"Wait now, Sam," Else interrupted. "Are you saying Coughlin and Doul Yank Gorman were murdered simply because they were new arrivals among an old, established group?"

"Stop saying 'murdered,' Else. All I'm saying is that they were new people in our midst, and they both caused anxiety among some people. Else, you must stop saying they were murdered."

"Oh, for God's sake, Sam! Will you give up on that? Everyone in Gohen knows that Mattie Mulhall shot his uncle Doul Yank Gorman, and everyone knows there was hanky-panky on Sally Hill where the priest died. And why are you bringing *The Valley of the*—?"

"I'm trying to paint in some background so Patrick will better understand any conclusions he may reach."

"Sounds to me like you're preparing Patrick . . . like you're getting ready to put . . . What do the Americans call it? Spin . . . sounds like you're preparing to do some spinning to keep Patrick from finding what he's looking for."

"Me a spin doctor? That's a good one, Else." Sam sat down. "By the way, did I interrupt something when I came back from the john?"

"Not at all, Sam," his wife said. "But I have often wondered in the past why you sound more intelligent when you came back from the loo. And now in my old age I have finally discovered it's because of exfusion and infusion."

"Yes, Else. I always feel a little bit inspired after peeing."

"Maybe you should start drinking more water," his wife said. The two of them laughed and Patrick joined in.

With the passing of the laughter, Patrick grabbed the ball and ran with it. "Lawrence Gorman, the returned Yank!" he said, like a conductor tapping the podium with his baton. "Lawrence Gorman may have given the farm to his nephew Mattie Mulhall in return for being cared for till he died, but it was Mattie who got the very short end of the stick. Mattie Mulhall would have been . . .

6

On the Kitchen Floor

1951

In which Peggy Mulhall, wife of Mattie, a.k.a. Matt-the-thatcher, diffuses her husband's anger at Eddie, a.k.a. Eddie-the-cap, Coughlin for interrupting a job on an ideal thatching day.

MATTIE MULHALL WOULD HAVE BEEN thatching the Coughlins' house except that Eddie Coughlin had eight big bullocks to sell, and the Fair Day in Gohen was on the third Tuesday of every month.

"It wouldn't have killed him to hold on to the bullocks for another month and not interrupt the job," Mattie Mulhall complained to his wife. "The man's a bit of an eegit, if you ask me. Why is he selling eight big animals all of a sudden?" he asked rhetorically, but he got an answer from his wife.

"Maybe he's going to buy a tractor," she offered.

"Tractor me hole!" her husband said, the edges on his words honed to a fine point by his annoyance at Eddie Coughlin.

With high and prominent cheeks, beaky nose and black hair, Mattie Mulhall could have been a conquistador if he'd had an upside-down tin bucket on his head. He had fierce black eyes with fierce black eyebrows. While his teeth were not bucked, they were as noticeable as his nose. His Adam's apple continued the line of prominence from forehead to trachea and it moved up and down his neck with every word spoken. One of his ancestors had been washed up on a beach on the west coast in 1588, part of the flotsam of the Spanish Armada. "Is this Spain?" the ancestor had asked a passing Paddy. "Spain, me hole!" the Paddy answered and gave the Spick a clatter across the head with a fish because he looked different. "And that's just for looking different. Leave our women alone." But the Spaniard had not.

"Couldn't he at least have told me last Saturday about going to the fair? Then when we finished yesterday, he was all offended when I said no to having Bridie pull the straw and serve me on the roof. I put the kibosh on that one right away—a woman running up and down the ladder with straw and scollops, and the whole world looking at her pink knickers!"

Mattie Mulhall was sitting in his kitchen having his elevenses. Slices of homemade bread, lathered with butter and rhubarb-and-apple jam, were piled on a willow pattern dinner plate in the middle of the table. A mug of milked and sugared tea was in his right fist.

Peggy Mulhall had heard her husband's complaints last night and at breakfast this morning. With her back to Mattie as she poked at the fire, she was only half-listening to the dreary dronings. But Bridie Coughlin's pink knickers suddenly presented her with a way to jostle Mattie out of his rut. "How do you know Bridie's knickers are pink?" she asked without looking around.

For a minute, the wife thought she hadn't even put a ripple in the husband's self-pitying wallowings. "Didn't Eddie ever hear of ladies first everywhere except up a ladder?" he asked. Then he said, "The only knickers color I ever saw was pink on a clothesline."

"My knickers aren't pink," Peggy said, and she already knew where she was leading her husband.

"What color are they then?" Mattie asked, and he took another slice of bread off the pile.

"That's something you'll have to find out for yourself."

With his teeth poised to chomp down into the rhubarb-and-apple jam, Mattie hesitated and asked, "What are you telling me, woman?"

And Peggy knew she had him. "Nothing, man."

Mattie Mulhall lowered the slice of bread and dropped it on the table beside his mug. His Adam's apple was yo-yoing. "At eleven o'clock in the morning?" he asked. "And your man," he lifted his eyes to the ceiling, "will be getting up any minute?"

"What are you talking about?" Peggy asked, and she heard her husband's chair scraping on the cement floor. She ran to the front door. The moment she slid the deadbolt into place, she turned and dodged around her husband. But, as she knew he would, he caught her from behind and clasped her breasts.

"Sweet mother of Christ!" he breathed into her ear. He pushed his pelvis against her, pulled her back into him, his fierce, welted hands strong on her breasts but tender at the same time, her clothing cushioning the hard skin of the thumbs that chased the nipples.

Without very much fat on her, Peggy Mulhall was a big woman. Her russet hair was full of tight curls, and her skin was as smooth and as delicately colored as a Royal Worcester teapot. She was three inches shorter than her husband's six feet.

"Sweet mother of Christ," Mattie said again, hardly enough blood left in his brain to send the message to his vocal cords.

The feel of his hot, turgid breath in her ear sent a welcoming torrent plunging down Peggy's body. "I'm weak at the knees," she moaned.

"The easier to pull them apart, said the wolf." The hot steam of Mattie's breath pierced her brain like a six-inch hatpin.

"Oh, Mattie," she shuddered, and she put her hands behind her to feel what he had to offer.

One of his hands fell off a breast, and then it was on her bare leg beneath her dress. The hand climbed to the waistband of her knickers and immediately plunged down. But at the edge of her hair the fingers stopped and stealthily stole through her hirsute copse. She had trained him to be gentle by being funny, instructing him in a posh accent, "Don't plunge into the plover, my dear."

But this kind of spontaneous aggression on his part made the usual subtleties redundant. All she wished right now was that he'd knock her down on the kitchen floor and stab her. With her toes, she pried off her shoes in preparation for what she knew he would do next. When they were excited like this, they understood each other best.

He bent down, pushing her knickers to her knees. He raised his foot, pushed the knickers down to her ankles and held them pinned to the floor with his boot while she pulled herself free. By the time Peggy had kicked the knickers away, his fingers were probing.

"Sweet mother of Jesus," he grunted, when he felt her hot, silken, welcoming, grand entrance.

She loved it when he swore during sex, like her ancestors of ten thousand years ago must have done when they were at it, tearing into each other in the dark, snarling and cursing and biting and scratching like cats. She loved the picture of the pelt-dressed man with the club on his shoulder dragging a woman by the hair into his cave. The size of that club!

While Mattie lowered her to the floor, she pulled the buttons of his fly out of their buttonholes. Then she lay back and pulled up the dress that separated them.

And then Mattie was nudging her front door, and she thought she would die, explode into a million pieces and go shooting off up into the stars. When he slipped in, she groaned like she'd been stabbed between the shoulders with the blade of a blunt scythe.

She had trained him not to treat her as if she were a cow and he a bull doing it to a cow: up, in, squirt and fall down as if hit on the head with a forty-pound mallet swung by a savage. Of course, she had done it in such a way that he never even knew he was being trained. And now, on the kitchen floor, he was holding back, but moving against her with such precision that every time they came together she saw streaks of forked lightning behind her eyelids. The instant he heard her neighing, he turned into a stallion at the mercy of instinct, and by the time the toes of his leather boots were scraping the floor she was screeching through her teeth like a pig with its snout caught under a gate.

She wrapped her arms around his rear and held his pelvic bone against her as the last of the spasms jerked him. For a moment she teetered on the fine edge separating pleasure and pain, moved her hands around to his hips, ready to give him the signal if she started sliding down the wrong side. But then she felt him slumping as if someone had reached up inside him and yanked out all the bones. "It's like he's entirely deboned all of a sudden." It was the only way she could explain how it felt to be under him after he being a stallion one minute and nothing but a sack of water the next. But she loved the feel of him still inside her.

An extra dimension was added to their rutting on the kitchen floor while the Doul Yank was still in his bed upstairs—risk of discovery. Estelle Butler, Peggy's friend since First Babies, often told Peggy where she and her Paul did it. Estelle and Paul liked to run the risk of getting caught; they often did it in the hay in their haggard; in a wheat field beside the main road from Gohen to Marbra, suddenly dropping out of sight and rolling around in the golden straw; they once did it standing up in a cemetery, she with her bare arse against a local politician's ornate and cold headstone. They had even done it in Peggy's front garden one night on their way home from the pictures in Gohen. When Peggy was disbelieving, Estelle told her where to look for the bent grass ten feet from her own bedroom window. In Peggy's mind, Estelle's galloping loquacity sometimes revealed things better left covered.

"That's it!" Mattie suddenly said. "I was wondering why they're thatching so soon again. I'll bet anything the priest brother is coming home from India. And that's why Eddie's selling the eight big cattle, too. I'll bet anything they're going to put in the water—have a lav for him when he comes."

Peggy didn't respond. Although she was still marinating, she wondered about the workings of men's brains: stallions one minute, geldings the next; ravishing sex one minute, building lavs the next.

Mattie stirred, and Peggy knew he was getting ready to disconnect. Even though she held her breath against the feeling she knew was coming, she still moaned at the surge of emptiness.

Mattie twisted over into a sitting position and bundled himself back into his britches. Peggy stood up and retrieved her knickers from under the kitchen table. There was a mud stain where Mattie had held them to the floor with his boot. She balled the knickers and threw them toward the bedroom door. While she smoothed her dress she asked, "So tell me, Mattie, what color is my knickers?"

"Damned if I know," Mattie said, and he stood up. "I'll find out tonight."

"Only if you take them off me."

"That's what I mean. This is something we should be doing oftener."

"What have I been telling you all this time?" Peggy almost said, but she stopped her unsubtle self, and overhead they heard the loud, intentional coughing which reminded them of the chains of their bondage.

Mattie lifted his eyes to the ceiling. "Doul Yank," he muttered. He downed the remainder of his cold tea, used the same magic finger that had turned his wife into an animal to scoop the unmelted sugar out of the bottom of the mug. He stuck the finger into his mouth and the sweetness gladdened his gums. "I'm going over to open the turnip drills in the Middle Field," he said as he put the mug down on the table.

"I'll hit the pighouse when the dinner's ready," Peggy needlessly said. Everyone in Clunnyboe knew the sound of Peggy's ashplant against the galvanized side of the pighouse was the Mulhalls' dinner bell when Mattie was working in the fields.

As he was going out through the kitchen door, Mattie stopped. He indicated his uncle's bedroom with the peak of his cap. "Maybe that's what your man needs—a good roll in the hay with a woman who's dying for it."

"She'd have to be more than dying; she'd have to be dead before he'd get her into the hay."

The kitchen door closed and opened again. Mattie stuck his head back in. "Don't forget what I said about your man in India," he said. "Aren't they a terrible closemouthed pair, the two of them, Bridie and Eddie, not saying a word? And wait till you see—Ned Bracken will be up there building a lav any day now."

Peggy still had other things on her mind. When her husband stopped talking, she lifted up the front of her dress and exposed her naked self to him.

"I married a slut," Mattie said.

The forced cough came from upstairs again. The signal had been given that Lawrence Gorman was about to rise from his bed. His cough gave the order for the preparation of his breakfast, that it should be waiting for him when he stepped onto the landing outside his bedroom door.

Mattie rolled his eyes to the ceiling. "The bastard Yank," he said, and he closed the door.

7

Wrestling on the Edge of a Cliff

1951

In which, Mattie Mulhall, a.k.a. Matt-the-thatcher, is enslaved by the conditions of a promised inheritance from his uncle, Lawrence Gorman, a.k.a. Doul Yank.

MATTIE MULHALL, THE NEPHEW, and Lawrence Gorman, the uncle, were entwined in a business relationship binding them together till death would them part. If nature followed her usual course, Lawrence would die first, but whenever Mattie Mulhall became apoplectically angry at his situation, the normal course of nature was threatened.

Of course, Mattie's Peggy did not try to calm the waters when one of Mattie's angry fits was already in its gathering stage. Mattie's fits always primed Peggy's own anger at the predicament in which she lived; and while Mattie's fit raged, she couldn't help insinuating that, had she been around at the time, the agreement which now bound her and her husband to Lawrence Gorman would never have been reached. Not caring that her husband couldn't hear her when his pounding blood was bottlenecked on its way to his brain, Peggy would pick the most suitable pearls from her collection: When you lie down with dogs you get up with fleas; If you sup with the devil, you must use a long-handled spoon; You made the bed, now the two of us must lie on it; If wishes were horses, beggars would ride.

Peggy knew her old saws were as useless as the useless scriptural passages thrown out by jaded priests as bandages for broken hearts and spirits. Her recitation of them was her way of knifing her mother-in-law.

The worst aspect of the relationship between uncle and nephew was that they lived in the same house, the uncle upstairs where his every fart and slashing piss into his metal bucket could be plainly heard. The sound of the lid carelessly dropped back onto the commode made the nephew's blood cells sprout spikes. But when Lawrence Gorman demanded the presence of someone from downstairs by banging the heel of his boot on the floor beside his bed, the nephew frothed like a distempered dog having a fit.

When Lawrence Gorman emigrated to America in 1912, he left behind a cantankerous, begrudging and bitter father who owned fifty acres of praiseach-infested land, as well as a defeated mother and two sisters, Lizzie and Helen. Because Lawrence had missed the *Titanic* by three weeks, many of Mattie Mulhall's laments began with the words, "If only . . ." and ended with, "the fucker would have taken a child's place in a lifeboat, thrown the child into the water."

According to Uncle Lawrence, he had become a shopman in America, and had once served as chairman of the Christmas Ball sponsored by his emigrant county society. To prove he had risen to such heights of organizational acumen, he still had a printed program, the original green fading out of the paper, with his name under the bold letters of "Chairman." He also had a *committee* photograph in which he himself was seated in center front of a large group of men, all with large mustaches, starched collars and shoestring ties, all with hair parted along the ridges of their skulls, all so tense-looking that each could have been sitting on a chair with a missing leg. The light from the photographer's flaring magnesium was reflected in the greased coiffure on every head. There wasn't a woman in sight.

The best-known Lawrence-in-America story was set in a speakeasy where liquor of doubtful purity was served. All the patrons' suspicions were laid to rest one night when a man drank a shot of the house whiskey and dropped dead at Lawrence's feet. Whenever the nephew heard this story being repeated, his thoughts began with, 'If only. . . .'

"Speakeasy" was one of the two American words Lawrence dropped when impressing a listener with the extent of his foreign travels. The other was "ketchup." Other than this expanded vocabulary, all he brought home from America were the clothes he wore, the art-deco metal commode and its lid, the Christmas Ball program and the committee photograph. He did not bring money.

During Lawrence's fourth year abroad, his oldest sister, Lizzie, married Mick Mulhall-the-thatcher, and from then on she was referred to, behind her back, as the Thatcherette—authorship for the name credited to Pascal Lalor-the-postman. Lawrence-in-America did not send a wedding present of dollars or anything else. On the day of the nine-month anniversary of her wedding, the Thatcherette gave birth to a boy and named him Matthew. When he heard about the new arrival, Pascal Lalor-the-postman did his sums and said, "Mick must have slipped his scollop into her thatch in the church porch."

Seven years after becoming a grandmother, Lawrence's mother died roaring. It was cancer of the breast that killed her, but superstition and prudery did not allow for the enunciation of either "cancer" or "breast."

Five years later, the younger sister, who had sported hectic cheeks since middle adolescence, finally surrendered to tuberculosis. Within six years of her funeral, Lawrence's father died while violently haggling over the price of a heifer with a Protestant on a Fair Day in Gohen. The local Protestants saw old man Gorman's sudden death, and his ignominious collapse into the fresh cowshite splattered all over the main street, as a sign of favoritism on the part of the God of Protestants.

In America, in 1935, Lawrence received a letter from the Gohen solicitor, William Stewart Howard, father of David Samuel, informing him of his father's death and of his inheritance of the family farm. Absent from the letter was any hint that the father had kept the farm in the family name at the expense of deeding it to "that useless little robin-shite in America." Unmoved by the tone of congratulations in the letter, unwilling to relinquish his new landowner status, but also doubtful about the wisdom of returning to a farm whose best crop was praiseach—that yellow-flowered, Attila the Hun of the world of weeds—Lawrence did not respond to Howard's letter.

Back in Clunnyboe, Lawrence's silence quickly mutated into the hope that he had died in America. His sister, the Thatcherette, began fantasizing aloud to her neighbors about the prospect of moving up the social and economic ladder when she became a landowner by default. Her husband would retire from the practice of his servile trade and, for the first time in his life, he wouldn't have welts on his thumbs and the palms of his hands from twisting and bending half-scollops into staple-shaped keys. "His hands are as rough as dry thistles on my body," she complained and boasted at the same time. No longer would he have welts on his knees from kneeling on the rung of a ladder on a sloping roof, and no longer would he have to work for a wage, eating his meals in other people's houses—"I won't mention any names"—where the cat walked around the table during mealtime with its tail up in the air. "Trying to eat the dinner and look at a cat's hole at the same time makes me sick. Them and their fecking cats!" was the complaint she had heard a thousand times. Eighteen-year-old Mattie-the-son would not have to finish out his apprenticeship to his father.

As time wore on, and there was still only silence from America, the neighbors began to notice a change in the angle of the Thatcherette's nose and in the way she spoke. With uptilted face, and seemingly suffering from a mild case of lockjaw, she began the process of separating herself from her landless neighbors. She spoke about the profits of ownership; the turkeys she would raise for the Christmas market; the eggs and country butter she would sell in the shops in Gohen; the buttermilk which the landless masses would buy at her back door, their jug in one hand and pennies in the other; the sheaves of rhubarb stalks she would bring on the back of her bike to the Fair Day in Gohen every third Tuesday of the month. She and her husband would have a farm to leave to their heir.

Up to that point in time, the only heir the neighbors had heard of was Her Royal Highness, Princess Elizabeth of York.

Then one day, Pascal Lalor-the-postman, his approach telegraphed more by the clomping of his wooden leg on the stairs than by his cheery "*Guten tag*," dropped a thick letter on the desk of William Stewart Howard, Esq.

"Nice stamp there, sir," he said. He limped around the desk and bent over the solicitor's shoulder. They peered at the tiny, blue portrait of Benjamin Franklin, and the solicitor said, "Wasn't he a fat old devil? Will you look at all the chins on him? Five cee. That's five cents, I suppose. What's five cents worth? About tuppence hapeney? Tuppence hapeney to get a letter from America to Ireland in two weeks! Isn't that a miracle altogether. Three thousand miles for less than thruppence." He slapped the envelope with the back of his fingers. "Do you have this one, Pascal?" he asked.

"I don't, but I do have the fifteen-cent airmail in brown. I got it from Missus Dunne-of-the-shop. Isn't that a bigger miracle altogether, sir? Twelve hours from Idlewild to Riananna for about sevenpence hapeney. Lawrence must be in a bad way if he couldn't..." Pascal Lalor blushed and brought his hand to his mouth. "I'm sorry, Mister Howard."

"I know you'd never say a word, Pascal." The solicitor pulled the middle drawer out against his stomach and brought out a scissors big enough to trim a box hedge. When he had carefully clipped the stamp out of the envelope, he gave it to the postman. Without looking at what he was doing, Lalor fiddled with the silver-colored, harp-embossed button of his navy-blue uniform pocket. Most people in Gohen would have recognized the soft, brown, leather purse he took out of his pocket.

"The best-known bit of leather in Gohen," Mister Howard said.

"Aye, the famous LSP—Lalor's Stamp Purse—for the sale of the new and the collection of the old. I'll see you later if there's anything in the second post. Thanks for the stamp." Mister Howard waited until the postman had closed the door before he took out the contents of the envelope.

Three days later, Mick and the Thatcherette Mulhall went to Gohen all dressed up in their ass-and-cart.

Mister William Stewart Howard, Esquire, Protestant and suspect Freemason, unaware of the Thatcherette's fantasies of fortune, was taken aback at the collapse he witnessed when he told her Lawrence was alive and well in America. Believing her distress was the result of her relief at hearing the good news, the solicitor, embarrassed by such a violent display of emotion, removed himself from the room to give Missus Mulhall privacy to compose herself. Standing outside his office door, Mister Howard heard words he had never heard coming from the mouth of a woman, and later told his wife how amazed he was at the language Catholics used to release their profound relief.

Back in his office, the solicitor faced the red-eyed, hat-pinned and green-hatted woman and her Sunday-suited husband across his desk. Holding Lawrence Gorman's letter in his hand, and without once looking at it, he told them about the emigrant's proposal. The Thatcherette's hopes soared or plummeted with each revelation. In the end they crash-landed into a tangle of anger and despondency when she heard that the terms of her brother's proposal would all be for naught unless the price of his fare home from America was forthcoming from the fortunate recipient of his largesse.

Mick Mulhall and the Thatcherette would have told Lawrence to drop dead if they hadn't been blinkered by the prospect of their son becoming a landowner. Even though they had been denied owner-ship themselves, it was their greedy need to get their child's hands on the land that blinded them to the eventual cost.

And now, sixteen years later, Lawrence-the-uncle Gorman was living upstairs, and Mattie-the-nephew Mulhall was living downstairs with his wife Peggy and two young children. The six-and-a-half-foot-high kitchen ceiling allowed for the constant reminder that Lawrence was living in their midst. The two children thought everyone in the world spoke in whispers when indoors.

It was Missus Mulhall, Peggy, who answered the banging boot-heel above, she who forced her way into the stale-aired, low-ceilinged bedroom that smelled worse than a ferret box that hadn't been cleaned in a year. She took care of Doul Yank's clothes. His shirt collars were starched and his trousers pressed after every use. She prepared the food he ate every day in the kitchen. A clean, white tablecloth and a bottle of ketchup were the two basic requirements at every meal. He did not like eggs, and on Fridays his dinner had to include fish. "Fecking fish, for doul bastard!"

On the shortest and longest days of each year Mattie paid one hundred pounds to his uncle, and would do so as long as the uncle lived. Failure on Mattie's part to take care of all the details of his side of the bargain would invalidate his right to ownership of the land when Lawrence died.

It had quickly became clear to the nephew that trying to wrestle a livelihood from the farm would be as easy as milking a tiger with sore teats. To meet his first payment to the uncle, Mattie had returned to work with his thatching father. At night he read *The Farmers Journal*. He labored painfully over letters to the Department of Agriculture looking for ways to defeat the praiseach. He reddened iron spikes in the turf fire and shaped them into harrow teeth on an anvil outside the kitchen door. He let his tilled land lie fallow for three consecutive years and harrowed it every month in hopes of defeating the praiseach by thwarting its germination. Finally, in a late spring near the end of the war, he proudly gazed across his fields and did not see one yellow weed. Like Theodore Roosevelt with a victorious boot on the belly of a dead rhinoceros, Mattie stood posed with one triumphant foot on the bar of the wooden gate. He heaved a sigh of success and gazed with pride at what he had achieved.

His moment of victory was disturbed by the sounds of feet swishing through the long grass behind him. It was the uncle setting out on his daily shoot, the shotgun resting in the crook of his left elbow.

"A job never got done by looking at it," Lawrence heralded in the stentorian voice he used that proclaimed himself as the repository of all knowledge in the universe.

Choking the words on the tip of his tongue—"Will you feck off, you fecking old Paddy-bollicks"—Mattie was too elated to completely hide his self-satisfaction. "This is the first time I've not seen the flower of the praiseach in one of my fields in June."

Lawrence hesitated in his onward pursuit of snipe, and said, "Even if I have willed the farm to you, those are *my* fields till I die. As well as that, any eegit could tell you that praiseach can lie dormant in a field for fifty years and, sure as shite, it'll be back, tall enough to bite you in the hole." The uncle resumed his progress to the hunt through the long grass.

With his foot still on the bar of the gate, Mattie twisted his head and, with his brain sizzling in hatred, looked after his departing uncle and prayed that Lawrence Gorman's gun would go off when he was climbing over a hedge and blow his fecking head off.

When the thirtieth payment was due on the farm, Mattie Mulhall was still thatching. His father had died eleven years earlier after suffering a stroke and falling off a roof in Clonaslee. Mattie was now servicing his father's customers and using every windy and wet day to take care of his own crops.

In her kitchen, on the third Tuesday of the month, as the sexually depleted husband was on his way to open the turnip drills in the Middle Field, Peggy Mulhall rushed from table to cupboard to fireplace preparing Doul Yank's breakfast. Very soon, the gentleman farmer would grandly descend the stairs carrying his art-deco commode out to the dunghill.

Peggy always contrived to have something to do in the farmyard while Lawrence ate. She was heading toward the kitchen door as the footsteps upstairs moved across the kitchen ceiling. With her finger on the latch, she gave one last glance back to make sure everything was in its place. Satisfied that the table was properly set and that nothing embarrassing was hanging on the kitchen clothesline she turned back to the door and in the corner of her eye she saw her discarded pink knickers on the floor at the bedroom door. Her hand instinctively went to her crotch. "Holy Moses!" she gasped, as she felt her nakedness under her dress. "Lawrence will think it was me who dirtied the knickers."

She skipped back across the kitchen, scooped up the knickers and went into the bedroom. While she sat on the edge of the bed and carefully twisted a clean pair over her shoes, she heard Lawrence going out through the kitchen door with his bucket.

Smoothing down her dress, she came back into the kitchen and crinkled her nose against the sour smell wafting in the wake of the commode. When she stepped out into the farmyard, the uncle had already got rid of his exudations and the still air was full of stink. He was already at the water pump sloshing the rinsing water around the commode. As she walked past him and said, "Good morning, Uncle Lawrence," he flung the water onto the graveled yard at her feet. She did not allow the diluted splashes of the old body waste to divert her off the straight line she was taking to the turf shed. But Lawrence's question brought her to a stop.

"Who was that you were talking to a few minutes ago in the kitchen?"

Because of the detestation she felt for him, Peggy found it distasteful to even look at her husband's uncle. When she turned around she kept her eyes averted from his face. But in her mind's eye, she saw the bridge of his arched nose pulling the rest of his face into a permanent sneer of disapproval; saw the dark pools of his unfeeling eyes, the gash of his hard mouth, and the deep wrinkles of his sallow face like contour lines on the map of a mountainous country. In her peripheral vision she saw the only pair of clean Wellington boots in the county, the shape of the ridiculous knickerbockers, the dark tie against the starched collar of the white shirt, the deep-green fedora with the feathers of various dead birds stuck behind the hat band like the aigrette in the turban of an Indian prince.

The vapors of the foul bucket swinging in his liver-spotted hand seemed to reach out to Peggy and insert themselves into her nose. "That was Mattie," she said in answer to his question.

Lawrence took the lid of his commode off the corner of the pump-trough. "That fellow will never be a farmer if he's in the kitchen at eleven o'clock on a day like today," he said, and the sound of the lid returning to the commode underlined his pronouncement.

Peggy said nothing. If she had lunged through the strictures which prevented her from saying what she would have liked to say, she would have brought about the immediate disinheritance of her husband. She was used to restraining herself.

"Your breakfast is getting cold, Uncle Lawrence," she said pleasantly, and she continued on her way to the turf shed. Inside her skull her maledictive brain said, "I hope it chokes you."

8

In the Sunroom

In which Elsie Howard, wife of David Samuel,
Esq., explains why the divide between Protestants
and Catholics in a tight community can make
the reaping of gossip difficult.

A LOUD CLATTERING at the front of the house intruded into the
sunroom. "The lion roareth," Mister Howard said, and his wife
stood up as if she were a thirty-year-old; her knees didn't even creak.

"The Thatcherette did seethe till she died," Elsie said. "And not
only because she didn't become a landowner; it was having to buy
Doul Yank's passage home that put a burr in her brassiere for the
rest of her life."

"Else, I think you're getting into the realm of gossip here, and
as well as that I doubt if the woman ever wore a brassiere. And how
a woman could get a burr in her brassiere defies the imagination,"
Mister Howard said.

"No, Sam, this isn't gossip and I am allowed a figure of speech.
This is what I saw with my own eyes and heard with my own ears. As
well as the ticket home there was the humiliation of not inheriting
the land. . . . Remember she had already prepared the neighbors for
her induction into the land-owning class. It was like that farmer in
Carlow who got the telegram and thought he'd won a fortune when

he saw the advertisement on the envelope for the Irish Sweepstakes. After he'd run around telling all his neighbors he'd won the Sweep, someone who'd had experience with telegrams told him the message was inside the envelope. The message was that his sheep in the far field had worms."

The lion's nose ring clattered again, and Elsie said, "That's a Catholic. They're more impatient at front doors than Protestants." As she walked out she said, "And that farmer in Carlow had never bought a Sweepstakes ticket in his life."

"Else has been the gatekeeper since the day we came home from our honeymoon many moons ago, Patrick. Even though I'm long retired, people still come knocking, especially the older ones I've known all my life. Else directs them to the new man, who happens to be our son. When you're a small town solicitor, many people don't differentiate between your office and your house. I don't think I've ever answered a knock on our front door."

"Your father was a solicitor too, wasn't he?" Patrick asked.

"Yes, and his father before him. We're a bit like the old Brehons that way—from father to son. The Howards are as much a part of Gohen as the River Owonass. My grandfather lived in this house, too, and my son says he's going to live here when Else and I kick our respective buckets. I tried to persuade him to get a house ten miles away so he won't be bothered night, noon and morning. Living in the same town is as bad as living over the shop—you're never free of the business."

"If your grandfather lived here, then this house is fairly old," Patrick said.

"It was being built in 1798, during the United Irishmen rebellion, for a Freemason by the name of Hogg. When the Gohen lads who'd been in the fighting in Monasterevin were brought back to be hung, they passed by here just as the lintel of an upstairs window was being put in place. One of the workmen called out to the Redcoats, 'Bring them in here, and we'll hang them from the lintel.'"

"Jesus," Patrick said.

"Jesus be damned! The Redcoats brought them to a house at the far end of the town and hung them by tying a rope around a rafter and throwing the poor buggers out through the upstairs window."

Missus Howard came back into the room. "The hang-them-from-the-lintel story," she said. "I wonder, if they had hung them from the lintel would your grandfather have bought it, Sam?"

"No, Else, I don't think he would. He was a great admirer of Wolfe Tone—fellow Prod."

"Even the Catholics admit that Tone was a *good* Protestant." Else sat down. "That was the G.A.A. club at the door selling raffle tickets; first prize is a pair of ducks; tuppence each, and I bought five books."

"We've been lucky with the Catholic raffles, especially the Gaelic Athletic Association—never won their ducks," Mister Howard said. "But Else is a great supporter of raffles."

"Anything to let the Catholics know we're as Irish as they are; that it's our country, too. And anyhow, Protestants play Gaelic games every bit as good as Catholics, even if they call us Left-Footers. We even speak Irish as good as they do."

Sam said, "The Catholics like to think the Protestants don't know what goes on among them, but we knew everything. The Catholics and Protestants work too close together for it to be any other way. But it doesn't work as well the other way around because there are far fewer Protestants. We are inclined to keep our own peccadilloes away from Catholic ears as a form of defense."

Patrick said, "But still things can seep out into the community no matter what defenses you have. That conversation between your father and mother about the language Lizzie Coughlin used when she was told her brother was alive was told to me as gospel truth."

"That's it," Sam said, and he clapped his hands. "I knew I wanted to ask you something. How could anyone have known what my father said in his own house?"

Neither Elsie nor Patrick rushed to answer his question, and the three of them sat in silence for a while. Finally, Elsie said, "Sam, you don't know how gossip works. You have to give a bit to get a bit."

Again they sat in silence until Sam finally exclaimed, "No, Else, you never—"

But Elsie cut him off. "Oh, Sam, don't blow a gasket. I never gave away any of your privileged confidences because you never told me any. And you listen to gossip as eagerly as everyone else."

"I never traded in gossip."

"But you listened to it."

"I will admit that like my father I had a good source of community news—the postman, Kevin Lalor's father."

"Community news! Patrick, Sam applies his self-serving alchemy to words to suit himself. And I wish there was no such thing as Protestant and Catholic. I wish religion had never been invented. It leads to all kinds of stupidity and stupid thinking. Do you remember a Willie Collins, Patrick? He would have been about your age."

Patrick was momentarily nonplussed by the sudden question. "Yes, we were in the Boys' School together. Didn't he get killed—?"

"Yes, about twenty-five years ago. A sawmill blade jumped out of its anchors and more or less split him in two from the waist up. He had a day off and was helping the Mangan lads with the sawing. Some Catholics said that Willie was killed by God because he was working with the Protestant Mangans on a Catholic holy day. The things people make their God do!"

Elsie's searing tone established silence in its wake for a few moments.

Then Patrick said, "Religion encourages people to do many strange things to ensure instant and painless entry . . ."

9

The Sister

In which Bridie, sister of Eddie-the-cap
Coughlin, expresses her anxiety to Annie Lamb
about the impending six-month visit of her
brother, Jarlath, a missionary priest.

To ENSURE HER INSTANT AND PAINLESS ENTRY into the hereafter,
Bridie Coughlin's spiritual exercises included attendance at
the Women's Sodality in the church at seven o'clock on the fourth
Sunday of every month.

Bridie recited morning and night prayers while kneeling beside
her bed. She prayed the rosary every day after dinner while kneeling
at a chair on the concrete floor near the fire; she said grace before
and after her three meals, her eleven o'clock tea, her four o'clock
tea and before her tea and slice of bread at bedtime; she dipped her
finger in the Souvenir of Lourdes holy water font inside her front
door and blessed herself every time she went out of the house; she
prayed the Angelus at 7 a.m., 12 noon and 6 p.m.; she did the Stations
of the Cross while in Gohen on her weekly shopping excursions;
she never passed the church without going in to say hello to Jesus,
lonely in his tabernacle; she attended the 7 a.m. mass every day during Lent and scrupulously observed the Lenten fasting laws; she had
observed the rituals of the nine first Fridays many times over; she

blessed herself when she heard the dead bell announcing a death in the parish and when she saw a flash of lightning and saw a falling star and when she heard the corncrake for the first time in the spring, whenever she heard a hen trying to crow like a cock and whenever she heard bad news. She wore various medals and scapulars next to her skin. But she had read in *The Messenger of the Sacred Heart of Jesus* that faithful attendance at the Sodality of Our Lady of Mount Carmel *guaranteed* the safe delivery of the soul to the hereafter in a handbasket lined with hay.

No matter how severe the weather, when it was time for the Sunday evening service Bridie hauled her bike out of the turf shed and headed off to salvation, her head scarf tied tightly under her chin. On the occasions when she pedaled the three miles against a harsh north wind laden with horizontal rain that felt like icy pebbles on her exposed face and ungloved hands, Bridie knew the octane of the credit she was stashing away in her heavenly storage tank was very high. She hoped Saint Peter, infamous for falling asleep at the wrong times, was paying close attention to her efforts.

Whenever her determination to get to the Sodality wavered in the face of gale-force adversity, Bridie simply made herself think of the post-Sodality visit to Annie Lamb in Clunnyboe. Above and beyond the promise of the mug of hot sweet tea and the two cuts of curranty cake lathered in butter, there was the gossip to be dispensed and the gossip to be gleaned.

And so it was, on the evening of the fourth Sunday of May, Annie Lamb was settling on a straight-back chair in front of the kitchen fire with a very tattered *Jane Eyre*. As she pulled her dress up to her knees and opened her legs wide to the heat of the glowing turf, the sounds of the spring storm howling in the chimney and the slates added to her feelings of coziness. There was no trepidation lurking in her breast that Bridie Coughlin would be rambling tonight, because only a madwoman would be out on her bike on such a night as this. The children were in bed, and Annie was wallowing in the prospect of four hours of uninterrupted reading. She sighed with contentment as the heat moved in and encased the upper reaches of her thighs with glowing warmth.

Annie opened her book with more anticipation than when she'd read it the first time. Because of the scarcity of books, but also because she loved the story, this was her seventh adventure with Jane and Rochester. As if tasting the first sips of a longed-for cup of tea, Annie slowly savored the opening words, letting them slip deliciously into every nook and cranny of her brain. *There was no possibility of taking a walk that day, the cold winter wind had brought with it clouds so somber, and a rain so penetrating, that further outdoor exercise was now out of the question.*

Annie heard a noise at the door. Thinking her husband, Simon Peter, was coming in with a basket of turf, and never suspecting for one moment that Bridie Coughlin was standing out there on the step, Annie, book in hand, went to the door and opened it.

She almost screamed at the apparition she beheld.

If only Annie Lamb could have imagined a buck-toothed, red-headed woman, smelling worse than the pelts she wore, who had lived locally in the days of melting glaciers, she would have seen that primitive's direct descendant standing in front of her now. Buck-toothed, red-headed, looking like she'd been dragged across the Shannon at the wrong end of a rope, Bridie Coughlin stood there in the dim light of the kitchen's paraffin-oil lamp. She was grinning with glee at her triumph over the elements, the grin as toothy and as gummy and as false as the grin of a performing orangutan.

At the last moment, Annie Lamb's strangled scream emerged from her lips high-pitched but reshaped into words: "Sure, Bridie, it's grand to see you," and she wondered what was hanging on the kitchen clothesline. She stood aside and, as Bridie stepped past her, the smell of the Sodality's incense ascended out of her permeated and waterlogged coat. Once again, Annie was reminded that she would never smell church incense without Bridie Coughlin's vaporous visage rising into her brain.

With eyes closed in resignation, a finger still between the pages of *Jane Eyre*, Annie closed the kitchen door and turned around.

Standing in the middle of the floor, Bridie was holding her head scarf. From the hem of her cloth coat, fat drops of water plopped down onto the concrete floor enclosing her in a wet circle. A pillar of steam rising out of the top of her head reminded Annie Lamb of a line drawing in the Penny Catechism showing the Holy Ghost descending onto the heads of the Apostles in the shape of tongues of fire.

The redness of Bridie's hair was that of a Rhode Island Red chicken's feathers. The strands, as straight and as scarce as the hair on an old coconut that's been in the sea too long, were as jagged as a young girl's who has been at her own hair with her mother's scissors. Her face, all teeth and gums and blond brows and popping eyes, was as eager for company as the gaping maw of an ascending baleen whale craves krill.

Bridie wrestled her body out of the sodden overcoat, and when she turned to hang it on the wooden rack attached to the parlor door, Annie Lamb whipped a pair of her husband's drawers off the clothesline. She rolled them into a ball and threw them onto the wide sill of the kitchen window among the untidy pages of the day's newspaper, children's caps and a ball of wool pierced with two long knitting needles.

With, "I was just saying, Annie, that a wet and windy May fills the haggard with corn and hay," and a teeth-jarring rubbing of her sandpaper-rough hands, Bridie went to the fire and turned her back to the heat. Steam rose out of her behind.

Annie Lamb had not yet recovered from the brutal intrusion. And as it became clearer how her evening had changed, a fierce disappointment came upon her, a disappointment all the more intense because of the time of month that was in it for Annie. She had the presence of mind to say, "I think I hear Fintan awake," and she went through the door leading to the three bedrooms. She shuffled through the darkness of the hallway to her own room and sat down hard on the hard edge of the hard bed, her cheeks already as runny as the face of a bawling child. It was only when she brought her hands to her face that she realized she was still holding *Jane Eyre*, still had her finger stuck inside holding her place at the first page. She let the book fall at her feet, and within seconds her shoulders were heaving.

Annie Lamb was a hormonally weepy woman, and the dam was full. The gates swung wide open. It took nearly four minutes of intense sluicing to flush out her emotional system. Then, as if she were slowly waking after a deep and dreamless sleep, she found herself relaxed. She dried her face in her handkerchief. The female-for-female sympathy she normally felt for Bridie had almost reestablished itself in her head.

Annie Lamb, wife of Simon Peter, mother of Mikey, Molly and Fintan, felt around in the dark at her feet until she touched her book. She stood up and dropped it on her side of the bed. She would start again by candlelight when she came to bed. As she went back to the kitchen, she took the man's handkerchief out of her apron pocket again and dabbed at her eyes.

Bridie Coughlin was already in full gossip stride when Annie entered the kitchen. Simon Peter had finally come in with the basket of turf and had been ambushed by a volley from Bridie's Gatling teeth. Annie could see plainly what Bridie, in her roaring hunger for human companionship, could not: that Simon Peter was an impaled worm writhing on a barbed fishhook. When he saw his wife coming through the door, Simon Peter sidled out of Bridie's line of sight and turned his eyes to Annie in a plea for permission to escape. His wife nodded in understanding.

With nowhere else to escape to, Simon Peter silently slipped through the door to the bedrooms. Annie brought a kitchen-table chair to the fire and quietly placed it on the bare concrete floor across from Bridie.

Bridie had not missed a beat during the changing of her audience, and she continued to spate out a stream of words without full stops, commas, hyphens or paragraphs. Even on the inhalation of her breath she shaped words that sounded like the gaspings of an asthmatic. From subject to subject she hopped with the ease of a stone skipping across a calm pond from the hand of a boy on the sunny afternoon of a summer's Sunday. Bridie didn't even notice Annie Lamb hadn't yet sat down, that she was taking the dripping, Sodality-smelling coat off the parlor door and hanging it on the drying nail in the wall of the chimney.

". . . Doul Yank in those knickerbockers of his and he talking to me through a hole in the hedge with two snipes hanging from his belt and he complaining about Mattie-the-nephew the day Eddie was at the fair—last Tuesday, it was. I was just saying, I couldn't take my eyes off the two snipes with their beaks as long as number eight knitting needles. I thought there was something quare about the birds, and it took me ages to figure out he had elastic garters around them to keep their wings all tidy-like against their bodies to keep them from flopping all over the place and getting in his way. 'In the kitchen having his elevenses with the sun splitting the trees,' says he, 'when he should have been off thatching or out in the fields working. That lad's not worth a pike's shite,' says he. The tongue of him! Then he starts talking about the snipes. 'There's wonderful medicinal qualities in the meat, and the grease is a great embrocation for the gout,' says he, 'all that suction out on the bog, sucking up nothing but goodness through them long beaks of theirs. If we could only live by suction we'd be as healthy as snipes ourselves. I've never met a sick snipe in all my days,' he says. And then he starts telling me about how he was going to send the snipes up to the Convent for the nun with the teebee, all plucked and drawn as if he would be doing the plucking and the cleaning himself and not Peggy-the-niece-in-law. I was just saying, by the way that man talks you'd think he was giving the nuns the snipes for nothing and he charging them half a crown a bird. A half a crown, mind you! Peggy has to paunch and skin the rabbits he shoots. He wouldn't get a bit of blood and guts on his hands. Embrocation, says he. That man's a ferocious eegit!"

With teeth flashing, spittle spraying and eyes darting, Bridie released the fetid energy that never ceased to build up from working side by side on their farm with her bachelor brother—two forgottens unnaturally paired in middle age in a relationship where unexpressed anger was pressurized, where dead-endedness and bitterness and regret and envy were the filters through which they both interpreted the world.

In tones full of sharp-edged judgment or cynical wonder, Bridie recited everything she had heard from every person who had spoken to her since her last post-Sodality visit. "But how," wondered Annie Lamb, "does she ever hear what anyone else has to say?"

Without her even noticing it happening, the doors to Annie's ears swung slowly shut until she was only hearing a distant drone, a sound like a trapped bee buzzing in a bottle. With arms folded loosely under her breasts, her eyes fell down toward the floor, and she began the exercises she had developed over the years that would keep her from nodding off and subsequently snapping into wakefulness, jerking all over the hearth like a poleaxed cow in a slaughterhouse, nearly falling off the chair.

Into Annie's descending eyes the hem of Bridie's brown skirt appeared; then came a few inches of the thin, hose-clad legs exposed between the hem and the man's socks—the tops turned down to the knotty calves. The thickness, the grayness, and the wooliness of the socks were loud declarations that Bridie Coughlin never dressed with an eye jaundiced by feminine delicacy. The brown booties, worn on Sundays only, twenty-nine years old and resoled six times by Ralph Behan-the-cobbler, were styled after the footwear of Robin Hood and Peter Pan in Mikey's comics.

With heroic determination Annie kept the doors to her ears ajar, and she heard Bridie talking about thatching, about her brother Eddie and about Mattie Mulhall.

"Eddie says to Mattie, 'Sure I didn't know till yesterday myself I'd have to go to the fair, and anyhow Bridie says she'll serve you on the roof. She can pull the thatch as good as any man, and the ladder won't be any bother at all, she's up and down the ladder at the reeks in the haggard oftener than myself.' 'Ah, Jazus, no Eddie,' says Mattie, 'sure I'd never have a woman on a ladder, it's terrible unlucky to have a woman on a ladder. If only you'd told me sooner I could have got one of the young Kearnses, but they're all on the bog wheeling turf.' 'Sure, I told you the minute I knew myself,' says Eddie. 'Bridie's as good as any man, Mattie, like a monkey on a ladder.' 'Begob, I won't have a woman on a ladder, and that's that,' says Mattie. 'No, Eddie, I'll do a bit of work on my own land tomorrow meself, open the turnip drills, and I'll be back on Wednesday. The only thing is I promised Willie Reid I'd start over at his place next Monday and I hate telling a man I'll be there and then not turning up. If you see anyone at the fair that lives out near Willie Reid, tell them I told you to tell them to tell Willie I told you to pass the word along that I won't be there till Tuesday.' And with that Mattie went off home leaving Eddie half afraid he might be in a bit of a snit, sort of afraid Mattie wouldn't come back to finish the job, he was so cross. 'For God's sake,' says I to Eddie, 'did you ever hear of Mattie Mulhall never finishing a job that he started?' I was just saying that he even finished the job on the roof his own father fell off of and got killed, was there a few hours after the funeral to get on with the job."

Long after her attention had lost its grip on Eddie and Mattie and thatching, Annie Lamb came to herself again. She found herself examining Bridie's face and, because she didn't know how long she'd been staring, she quickly pulled her eyes away. But even so, Bridie's skin was trapped in her mind. Like the leather of an old discarded boot, there were cracks and wrinkles in Bridie's skin telling the story of exposure and abuse. Like the real laboring farmer that she was, Bridie even had the line on her forehead an inch below the hairline— the track of corpse-white skin protected by the man's peaked cap she wore winter and summer in the fields and the farmyard. Her eyes were slightly apop; the gashed mouth framed in thin lips curled for-ever in disappointment; the nose a severely bowed bridge covered in skin as lifeless as the leaf of an ash tree lying in a December ditch.

The desperation that had first appeared as she approached the last of her child-bearing years had been etched permanently into Bri-die's eyes by the dreadful realization that no man would ever woo her. And now, many years later, the etchings were still plain to see.

"Wasn't the Martyr very cagey about drawing the horse in the Grand National in the Protestant raffle?—never told a soul. Tuppence the ticket cost her, and the horse came in third. If she'd only drawn the winner she'd have won a hundred pounds, but Eddie says, 'It's just as well she didn't or she'd a died with the fright.' Some Protestant won that of course, money attracts money, or as I was just saying, have a goose and you'll get a goose. The second horse went to a Protestant, too, fifty quid. Eddie says they had to make sure a Catholic won something to keep the Catholics buying the Protestant tickets the next time around, so they went through all the stubs till they found the one belonging to the Martyr Madden and gave her the horse that came in third. Fifteen quid, the most money the Martyr ever had in her life, and she told no one. Only Eddie was talking to Mister Morgan-of-the-shop we'd never have known, and the Martyr eating her breakfast and dinner and supper in our house six days a week. Eddie says the Martyr wouldn't tell anyone in case they'd ask her for some of it or for a loan she'd never get back. I was just saying, did you ever notice how the Protestant prizes are always bigger than the Catholic ones? Protestants give money, Catholics give ducks and who, I ask you, wants two more bloody ducks around the place? Duck dung is a terrible nuisance, and they do it everywhere. I was just saying, I'm always stepping in duck dung. And as well as that the raffle was for the repairs on the Protestant church, and the Martyr shouldn't have supported that. I'd let it all fall down on top of them, and that'd show them who is right."

Bridie's train of thought lurched onto another track and careened ahead at full speed. Annie Lamb stored away the news of Biddy Madden's winnings in a cerebral pigeonhole, and her barely focused eyes fell down onto Bridie's lap.

Bridie's hands, resembling the scaly feet of a turkey, were resting in the clothed valley between her thighs. Annie knew that on the surfaces and in the bones of those hands was carved the history of Bridie Coughlin; a story etched by newly-surfaced stones picked off the land every cold and wet springtime; by the thorny briars furiously gathered with barley straw into sheaves at harvesttime; by the razor edges of clutched grass slipping through fingers when a handful of bum-wiping fodder was gathered under a hedge. The hands had been permanently marked with dirt pressed into the skin by the hard handles of dung-spreading forks; by the jerking reins of toiling and fly-annoyed horses; by the spring-loaded handles of castrating pincers that changed bull calves into bullocks; by the staining juices of weeds angrily pulled from the long drills of sugar beet and turnips and mangels and potatoes; by the handles of two-pronged, hay-pitching forks; by the rough twine used for tying the necks of coarse burlap sacks full of wheat and barley and oats at harvest time.

Not all the perfumed soaps in all the chemist shops in the world could soften and clean those hands; neither could the oleiferous glands, elbow-deep inside calving cows; nor the grease of butter scraped off the sides of churns; nor the slime of eggs hand-mixed into weekly dough; nor the milk used to wet caressing fingers on cows' teats; nor the diluted Jeyes Fluid swished around empty chamber pots; nor the rough tongues of suckling calves learning to bucket-drink from fingers hidden under the surface of the milk; nor the rubbing of salt into pigs' meat after the yearly slaughter; nor the squashing of potatoes in milk for the dogs' dinners; nor the mixing of delicate mashes of boiled eggs and chopped dandelion and nettle leaves for newborn turkeys and chicks and goslings and ducklings. On her waking bed, Bridie's hands, clutching a set of rosary beads on her chest, would be as scarred and as stained as they were at this present moment.

The sound of Bridie's other brother's name whispered along the tendrils of sleep creeping across Annie Lamb's brain. She changed her position on the chair, hoped she was giving the impression she had been paying attention all along.

"... until the Suez Canal was open for passenger ships. He'll never go around by Good Hope again after that journey back just when the war started. Sure, he was terrible lucky to get back at all then, and he can't even hear the word 'Africa' now without feeling like he's going to die. He vomited all the way down the one side of Africa and across the bottom of Africa, too, and halfway out into the Indian Ocean he said in a letter. The middle of June he'll be in Southampton and two more days home from there. I was just saying that's why we have Mattie doing the bit of thatching, so the place looks a bit decent when Jarlath gets home. The Martyr will do the whitewashing inside and outside. But she's a terrible woman with the splatters. He's used to all

them nice things out in India, especially since he became the princi-
pal himself and three other priests helping him and the rest of them
lay teachers, over a hundred of them altogether, so that'll tell you
how big the school is; hundreds of children and they all Indians. It's
as good as an English school, he says, but then didn't Dinglish build
it and they pay for the running of the whole thing, too, just too glad
to have someone like Jarlath and his likes to do the work for them for
next to nothing. Dinglish, you know! They're all over the place like
the scour of a sucking calf. He's going to see a lot of changes since he
was home before the war."

Then Bridie took off at a gallop about the new Protestant minister's
wife who would cut the socks off you with her style. It was Bridie's
opinion that a minister's wife had no business looking as good as that,
it being almost a mortal sin for a minister to have a wife that looked
as good. Wouldn't it be better for a minister to have a wife who was a
bit on the dowdy side, a bit fat and wearing black, instead of a young
one making the rest of the women in the world look shapeless with
her indecent figure? And the seamless nylons!

As she pursued the shapely and stylish Protestant wife around
the town, yipping like an irksome terrier at her heels, Bridie tightly
pulled her shapeless cardigan around her own timid chest as if to
shield it from comparison with the Protestant promontories.

And Annie Lamb, who had fallen behind Bridie in her relentless,
begrudging pursuit, was thinking about a secret she had told Sheila
Feeney, her very best friend since their first day in First Babies in
the Convent School, married in Gohen to Quick Quigley-the-road-
sweeper. Since early adolescence, when she had first realized what
married people do with each other, Annie Lamb discovered she had
the gift of imagining couples copulating. It was an instinctive thing
with her, this instant placing of the woman on her back on the bed,
the man on top sawing away. It didn't matter if the couple was coming back from the altar rails at Mass looking as solemn as saints, or
whether they were jogging to the fair in their ass-and-cart; they simply
became suddenly naked in Annie's head with the man between the
woman's spread legs, whacking away like the big dog she'd once seen

doing it to a small bitch in the Protestant part of the parish cemetery. It didn't matter to Annie if the couples were young and halfway handsome or old and ugly and fat as old pigs; she had a wonderful facility for undressing them in a flash and, until she told Sheila Feeney about what she could do, she thought everyone else did the same thing, at least women. 'And what does Quick look like when we're doing it?' Sheila had laughingly asked. 'Like a dunghill cock with a hen,' Annie had said. 'Up, flutter and down again, maybe because his nickname is Quick.' 'But his nickname is Quick because he's so slow about everything. Long and thick, and not too quick, is what he whispers in me ear when we're at it, and me under him trying not to laugh. I snorted the first time he said it and I shot him out of me.' The two friends had laughed until they got stitches in their sides, their backs to the railing around the churchyard after running into each by accident.

Annie Lamb surfaced for a few seconds to make sure Bridie Coughlin's soliloquy was not in need of sustenance from the sidelines.

" . . . and every Protestant minister I've ever seen in my life looked like he needed a good feed of cabbage and spuds with a good mug of buttermilk. And every Protestant minister's wife I've ever seen in my life had thick legs, not like this one . . ."

And as Bridie Coughlin continued to pester the Protestant minister's wife, Annie Lamb was looking at the minister and his wife on their bed. Because the wife looked beautiful and delicate, the husband was delicate in his movements. Raised on his outstretched arms above her, he was sliding in and out so slowly he could have been keeping time to a solemn Protestant funeral hymn he was hearing in his head, or else doing press-ups like those soldiers training in the newsreel in the Picture House in Gohen during the war. The woman beneath him had a pair of compact breasts on her chest, not a couple of old sagging sacks falling away on each side into her armpits like Missus Dempsey. Every time he completed the gentle lunge, the minister's wife, with skin of milk and hair of honey, moaned. Down along the female body Annie Lamb's eyes crept, down to where the two people were joined, and she waited with bated breath for the man to raise himself so she could see the Protestant ministerial mickey. But the minister remained buried in his bride. Suddenly, his elbows collapsed and he sank down onto his wife. They dissolved into a pair of writhing eels on the bed, he moaning and she screaming through clenched teeth and sealed lips, the way a mother must in case her young children might think she was being murdered. Annie Lamb checked in with Bridie Coughlin again.

". . . and the Martyr's mind is going quicker by the week. There she was gathering the eggs out of the nests in the side of the hayrick, and she saying it over and over and over to herself. I was just saying, I don't know how long more we'll be able to keep her around the place. Last week she heeled up in front of Eddie and let fly with her water before he could get away, cutting the stones out of the yard with her squarts, not the stitch of a knickers on her. She's always muttering to herself, 'The Protestants. The Protestants. I have my bag and my handkerchief. I have my bag and my handkerchief. What's so funny, what's so funny?' Nearly whispering it to herself, and I just after saying, that only I have the ears of a rabbit I wouldn't know what she was saying. They say a rabbit can hear the grass growing."

Annie Lamb's mind drifted from the Protestant minister's sexual ministrations to her own nuptial bed, to the warmth she always felt when she was entangled in Simon Peter after their own sessions of moaning and tight-lipped screaming. The feel of his hairy skin on her skin, the feel of his body from face to toes, the feel of his entwining arms was better than any miracle at Lourdes—God forgive me. Annie Lamb loved the satisfaction of her skin-hunger, and when she heard her visitor in the distance, Annie realized that Bridie, since the time she had been held as a child, had never had another person put entwining arms around her body, clothed or naked. Bridie had never died and gone to heaven in another human's arms. And Annie Lamb realized, as she forced her brain back into the sterile stream of Bridie's steady flow of verbiage, that this very absence in Bridie's life was the foundation of Annie's sympathy for her. "Anyone who doesn't skin with another must be lonely to the point of being mildly mad."

As she surfaced out of her reverie and was pulled deeper into Bridie's swirling and polluted eddies, Annie wondered if the man's life that Bridie was living, side by side with her brother, somehow made her less of a woman, robbed her of little things that Annie herself took for granted: the feel of a husband's strong hand on one of her arse cheeks; the dirty talk about sex she and Simon Peter used when they were alone; walking past her husband and running her hand softly across the front of his trousers; the rough grab and kiss in one of the sheds when there was no danger of being discovered by the children; the sudden sex, almost frightening, in the dark in the loose straw at the foot of the straw rick, hands tearing at clothing, bodies heaving and plunging with ferocious animalness; the feel of a sleepy child in the lap in front of a fire.

As she straightened her back against the hard wood of the kitchen chair, Annie Lamb surreptitiously glanced at the clock on the wall. It was time to make the tea. She picked up the long tongs and poked the fire. The ever-hanging kettle changed its tune.

". . . that time the Civil Servant went off to Germany to hear the operas and saw Hitler. Wasn't he terrible brave to do that, and Hitler going around shooting people by the hundred. I would have died, and he only a few feet away from him."

Annie stood up and took the tea canister off the high mantelpiece.

"I was just saying, I'd love to hear the operas myself, all that music and singing. Sure, there's nothing like a bit of music. Sometimes when we're out in the fields, and the wind's blowing the right way, we can hear the pipe band practicing in the football field in Gohen; the big drum and Bill Brophy on the pipes sending songs into the sky like he was a lark gone mad. I think if you go to the opera, you have to dress up. I'd have to buy a new hat and maybe a wristwatch."

Using the corner of her apron to protect her hand from the heat of the kettle's handle, Annie Lamb poured the spluttering water and put the teapot near the fire to keep it hot while the tea drew.

"Wasn't it a fright during the war with no tea to be bought at all? That's one thing Jarlath wasn't short of in India and he would have sent us tons only he knew it would have got sunk with the ship it was on. That was the time all the ships were going to the bottom of the sea like stones, sunk by Hitler. Wasn't he a terrible man altogether?"

From under the kitchen table Annie Lamb swung another chair across to the fire. She put the steaming teacup and the plateful of butter-laden, curranty cake down on the makeshift table.

"Ah, sure, you shouldn't have bothered with tea at all, Annie," was Bridie's way of thanking Annie for her hospitality. She filled her mouth with the sweet cake, slurped loudly at the edge of the cup and continued talking. "Eddie will be sitting there staring into the fire waiting for me to make the tea for him when I get home. I was just saying, if I fell off the bike and got killed going home, wouldn't Eddie be found dead in the chair in front of the fire, dead of starvation because I never got home to feed him? All dried out like an old rabbit skin."

With her face glowing from the heat of the fire and her mouth still full of the taste of sweet tea and curranty cake, Bridie Coughlin stood up and brushed the crumbs off her skirt onto the floor. Meanwhile, Annie Lamb retrieved the blue coat from the drying nail in the chimney. As she held it up, Bridie put her arms behind her and backed into the sleeves. When the coat swung around her, she said, "Oh, God, Annie, but the coat feels so nice and dry and warm. You're the only one who'd ever think of having it nice and cozy for a body. That's one of the things that's going to bother Jarlath when he comes home, the cold. It always does. He'll be here for six months. Do you think I'll be able for him, Annie? Him with his servants to look after him out in India, and they with running water and the electric; fans in the ceilings to keep them cool, no less. Fans, mind you! I was just saying, it's not fans he'll be needing when he comes home. It's a good fire he'll be wanting the whole time to keep himself warm."

Annie Lamb threw her husband's topcoat over her head and around her shoulders. When she opened the kitchen door, a gust of watery wind blew in on her face.

Adjusting her scarf one more time, Bridie Coughlin put her head down and stepped out into the dark. "Now, you shouldn't be bothering coming out to see me off, Annie," was her way of thanking Annie for her consideration.

Out on the road, Bridie took hold of the bike's handlebars as if they were the horns of an uppity bull calf she was about to wrestle to the ground with a view to castrating him. A gust of wind howled around the two women as Bridie switched on her flashlamp and turned her bike in the direction of home. "Sure, Eddie says I'm as tough as a noul galvanized bucket, Annie. I'll be home in no time because once I get to Tuohy's Corner the wind will be in my back." And then, like a lone, lost crow blown across a stormy sky, Bridie was gone.

10

In the Sunroom

In which Elsie Howard and Patrick Bracken contemplate the role of luck in human affairs.

"DEAR GOD," MISSUS HOWARD said. "What a joyless life! I remember Bridie Coughlin, and I knew others like her who spent their lives teetering on the edge of madness. Life can be such a mean, miserable and nonstop grind for some, the nonstop fretfulness; the bitterness. How unlucky some people are!"

Silence fell into the sunroom. If there had been anyone in the garden looking in, he would have seen an old couple gazing out, their eyes lost in the distance; he would have seen the back of a man's head, his elbows on his knees and his face enclosed in his long fingers like a hazelnut in its cupped September husk.

Even when the silence dragged on, Patrick did not feel uncomfortable. He contemplated the role of luck in people's lives, in his own life. He saw his professional life as a road that crossed other roads; where the roads crossed, a square was formed; in those small squares, chance meetings had occurred and he had taken advantage of them by making connections. Was that what luck was? Finding oneself with someone else for a few moments in a coincidental meeting?

Was making your own luck just another name for the survival of the fittest? For the most calculating? For the brightest? For the slyest? For the most devious? For the more self-assured? But Patrick knew he had also made his own luck by lying in wait in the corner of the square for the certain arrival of that other person.

In the corner of his eye Patrick thought he saw Elsie's fingers wiping at tears. He looked directly at her and, indeed, she was surreptitiously spreading the tears on her face to make them evaporate quickly. He heard her sighing softly.

"You're sighing, Else," Sam said, and he changed his position, brought himself back into in the sunroom.

"Yes, Sam," Elsie said, and she shook herself out of the sadness that had sprung her tears. "God, I was so lucky! It's all a matter of luck"—she held up her hand to Patrick—"and I know we make our own luck to a certain extent, but pure luck, pure coincidence is a real part of it all. The Bridie Coughlins of this world didn't have any luck at all." She stood up. "Patrick, your story about Bridie reminded me: I have a curranty cake, and I'm going to make a fresh pot of tea." She stood up and collected the three used cups. "Did your mother make a curranty cake every Saturday for Sunday?"

"No, Else, she didn't. But Missus Lamb did, and her son Mikey brought some to school for his lunch on Mondays. That's how we started being friends—when he gave me some."

"Imagine!" Missus Howard came to a stop near the kitchen door, cups and saucers in her hands, "You married the woman you married because her brother gave you a piece of cake when you were children. Life is full of coincidences."

Mister Howard said, "Else loves coincidences, Patrick. She believes they are foreordained by fate or God or the fairies or Mao Zedong."

"Sam has no room in his head for anything except logic, Patrick," Elsie said. "And no more about the return of the natives till I have the tea made." She went into the kitchen.

Sam threw his voice after her. "The word 'coincidence' is invariably used incorrectly in an effort to remove the randomness from our lives."

The sound of flowing water stopped in the kitchen, and Elsie came to the door with the kettle in her hand.

"Patrick," she said, "I had to give Sam many infusions of romance over the years. But every now and then he falls into remission and his logical self flares up." She retreated.

"That's true," Sam said to Patrick, and he raised his voice again. "She has treated me, but I had to treat her too; exfuse her romanticism and infuse her with a good dose of logic every so often, especially when it comes to coincidences."

Elsie came back with a plate of sliced curranty cake. She said, "You're just being stubborn and annoying with that new word of yours: 'exfuse.' Look it up in the dictionary, and you won't find it. And will you stop boring Patrick with your coincidence speech, Sam. You'll drive him away before we find out what he has to tell us." She went out again.

She failed to derail her husband. "It's only when we seize the randomness and rename it that coincidence enters in. We invent coincidence in order to convince ourselves that there is some purpose to our lives."

Elsie came in with three mugs on a small tray. "There's more tea in a mug than a cup," she said. When she held out the tray, the two men took their tea. "I forgot the plates," she said as she put the tray down on the table. "Randomly, I forgot the plates and if I fall and break my hip when I go back to get them it will be a coincidence that I broke it while Patrick was here because if he wasn't here I wouldn't have broken it." She went out and came back immediately with three plates. As she handed them around she said, "Coincidently, gentlemen, I did not break my hip; isn't that a coincidence?"

"Jesus!" Mister Howard said. "I'm sorry I mentioned it."

"Wasn't it a real coincidence that you did?" Elsie said, and Patrick almost sputtered tea.

"She never knows when to stop," Sam said, and he smiled.

Patrick complimented Missus Howard on the quality of her cake.

"Is it as good as Missus Lamb's?" she asked.

"You're fishing for a compliment, Else," Sam said

"Patrick can tell the truth," Missus Howard said.

"Nothing will ever taste as good as Missus Lamb's curranty cake, Else, because until I tasted hers, I had never eaten curranty cake."

"Curranty cake and sex and everything else in the world," Sam said. "There's nothing like the first time." The two Howards, unembarrassed, floated off into their memories for a moment. When they showed signs of returning, Patrick said, "Even though most people called him . . ."

11

The Civil Servant

1951

In which it is seen why it had to be Kevin Lalor,
a.k.a. the Civil Servant, who discovered the body
on the hill on a summer morning in 1951.

EVEN THOUGH MOST PEOPLE CALLED HIM Kevin to his face, they always
referred to Kevin Lalor as the Civil Servant. Lalor was secretive
by nature and inclination, but over the years his neighbors had
drawn inferences from what he didn't say as much as from what he
allowed to escape. Some facts were inescapable.

Kevin Lalor was the only child of Betty and Pascal Lalor, both
now living in a council cottage in Gohen. The quoins at the corners the windows and door were painted red. The front door was
red too, and the house white. A low wall with a red gate kept cattle,
horses and dogs from plundering and dropping their dung in the
small flower garden. Townspeople often said to each other, "Isn't the
postman's house as neat as a pin. It could be on a Christmas card."

During the First Battle of the Somme a piece of exploding shell
hit Pascal Lalor above the knee and left the two parts of his leg connected by a sliver of flesh. As the battle raged and soldiers ran past
him into a storm of bullets fired from German machine guns, Lalor
drew on reserves he never knew he had. He sat up in no-man's land

with his back to Ypres and his front to Tyne Cot, used the belt of his water can as a tourniquet, finished the shrapnel's job with his bayonet, took the boot and sock off the dead leg, looked at its sole, and threw it away. With boot and sock clutched to his chest, he fainted from shock and loss of blood. Nineteen hours later, a searching stretcher-bearer stepped on Lalor's stump in the dark, and Pascal came moaning back to consciousness and salvation. While a nurse in a field hospital gave him an injection of morphine in preparation for the cleaning, trimming and sewing of the stump, the boot and the sock were pulled from his clutching arms. As he floated back from morphine heaven, Lalor lingered in a layer of dense anxiety in which an English officer berated him for losing some of His Majesty's ordinance. "Damn your lost leg, Pat. The boot and sock were army issue! Your pay will be docked."

In 1917, from the bus stop in Gohen, Pascal Lalor rode home from the war on a black, army issued, fixed-wheel bike, the right leg doing all the pedaling, the left wooden leg hanging straight down and resting in a stirrup a few inches above the ground. In his pocket was a pension from the King and a piece of paper entitling him to a civil service job. In 1917 he married the woman he had left behind, and nine months later he was a father. When the ownership of the country finally came back into Irish hands in 1922, Pascal Lalor managed to hold on to his postman's job, even though he had been exiled to the edge of society for having joined the British army. The old soldier would not have minded being called "Limpin Lalor" had the tone been sympathetic. But not only was the nickname used without neutrality, there was a jeer in it that rankled every time Pascal heard it.

On the strength of his father's British army pension, his postman's wages and a small scholarship, the son, Kevin Lalor attended the Christian Brother School in Marbra and received a secondary education. For five years Kevin traveled the seven miles of the Bog Road on his bike twice a day. He never missed a day in five years, and he won a dictionary for perfect attendance. But his most public academic achievement was the publication of his winning essay in *The Leinster Express*. The secondary level was as far as he traveled in the meadows of academia. He was eighteen when he got the job in the courthouse and quickly became known as the Civil Servant to everyone in Clunnyboe and Drumsally and Gohen. Seventeen years later he was the person who issued licenses for bulls, stallions, boars, dogs, guns and wirelesses throughout the county. When his parents moved into Gohen, Kevin decided to stay on in the rented house he had been born and bred in.

It was not only on account of his collar-and-tie job that Kevin Lalor was regarded by all his neighbors, except the returned exile Lawrence Gorman, as being a cut above everyone else. He occupied a lofty niche in society because he had once seen Hitler. The Civil Servant had expressed his relief on several occasions that he had not seen the apparitions at Fatima or Lourdes: "Otherwise, I'd be canonized altogether," he was heard to say once while eating his lunch sandwich of butter and jam in the courthouse.

It was unusual in those days for the people of Clunnyboe, Drumsally and Gohen to have visitors in their houses unless they were sufficiently well off to have nice furniture instead of the scarce, vernacular creations and wooden boxes that most people had. The only way his neighbors knew about the inside of Kevin Lalor's house was through the child Mikey Lamb. When questioned, Mikey Lamb spoke of cleanliness and warmth. There was an armchair with a cushion. There were thick books and a crystal set, thousands of postage stamps stuck into albums, a gramophone that played strange-smelling records. And on the records women sang in high voices like they were cross, and men sang like they were giving orders to everyone else in the world. And there were always two white shirts hanging upside down on the kitchen clothesline. Pictures of ducks and hens and geese hung on the kitchen walls as well as a framed copy of the essay that won the prize in *The Leinster Express*.

Kevin Lalor left his house at ten minutes to seven, six mornings a week, no matter what the weather was doing. On his clean, black, stout Raleigh bike, with its dynamo, bell and pump, he rode to his job in Gohen. A broad rubber band, cut from an old inner tube, danced in the center of each wheel and kept the axles shining. In bad weather

Lalor wore his khaki gabardine coat, his sandwich in the left pocket, and his peaked cap. When the weather was good, he traveled in his suit and cap, with the folded overcoat tied up in its own belt on the spring-loaded carrier above the back wheel, the sandwich in the left pocket of his jacket. And, even though the chain had a gear-case cover, Lalor always wore bicycle clips at his ankles to keep the cuffs of his trousers clean. Locally, this had given rise to the adage aimed at the over fastidious: "You're as bad as the Civil Servant with his gear-case and bike clips." In his seventeen years of employment, Kevin Lalor had not missed a day's work. And it was because he was always the first person to travel the Lower Road every morning that he was the one who found the body in that summer of 1951.

12

The Bike

1951

In which Mikey Lamb, age eleven, confides more in Kevin Lalor, a.k.a. the Civil Servant, than he does in his own father, Simon Peter.

On a Friday evening in May, a few minutes after eight, Kevin Lalor was slouched in his armchair in front of the dying kitchen fire. At the end of his stretched-out legs, his feet rested on a low, three-legged stool. The two shirts hanging on the high clothesline above him were like the headless carcasses of eviscerated two-legged goats.

The whitewash on the walls of the small kitchen would have been whiter had there been more light. Through the small window only enough twilight seeped for Lalor to see the holes in the toes of his ancient, colorless slippers. Brown linoleum, its geometrical pattern faded into the gloom, covered the concrete floor. The dresser, with its display of glistening willow pattern dishes, plates, saucers, cups, eggcups, sugar bowl, teapot and milk jug, were bequests from his parents when they moved into Gohen. Lalor was not neurotically fastidious, but he did like order and cleanliness.

The three pictures hanging on the walls had been there in his childhood, and the farmyard scenes they depicted were still a comfort to him, like an old blanket. It wasn't what was represented in the pictures as much as their colors which evoked feelings of security and contentment; the flaming reds and flat blacks of cockerel, russets of hens, whites of kittens' paws, roans of cows, yellows of goosey beaks, evanescent blues and greens of drakes, dull browns of ducks, golds of straw, purples of elderberries. Lalor often allowed the colors to gather him up and swing him back through the years into his childhood.

Kevin Lalor was a thin man. He was considered by most people to be delicate, by which they meant he would never enjoy old age. Lawrence Gorman used "rake handle" to describe the neighbor who passed his house twice every day on his bicycle.

The Civil Servant wore thick glasses that magnified his eyes and made them look wet. At thirty-five he was unmarried, and, as far as anyone knew, he had no interest in finding himself a wife. He was simply one more bachelor in a country of tens of thousands of bachelors. However, Lalor considered himself a firmly grounded rock in the sea of mild insanity in which the isolated unmarried existed.

As he sat in front of his dying fire, Lalor moved the tuning coil of the crystal set attached to the piece of polished board on his lap. In the earphones, a man's voice was giving the weekly roundup of the prices from the Dublin Cattle Market. Weathers and hoggets were mentioned, and as the announcer's voice began to break up in the ether, Lalor felt something hard pressing into the back of his neck. As the hairs on his body stood to attention, a screechy voice cut through the earphones: "Stick 'em up!"

In the same motion, Lalor tore the earphones from his head, grabbed the crystal set off his lap and jumped up, shouting, "In the name of the sweet Christ almighty, Mikey, you frightened the hell out of me." And there, passing gas behind the cushioned chair, in his soiled work clothes, his undefeated hair like a battered wire brush, his eyes as big as pennies, stood Mikey Lamb with a silver six-shooter in his right hand and an empty leather holster on his right hip. In his frightened face his top lip was drawn up off his front teeth, and the galaxy of freckles across his cheeks and nose was dark against his white face. Water welled into his eyes and quickly ebbed away.

With his hands full of wire, earphones and the pieces of his crystal set, Kevin Lalor continued to give sound to his fright. "What were you thinking about to sneak in on me like that, for Christ's sake?"

"But you told me to come over with the bike tonight," the child said. He bit his trembling bottom lip and lowered his head.

"But, Jesus, you shouldn't have sneaked in on me that way."

"But I knocked. And then I stood there and said hello, Kevin. I thought you heard me, and I thought you were playing with me."

"Oh, for Christ's sake," Lalor sighed. "I'm sorry. I didn't hear you. Jesus! I suppose I frightened you too when I jumped up."

"You did so. You frightened the life out of me, so you did." Mikey put his gun back into its holster on his hip, and from the cast of the child's face, Lalor saw that the thrill of showing off the new toy had turned to ashes.

The Civil Servant put his tangle of wires and gadgets on the kitchen table. "Where did you get the gun?" he asked.

Mikey drew the six-shooter out of the holster with a flourish. He pointed it at Lalor. "I swapped the spyglass for it."

"You didn't!"

"I did so."

"Who swapped with you?" Lalor took the double-wicked paraffin-oil lamp off the wall. He removed the tall glass globe and shook the oil well.

"Dumpy Dolan from Tile Town," Mikey answered, using the nickname for Saint Martin's Terrace in Gohen, where all the houses were roofed with red Spanish tile. Everyone who didn't live there believed that the desperate, the depraved and the hungry dwelt in Tile Town. Occasionally, at nighttime, entire families living there disappeared into England leaving behind their debts to grocers and drapers and rent collectors. It was the hunger and the desperation of its inhabitants that made outsiders afraid or suspicious of them.

Shapeless shadows danced on the white walls as Lalor dragged the safety match along the sandpaper strip on the box of Friendly Matches. When he touched the match to the lamp, Mikey watched the flames creeping across the wicks.

"Where did Dumpy Dolan get a gun like that?" Lalor asked, and he hung the lamp back on its nail in the wall.

"His uncle brought it home from England."

"Give me a look." The Civil Servant held out his hand.

"It has ivory handles," Mikey said, as he gave over the weapon.

In Lalor's big hand the gun was small. It was light and cheap, made not to last very long. The ivory handles were painted tin and the paint had already begun to peel off the barrel. The Townies had fooled Mikey again. The gun was a cheap toy; the spyglass would have withstood the salt of the seven seas forever.

When he handed the gun back, Lalor saw the red scrape on Mikey's right cheek.

"Watch this, Kevin."

Lalor watched as the boy awkwardly and self-consciously spun the gun around his finger in the trigger guard. Mikey missed the holster when he tried to slam the gun in. It fell on the floor with a clatter. "Gene Autry never misses," he said, as he picked up the gun, "and he doesn't even look at the holster when he does it."

"What happened to your face?" Kevin asked.

The boy bent his head as he stuck the gun into the holster. "Dumpy Dolan wants the gun back," he mumbled, as matter-of-factly as he could.

"And you don't want to give it?"

Mikey still fumbled unnecessarily with the gun. He didn't look up. "It's mine. It was a fair swap."

Lalor bent down to the turf basket and put some fresh sods on the fire. "When did you do the swapping?" he asked.

"Last week."

"What day last week?" Lalor used a cured turkey wing to sweep up the fallen turf crumbs between the basket and the grate.

"Monday."

"That's nearly two weeks ago. And when did Dumpy Dolan say he wanted his gun back?"

"On Tuesday."

"This week or last week?"

"Last week, the day after the swap."

"And why didn't you give it to him?"

"I hadn't it with me. I left it in the knife-and-fork drawer because I knew he'd want me to give it back. Everyone in the school said I got the good swap and he got the bad one because they're always playing Cowboys and Indians in Tile Town and now he has no gun."

"Did he beat you up every day since last Tuesday week?"

"One day he wasn't in school, but Elbows Kelly got me for him that day."

Kevin Lalor finished attending to the fire. He straightened up and looked at Mikey. "Show me your wrists," he said.

Mikey put his hands in his pockets. He looked at his unpolished and scuffed leather boots. "My wrists are all right," he mumbled.

"If you don't show them, I won't mend your bike."

Mikey held up his hands and stretched his arms out of their sleeves. The wrists were marked with red blotches where bony fingers had grasped them like two wrenches. The Indian torture was inflicted when the two wrenches were twisted against each other. "Dumpy Dolan told me today if I don't bring in the gun on Monday, his uncle is going to paralyze me."

Kevin Lalor unhooked his crystal set from its aerial where it came in through a hole in the wooden window casing. "They've beaten you up for nine days in a row," he said, "and you still wouldn't give the gun back! You're as stubborn as a mule, Mikey."

"It was a fair swap. Can I sit in the armchair?"

"Yes, but mind your boots."

Mikey sat into the cushioned chair, adjusted the gun on his hip to make himself comfortable.

Lalor asked, "What do your father and mother say about getting beaten up every day?" He untangled the wire of the earphones from the components of the crystal set.

"They don't know."

"They don't know you're getting half-killed every day! How did you explain that scrape on your face?"

"I said I ran into Dumpy Dolan's head when we were playing stag."

Lalor folded the earphones into their polished case. "Do they know you made the swap?"

"They do. Daddy's cross because he was watching Mattie Mulhall thatching the Coughlins' house. He told me he won't let me go to the pictures anymore till I swap back. Can I listen to your crystal set?"

"There's nothing on besides the Dublin Cattle Market."

"Doul Yank told Daddy the Coughlins are thatching their roof because their brother's coming home from India."

Lalor's hands hesitated on the brass latch of the crystal set case. "Mister Gorman to you, Mikey! So that's why they're thatching! I was wondering about that. The next thing they'll do is whitewash the house."

"How do you know?"

"That's what everyone does when someone important is coming to visit." The Civil Servant put the lacquered black box on top of the dresser. Since Mikey had toddled up the road for the first time with his pants sagging between his legs and he as ripe as a dungheap, the top of the dresser had become the place to keep things out of his reach.

"A brother isn't that important."

"If you haven't seen him for a long time, he becomes important."

"What's he doing in India, the brother?"

"He's a teacher, a missionary, a priest."

"We just finished India in school. They have funny names for things. The rivers are the Godavari, the Narmada, the Indus, the Ganges, the Sutlej, and the Juma." Mikey rattled off the names as if he was reciting the two-times-two multiplication table.

"How about the cities?" Lalor asked, always amazed at Mikey's intelligence and his lack of common sense. He enjoyed playing these classroom games with the boy who didn't know how bright he was.

"Bombay, Calcutta, Karachi, Madras are port cities. Ahmadabad, Cawnpore, Delhi, Hyderabad, Lucknow—"

"Mountains?"

"Eastern Ghats, Western Ghats, Himalayas, Karakoram, Nanga, Rahaposhi—"

"States?"

"Assam, Bengal, Bihar, Andrah Pradesh, Uttar Pradesh, Punjab, Sikkim—"

"Natural resources?"

"Asbestos, coal, copper, gold—"

"Agriculture?"

"Camels, cattle, goats, rice, sheep, sugar, tea—"

"Industry?"

"Chemicals, iron, steel, textiles—"

"Size?"

"One and a quarter million square miles."

"How many Irelands would fit in India?"

"Thirty-nine."

"Seas?"

"Indian Ocean, Arabian Sea, Bay of Bengal."

"Who used to rule India?"

"The English."

"What were the English called in India?"

"The Raj."

"Get the bike."

"Was I good?"

"Full marks."

"Let me read your composition out loud before we do the bike, Kevin."

"You've read it a hundred times."

"I'll read it quick."

"No, not tonight, Mikey."

"What did you do with the five pounds you won for it?"

"Mikey Lamb. How many times do you want me to tell you?"

"But I like hearing it."

Lalor took on the tone of a bored child reciting a poem. "I went to the post office. I bought a postal order. It cost two pounds seven-and-sixpence. I put it in an envelope with the order form.

I sent it away to Rugby in England. Two weeks later the postman, who is my father, gave me the parcel from Rugby. When I opened it, there was the crystal set."

"I bet you couldn't wait, Kevin. Do you remember the time I sent the flaps of the cigarette boxes to Capstan for the pack of cards and it took months. I waited for the postman every day for ages. Did you show . . . ?"

"Mikey Lamb! Go out and get your bike, and there better be no dung or muck on the wheels."

"I made sure to miss the dung and the lane is dusty."

The boy left the kitchen door open, and Lalor heard the bike bouncing off the ground as Mikey knocked the dried muck out of the mudguards. Then he was back with the bike, a wheel scraping against something with every full circle it made.

"For God's sake, Mikey," Lalor said, when he saw the broken rear mudguard and the crooked front wheel. "What the hell happened to the wheel?"

"The Tilers knocked me off, and Dumpy Dolan jumped on the wheel when the bike fell."

"What happened to the mudguard?"

"Elbows Kelly kicked it."

Lalor grabbed the bike by the frame and turned it upside down. He went to the dresser, reached up and felt around near the stamp albums. He touched the cloth bag of his tool kit. "That wheel will never be right again no matter how hard we try to straighten it," he said.

Mikey kept the bike steady on its saddle and handlebars. Lalor, with his hands eighteen inches apart, grasped the front wheel and pushed one against the other. He spun the wheel, and sat on his hunkers trying to detect the wobble still hitting the fork. After more straining and sitting, he spun the wheel, and it finally sang silently on its ball bearings.

As Lalor went to the back of the bike to inspect the mudguard, Mikey asked, "Do you want to hear a riddle?"

"Is it a good one?" the Civil Servant asked.

"It's a great one. Supposing, supposing three men were frozen; one died, how many were left?"

Lalor said, "Get out of the way while I turn this back on its wheels." He picked up the bike and twisted it in the air. As the tires bounced on the kitchen floor, he said, "Well, I suppose the answer isn't two. Tell me the answer."

"None, because it was only supposing," Mikey said gleefully.

"That's a stupid riddle," Lalor said.

"That's what you always say when you don't know the answer."

"Well, that's the stupidest one you ever told me. I don't think this mudguard can be fixed. Will your father mind if I break it off?"

"Daddy says you're the mechanic."

"Be jakers! Is that what he said?" Lalor bent the piece of mudguard up and down. "I'm the mechanic!" When the metal broke, he said, "Well, this mechanic says that the owner of this bike should give the six-shooter back because this mechanic is getting tired of fixing what Dumpy Dolan breaks. And as well as that, this mechanic knows the six-shooter is going to break soon and then there will be no way of getting back that sailor's spyglass."

"A sailor's?"

"Probably a pirate's."

"You're codding me, Kevin."

"Well, it's such a good one it could have been stolen by a pirate. Here, take your bike and go home."

"Let me stay for a while!"

"No. I have a good book to read, and I'm going to finish it tonight no matter what."

"Let me look at your stamps."

"Mikey Lamb! Take your bike and leave me in peace." Lalor went to the kitchen door and opened it wide. "Hurry up and don't let all the heat out of the house."

When the bike was half in and half out, the boy stopped and asked, "Does it pain you much when you're getting paralyzed?"

"It's terrible, and for the rest of your life you can't move a muscle. You just lie there in a bed wetting yourself and dirtying the sheets, and some big, cross nurse with a red face and fat arms feeds you nothing but lumpy porridge with no sugar or milk on it. Go on, go home."

With mouth open, Mikey wheeled his bike out into the failing light. Kevin Lalor closed the door and smiled to himself as he went to the kitchen windowsill and picked up *The Good Companions*.

13

The Trap

1951

In which the Civil Servant assists Mikey to plot
the entrapment of a Tiler into friendship.

WITH THE BUTTONS UNDONE, the flaps of Kevin Lalor's short coat
were floating on the breeze created by the speed of his bike.
The muck of the Lower Road had dried during the past rainless
two weeks and his bike's fat tires were leaving a low trail of dust in
their wake. The dismalness of a wet spring had suddenly changed
into the glory of high summer. There was warmth in the air from a
sun that had been shining for eight consecutive days. The clear-sky
sunshine was affecting the brains of the populace as powerfully as
the moon lifting forty-foot tides into the Bay of Fundy. Even the
cattle, lately released from the long winter housing, showed their
appreciation of the sun by mindlessly breaking into sudden gallops, throwing their back legs into the blue sky and splitting the air
with crackling farts.

The fields had responded to the weather with a profusion of
growth. Almost overnight the vibrant green grass of the countryside was littered with white-petaled daisies and yellow dandelions,
golden buttercups and custardy cowslips, lilac cuckoo flowers and

yellow-flowered trefoils, red clover and white cow parsley and bright-blue bluebells.

The birds had gone mad entirely, peeping and cawing and whistling and singing and shouting and pecking and hopping and swooping and flying, just for the sake of flying. Soaring swallows traced black lines across the blue sky, twisting and twirling and testing the far-out limits of aerodynamics.

Kevin Lalor's bike was a magic carpet, and his body was not registering the passage of dried-up potholes beneath his fat wheels. Something unusual was going on in Lalor's body. A hot emanation, intensified by the generosity of the sun, was centered in the area of his diaphragm. It was a sensation he had experienced only once before—when a Norwegian soprano had sung an aria on the stage of the Festspielhaus in Bayreuth. She had sung to him alone in a voice purer than gold refined a hundred times. The beefy, ponderously-breasted, yellow-wigged, Viking-helmeted soprano in makeup applied with a trowel was the most beautiful creature he had ever beheld.

And now, ten years later, his diaphragm revisited by an identical feeling, Lalor knew he had been smitten through both ventricles by a love-shaft as thick and as blunt as the handle of a dungfork. However, he was mature enough to recognize that Cupid's darts connect the heart to the testes in such a way as to knock a man's equilibrium off its axis.

Ever since he had heard Deirdre Hyland speaking three weeks ago, the Civil Servant had been keeping a tight lid on the explosive mixture of emotional and sexual giddiness which he knew could change his life in an instant of indiscretion. What his giddiness was driving him to whisper in Miss Hyland's ear was, "I'm insane with the love of you. I want our beings to meld into each other like two pieces of baker's dough kneaded into one loaf. I'm totally mad with the want to be naked with you. I want to put my mouth on your mouth, on your breasts at the same time in soft green grass in a sunny field. I want to be inside you forever. I want to be so much inside you that I will be able to see the world out through your eyes." But Lalor, having inherited the same iron will that had allowed his father to finish with his bayonet what a German machine gun's bullets had begun, had held in check the feelings in which he was so painfully laocoöned.

Deirdre Hyland was twenty-eight, and she had passed the Civil Service examination nine years ago. While waiting for a position to present itself in the Courthouse in Gohen, she had worked in the back office in Humphrey Smiley's Hardware and Farm Supply Company. There, to the monthly annoyance of farmers in debt, she had established a reputation for steely efficiency in the management of accounts payable. When the farmers complained to each other about Deirdre Hyland in their nasty testosteronic way, they associated the monthly reminders of their indebtedness with the premenstrual symptoms of their tormentor.

However, for another reason completely unrelated to her business efficiency, every man who came in contact with Deirdre Hyland felt threatened, whether or not he was a farmer. The men gave vent to their imagined emasculation by declaring loudly to each other, "The way she talks! Who the hell does that bitch think she is?"

Deirdre Hyland said meat when everyone else said "mate"; for her, "bate" was beet, "sate" was seat, "buhher" was butter, "waher" was water, "munny" was money, "cowshite" was farmyard manure and "ferninst" was not a word at all. "'Opposite' is the word," she had told one ancient bachelor farmer who enragedly gaped at her as if eyeing the bastard cattle jobber who had just pulled a fast one on him in the buying of a bullock.

It was precisely because she spoke properly that she was a threat, not only to the men of Gohen and its environs, but to the women too.

As well as pronouncing and enunciating her words correctly, Deirdre Hyland was five and a half feet tall and capable of looking most people in the eye. She kept herself presentable with the frequent use of soap, water and hairbrush. She had straight, clean, white teeth; her skin was clear. Clever and creative use of her lean wardrobe enabled her to give the impression she had more than she actually had. She wore low-heeled, step-into shoes. She was beautiful to look at, as beautiful as the Protestant minister's wife. If she had used makeup, she would have been called a slut.

Kevin Lalor had often seen Miss Hyland on the streets of Gohen and on the same streets had heard many disparaging remarks about her. But it wasn't until Deirdre came into his office to introduce herself on her first day as the latest addition to the buildings-permit office, that he had heard her speaking. Feeling the same dismay as if he had run flat-out into a stone wall in the dark, Lalor felt the passage between his heart and his testes savagely excavated as he attempted to get out of his chair to greet the new arrival. By the time he got up on his underpinnings there was no blood left in his brain, and he was rendered stupid. He could not remember what he had mumbled in response to her introduction.

Now, three weeks later and still wondering what foolish things he had muttered, Kevin Lalor free-wheeled around Tuohys Corner on the Lower Road, and there, sitting on the grass verge of the lane, his feet dangling over the edge of the drain, was Mikey Lamb. The boy was clutching something to his belly and, pensively, he was staring down between his boots into the water. The narrow end of the birthday telescope was sticking out of his breast pocket. When he heard the song of bicycle tires on the lane, the child slurped at a dangling drool and closed his mouth. He looked up and yelped, "Kevin, I've been waiting for you for ages."

It was a jam jar, full of murky water and seething with tadpoles, that Mikey was holding. As he plonked it down, some of the water sloshed over the rim. Stranded black tadpoles wiggled furiously in the grass.

As Lalor slowed down, he lifted his rear end off the saddle. When he came to a stop, he put his feet to the ground each side of the bike, the bar between his legs touching the shrinking remembrance of Deirdre Hyland.

"Look what I found," Mikey said, and he lifted up a dead rabbit by its back legs. He pointed to the back of the neck. "Look where the weasel got him—chawed his way down to the bone. You can see the joins in the neck bone like when you suck the meat out of a chicken's neck. And look at the eyes. The crows got them." He put his left hand under the rabbit's chin and lifted the head onto the center of Lalor's handlebars.

"Will you get that yoke off my bike," Lalor said. "You could get a disease from dragging a dead animal around."

"Sure, it's only a noul rabbit, Kevin. How could I get a disease off it and we eating rabbits all the time?"

"The crows and the weasels haven't been at the ones you eat and they haven't been dead for a week either. Throw that thing over the hedge and let the scall crows finish it off."

Mikey swung the rabbit around his head several times. He finally released it, and as it sailed over the hedge trailing a streak of very yellow rodent urine, he whooped like an Indian doing a war dance in the pictures, tapping his rabbit-haired fingers against his lips.

"Is that what you stopped me for, to show me a dead rabbit?" Lalor asked, but he wasn't annoyed. In fact he was feeling expansive, his patience with the boy related in some circuitous way to the foreign feeling glowing like magma deep in the area of his testes. "I saw you today—" he said, but Mikey cut him off.

"Aw, Kevin, let me tell you. That's why I stopped you. Mister Tracey sent me to the bank with Brendan Healy today, and he said I'll be doing it all next year by myself."

Everyone in Gohen, Drumsally and Clunnyboe, knew that the teacher cum Picture House manager, Mister Tracey, counted last night's takings on his desk first thing every morning—inspectors from the education department never made terrorist appearances before ten o'clock. While the master counted, his students practiced their penmanship—rounded shoulders and ankles for English letters, pointed ones for Irish, and six of the hardest for the child who mixed up the two styles.

"That's great, Mikey," Lalor said, even though he was surprised the teacher had singled out the boy for this particular job. It was commonly believed that the student who could be seen from Lalor's courthouse window carrying the money in a cloth bag was the most mature and trusted of his peers. Because his job demanded absence

from the classroom for almost an hour every day, he was also considered to be one of the best students in his class. In Lalor's mind, Mikey
could afford to miss the classroom instruction, but if he was the most
mature boy in his class then the rest of the children must have been
still fighting their way out of their nappies.

"Brendan Healy did it all this year, and now he's showing me how
to do it for next year. He told me about Mister Gorry on the way to
the bank, and I nearly burst out laughing when I saw him twitching
and blinking all over the place, like Brendan said. And the way he
pushes his glasses up on his forehead when he wants to look at you!
You should see how quick he counts the money—you'd hardly see his
fingers moving when he was counting out Doul Yank's fivers. There
must have been a hundred of them. And the pennies in our Picture
House bag zipping across the counter like bullets."

"Not Doul Yank. Mister Gorman to you, Mikey. And all those
fivers, I think you were seeing things," the Civil Servant asked, hoping to get more information about Doul Yank's business transaction.
But his sly probe was not successful.

"What does Mister Gorry shave his head for, Kevin?"

Knowing how deeply a person's name can be embedded in a
piece of gossip, Kevin Lalor did not tell Mikey that Mister Gorry
was as eccentric as a brain-damaged hen, that his facial and cervical
twitchings were the stuff of cruel imitation in Gohen, and that it was
believed he kept his pate in a state of hairlessness because of his terror of fleas. He didn't tell Mikey that Mister Gorry was called Hairy
Gorry. The more reckless gossipers claimed that Hairy also shaved
his belly hairs, and that the ensuing itchiness was why Mister Gorry
made so many lightning grabs at his crotch.

"Some people like bald heads, Mikey," Lalor-the-discreet said.

"But how can he shave the back of his head if he can't see it?"

"Maybe he's done it so often he can do it with his eyes shut, like
me shaving myself."

"You can't shave with your eyes shut, Kevin."

"I could if I had to."

Mikey changed the subject. "The Coughlins bought a motor car. Doul Yank saw Eddie—"

"Mister Gorman, to you, Mikey."

"He saw Eddie learning how to drive it in the Beech Field, and Bridie was out waving all over the place and jumping out of the way. And you were right about the whitewashing. Doul Mister Gorman said Missus Madden was as white as the walls. And you were right about the brother coming home from India, too. Is he the one in the composition on your wall, Kevin?"

"That's him, the man who was sent east to India," Lalor said.

"Bridie told Mammy he was in the Suez Canal. How did you figure out the whitewashing and the brother before anyone else, Kevin?"

"Deduction," Lalor said.

"What's that?"

"If you see a fox's tail sticking out from under a bush, you know there's a fox hiding in the bush. When people make their roof look good with new thatch, you know they'll make their walls look new as well. If they didn't, it would be like putting on a pair of Wellingtons covered in cow dung when you have a new suit on."

"But how could you tell the brother would be home from India?"

"If you thatch your house when it was thatched only a few years ago, you must be expecting someone important to visit you, and the only one the Coughlins have to visit them is their brother in India."

"Isn't that what Sherlock Holmes does—deduction?"

"Yes, he deduces. And talking about deduction, Mikey, how badly did the Tilers beat you up in school today?"

The boy's mouth dropped open, and before he could put a lie together, Lalor said, "Don't make up a story for me, Mikey."

"How did you know, Kevin?" Mikey asked. "They all grabbed me and dragged me to the back of the ball alley. I thought they'd leave me alone after swapping back the telescope."

"What did they do to you?"

Suddenly, Mikey's eyes were swimming. "Twisted my arms up behind my back; and pinned my head to the ground by the ears and

93

pressed my nose flat on my face; and put their hands up the leg of my trousers and twisted my balls; and bent my fingers back; and stood on the backs on my knees; and gave me the Indian torture. Look." Mikey pushed his arms out of his sleeves, and his wrists appeared to be badly chilblained. He used the back of his right wrist to swipe at a running tear on his cheek. "How did you know, Kevin?"

"Deduction, Mikey." Kevin Lalor reached out and awkwardly rubbed the top of the child's head. The hair was as coarse as the coat of an Irish terrier.

"But what was there for deduction? Where's the fox's tail?" Mikey wiped his nose with his sleeve.

"It's very easy, Mikey." Lalor leaned forward and rested his elbows on the bike's handlebars. "Why do you think the Tilers grab your lunch every day and run away with it?"

"Because they're bullies."

"No. Because they're hungry, Mikey. Why do you think they break your bike?"

"Because they're bullies."

"No. Because they're poor, and if they can't have a bike they don't want you to have one either."

"But we're poor too, and even if I hadn't a bike they'd still beat me up just because they're bullies."

"They'd still beat you up, but only because you're the best in the class. The only way the Tilers can be better than you is by beating you up."

"But why did they beat me up today?"

"Because Mister Tracey made you special by choosing you to bring the Picture House money to the bank."

"Then it would be better to be thicker and poorer."

"There's nothing good about being thick or poor."

"But there's no way around that. You can get beaten up because you're good at your lessons and have a bike, or you can be thick and have no bike and not get beaten up. Neither is good."

"Maybe there is a way to be best in the class and to be friendly with the Tilers at the same time."

"No, there's not."

"Yes, there is."

"What is it?"

"Try to figure it out yourself."

Mikey kicked the toe of his boot into the dusty lane. "I've tried to be on their side a whole lot of times, but they won't let me. When I follow them around they throw clods at me and make pig sounds at me and tell me to go home to my pighouse. They'll never let me be on their side."

"Supposing you pick out one of the Tilers and become friends with him."

"But the rest of them would still beat me up."

"They might, but if one of them is your friend the rest might stop beating you up."

"But that means I'd have to make friends with a tough one, like Elbows Kelly, because he's the only one they're all afraid of." Mikey viciously kicked at the little depression he had made with the toe of his boot.

"Will you stop doing that? You're ruining your boot. How about making friends with one of Elbows Kelly's friends, someone who isn't too tough?"

"Like Barlow Bracken? But how, Kevin? I've tried to play with Barlow Bracken, and he always tells me to frig off."

"He has to do that to stay friendly with the rest of the Townies. Give him a piece of the curranty cake you bring for lunch on Mondays."

"But that's only curranty cake."

"How many Tilers bring curranty cake for lunch on Mondays?"

"I don't know."

"None, Mikey. Their mothers are too poor to make curranty cake. That's why they're always grabbing it off you and stuffing it into their mouths while they're running away. Give Barlow Bracken some of the curranty cake on the sly and he'll soon become your friend."

Mikey's eyes began to brighten as his imagination took off with Lalor's suggestion.

"Let him ride your bike a little bit on the way home now and then. Help him with his sums."

"He doesn't want any help with his sums or anything else. He got first place and won sixpence for the best composition."

"Ask your father to let him come to your house to play. When there's apples in your garden, bring him one."

Mikey was now smiling broadly, and he offered his own suggestion. "If Mister Tracey has two money bags for the bank on Monday mornings, I could ask him to let Barlow Bracken go with me."

"There you are!" Lalor said. He reached out again and rubbed the wiry hair.

"Maybe he'd come out to our house to play and maybe Mammy could give him rhubarb for his mother when he'd be going home. But how would he get out to our house?"

"Maybe you could carry him on the bar of your bike after school."

"And I could carry him back some of the way too." Mikey was grinning at what his imagination was dishing up—Barlow Bracken on the bar of his bike, the two of them laughing. "Wouldn't it be great, Kevin? And it's all like putting bait in a trap, only I wouldn't be trapping Barlow Bracken, but everything would be like bait to catch him like Daddy putting a jam jar half full of water under the apple trees to catch the wasps."

"Now you're talking, Mikey, but don't try everything at the same time. Give him the curranty cake for a few weeks before you do anything else. You can't let him know what you're up to."

The boy was grinning. "I'll buy him a Peggy's Leg tomorrow."

"No, Mikey. You can't do that. If you start doing a whole lot of things he'll know you're up to something, and it'll all backfire. Here's what you have to do. Tear a page out of your copy and write tomorrow's date on the first line, then the next date on the next line until you have all the school days to the beginning of the summer holidays filled in; then write down on each line what you're going to do for Barlow. But on most of the lines write 'nothing.' The first week, do one nice thing; the second week, do two things. But once you have the list made up, you must stick to it. Bring the list up to me when you have it done, and we'll go over it together."

"Oh, Kevin, it all sounds like a plot. I'll be like a secret agent in *The Commando*."

"You'll have to be very careful, Mikey, because if the Tilers find out you're a secret agent, they'll only beat you up all the more."

"They'll never get me to admit anything, Kevin, no matter how much they torture me. I'm going home to write down the plan." Mikey's feet spun in the dust of the lane.

Lalor called after him, "What about the tadpoles, Mikey?" He pointed to the jam jar in the grass.

The boy ran back and emptied a waterfall of tadpoles into the ditch. He didn't notice that he was stepping on the marooned tadpoles in the grass. Without another word he ran off home, the empty jar in his left hand.

Lalor sat back on his saddle, and before he had gone three yards, Deirdre Hyland had elbowed Mikey Lamb out of his brain. But then he heard Mikey calling after him, "KAY-ven, KAY-ven!" The Civil Servant steered to the side of the lane and circled around to where he'd come from. Mikey was running toward him, the jam jar clutched into his belly. When they met, the boy was breathless and as pent as a steam engine.

"I forgot to tell you the one I heard in school today," He had to take several breaths before he could deliver his lines. "Julius Caesar made a breezer off the coast of France. Napoleon thought he'd do the same and did it in his pants."

Lalor guffawed, and a triumphant grin split Mikey's face. "I made you laugh, Kevin." He turned around and ran home.

14

In the Sunroom

In which Patrick Bracken confirms to Sam and
Elsie Howard that his friendship with Mikey
Lamb only lasted the length of one summer.

"Patrick," Mister Howard interrupted, "by my mathematics you
and Mikey could not have been friends for very long."

"That's right, Sam. Of course we kept the friendship going
when my family moved to England, but we had only been friends
for that one summer in nineteen fifty-one. We left for England in
September."

"Mikey only had you for a few months!" Elsie said. "But he must
have been . . ."

"Devastated," Patrick supplied the word. "We were all devastated,
Else. Our family didn't survive as a family."

"Maybe Patrick would prefer not to talk about this, Else," Mister
Howard said.

"No, it's all right," Patrick said, and he lifted his hand to divert
Sam's concern. "Most of the pain has leeched away, but whenever I
smell coal smoke I hear the train speeding through Yorkshire in the
dark and I see the stump of a candle in my father's hand."

15

Emigration

1951

In which the uprooting of the Bracken family from their home in Gohen and their resettling in Bradford brought with it triumph and anguish.

IT WAS THE STUMP OF A CANDLE IN HIS FATHER'S HAND that Barlow Bracken saw first that night when Pops gently shook him awake. Then it was his face bent down and lit from below by the small flame—a Rembrandt face shining in the dark.

Barlow was annoyed, wanted Pops to stop shaking him out of the warmth of the bed onto the cold concrete floor.

"Wake the two lads," Pops said quietly, and he began to gently awaken the girls in the other bed.

As clearly as in brutal Bergmanesque blacks and whites, Barlow saw his father spilling drops of grease onto the windowsill and setting the short piece of candle in it. Slow shadows moved on the walls and ceiling, as shapeless daubs of black.

As Pops went into the darkness near the door, he responded to Barlow's question in a tired voice. "I'll tell you all together when everyone gets their clothes on and comes into the kitchen. Put on your socks and shoes, the weather has changed. Everything's damp."

The children sat around the kitchen table shivering, the three boys with hands buried in crotches, the cold kitchen reminding Barlow of the Lambs' warm kitchen and the lovely smell when Missus Lamb grated nutmeg into the curranty-cake dough on Saturday nights.

Kits, the youngest, clung to her older sister, AnneMarie, whimpering like a puppy seeking comfort at its mother's belly.

Four half-sized tea chests cluttered the floor, the silver paper still lining the insides, *Ceylon* stenciled in black letters on the outsides. On his knees, Pops drilled into the sides of the thin plywood boxes with violent twists of his penknife's blade. He poked short lengths of strong twine into the holes and made carrying handles. When Missus Bracken came out of the bedroom with her arms full, Pops looked up and said, "Barlow, help your mother with the sheets."

As he folded the bedclothes with Mother, Barlow felt the body warmth still lingering in them. Mother pressed the sheets into one of the tea chests, and then stood at the end of the kitchen table, her hands folded on her belly beneath her apron.

"Tell them now, Pops," she said.

Pops, still kneeling on the floor, put the long, strong, dirt-inlaid fingers of one hand on the edge of the table. He glanced up at Mother at the other end, lowered his eyes to the tabletop and spoke very quietly.

"We're all going to England," he said.

The five children looked down at him, their mouths like gawping perch in the canal on a hot day, blind to the impaled red worm. There was a long, long silence. Pops eventually lifted his head as if to check whether anyone had heard him. He was crying, and the children had never seen him crying before. Out of the corner of his eye Barlow saw his mother bringing the apron to her face.

AnneMarie asked, "When, Pops?"

"Tonight, Annie," he said, using his pet name for her. "Mister Coss will be here with his motor at one o'clock."

Whether it was from the sleep still in their brains, or whether it was from being stunned by the news, the siblings continued to gape at their kneeling father.

"Why, Pops?" AnneMarie asked, and Pops was unable to answer. He kept swallowing, and then Mother said, "There's no more work here for Daddy, AnneMarie. There's work in England, and we'll have money."

Without any sign that it was on the way, a sob jumped out of AnneMarie. Tears shot out of her eyes onto the table, and an animal wail followed immediately after the sob. Barlow started crying, wailed like AnneMarie. Then the others joined in, and then Mother was on her knees crying too, seven foreheads on the backs of hands around the kitchen table. The sound of the wailing rose and fell, turned and fled higher in a fluid motion like a flock of starlings in an autumn sky blindly following the rules of group movement. Perhaps crying out loud—bawling—was the best curative at that moment; perhaps it drained off some of the shock and left everyone with clearer heads to deal with what was ahead, although none of them could imagine what was ahead, not even Pops and Mother. The crying finally eased off, and it was as if the flock of starlings had glided to rest in a leafless ash tree.

It was Kits who helped dispel the spell of anguish, who made everyone laugh nervously with her innocent question. "Are we going all the way to England in Mister Coss's motor car?"

"We'll be in the motor as far as Dublin," Mother said. "Then we'll be on a ship, and then we'll be on a train."

"A ship, a train, a motor," Kits said with excitement, and her innocent expectations were a weak drizzle of sanctifying grace on the family.

When the delft and pots were packed between the clothing, Barlow helped his father tie strong twine around the tea chests, carried them out to the side of the street with Pops while Mother and the children put on their coats and hats.

Tile Town was dark and silent; the first blanket of winter dampness had descended with its penetrating chill. The church clock struck one and the lights from Mister Coss's motor came around the corner at the end of the street. He must have been waiting for the sound of the church bell, listening with his window open. Like a stealthy, large black cat, the motor came toward the waiting, silent family. In less than five minutes the luggage was in the boot and tied on the roof and everyone was in the motor making space for each other.

None of the passengers had been in a motor car before, except for Pops; he'd been in Paddy Kavanagh's lorry when Paddy was drawing sand from the Ridge for the new reservoir. But despite his motorized traveling experience, Pops, like the rest of the family, felt his stomach heaving into his lungs every time Mister Coss's motor sped over a hill in the dark.

The significance of the giant step that took them from Tile Town to Bradford in Yorkshire hit home most painfully on the children's first day in an English school. The English children pointed to their clothes; they did not understand the speech of the Irish villagers. After Barlow trepidatiously asked for directions to the lavatory, his teacher asked him if he spoke any English. It was made brutally clear to them that they were smelly and raggy. They were lost in a warren of unfamiliar buildings and systems, and on the second day they left their flat crying, Mother encouraging them with promises that everything would quickly change for the better.

And so they all survived to some degree, except AnneMarie and Ned, the father. AnneMarie never found her way out of the thickets of strangeness. From being the most outgoing of the family, she quickly sank into black and prolonged moods. Three years after the move from Ireland and two days before her seventeenth birthday, she walked the four miles to Shipley and drowned herself in the Aire—lost angel of a ruined paradise, she left no message.

But she did leave six people forever changed, Pops more than anyone. With AnneMarie's suicide, he began a slide into depression that ended with his death eighteen months later in a red-bricked asylum with two thousand beds. He weighed six and a half stone at the time of his death, and the hospital people gave his dentures to Mother in a pre-used, brown envelope, a cancelled stamp with the King's head on it. They buried Pops with AnneMarie in a crowded cemetery in Bradford. Besides themselves there was no one at the funeral. It was a withering blow for Mother, who had never before even imagined that a funeral could be so poorly attended. At the graveside she howled like a dog whose litter has disappeared and can't be found.

The four children and Mother stumbled on for several years before they found their feet. Mother got a job in a bacon factory—big bits of pig carted in one end and carted out the other end in thin slices, weighed and packaged. As the children got older they got jobs and contributed to the running of the rented half-house. As their second Christmas in Bradford approached, Barlow sent Mikey Lamb a parcel of twenty-seven English comics that had already passed through many hands.

By the time Barlow graduated from university, Mother had became a supervisor in the bacon factory where she oversaw the high jinks of two hundred men and women from Trinidad and the adjacent islands where the natives play cricket. When she had begun in the bacon factory as a floor sweeper, she had worked there for two months before she realized the Islanders were speaking English. When she eventually retired, some of the old hands congratulated her for working so hard to learn English.

Kits eventually married a decent man who was a teacher like herself. One of the brothers, Liam, ended up as the manager of the factory where Mother had worked. The other, Anthony, became a well-loved secondary teacher in Bradford, and he married a nurse who had been born in Fermoy in County Cork.

16

In the Sunroom

In which Patrick Bracken wonders if he has unsettled Elsie and Sam Howard by unwittingly resurrecting a sad remembrance.

"IT'S STRANGE HOW THE MIND holds onto odd details," Patrick said, "how some insignificant things refuse to sink out of sight in our memory and stay afloat despite our best efforts to sink them—like Pop's teeth in that torn, brown envelope."

For a while there was silence in the room until Sam said, "That's not a happy story, Patrick."

Elsie said, "It was a terrible price to pay to survive—AnneMarie and your father. The death of a child; your mother left by herself to cope . . ." Elsie's voice trailed off, and she looked over at Sam, but Sam was not looking at her. He was gone into his own thoughts, looking at something in a dark clump of shrubs in the garden.

Elsie turned to Patrick and, with movement of hands and pursing of lips, tried to convey something that Patrick did not understand. When he did not respond to her gestures, she stood up and went to her husband. She put her hand on his shoulder and asked, "Would you like another cup of tea, Sam?"

Sam dragged himself back into the sunroom. He put his hand on Elsie's hand. "No thanks, Else. I'm fine. Fine." He looked at Patrick. "I wandered off there for a minute, didn't I, Patrick? Sometimes I wonder if I can feel Doctor Alzheimer breathing down the back of my neck."

Elsie went back to her chair. "Doctor Alzheimer is not within an ass's roar of your neck, Sam, never mind within breathing distance. You know and I know where you were wandering, and it's all right. Just don't use Alzheimer as a cover-up. Alzheimer's is nothing to be funny about."

Howard held out his hands to fend off his wife's words. "All right Else. All right." There was impatience in his voice.

"I'm sorry, Patrick," Missus Howard said. "You probably feel we're speaking around you, and that is not polite."

Patrick did feel as if the Howards had been speaking around him. He wondered what had introduced the distraction into the sunroom. He decided he would wait for the go-ahead from either of them before he continued with what he knew about Father Coughlin and Lawrence Gorman. Whatever it was that had arisen between Sam and Elsie took several minutes to settle back into place. He was surprised that Elsie allowed the silence to linger so long, wondered if she was trying to force something out of Sam.

Finally, when Sam did speak, Patrick felt that his question was just a sound to break the silence, "The others, Patrick, the other ones you spoke to before you came to us to hear what we have to say—was it difficult to get them to talk about all this?"

"Generally no," Patrick said, and he used Sam's verbal rattlings to repair the rhythm that had been upset. "A few were reluctant, but once they got going it poured out like water spilling over the lip of a spring. Only once did I find myself laboriously pulling teeth . . ."

17

The 3,367th Journey Home

1951

In which the great white missionary, the Reverend Father Jarlath Coughlin, arrives in Gohen from India and is met at the bus stop by his brother, Eddie-the-cap, and his sister, Bridie, who carries his two suitcases to their new car.

L ABORIOUSLY PULLING A CLOUD of blue smoke along the ground after itself, the green bus loudly moaned its way across the Plain toward its final stop outside Gohen's Central Hotel. It was a bus with half its face missing, as if a giant with his giant penknife had cut out a front corner. Toward its rear end, tied in six places to the wooden roof rack, a canvas cover rippled and snapped in the wind and lent the bus an air of urgency which it did not possess.

On the sides was painted a golden logo of concentric circles with trailing and forward tangents—an abstraction of a speeding snail with its house on its back conveying the promise of meteoritic conveyance of passengers all around Ireland. Beneath each logo were the initials C.I.E.—Coras Iompar Eireann, Ireland's Transport System.

Sitting in the part of the bus missed by the giant's knife sat Joe Corrigan in his silver-buttoned, dark blue uniform and peaked cap. Since he had steered the bus out of Portarlington and onto the last stage of this day's journey, Corrigan's thoughts of things to be done when he got home were making him weary; park bus in Bill Moore's shed, ride bike two miles home, say hello to Missus, change into old clothes, eat colcannon and two fried eggs, get up on bike again and head off with Missus to the bog to cut a few barrowloads of turf. Then home again in the ten o'clock's twilight on the bike. "God! I hate this time of the year, this rushing home, rushing the colcannon, rushing out again."

Before he got the bus job, Joe Corrigan had loved working on the bog with the lads. Going there to take care of the turf was going on a picnic—the hard work in the freshness of the heathered air giving a fellow a roaring hunger; boiling the kettle over a hot fire of bog deal; spooning the mixed tea and sugar into the boiling water; sitting on the turf bank drinking mugs of strong, sweet tea and eating lashings of homemade bread plastered with homemade butter, and if a fellow was lucky at all, a handful of fresh scallions laced with salt. The loud laughter of the lads.

But this rushing to get the bog work done in the few evening hours that were now available to him had taken all the joy out of bog work. And the midges came out in the evenings when the weather was right for them—clouds of them, millions in each cloud, tiny bastards with teeth of eels. A fellow could rush to the bog and leave five minutes later because the fecking midges were out. Corrigan had once heard someone disparagingly referring to a miserable village as the place where the midges et the bishop. With one hand resting lightly on the steering wheel, he grunted at the remembrance. At some other time he would have smiled at the image of the bishop beating off the clouds of insects with his miter and his maniple.

Although he knew the bog work would eventually have to be done, there were times when he was glad it was raining on this last stretch of the journey. But today there was no rain, there wasn't even a wisp of cloud in sight.

"Feck it," Joe Corrigan said aloud. "Feck it."

For six days a week for eleven years, Joe Corrigan had driven the C.I.E. bus from Gohen to Dublin and back again. He left at seven in the morning and returned at six in the evening. All along the road between the country and the city, people told the time of day by the passing of his bus.

In a country still jittery in the triple aftershocks of the departure of the English, the Depression and the War, people envied Joe Corrigan his job. In a country where people seldom traveled outside their own townland, Joe Corrigan's daily adventure to the big city was envied. When these envies were expressed to him, Joe Corrigan gave divine praise for his good fortune—"Sure I'm a terrible lucky man, thanks be to God." He knew that if he simply said, "Sure it's just another fecking job that gives a fellow piles," people would think he was an ungrateful get.

Joe Corrigan was a counter. Anything that could be counted he counted, and he counted things because he was bored to fecking death with this fecking job. On this evening in June 1951, Joe Corrigan was making his three-thousand-three-hundred-and-sixty-seventh trip home from Dublin.

Corrigan was so familiar with the road between Portarlington and Gohen that he couldn't have been more contemptuous of it. The straight-as-a-die Four-Mile-Stretch outside Port was a brain paralyzer. Only he was afraid one of the passengers would see him, he would read his book. Every fecking whitethorn bush, every twisted elm, every ash tree coated in ivy, every bunch of stinging nettles, the forests of cow parsley, the clumps of elder, the nests of man-eating blackberry briars, everything ugly and smelly and thorny and mean that grew on the sides of the road was familiar to Joe Corrigan, and he hated the whole lot of it. He would have to watch all this stuff going through its life cycle until the weak grip of winter finally choked it and left it to rot above its own roots.

Joe Corrigan stared into the four miles ahead, and he saw neither bike nor ass's cart; nothing but a lonely level stretch, eight minutes of ugly, and at the end of it a feed of colcannon eaten in such a hurry that he'd get heartburn, and then the fecking bog.

He tried to distract himself in the usual way by playing the game he had devised; name every passenger remaining on the bus, even though at this tail-end of the journey there were never many people left. However, he couldn't get his brain going, and his eyes became trapped in the surface of the road disappearing under the nose of the bus.

But, eventually, the face of one of his remaining passengers worked its way, unbidden, into his brain, a very brown head belonging to a man wearing a roman collar and a black suit. The man's hands were brown too. He could be a foreigner. If he was an Irishman, he had certainly been living in a foreign country with a shining sun. But whether they were Irish or foreign, Corrigan had no time for clergymen; they were bloodsuckers, and he was not afraid to let his views be known. At his mother's funeral two years ago, the parish priest, Father Mooney, had arrived late for the graveside prayers with his bag of golf clubs on the backseat of his car. As the priest headed off again while the last Amen was still clinging to the field of headstones, Corrigan had gone after him, had called him by shouting, "Hey!"

Blinded by the volatile mixture of anger and grief, the son had invaded the cleric's facial space and chiseled out his harsh words through gnashing teeth: "I hope my mother's funeral didn't interrupt your golf game, father." *Father* had come out colored with many shades of meaning—prick, bollicks, fucker, cunt, bastard.

"You're upset, Joe," the priest had responded, his face reddening.

"Fecking sure I'm upset," Joe had spat out, and before he turned back to his mother's still-open grave, he snarled, "Fecking priests, fecking parasites. Go back to your fecking golf where you belong. You don't belong here, that's for sure."

Priests! Joe Corrigan was frightened of no man. Like Boadicea, whom he had read about in a poem, he scorned the idea of anything Roman, as well as any person who patronized. "'You're upset, Joe!'"

As the bus reached the end of the Four-Mile-Stretch, Corrigan turned the steering wheel slightly to the left, at the same time pressuring the accelerator to get up speed for the hill ahead. The image of the brown clergyman evaporated when, up ahead, he saw Paddy Kavanagh giving his lorry a rest on the small landing halfway up Beggses Hill on the Esker.

Corrigan took his foot off the accelerator, pushed in the clutch and let gravity bring the bus to a stop. As he switched off the engine, he made the decision that, no matter how long it took Paddy Kavanagh to reverse his sand-laden lorry up the rest of the hill, the delay was going to rule out any bog work this evening.

Suddenly feeling better than he'd felt all day, Corrigan opened the door and swung down out of his high seat onto the road. He pulled his trousers out of his secondary pair of cheeks. After throwing his cap back up into the cab, he rubbed the itching sweat-track out of his silver hair with the fury of a dog's paw attacking a biting flea. After smoothing down the disturbed hair, the bus driver put his hands on his hips and arched his shoulders back. He saw Paddy Kavanagh getting out of his lorry and cupping his hands around his mouth.

"Can you give me five minutes, Joe?" the lorry driver called.

Corrigan cupped his own mouth and called back, "No hurry, Paddy. Take your time." Kavanagh waved his thanks and slowly walked around his dilapidated lorry inspecting, kicking, poking, tugging, hoping. Another man got out of the lorry's cab, and even though he could not make out his features, Corrigan knew it was Ned Bracken. "Poor old Ned. Takes any kind of work that comes his way. Shoveling sand all day is a killer."

Corrigan bent at the waist, let his hands and head hang down until he felt the blood in his finger tips and eyes. This evening he was going to enjoy his colcannon and his eggs, and if the midges allowed, go for a walk with the missus along the river bank into the town for a half-one in Lee Reilly's snug. His face was purple when he straightened up. He shook the pins and needles out of his fingers. When the feeling of fullness leaked back down out of his face, Corrigan bent over again, enjoying what the stretching was doing to his cramped shoulders and lower back. Between his legs he saw feet approaching and knew it was Ned Geoghan, the conductor, out for a stretch too. The feet stopped, and a voice that was not Ned Geoghan's said, "Excuse me, driver."

Although he responded to the imperious tone as slowly as he could, Joe Corrigan straightened up too quickly and brown clouds and streaks of light fled across his eyes. He put his hand on the bus's mudguard and turned around. The brown clergyman was standing four feet away. The scarcity of the long, golden hairs lying across the dome of the churchman's head highlighted his brown baldness, and it was this extra expanse of tanned skin that convinced Corrigan this man was from a country of dark-skinned people. The sparkling, clerical eyeglasses were set in gold-colored frames. The large, golden face was without blemish, well-fed without being fat. It was very obvious that the clerical suit had been fitted by a tailor. The black shoes were without animal dung, dust, dirt or muck—a veritable miracle in this land flowing with muck and shite.

Before the C.I.E. driver could say anything, the clergyman asked, "What are you doing?"

Despite the scorn he held for priests, Corrigan almost reacted on a nun-instilled instinct—*almost* started the motions of tugging his forelock out of respect for the cloth. But he easily checked himself. "If it looks like I'm stretching, then it's stretching I'm doing," he said. To show how much he had recovered from the nunnish brainwashing, Corrigan stretched his arms above his head and stood on his toes. "Aaaah," he said. "There's nothing like a great bloody stretch."

"And what are the rest of us supposed to do while you're out here enjoying your stretch?"

Corrigan saw sparking anger in the cleric's eyeballs. Keeping his arms above his head, he said, "Oh, I would never make a suggestion to a man of such standing as yourself, but since you ask, you might like to walk on ahead and I'll stop when we catch up with you so you can get back on the bus again."

The sparks in the priest's eyes became flames and, in his peculiar accent, now obviously underpinned with an Irish lilt, he said, "My good man, I paid for a seat on this bus to get to Gohen by six o'clock. I suggest that you suppress this sudden urge to perform calisthenics out here in the countryside, that you get back in your bus and drive it to Gohen without further delay."

Unblinkingly returning the imperious stare, Joe Corrigan jerked his thumb over his shoulder and said, "My good man, there's a lorry stopped in the middle of the road ahead of us. It'll be out of the way in five minutes."

The clergyman looked up at the lorry sitting on the landing on Beggses Hill. "I should have known," he said, meaning *I'm surrounded by fools*. He turned around to go back to the bus, but before he had gone two steps, Corrigan called after him, "Hey!" The priest stopped, but there was a split-second hesitation before he turned around. He glared at the driver.

"If you'd asked politely like any decent man would do, you wouldn't have made an arse of yourself," Corrigan said, and he resumed his calisthenics.

Five minutes later Paddy Kavanagh got into his truck and Ned Bracken cranked the lorry's cooled engine to life. The clanging of metal was heard in the land as Kavanagh wrestled with gear lever and clutch. He stuck his upper body through the window and twisted his head toward the rear of his lorry. The engine groaned like an old woman changing position in her bed. In many forceful streams, smoke spewed out of the many-holed exhaust pipe and enveloped the sand-lorry. The groaning cloud slowly backed up the face of Beggses Hill like a doubtful saint wobbling up to heaven on a porous cloud. For one breathless moment it seemed to teeter, exhausted, on the crest before it slipped from view. Ned Bracken, walking to reduce weight, disappeared into the smoke.

His backside against the front of the bus's mudguard, his arms folded across his chest, Joe Corrigan gazed at the spot where the lorry had sunk like a ship on the other side of a rolling wave. He heard footsteps approaching, but he didn't turn around. It was the priest again. He stood beside Corrigan, too close, and asked, "Are we going to stay here all night?"

"I don't know about you, but I'm not," Corrigan said, and he didn't move, didn't look at his inquisitor, just kept looking at Beggses Hill.

"When can we expect you to grace us with the service we paid for?"

"If you're asking when will we get moving again, the answer is, in about two minutes. That's how long it takes Paddy Kavanagh to turn his lorry around."

"And then I suppose we'll have to stay behind him all the way into Gohen."

"You're right at that! But I wouldn't worry about it," Corrigan said. "Paddy's able to get his loaded lorry up to ten miles an hour on the level."

"My good man, I've been traveling for a long time and I—"

Corrigan turned and bestowed on the cleric the look he reserved for cat shite stuck to the sole of his shoe. He spoke quietly and firmly—menacingly almost. "My good man, I've been traveling a long time myself. The other people on the bus have been traveling a long time. Paddy Kavanagh started loading his lorry at seven o'clock this morning, and it'll be dark by the time he throws off the last shovelful of sand." He ran appraising eyes down along the body of the cleric, then locked onto the ecclesiastical orbs until the clergyman blinked and left.

Trailing Paddy Kavanagh's lorry, the bus arrived twenty minutes late in Gohen. While he was still fifty yards away from the Central Hotel, Joe Corrigan eyed the few people waiting to meet his passengers and deliveries. The young Bracken chap, his blond hair making him as obvious as one dandelion in an acre of lawn, was there as usual, waiting for the box of reels for the Picture House. Simon Peter Lamb's boy, sitting on his bike with his hand on the Bracken boy's shoulder, was there too, as Corrigan knew he would be, waiting for the box of day-old Rhode Island Red chicks under the canvas on top of the bus. Jimser Conroy, huge gut held up off his thighs with a leather belt strong enough to hold a howdah on an elephant, was standing in the front door of his two-storied hotel, stoically hoping the bus was bringing him some custom. And of course, Con-I'll-have-it-for-you-tomorrow-Carroll, the draper, was there waiting for his delivery from Clerys of O'Connell Street. There was no one else, except the mad-looking Coughlin woman from Drumsally on the far side of the Esker, but it was likely that she was just passing and had stopped to gawk.

"Maybe your man is coming to see Father Mooney," Corrigan thought, "and maybe Mooney's on the golf links."

No sooner had the bus come to a stop than Corrigan could hear Ned Geoghan clambering up the metal ladder at the back. Switching off the engine, the driver climbed out of his cab and swung the door shut. As he went to the back of the bus to help with the unloading of the luggage and deliveries, the Coughlin woman strode past him. At the same time, the cleric with the golden hair stepped onto the footpath and looked around. The Coughlin woman, wisps of her thin red hair escaping from her hairnet, went directly to the priest and stood in front of him.

As he went by, Corrigan heard the churchman saying, "I hope you bought the motor."

Ned Geoghan handed down the two brown suitcases, and Joe Corrigan placed them on the footpath. There were no nametags on them, just large black numbers inside white-starred labels. Then came the Clerys package, and when he turned around with it, Con-I'll-have-it-for-you-tomorrow was waiting for the hand-off at Corrigan's elbow. "Good man, Joe," Con said, and he strode off with his little bit of profit under his arm.

When Ned Geoghan handed down the box for Simon Peter Lamb's wife, the scrabbling feet of the dozen day-old chicks inside could be heard. As he called over the Lamb boy with a flick of the peak of his driver's cap, Corrigan saw that the Coughlin woman and the priest were gone, were walking up the street. The woman was carrying the two suitcases.

The Lamb child wheeled his bike over and, when the Bracken boy yanked up the spring-loaded arm, the bus driver put the box on the carrier over the back wheel.

"Is your name Billy?" Corrigan asked, as Bracken carefully set the carrier arm against the box of livestock.

"No, sir. Barlow."

"Barlow, as in Bartholomew?"

"Yes, sir."

"I just saw your father in Mister Kavanagh's lorry." Corrigan turned to the Lamb boy. "And you're one of Simon Peter's lads?"

"Yes, sir. Mikey."

"Your mother was a Hayes, wasn't she?" Corrigan said. "And

you're a real Hayes yourself to look at. Tell me now, Mikey, how is it that day-old chicks don't die of the hunger and they not fed since they were born?"

"When they come out of their shells, sir, they still have a bit of the egg yolk in their stomachs and that keeps them going for a few days until they learn to pick."

"But isn't the yolk the yoke they hatch out of?"

"It is, sir, but when the guts are made, they're made around a little bit of the yolk and that's still in there when the chicken is hatched."

"Be Janey! I've always wondered about that, and no one was ever able to tell me. Where did you find that out?"

"In a book, sir."

"I love books, myself. There's nothing like books for finding out things," Joe Corrigan said. "Did you ever hear of Boadicea?"

"No, sir."

"Well you will someday. She was one great woman even if she was English."

Ned Geoghan had climbed down the ladder with the flat box of reels in his free hand. "What does Mister Tracey pay you for doing this?" he asked, as he handed it to Barlow.

"Tuppence a day or into the Picture House for nothing."

"I suppose you see every picture, then?" Geoghan asked.

"No, sir," Barlow Bracken answered. "I give the money to my mother."

"That's a good lad," Corrigan said. "How old are you?"

"Eleven, sir."

"Only eleven and you helping out your father and mother with the money. You're a good lad, Bartholomew Bracken."

Barlow Bracken blushed.

With Ned Geoghan the only person left on the bus, Joe Corrigan drove up the empty street toward Bill Moore's shed. When he went around the bend at Lee Reilly's pub, he saw the Coughlin woman and her brother Eddie-the-cap and the brown priest standing at the back of a black Morris Minor. The lid of the boot was open, and the perpetually becapped one was lifting a suitcase into the car.

Rules are rules, and the C.I.E. rules said the bus could not be reversed unless the conductor stood outside to guide the driver. And so, Ned Geoghan, keeping himself in the frame of the rearview mirror on the side of the bus, guided Joe Corrigan into the shed. With a final sighing of springs the bus came to a stop and when the engine was turned off, the silence in the shed was loud.

As Corrigan turned the key in the door lock, Ned Geoghan came up from the depths of the shed. "Were you talking to that priest at all?" Corrigan asked.

"I never heard such a fussy old bollicks," Geoghan replied. "He pissed and moaned the whole way home. You'd think he was the king of England, the way he was going on, complaining about everything."

Side by side, they strolled to where their bikes were lying against a disused manger.

"God, he was real snotty to me. Did you see he was met by that quare Coughlin one and Eddie-the-cap?"

"He's their brother home from India for his holidays."

The two men rested their bikes against the low wall outside the shed.

"He's the brother of them Coughlins?" Corrigan echoed. "I never heard of the Coughlins having a brother, never mind a priest in the family."

Corrigan and Geoghan each pulled in a big half door and met in the middle.

"He's their brother, all right—away for years. And he belongs to some religious order or other, so he kind of disappeared when he was about twelve. He told me he's been traveling for three weeks from India and that the journey from Dublin to Gohen was the worst part."

"He's a miserable old bollicks," Corrigan said, as he locked the two doors of the shed together with the heavy chain.

"Well, if he's not miserable himself, he makes everyone around him miserable," Ned Geoghan said. He put his left foot on the bike's pedal and pushed off. As he swung his right leg over the saddle, he said, "I'll see you in the morning, Joe."

"Right y'are, Ned!"

When Joe Corrigan rode his bike out onto the street, Mikey Lamb was wobbling by on his bike with Barlow Bracken on the bar, Bracken holding the film reels to his chest with his free hand. When he caught up with the boys Corrigan slowed down. "Will I give you a push to get you going, lads?" he called from behind.

"Yes, please, Mister Corrigan," Mikey Lamb replied.

"Hold on, so," said the driver. "Here I come." As he sidled up beside the boys' bike, he could hear the peeping of the chicks in the box on the carrier. He put his right hand on the small of Mikey's back and gave him a boost forward.

The wobble went out of his bike as Mikey pedaled furiously and got up a head of steam.

"Thanks, Mister Corrigan," the two boys called together, and Joe Corrigan turned off into Long Barn Lane and headed home to his colcannon and two fried eggs. He was bursting with the good news for his wife that instead of the bog tonight, they were going to walk into Lee Reilly's for a half-pint each. He'd tell the Missus how a chicken gets hatched around a piece of egg yolk.

Their riverside walks sometimes ended with great action between the sheets before they went to sleep, neither of them with a stitch on.

18

The Terrible Thought

1951

In which Estelle Butler, lifelong friend of Annie Mulhall, niece-in-law of Doul Yank, dispenses delicious gossip, but Annie is too distracted to enjoy the dished dirt.

FOR SOMEONE ACCUSTOMED to traveling along rutted, overgrown lanes in an unsprung, iron-shod, and chain-encumbered cart, there was an elegance to traveling on a smooth, tarred road in a trap with rubber-tired wheels, sensitive springs and leather draughts. A person could chat without having to compete loudly with clanging iron and jangling chains—not have to worry that the conversation would go over the roadside hedges into greedy ears.

Peggy Mulhall, wife of Mattie, niece-in-law of Doul Yank, was sitting in Estelle Butler's trap, very pleased with herself in her cushioned seat. The two women, friends since First Babies, were facing each other, their knees occasionally touching. The only sound, besides Estelle's voice, was the unrushed clip-clopping of the pony's hooves.

Peggy's satisfaction would have been more complete if only she could have banished her thieving uncle-in-law from her mind. She was so needful to talk with her friend about Doul Yank that she was impatient for Estelle to finish dispensing her accumulated gossip. Besides a few hums and haws, Peggy did no speculative wallowing in Estelle's latest news, hoping that her restraint would speed things along. Peggy sometimes resented Estelle's selfish command of the conversation. Sheila Quigley, wife of Quick, and their mutual friend, had no qualms about silencing Estelle's mad loquacious gallops with a vocal tackle of her own.

Father Jarlath Coughlin had visited Estelle, Paul and their two girls on Thursday evening. "It's hard to imagine he's the brother of Bridie and Eddie. He's so . . . he talks so nicely—little ups and downs like he's nearly singing. And it's almost a sin how clean he is. Not a speck under his fingernails, and you know the way the dirt gets ground into a man's hands? Well, he has the cleanest hands I've ever seen on a man, or a woman for that matter, cleaner than the Protestant minister's wife. And you'd cut yourself open on the creases in his trousers, they're so sharp. The girls could see the red of the fire in his toecaps. But the best of all were the cufflinks. His brown skin, the black suit, the white shirt and the gold cufflinks—he looked so . . . so perfect, so rich, so refined. That's exactly it—refined. Cufflinks made of *gold*, mind you. And the gold rims of his shining glasses! Paul beside him in his old clothes and Wellingtons looked like a pile of fresh horse dung with steam rising; such perfect skin and it so brown and clean you'd love to get bare with him between the sheets even if only to feel him all over. I'd say he even has a golden rod." Estelle slapped Peggy on the knee and sent a stream of laughter arcing over the hedges. Peggy forced a smile. In Peggy's mind her friend's name had always lent Estelle a certain degree of poshness—"Estelle" sounded a bit Protestant. And so, Peggy was always mildly surprised when vulgar stuff came out of Estelle's mouth.

Doul Yank's thievery was turning into an ache in Peggy's stomach.

"He's terrible interesting, and as brown as a hen egg. The girls only wanted to see the pictures in the stereoscope. They were pretending to do their homework, waiting for him to finish telling Paul and me about the Hindus and the Muslims and what's going on since the English left. There's been terrible killing, and I'm afraid the girls might be having nightmares. Of course their ears pricked up entirely when he started whispering to Paul and myself about what the Indians

119

do to each other with those terrible machetes, chopping the hands and arms off each other with one swipe. Can you imagine someone coming at you swinging a billhook? I'd die of the fright, myself, before he even got near me—dirty my knickers at least. Go up!" As if to get away from the image of the amputating billhook, Estelle slapped the pony's rump with the flat of her hand. The pony made a feeble buck within the confines of its tacklings, told Estelle with its arse to feck off.

"Doul . . ." Peggy began, but Estelle didn't hear her.

"The stereoscope is a great contraption. There's two pictures exactly the same stuck to a piece of cardboard beside each other. You put the cardboard in a frame and look through two eyeholes with glass in them and the two pictures become one picture and you'd think there's space between the people far back and ones near your eyes. The pictures were great and terrible at the same time. You'd think you were standing right there in the middle of everything, but the people in them were terrible skinny and mad looking. One man wearing a sheet had bits of sticks for crutches and a lump of a stump hanging there like the end of a sausage tied up with a twist of twine. There wasn't a blade of grass anywhere, just heaps of dust and rocks, and a few cows with their hips sticking up like two sticks in an empty sack and humps between their shoulders. There was one man on his hunkers with nothing only a rag around him, and the boniest knees you ever saw, and the thinnest legs—God! I'd hate to see *his* privates—two raisins and a dead minnow. He was stripping the skin off a cow, and big birds looking down at him from the bushes. Any animal is terrible to look at without its skin, all bloody and gutsy. Only certain people are allowed to skin cows, and only the vultures and the kites are allowed to eat them, and people dying of the hunger in the streets every day. The cows are sacred, and if a Hindu eats beef he's finished for ever, straight to hell with him. Did you ever hear the likes? The cows go anywhere they want and do their dung all over the place. Sacred cows, I ask you! The girls couldn't look at half the pictures, after all the looking forward. There was another with a man holding the body of a monkey by the feet in one hand and its head in his other one. It reminded me of John the Baptist's head on the plate in that picture in the convent. How do the nuns pass that every day going in to eat?" Estelle rippled the reins along the pony's back, but the old pony would not be bullied, and its steady trot did not change.

Peggy quickly loaded her lungs, but Estelle wasn't finished yet.

"When the English wanted to torture a Hindu, they pushed beef down his throat and rubbed cow fat all over him. They tortured the Muslims the same way, only with pig. Aren't the English a terrible crowd altogether? Father Coughlin said now that they're gone out of India, his school has to raise all its own money, that neither the Hindus nor the Muslims will support a Catholic school. He hopes the people of Gohen and Clunnyboe and Drumsally will be very generous. When he left, Paul said, 'That's why he came home—to raise money. He'll be back with the hand out.' There we were thinking he was visiting us just to be nice, to show us the pictures, and all he was doing was softening us up for a donation to his school. I hate when people do that—you think they're all friendly, and then you find out they're after something. Asking the likes of us for money for a school in India and we lucky if we can afford to go to the pictures once a month. Go up." Again, the leather reins rose and fell, and the pony took no notice.

"Doul Yank . . ." Peggy said, but Estelle was already off at full steam on a different track. "And did you ever think you'd see the Civil Servant riding down the road with a woman, and the woman Deirdre Hyland, no less? I thought that one would only marry a vet, or a doctor or a solicitor or a draper. God, she has terrible notions that one, talking with an accent like she was from London or somewhere. And the Civil Servant taking to her like a duck to water. I'd love to be a fly on the wall the night of their wedding. Imagine the Civil Servant with nothing on, only his glasses. Hyland without her clothes! It's the real proper ones you have to watch out for. She'd be the kind to surprise everyone, and it wouldn't surprise me if she'll surprise the son of Lalor by falling to her knees in front of him to worship his relic." Estelle exploded in laughter.

And Peggy smiled. While the loud laughter soared, Peggy's inward eye saw Doul Yank with his fistful of brown five-pound notes that rightly belonged to her and Mattie, saw him sloping out of the bank like a horrible snake in the grass. If Mikey Lamb hadn't seen him, she and Matt wouldn't have found out till the bollicks was dead. And by that time Doul Yank could have taken out the entire value of the farm. And what was the fecker doing with the money?

Estelle leaned in and brought Peggy back by putting her hand on her knee. "It won't be la-di-dah-Deirdre when Lalor gets going. Can you picture it? Then all the refinement gone out the window, and she grunting and sweating like an old sow under a boar, squealing for more." Estelle threw back her head and made a whinnying noise that segued into mirthful laughter. And before the laughter had run its course, she was talking again, her voice so tautly pitched it was in danger of collapse. "If they don't go away for a honeymoon, I swear I'll be outside their window on the first night. Even if they do go away, I'll be there outside the window their first night back."

During Estelle's commentary, Peggy suddenly grew weary of her attempt to talk about Doul Yank; had grown weary of Doul Yank sitting inside her head. "What is there to talk about anyway? Just that he's borrowing money against the farm that's supposed to be ours when he dies."

Her eyes wandered into the finely inscribed curlicues and flourishes painted on the curving shafts of the trap; they followed the open circles within open circles, all joined together with roaming lines that could have been stylized, thorned vines, and in these vines Peggy's mind numbly came to rest and she heard all over again what Mikey Lamb had told her and Mattie, what Mikey's father and mother made him tell them.

"Brendan Healy and myself were waiting with the Picture House money, and Mister Gorman was leaning across the counter whispering to Mister Gorry, and Mister Gorry got this big book from under the counter, and when he found the right place, he spun it around and said, 'Sign there, Mister Gorman.' And when Mister Gorry was counting out

the fivers, his fingers were a blur like a wheel in the pictures, and Mister Gorman spread himself all over the counter like a turkey with its wings around the young ones when there's a hawk, so no one would see. But I stepped over to the side, and I could see the brown fivers flying through Mister Gorry's fingers so quick you could hardly see them. I thought there must be a hundred fivers, and then Mister Gorry picked up the pile and went through it again very slow, and I counted, too, and there were only twenty fivers. Mister Gorman put the money in his inside pocket before he turned away from Mister Gorry."

When she finally dragged herself out of the painted thorns, the spire of the Protestant church in Gohen was peeping above the elm trees surrounding Blennerhassets' Stud Farm. Estelle was laughing again, and she gleefully gave the pony a sharp thwack on the arse with the end of the reins. The somnolent pony jerked awake and, with unexpected alacrity, broke into a short and angry gallop, causing the trap to undulate jerkily like a boy-blown paper boat in a basin. Noises of apprehension sprang out of the women and each clasped the side of the trap. Then dramatic sighs of relief escaped from Estelle when the pony suddenly returned to her previous gait.

They passed the Blennerhasset Stud Farm and Estelle, still blind to her friend's distraction, chattered on about the preparations the Coughlins had made for the homecoming of their brother—new thatch, new whitewash, and new geranium. Peggy's eyes wandered off again until they came to rest on the brass railing on the front of the trap with its upcurled ends channeling the leather reins from the driver's hand to the brass ring embedded in each side of the pony's straddle. As her eyes lost their focus, she eased herself into the gentle rocking motion of the trap. Just beyond the brass rein-rail, the blurred haunches of the pony hypnotically muscled with each step trotted, and a distant clipping and clopping was synchronized to the rising and falling of the haunches. The swaying of the pony's head, the movement of the haunches and the unending flow of tarred road into her eyes' edges harmonized into a symphony, and Peggy's brain threw up silhouettes on a distant horizon.

And there was Doul Yank in his snipe-shooting uniform and with his snipe-shooting double-barreled shotgun, heading across the fields on one of his snipe-shooting safaris, and Peggy heard the words Mister Howard had spoken to her husband: "*Death is the only thing that can stop Mister Gorman from taking the money out of the bank and using the farm as collateral. Remember, it's his till he dies.*"

Peggy Mulhall pulled in such a loud chestful of air that she sounded like a victim of apnea who has seen the glow of the Pearly Gates but who has opted to come back to her warm bed for another while. Estelle asked, "Are you all right, Peggy?"

But an ass-and-cart came into view around the corner ahead and distracted Estelle. Spud Murphy, the bell ringer, public masturbator and general factotum of all the Catholic institutions in Gohen, was on his way to the Blennerhasset Stud for a load of Protestant horse dung for the nuns' flower garden. Even the nuns believed that Protestant horse dung had greater potency than Catholic horse dung because Protestant oats had the same good qualities as the barley they sold to Mister Guinness for his porter. Despite the unusually hot sun, Murphy was wearing his standard general factotum uniform of ragged cap, buttoned-to-the-throat dirty gabardine overcoat, and turned-down Wellington boots. In the center of his noisy conveyance Spud was standing up with the reins casually caught in the fingers of one hand. One flap of his overcoat was pushed aside, and the other hand was in his trousers pocket, sufficiently active to suggest that he was working himself up to a public performance. His entire body was turned slightly toward the center of the road, and he was showing off his cartmanship to the best advantage. He was in complete syncopation with the forward movement of the cart, his knees allowing for the short ups and downs of the backband in the straddle. The onlooker would have been convinced that, no matter what the ass did to throw everything out of kilter, Murphy would maintain his heroic pose. In another context he could have been a David in Carrara marble or a plumed chevalier laughing at a Dutch painter.

Estelle was not impressed. "Off to the stud for a load of Protestant horseshite, Spud?" she called, and she nudged Peggy Mulhall's knee.

"Missus Blennerhasset always gives me tea and jammy bread, with sugar in it," Spud called back, nonsequitoriously, and his hand inside his trousers went into high gear.

"Be gob, she's a decent woman," Estelle called back, as the cart and the trap passed on the road, each gliding past its background of high margin-grass and leafy bushes.

"That's a grand trap you have there," Spud called back, almost turned completely around in the distancing cart, not showing the slightest concern for his balance. "Grand soft wheels and springs, and I wouldn't have the bones shook out of me at all. Yeer two fine looking women. Ohyaah!" He suddenly bent over.

"Isn't he a terrible yoke," Estelle said. "How many times has Father Scully told him to stop pulling his wire in public? All the clouts he's got from every man in Gohen, and he still does it. And will you look at him? You'd think he was in Duffy's Circus, standing on the back of a galloping horse and holding onto nothing except his willie."

Even though the esquire's words were still ricocheting around her skull, Peggy smiled for Estelle. She was intensely relieved that she had not mentioned Doul Yank to Estelle, had not let loose her raging anger. A thought, too terrible to be told to anyone, had crossed her mind. She was so alarmed at the thought that she pushed it away, afraid that Estelle might see what she was thinking. Jesus! She felt her back begin to itch from a sudden surge of sweat. Quickly, she burst out, "What had you in the house for Father Coughlin to eat?"

"Nothing, only bread and butter and jam. I wasn't expecting him for another week."

The high wall around the Protestant churchyard threw back the sounds of the pony's hoofs on the road.

"I'd better get something. He might come to see us soon," Peggy said. "Maybe a bit of ham and a tomato and a pan loaf and a bit of Coleman's mustard. And maybe a few chester cakes as well."

"God! Don't give him too much, or he'll think you'll be giving him a big donation when he comes begging. If I were you, I'd give him nothing but tea and bread and butter. No jam."

On the streets of Gohen, people began to appear who needed to be greeted, and as the two friends nodded, waved and good morninged, the pony, unguided, trotted along the main street and turned into the yard behind Ramsbottom's shop, where it knew it would have a long sleep standing up in the shafts.

19

In the Sunroom

In which Elsie Howard begins to tell Patrick Bracken, once called Barlow, about a family tragedy, but Sam unwittingly interrupts and talks about the same tragedy he has kept buried for a long time.

"STOP, PATRICK," MISTER HOWARD said. He began to struggle out of his chair. "Le bladaire runneth over again," he said when he'd stood up.

"Sam!" his wife said. "There are other words for this bodily need of yours. You could at least say you're off to exfuse."

"I did use my French to take the vulgar edge off. I'm off to exfuse, Patrick," Sam said. "But no matter what you call it, there's no getting around the fact that *le vessie vieux* is shrinking. And the hands are shaking, and the underpinnings are beginning to go. Getting old—being old—is one big pain in the arse. I never thought it would be like this. And the damn thing, old age, creeps up so subtly that you don't even notice it. One day you wake up and you're old. It's so disappointing." He shuffled a few steps as he tried to work up a head of steam. "So disappointing," he said again and leaned a hand on the door jamb.

Missus Howard turned to Patrick. "Sam thinks he should still be able to run a marathon, even though he hasn't broken into a run since he robbed Morgans' orchard when he was twelve. One of the newly minted garda took him by the ear up to his father's office. He would have been on the books only he had a friend—his father—in high places."

Sam turned around. "I never shot a swallow with a pellet gun," he said. "That's what *she* did, Patrick. Shot a swallow, and her father had told her a hundred times that if you kill a swallow your cows will milk blood. She shot it while it was sitting on the peak of the roof of her own house, and it rolled down the slates and fell at her feet. She still feels guilty."

"I do. I still feel guilty even though it was seventy years ago."

Sam leaned his shoulder against the jamb. "She might be guilty about shooting a swallow, but she has no problem asking me to put a pellet into a cat's arse while it's doing its load in her flower beds."

"There's a difference, Sam, between an innocent swallow and a crapping cat."

"A crapping swallow dropped its load into some fellow's eyes in the Bible and blinded him. He probably thought all swallows should be wiped off the face of the earth. And there's no such thing as an innocent swallow and a guilty cat. Both are behaving within their instinctive rules, and neither has any feelings about what they do. It's we who ascribe bad intentions to them."

Patrick asked, "If we ascribe goodness or badness to the normal behavior of animals, then who decides where the line is, which life form should be on which side of the line—fleas and honeybees, for instance; goldfinches and scall crows; wasps and wagtails; maggots and mute swans; unloading cats or purring kittens?"

Sam said, "There's a sect in India called the Jains, and there's no dividing line for them. They believe in the sacredness of every form of life, some of them going so far as to wear masks so they won't inhale and kill small flying things. Some have servants to sweep the ground where they're going to walk so they won't step on any creepy crawlies."

"That's a bit mad," Elsie said.

"Not for them," Sam said. "Patrick put his finger on it: who decides what deserves to die and what to live? We decided a long time ago that fleas don't deserve to live, but that squirrels do. We wipe out whole colonies of ants, but we'll free one honeybee from a spider's web. We'll chop a rat into little bits with a spade but pick up a kitten and stroke it and even kiss it. That line, and what goes on which side, can be pushed up into the human life form. Look at what Hitler and the Nazis did: they put millions of people on the far side of the line and did away with them like they were fleas. Look at Stalin."

"We don't have to go to Europe or Russia looking for examples, Sam. Each side in any warring situation is less than human to the other side," Patrick said.

"You're right, Patrick," Elsie said. "Look at the way we treated Spud Murphy in our own town of Gohen. Spud was relegated to the other side of the line because he wasn't all there. We didn't kill him, but once he was on the far side of the line, all the men felt free to give him a whack or a kick whenever they felt like it, and who objected? Everyone laughed."

Again the three of them fell into contemplative silence. Then Sam asked, "Do some people *place* themselves on the far side of the line with the rats and fleas of the world?"

"That doesn't matter. They still must not be mistreated," Elsie said.

"Of course not, but you haven't answered the question."

"What you're asking, Sam," Patrick said, "is do some people make it easier for others to mistreat them? You said yourself that Father Coughlin and Lawrence Gorman behaved so badly they had no one to stand up for them when they died. They made it easy for people to dislike them."

"But did they go to the other side of the line by their behavior or did we place them there?"

Elsie said, "It's all a matter of likes and dislikes. We don't like rats, and our dislike makes it easy for us to kill them. Nobody liked Coughlin or Gorman, and it was easy for everyone to simply bury them and get them out of the way. Look at the priest—from the minute he stepped onto the bus in Dublin, he was a pain in the backside. Gorman was as big a pain. Both of them thought the world was all about them.

It's easy to dislike people like that. And yes, Sam, I think some people cross over the line and join the rats and the fleas, but at the same time that doesn't entitle the rest of us to treat them like the rats and—"

"That's a different question, Else," Sam interrupted. "That's a moral question with a simple answer. And I agree that some people do have the unfortunate knack of appearing to join the rats and the fleas. It was only Spud Murphy's mild insanity that saved him to some degree, but the other two—they had such weak egos that they behaved as if the universe revolved around them. After a while, the people get tired doing all the revolving. Gorman and Coughlin probably grew up in houses where their mothers were adoring satellites. I am now off to exfuse because le bladaire is about to exfluse."

"Exfluse?" Elsie asked.

"French for explode," Sam said, and he left.

When Sam turned the corner out of the kitchen, Missus Howard leaned toward Patrick, her voice low. She spoke fast, her eyes constantly turning to where her husband would reappear when he had finished in the bathroom. "Patrick," she said, "when you were talking about your sister drowning herself in Shipley, I wanted to tell you that one of our sons killed himself in Canada, but it upsets Sam too much to talk about it."

"Oh, Jesus. I'm—" Patrick said, but Missus Howard held up her hand.

"How were you to know?" she asked. "Of course it's still a terrible pain for both of us. Sam listens to my sadness but never talks about his own. David was his name, a lovely sensitive boy. He won a scholarship to study architecture in McGill University in Montreal. He had Trinity behind him, and he would only be away for four years. The plan was that he'd come home to visit after two years; travel wasn't what it is now. He did wonderful . . ." Missus Howard saw her husband returning.

Sam Howard stood in the doorway and looked at his wife. "Else, I'm going to tell Patrick about our David," he said, as if asking permission. "If it's going to upset you, then maybe you should—"

"Oh, Sam! I always want to be where our David is spoken about, and it doesn't matter a damn if I cry," his wife said. As Sam turned and went to his chair, Elsie looked at Patrick, raised her eyebrows and opened her hands like she was releasing a bird. Gladness and sadness fought for her face.

"Patrick," Mister Howard said. "You told us the painful truth about Mikey Lamb. You told us about your sister AnneMarie, how she went off one morning and . . . and killed herself. You told us about your father dying in the mental institution. I want to tell you something in return." Sam Howard paused for a moment, swallowed hard. "We had a son, David, who killed himself, too." His eyes filled with water, but it did not flow. He held out his hand to Patrick to forestall an interruption. "David was a lovely child, curious about everything, full of delight at everything he found. It was like . . . it was like he never lost his sense of wonder, always in amazement as if he'd only been hatched two minutes ago; he made you see things that you'd been looking at all your life without seeing them. Even his adolescence was peaceful for him and for us."

For a moment, Mister Howard paused, looked at something in his memory and left it in there. The water in his eyes had ebbed away. "David won a scholarship to a university in Canada, McGill in Montreal. He wanted to be an architect. He wasn't there a year when he fell for a girl from Boston. Of course, we didn't know . . . it was only after he died that we . . . he did mention her in several letters, and Else divined in her female way that David had found the woman he would marry. Her name was June Whelan. The plan was that at the end of his second year he would come home and bring June with him. The night before they were due to leave, a young man was side-swiped by a city bus, and he lost control of his motorbike. The bike went up on the footpath and whipped June out of David's hand and broke her neck. She died immediately. We knew nothing except that we got a telegram from David saying their departure was delayed for a week. Our David did the same as your AnneMarie—only he stepped out in front of a train. You can imagine what the . . ."

Mister Howard stopped again, and his mouth opened like that of a child who has been visited with a devastation of adult betrayal. Sam's eyes flooded again, and for a moment the surface tension held the tears in place, but the dam pushed from behind and the rivers of sadness ran down. But he still managed to speak. "Else and I have some idea what it was like for your family when your AnneMarie died, and I feel very sad for your mother and father even though they are dead now." He paused again and looked over at his wife. "How did I do, Else?" he asked, and Elsie stood up and went to her husband. She stood beside his chair and pulled his head into her chest. "That was grand, Sam, grand. Our David was a beautiful child. Everything about him was beautiful."

Sam's body was gently rocking in his wife's embrace as Patrick went to the door leading out into the garden. He closed it quietly and walked over to the small fish pond. Lengths of string tied across the shallow water protected the goldfish from birds. A fist-sized stone beside the pond was surrounded with broken snail shells—a thrush's midden. Patrick sat on the wooden bench and let his eyes get lost among the water plants. When his chilled body shivered him back to the present, he found himself hunched over, his face enclosed in his hands and water running down his wrists into his shirt cuffs. He felt drained as he returned once again from his remembrances, from the numbness of his family as the distressed policeman stood in the doorway telling them about AnneMarie. Patrick dried off his face and hands and stood up. He watched the fish moving languorously through the stalks of the plants, and he breathed his body back into its normal rhythms.

Twenty minutes later, when Patrick returned to the sunroom, Else was standing at the table holding a green teddy bear.

"Patrick," she said as she turned the bear toward him. "We gave this to David on his fourth birthday."

"He called it Saint Patrick," Sam said.

"I've had it wrapped up in a pillowcase for years and hidden away. I'd take it out every so often to give it a hug and have a good cry." She moved the bear's legs at the hips and placed it against the china table lamp with ceramic roses strewn on its base.

"You weren't the only one, Else. I discovered your hiding place a long time ago, and I hugged Saint Patrick and cried for David, too."

"Oh, Sam, Sam, Sam. Men, men, men." Elsie, tears flowing on her cheeks again, went to Sam and put her hand on his head. "Why do men have to hide their grief? We are going to keep Saint Patrick here in the sunroom. We are going to keep David in the sunroom and not worry about the crying."

"That's what we'll do, Else—keep David out in the open." Then he turned to Patrick. "It was David who named the lion on our front door MGM but not because of Metro-Goldwyn-Mayer. He had a friend when he was small, Malachy Gillespie. David once told Malachy's mother that she looked like our lion."

Elsie kissed her husband's bald and freckled head. "And, unfortunately, he was right. Poor Missus Gillespie was living proof that the ancient Irish had sexual relations with animals outside their own species."

Patrick's jaw dropped, and Sam said, "Jesus, Else!"

"Oh Jesus yourself, Sam. The truth always has a way of squeezing itself into the sunlight no matter how unpleasant it is." Else went to her chair and sat. She reached over and touched the bear's paw. She looked at Patrick, "Your story about AnneMarie restored David to Sam and me. And I'll leave it at that for now."

"But I have to say," Patrick said, "that both of you have my sincere sympathy for the loss of your son."

"Thank you, Patrick," the Howards said in unison.

The sunroom was silent for half a minute. Finally, Sam said, "We're fine for now, aren't we, Else?"

And Else said, "We're grand, Sam. Grand."

"Then let's get back to the happenings of nineteen fifty-one," her husband said.

Patrick hesitated for a moment as if putting a long train back on its tracks. Finally, he said, "Everything about Simon Peter Lamb's farmyard was gray . . ."

20

In the Burnished Pewter Bowl

1951

In which Barlow Bracken, age eleven, comes
home after school with Mikey Lamb and sees his
future wife, Molly Lamb, for the first time.

EVERYTHING ABOUT SIMON PETER LAMB'S FARMYARD WAS GRAY, except
for the doors of the various sheds. They were of the blackness of
tar, being coated once a year to protect them from the damp—outside,
inside and the four edges. The doors were two hundred years old.

The yard was surfaced with gray gravel, pounded into solidity
by years of hooves and feet—human, bovine, porcine, equine and
avian—and the iron-shod wheels of carts and farm machinery.

The buildings which gave the yard its rectangular shape were
built of gray stone, the irregular lines of pointing between the stones
a mixture of gray sand and gray cement. The south side of the gray
rectangle was edged by the dwelling house, with the turf shed at its
far end. Splashes of lichen, in yellows and purples, spotted the gray
slates covering the roofs of all the buildings.

When mountainous clouds lowered the sky, the grayness of the
farmyard was depressing. When rain cascaded out of those clouds
for unending days, the grayness of the yard was the color of desola-
tion, its soddenness that of the deck of Noah's ark.

But when the sun did shine, the grayness was transformed into burnished pewter; the stones in the walls stored and reflected the heat; the purplish-greenish-yellowish lichens on the dry slates and in the wall crevices took on colors which were not visible for the rest of the sopping year. In the summer sunshine, when all the animals were afield, the farmyard was a beautiful place, with only the random hen, turkey or duck dropping creating unpleasantnesses to be avoided.

Three weeks after the arrival of Father Jarlath Coughlin from India, the youngest of the Lamb children, Fintan, was pulling a cardboard box around the farmyard. Without its lid, and showing signs of wear and tear, it was attached to the boy's fist by a piece of raveling binder twine. On the outside of the box were words pleading for the safety of the day-old chicks within. But there were no chickens. Instead, reacting tremulously to every bump and hollow in the yard, was a punctured, yellow, rubber duckie with a red beak—the anachronistic bathtub birthday present from the misguided aunt in Yorkshire two years earlier.

The child's brown hair had not been combed, and the thatch on one side of his head was flat from its last sweaty contact with a pillow. Held up with gray braces, his knee-length, brown corduroy trousers had once belonged to his older brother, Mikey. Two of the three buttons of his green jersey, also a hand-me-down, were in the wrong buttonholes. One of his fawn ankle socks had disappeared into the once-white canvas shoes reluctantly handed down by his older sister. "I don't care if they're too small for me—they're my first communion shoes," Molly had complained, "and he's always walking in hen dung."

Dust had stuck to the drools around the boy's mouth, and he looked dirtier than he actually was.

As he dreamily floated in the sunny pewter bowl, Fintan gently clicked his tongue and made the sound of a trotting horse, audible only to himself. Behind him, the sprung brougham, decorated with the most intricate and colorful lines of marquetry and cornices of filigreed silver, luxuriously glided over a surface as level as a tarred road, while its crowned princely occupant, in robes of red and yellow, sat in the soft upholstered seat looking out, admiring his castle in the distance. Around and around the castle the boy drove his four white horses.

In the castle, during the daylight hours, a dozen Rhode Island Red chicks dwelt, all three weeks old. The cuteness, the cuddliness, the chirpiness were all gone, and twelve scraggly chickens, caught between losing their down and growing their first feathers, scrambled awkwardly around in their own dung on lanky legs which were not yet completely under the control of their owners. They carelessly bumped into each other in their large chicken-wired box, stepped on each other's toes, and generally exhibited a selfishness unencumbered by any concern for their brothers and sisters. Their toneless squawking was not unlike the breaking voices of adolescent boys. With one of their monocular eyes, all the chickens nervously followed the orbit of the circling boy with the cardboard box in tow. The birds did not yet know the difference between a child lost inside his own head and an attacking cat.

Inside the kitchen window, stooped over the kitchen table with one eye on what she was doing and the other on the chicken frame, Annie Lamb was thinly slicing a tightly packed bunch of stinging nettles with a kitchen knife, the blade sharpened to within a whisper of its existence on the wall of the sandstone pump-trough in the yard. The pungent smell of the nettle sap wafted up into Annie's face and made her nose run. The sound of water vigorously boiling four eggs in a battered saucepan on the open fire bubbled around the kitchen. As she glanced through the window, Annie saw the shape of her youngest son in the apogee of his journey around the chickens.

She moved her gloved left hand down along the bunch of nettles to give herself more slicing room, rubbed the back of the knife-wielding hand across the tip of her nose. She sliced.

This morning, one of the farmyard's two semi-feral cats had made an assault on the chickens by jumping over the side of the frame, only to unexpectedly discover the frame had a top. The cat had not been aware that its stealthy approach had been observed or that, at the very moment it had launched itself into the air, Annie Lamb had stepped out through her kitchen door with a knobby ashplant in her hand. No sooner had the cat found itself mysteriously suspended above the chickens, with its feet enmeshed in an uncertain surface, than the knob of the ashplant made contact with its arse. The cat's wild screech unleashed terror into Annie's veins and, before it had scrabbled its way off the chicken wire, the cat had received another whack sending it staggering across the yard and into the darkness of the cowhouse to lick its wounds. By the way the chickens were still behaving, Annie knew they had not yet recovered from the hysteria induced by the sudden attack and ferocious counterattack which had taken place in the sky above them.

In Annie Lamb's world, cats had one role to play in God's plan, and that was to keep the mouse population in check.

Releasing the pressure of her left hand, in which she kept the nettles bundled, Annie shook off her husband's too-big, stained leather glove. She straightened up, pushed her shoulder blades against each other and rested from her task for a moment.

She looked at Fintan with his box and duckie. When the two older children were at school, the child often spent hours circling the yard in a daze; the lullaby of the box on the rough gravel imprisoning the boy in his own world. Once, for a few fretful days, Annie had tortured herself with the worry that he might be demented and had only been satisfied when Doctor Roberts had snapped sense into her—"The child's supposed to talk to himself, woman!" As she gazed at her child, Annie Lamb was overwhelmed by a rush of maternal feelings. When she instinctively hugged herself, a primordial moan squeezed through her clenched lips. A mother frog or elephant or crocodile or ostrich could have made the same sound.

And then, yahooing and yip-yipping and slapping the soles of their boots on the hard ground, Mikey and Barlow Bracken came bounding into the yard through the haggard gate, each with a bunch of dandelion leaves in one hand, while the other hand urged on the imaginary horse each was riding, their legs and knees imitating the galloping of half-tamed stallions. Even when the cowboys loudly jumped over the passing princely conveyance, Annie's youngest child remained oblivious to the world outside his own.

Mikey had not yet changed out of his school clothes.

Through the kitchen door the two stallions pranced and when they reached the kitchen table, they proudly laid down their contribution to the chickens' mash. "Janey Mack," Annie Lamb said, "there's enough dandelions there to feed a cow."

"We got them in Dan Deegan's kitchen, and there's armfuls in the other two rooms as well," Mikey exclaimed. "Barlow found them, and we saw Father Coughlin in the spyglass sitting in the chair outside the front door." He put the spyglass in the cutlery drawer.

"He's all wrapped up in a blanket, and has a cap on," Barlow Bracken said. "I never saw a priest not wearing black clothes."

"I'd say he has the black clothes on under the blanket," Annie said. "He's not used to our weather yet after all that sun in India."

"When we get too cold we go to bed," Barlow Bracken said.

"I'd love to live in a place where the sun shines all the time," Mikey said.

"We saw Missus Madden bringing him out a teapot on a tray," Barlow said. "Their teapot is made of the same stuff as our cups."

"Delft," Annie Lamb said, "and it's their best teapot for the priest."

"Can Barlow come down to see the pictures when Father Coughlin comes to our house?" Mikey asked.

"He can, Mikey, but we won't know when Father Coughlin's coming."

"If Barlow's not here when he comes, I could ride into Gohen and get him on the bar of my bike."

"We'll see, Mikey," his mother said.

"Do you think Father Coughlin will come to see us, Mam?"

"He's going to see everyone in Drumsally and Clunnyboe, so I think he'll come here, too."

"Can we crack the eggs, Mam, and mash them up?"

After adjusting to the sudden switch of subject, Annie went to the fireplace, smiling to herself. This volunteering—this begging—to help with the feeding of the chickens was definitely due to the presence of the school friend. Using the corner of her apron, she lifted the saucepan off the turf fire and brought it out into the yard to the pump trough, the two boys trailing behind her.

"Can Barlow pump?" Mikey called.

"Of course he can," Annie said, and she realized she was speaking differently because of the stranger in the house. "I'll show you how to do it, Barlow. Put your hand down here." The boy wrapped his hand around the tail of the iron handle just above the knob.

As Annie Lamb encircled Barlow's hand with her own, she remembered how one time she had been grooming Mikey's hair with the fine-toothed comb. When she found two fleas, she asked her son who was sitting beside him in school; when Mikey had answered, "Barlow Bracken. Why?" she had said, "I was just wondering." Now, with her hand on his hand, her sleeve touching Barlow Bracken's hair, Annie said to herself, "Sure, what's a few fleas, especially when he's such a nice lad."

"Nice and slow now, Barlow. Up and down," she said to the beat of the pumping handle. "Nice and slow. Just like that. Up and down. Nice and slow. Now I'm going to take away my hand and you keep doing it. Up and down. You're doing it right." And Barlow Bracken grinned as the steady stream poured out of the spout of the pump.

As the sparkling water flowed over the boiled eggs, Barlow said, "I wish we had a pump like this."

"Oh, Barlow," Annie Lamb said, "I wish we had a tap in the kitchen like your mother has. She doesn't have to rise it when the weather's dry or thaw it out in winter."

"What's that, thaw it out?" the boy from the town asked.

"When the water in the pump freezes in the winter, Mikey's father has to wrap straw around it and burn it to melt the ice."

"It blazes up real quick, all red and yellow blazes," Mikey said, "and then it's gone in a minute, and the black ashes float up over the roof of the house like inky scribbles."

"That must be great," Barlow Bracken said, his imagination sparkling in his eyes. "Great things are always going on here, and your house is so big and there's so many places to hide, and there's the straw rick for jumping off, and the hens' nests in the hayrick, and

Dan Deegan's kitchen full of dandelions, and the piles of potatoes in the pits, and all the dark corners in the sheds, and a fire in the kitchen all day, and the cat with the kittens, and the twelve chickens and the two goslings and the little ducks, and yellow blazes around the pump in the frost." Barlow Bracken, dismayed at his eruption of loquacity, put the fingers of one hand to his lips and looked up into Annie Lamb's face as if he'd said a bad word.

Annie Lamb didn't burst the child's bubble, but she gently squeezed it. "Sure, it's like you having water coming out of a tap in your kitchen and *you* not even giving it a second thought, while *I* keep thinking that water in a tap in the kitchen is great altogether. And *you* think things here are great, but every day someone has to collect the hens' eggs or go out to look for dandelions or get the potatoes out of the pit and wash them or bring in the turf to keep the fire going or get the chickens' food ready for them. What looks great to you right now looks like a lot of little jobs to Mikey that he has to do every day. We think it's great for you that you live in the town where the roads are tarred and never mucky like our lane always is, that you don't have to keep looking down so you don't step in a hen dung or goose dung or cow dung or duck dung." She rumpled Barlow's hair and was annoyed at herself when she thought of fleas again. "Well," she said in a changed tone of voice, "the eggs must be cooled off by now." She put the saucepan in the trough and left the boys with instructions about saving the shells. "And you can mash up the eggs out here, too," she said from the kitchen door. Annie Lamb did not like the smell of hard-boiled eggs in the nude.

"The shells get dried out on the hob and then get smashed up for tomorrow's mash," Mikey told Barlow.

"Nobody eats eggshells!"

Mikey said, "Young chickens eat them to make their bones grow, and hens eat them to make the shell for their next egg."

Ten minutes later, like two acolytes leading a priest onto an altar, the two boys led the way from the kitchen door to the chicken frame. Behind them, in the same battered vessel in which the eggs had boiled, Annie Lamb carried her mixture of stinging nettles, dandelions, mashed eggs and smashed eggshells. Each acolyte held a chipped, dinged, many-patched enamel basin which, at some point in its life, had been used in the bathing of babies, the daily washing of the pots and pans, the kneading of dough, the Saturday night shaving of the man of the house, the gathering of eggs, the timely catching of emissions from young bodies with their various sphincters still in training, the daily washing before school, the soaking of aching feet, the transportation of dinners to distant fields, the mashing of boiled potatoes, the weekly brushing of teeth and the mixing of the currant cake.

The procession of victuallers crossing his path knocked Fintan out of his reverie. His cardboard box came to a halt, and he gawked with mouth ajar, satisfied himself that he knew the intruders of his dreamy kingdom.

When the aviary was reached, Missus Lamb divided the mash between the two enamel basins, each boy holding up his receptacle as if presenting an offering to a god. Meanwhile, the chickens rushed in the direction of the food and piled on top of each other on the far side of the wire each trying to prove it was the fittest to survive. Claws and beaks attacked the imprisoning wire; wings flapped, feathers flew and squawks filled the air.

As Annie Lamb prepared to remove the cover of the opening, Barlow Bracken said, "You put your basin in first, Mikey."

Mikey was intimidated, too, by the beak and claw battle being waged within inches of where he was standing. But the shame of being seen fearful of a few chickens, and his desire to impress his new friend, forced him to step up to the opening his mother was making. He sat down on his hunkers and, with his free hand, defended the ever-widening pass of Thermopylae against the barbarian attack. He steeled himself against beak and talon. The moment the gap was wide enough, he slithered the laden basin across the gravelly floor into the center of the frame. The chickens gave chase and attacked the food as if it were a rat invader.

It was while the chickens were distracted that Barlow Bracken pushed in his basin of food.

Fintan came over with his cardboard box and stood there with the others looking down at the chickens gorging themselves, jerking their heads backward and forward in the effort to move the food along their gullets and into their craws. When the last speck of food had been pecked, the stunned birds assembled around the battered and patched saucepan that served as their water dish. Trapping a drop of water in their beaks, they lifted their heads and elongated their necks to afford a smooth passage for the water as gravity pulled it down their throats.

And in answer to Barlow Bracken's question about this cervical stretching, Mikey casually explained the esophageal workings of a chicken, impressing not only Barlow Bracken, but himself. Barlow Bracken's ignorance of country and farmyard ways was making Mikey realize how much he himself knew. During the explanation, Fintan, with rapturous visage, gaped at his brother as if he were seeing a heavenly vision.

As the lecture on the drinking disabilities of chickens came to a close, the latch of the wicket door rattled, and everyone looked away from the wire cage. With the ease of someone who has done it many times, Molly Lamb was pushing her bike through the narrow doorway. She stopped, held the bike's saddle with her left hand, turned around and caught the edge of the door. As the door gently swung back into its frame, she deftly followed, and assisted the latch back into its catch. She was wearing a yellow dress with its own white cloth belt, and the straps of her schoolbag were hooked to each other on her chest. It was only when she turned around that she realized she had an audience, but she did not immediately see Barlow Bracken. "What are you all gawking at, Mikey?" she asked.

"We're looking at you with your eyes so blue and your face is—"

"Mikey!" his mother cut him off.

Barlow Bracken looked at Molly, and her face was not like a kangaroo's at all. Instead, for one blinding moment, she was a saint in a window in the church, all colors and niceness.

Fintan said, "Molly Polly," and he trotted off to his sister with the box in tow. As the others stood watching, Molly bent down and scooped her baby brother off the ground and landed him, legs held wide apart, on the carrier over the back wheel. Then, beeping like the Dublin bus, she rode around the yard, Fintan holding the saddle with one hand while he looked back at his box with its punctured occupant bouncing around in his carriage like a drop of water on a frying pan.

It wasn't until she had made a full circle of the yard that Molly saw there was a strange boy standing beside Mikey. Instantly, the Dublin bus stopped beeping, and Molly was off the bike, dragging the surprised Fintan off the carrier. She ran with the bike to the kitchen door and leaned it against the wall. Red-faced, she disappeared into the house.

Fintan gaped at the kitchen door and said, "Molly Polly?"

Annie Lamb said, "Mikey, you have to change your clothes now and bring tea to the men in the fields."

"Can Barlow come with me?"

"No. Barlow should be getting on home. You can give him a lift on your bike to the top of the Esker. The next time you come, Barlow, ask your mother first. She'll be worried to death about you."

"My mother doesn't mind as long as I get home at five o'clock," Barlow Bracken said. "I have to do my homework before I go to the bus for the picture reels."

"She's right too," Missus Lamb said. "Homework is terrible important. Mikey tells me you're very good at your lessons."

"But Mikey's the best in the whole school," Barlow said matter-of-factly.

Before he left, Missus Lamb gave Barlow two slices of her brown bread stuck together with butter and blackberry jam. With his schoolbag on the carrier, his rear end on the bar of Mikey's bike and one hand holding the middle of the handlebars, the Tiler ate his sandwich with the enthusiasm of a three-week-old chicken. When he'd finished licking his jammy fingers, he said, "It's well for you, Mikey."

"What's well for me?" Mikey asked.

"Everything; all the sheds and the animals. Your father must be terrible rich."

"He's not rich at all," Mikey said. "You go to the pictures more than I do, and you can play all the way home after school. I have to come home real quick to do my jobs."

"Still!" Barlow persisted.

"Still what?"

"Your father's so rich your mother gives boiled eggs to the chickens."

"That's only the way she feeds them. She gives potatoes to the pigs, but that's only because that's what pigs eat, not because my father's rich."

"And your mother gave me jam and bread in the middle of the day."

Mikey almost said, "Sure, that's nothing." But even though he wasn't old enough to hear the poverty behind Barlow Bracken's words, he did realize that what was ordinary food for him was extraordinary for Barlow Bracken. All at once, Mikey saw jam and bread in a new light.

For the last part of the journey up the Esker, the boys changed places on the bike.

"Duck dung," Barlow Bracken said, and laughed out loud. "Wasn't your mother funny about duck dung?"

"What do you mean?"

"Just the sound of it—duck dung. It sounds funny." As they wobbled along on the bike, they sang out together, "Duck dung, duck dung, duck dung," and the sound of their voices was absorbed by the lush greenery around them. When they finally crested the hill, they parted, and Barlow Bracken, with one final "Duck dung," trotted off toward Gohen, his homemade cloth schoolbag bouncing on his right hip, its strap over his left shoulder.

When Mikey arrived home, he changed into his old clothes and went back into the kitchen just as his mother was wrapping sandwiches in a tea towel.

"What was wrong with Molly when she put down the bike and ran in out of the yard?" he asked his mother.

"She was embarrassed because she didn't know Barlow was looking at her."

"Why would that make her embarrassed?"

"It's hard to explain. You'll have to hurry over to the field. The bellies will be falling out of the men."

"Barlow ate half of one of the eggs for the chickens when we were shelling them out at the pump trough," Mikey confessed. Even though he knew he was risking having Barlow banned from coming again, he was unable to carry out the deceit against his mother.

"Sure, the poor child," Missus Lamb said, as she pushed a stopper of twisted newspaper into the neck of the tea bottle. "His poor mother! They're very poor, even though his father is a terrible hard worker. I don't know how they make ends meet at all. Try to get Barlow to come again, Mikey. He's a very nice boy. Off with you now, and don't bang the bag or you'll break the bottle."

When Mikey stepped out into the farmyard, he saw Fintan sitting beside the chicken frame. The rubber duckie in the child's hand was deep in conversation with the chickens. Neither duck nor boy noticed the passing of the big brother.

21

The July Fair Day in Gohen

1951

In which Simon Peter Lamb is told of the egregious behavior of Doul Yank by Mattie-the-thatcher Mulhall and of the cruelty of the returned missionary priest by his voluble brother, Eddie-the-cap Coughlin.

O N THE THIRD TUESDAY OF EVERY MONTH, the Protestants and Catholics of Gohen were united not by Christian love, but by their common annoyance at the local Protestant and Catholic farmers.

On the third Tuesday of every month, the farmers from the surrounding countryside drove their saleable livestock into the Square in the town. There were no pens for the animals, no corrals. The cattle were herded up against the front walls of the houses and shops and kept in their places with flailing ashplants and hard, loud shouting. Each farmer might only have three animals, some one or two. But sixty or seventy farmers, each trying to control a restless, noisy, ever-moving and multi-membered organism with the assistance of a child or a hired man, took up a lot of frontage along the footpaths.

The urban homeowners, not used to what the farmers were inured to, and fearful of an encounter with an uncontrolled animal, timidly stepped through their front doors in the pursuit of their own polite livelihoods. They immediately encountered the stinking, greenish bovine waste that seemed to be everywhere—in neat piles like miniature extinct volcanoes where a standing animal had relieved itself, or spread out in a line like huge individual splashes of sloppy pancake mix where an animal had simply let go while in motion. Even the fronts of the houses and shops became daubed with streaks of dung as cattle in the act of spouting turned their arses against the walls.

Startled animals, making sudden moves to escape perceived or imagined threats, slipped in their own dung and banged their chins on the hard road surface, or, to their own amazement and the merriment of the onlookers, ended up like dogs sitting on their back legs, struggling to disentangle themselves.

The simile which united a heavy downpour of rain with a cow pissing on a flat rock was on display all day. The possibility of encounters with out-splashes of bovine urinary waterfalls had to be anticipated with every step gingerly taken on the dung-stained streets.

The coarse and dirty farmers in their coarse and dirty clothing sent their hacked-up sputum across the road like hailstones dancing on hot galvanized roof in summertime. Globs of nasal mucus were recklessly snorted onto the pavement by the placing of an index finger over one nostril and the shunting of air through the other with enough pent-up force to take the flame off a blowlamp. And over all the confusion, stretched like a giant circus tent, was the constant, loud bawling of the hungry, thirsty and frightened animals: big, boney, unmilked cows whose swollen udders were supposed to fool the jobbers and the jobbers the ones who had invented the trick; blatantly ungraceful and awkward bullocks, their lack of any intelligence every bit as obvious as their lack of testicles; young heifers giving off enough oestral scent to awaken memories in the bullocks and cause them to mount whatever was nearest them and go through the instinctual motions of rutting—the owners shouting at each other to do something about their fecking animals; young calves—fleet of foot and full of energy and fright—slipping in the dung underfoot, ruining their silken coats when they fell.

Young boys dressed in above-the-knee trousers, leaking Wellingtons and torn clothes, none too surreptitiously pissed against the walls of the houses and shops. The boys, working under the direction of the loud, angry and commanding voices of their fathers, could not afford to look for cover, lest in their absence the animals in their care bolted into the surrounding mayhem.

On many fair days it rained, and the rain was just one more element adding more sloppiness and slipperiness to the streets and footpaths.

However, on the July fair day of 1951, the sun was shining warmly on Mikey Lamb and Barlow Bracken as they kept two bullocks cornered against the yellow-washed wall of Horans' Bakery. The bullocks had calmed down after the long, early-morning journey over the Esker from Clunnyboe. The two big bullocks stood motionless in the hot sun, their heavy heads hanging and their chins within inches of the dungy footpath. The boys constantly glanced over their shoulders to see if there were signs that Mister Lamb was making headway with Mister Thompson-the-cattle-jobber.

"Say it once more," Mikey said to Barlow.

Bracken quietly chanted, "Don't eat Horan's bread. It'll stick to your belly like a lump of lead. Your mother will just wunder when she hears your clap of tunder—don't eat Horan's bread."

Mikey repeated the rhyme several times to commit it to memory. "Now I'll remember it for Kevin Lalor. He never laughs out loud at my jokes or riddles, but I know he's always laughing on the inside."

Since Barlow had taken up residence with the Lambs, Mikey had begun washing his face, brushing his teeth and using Brylcreem to flatten his rebellious hair.

"I have one for you, Barlow," he said. "Missus Brown went to town to buy some macaroni. She blew a fart behind the cart and paralyzed the pony."

Mikey let his head hang down and held his arms out at his side to imitate the paralyzed pony. And Barlow Bracken laughed out loud. Then he repeated the rhyme and copied Mikey's pantomime. The two boys laughed, and when Mikey glanced around at the seller and the buyer, he saw his father spitting on his hand.

"He sold them," Mikey whispered at Barlow. "In a few minutes we'll be able to go to the hucksters' stalls."

When Barlow looked, Mister Thompson spat on his own hand and slapped it into Mister Lamb's upturned wet palm.

"They never need a middleman," Mikey said.

"What's that?"

"When the buyer and the seller can't agree about the price, another man joins in. It looks funny with the middleman talking and at the same time trying to slap the hands together that don't want to be slapped. You'd think they were all fighting. And then they agree, and it's over all of a sudden. But Daddy likes Mister Thompson, and Mister Thompson always gives me sixpence when we drive the cattle to the yard behind Humphrey Smiley's."

"Sixpence! Will he give me sixpence?"

"Even if he doesn't, I'll give you half of mine," Mikey said, not so much out of a desire to share, as out of his insecurity about Barlow Bracken's friendship. Even though everything had worked out exactly as Kevin Lalor had said it would, Mikey was still using bribes to insure Barlow's reciprocity of feelings. Even though Barlow was living with the Lambs for this first week of the summer holidays, Mikey was not fully convinced of his good fortune in having a friend.

Barlow Bracken looked back at the two men. "They're standing real close together and Mister Thompson is counting out money."

But Mikey, as if his feelings of insecurity were suddenly externalized, swiped his ashplant at a perfect volcano of animal waste, sent a fine shower of the dung flying toward four huddled and talking men. "Quick, Barlow, look this way and don't turn around no matter what happens."

"Who the hell's throwing cowshite?" a voice bellowed.

"Jeepers!" Mikey whispered, his face flushed with fear. "Pretend you didn't hear him. Pretend we're minding the cattle." They separated and approached their two bullocks and roused them from their stupor.

By the time the boys regrouped, the four men had given up trying to detect the dung-thrower and were pointing to specks of shite on each other's faces.

"Why did you do that?" Barlow asked.

"I wasn't thinking," Mikey said, "and I just made a swipe at the cow dung."

"Your father is giving change to Mister Thompson," Barlow said.

"That's not change. That's the luck money. The seller always gives some money back to the buyer for luck. Most of the time when they can't agree, it's all about how much the luck money will be. Nobody ever tells how much they get for their animals, so don't ask my father. That's why they're over there, so we won't hear them. Sometimes when there's bargaining going on near us, my father sends me over to stand around and find out what price the men are talking about."

"A spy," Barlow said.

"A spy in the war hiding and listening."

Barlow said, "If Mister Thompson gives me sixpence I'm going to bring it home to my mother."

"Aw, Barlow. Keep it and buy something off the one of the hucksters."

Mister Thompson had two silver sixpences hidden in his hand when he came over to the boys with Simon Peter Lamb. "Well, Mikey, your father robbed me again," he said. "You're Ned Bracken's son?" he said to Barlow.

"Yes, sir."

"I hear you're becoming a farmer, down living with the Lambs for a few days. What's your name?"

"Barlow, sir."

"Well, Barlow, don't let this scallywag make you do all his jobs for him. I see he's trying to be a gentleman farmer now with his hair oil." Mister Thompson put his hand on Mikey's head and ruffled his hair. "Be jakers, you must have put a whole jar of Brylcreem on this morning, Mikey." He wiped his greasy hand on the seat of his trousers. Mikey blushed, and he and Barlow stood open-mouthed in front of the friendly jobber. "Now, lads, I want you to pretend you're cowboys and drive these two boney yokes down to Smiley's yard for me." Mister Thompson glanced at Mikey's father, a twinkle in his eye. "If you become a cattle jobber instead of a farmer, Barlow, the first rule is always to insult the animals you're going to buy. Then you start bargaining, and when you buy an animal, always let the farmer think he got the best part of the bargain. Here's sixpence each for pretending you're cowboys."

The boys held out their hands, and their eyes became misty with excitement as the coins were placed in their palms. "Thank you, Mister Thompson," they said in unison.

"If the cattle aren't in Smiley's yard when I go down with my lorry, I'll call out the sheriff and a posse. And you know what happens to rustlers, don't you lads?"

"We do, sir," the boys replied.

"They get hung, sir," Barlow added.

"From the nearest tree," Mister Thompson said, and he leaned down and whispered into Mikey's ear. "And they get hung, too, for spraying cow dung all over their neighbors. I didn't tell your father."

"I wasn't thinking," Mikey whispered back, feeling compelled to defend himself, but Mister Thompson had already turned to Mister Lamb. "Thanks, Simon Peter," he said, and he touched Mister Lamb on the shoulder. Mister Lamb touched the touching hand and bade Mister Thompson goodbye. Mikey ran after Mister Thompson and tugged at his jacket. "I wasn't thinking when I hit the men with the cow dung."

Mister Thompson smiled down. "I know you didn't mean it. But the next time you're going to do it, tell me first. There's a few oul lads I'd like you to get for me." Again he ruffled Mikey's hair, looked at his greasy hand and said, "Be jakers!"

They were only five hundred yards from Smiley's yard, but it was fifteen minutes later when Mikey swung the gate shut on the two bullocks. The animals had poked their heads through the door of Horans' Bakery; had walked into other farmers' groups of livestock; had been seen as a threat to the stall of the fishwoman who screeched in a Dublin accent—in her ignorance threatening to rip out of the bullocks what had already been removed when they were calves. Barlow, still not convinced that a big animal is afraid of a small, arm-waving boy, nervously jumped backward and sideways whenever the animals made unexpected moves.

As Mister Lamb secured the gate in Smiley's yard, he told the boys they could ramble around the fair until Spud Murphy rang the Angelus, and then they were to meet him on the street outside the hardware shop. He gave them sixpence each. Barlow's eyes bulged. The boys bolted back out onto the street and disappeared.

As Simon Peter stepped back in the mayhem on the streets, he reassured himself by touching the trousers pocket where he'd stuffed Mister Thompson's money. And as his fingers felt the bulge of the ten-pound notes, his shoulder hit up against the becapped Eddie Coughlin.

"Simon Peter," Coughlin exclaimed, and he held up his two hands, each with a piece of a four-grain fork. "Did you ever notice that a tool always breaks at the wrong time? I'm bringing this into Smiley's for them to weld it, and the turf bucking mad to be turned. I was just saying before I got up on the bike, if it's not one thing it's another. There we were all day yesterday bringing Jarlath up to the Mater Hospital in Dublin with his appendix. A great day for turning the turf, and we had to spend the whole day getting lost in Dublin. Between you and me, I don't know why the hospital in Marbra wasn't good enough for him. Nothing would do but we take him to the Mater. I'm just after telephoning them from the telephone in the Post Office—sixpence, the hures—and they told me they took it out last night and it was a lucky thing it hadn't bursted, there would have been poison all over the place inside him and it would have taken hours to clean him out or he could have died, too. Eleven stitches, and now Bridie and myself will have to be going to see him on Sunday to bring him apples and pears. A whole day it will take, and if he'd only gone to Marbra we could have gone to see him every night. But that's the way he wanted it. 'Take me to the Mater,' he says, and when Bridie says to him that Marbra was a lot closer than Dublin, he nearly et the face off her. There we were driving over the River Liffey a thousand times and up and down roads blocked with motor cars and lorries and double-decker busses and everyone blowing their horn at us. I haven't sweated as much since the hay. As far as I can see, there's no one in Dublin who knows where the Mater Hospital is. One fellow would point us in one direction, and when we'd get there another fellow would point us back again. It was five o'clock when we pulled in through the gates, and Jarlath stretched out on the backseat making more noise than a stuck pig the whole way there. I was just saying to Bridie that I'd rather thin seven acres of sugar beet on my hands and knees than drive to Dublin again. But what can we do? We'll have to drive up there again to bring him apples and pears. There's nothing like fresh fruit for the evacuation of the bowels. Did you ever see a cow shiting after a feed of apples? Put the squarts over the moon, she would. I'll tell you something, Simon Peter, even though he's my own brother and a priest at that, I could have hit him with a swingletree to get him to stop roaring. He made Bridie stay in the car when we got there, and I brought him in, and he kind-of half hanging out of me. The minute the nurses saw the white collar and the black suit, he was put in a wheelchair and whisked off, and me left standing like an eegit for a long time till I decided I was forgot about so I went back out to Bridie. It took us till nine o'clock to get home, and not a cow in the house milked. And then, first thing this morning, this bloody fork broke, and I had to leave Bridie on the bog working away; just snapped like a twig. Bloody into it, says I to myself, what's going to go wrong with this fecking turf next. It wouldn't surprise me if it rained from now till Christmas Day, and we not with a sod to burn. And I after riding in already this morning to telephone the hospital on the telephone and going home again and off to the bog only to have the bloody fork break before I had turned twenty sods; nothing's any good since the war. And the telephone! I never used a telephone before, and I walked into the Post Office and said to Miss Bergin, 'Where's the telephone?' I went straight into the box and stood looking at this yoke for a minute. Then I picked it up and I says, 'How is Father Coughlin? He was brought in yesterday with an attack of the appendix.' Then I heard someone saying, 'What number do you want, Mister Coughlin.' 'I don't want any number,' I said, 'I just want to know how my brother is.' 'Where is your brother, Mister Coughlin?' she asks. 'Be gob, if you don't know where he is, how could I know where he is? I left him in the hospital yesterday with the appendix.' 'In what hospital, Mister Coughlin?' says she. 'Your hospital,' says I. 'The Mater Hospital in Dublin.' Then she tells me to wait, and after a while I hear this sound like a buzzing bee in the telephone. Then she says, 'The Mater Hospital. Can I help you?' 'Didn't I tell you? My brother Jarlath,' says I, 'he had an appendix yesterday, and I want to know how he is.' 'And what's his name?' says she, and I nearly said, 'Be Janey, you're a terrible eegit of a woman, and I only after telling you his name.' So I told her again and then I had to tell her my name and she asked me if I was Jarlath's father and she must have walked a mile and a half to find out about him and it costing me by the second. Jarlath's father, I ask you! When she came back, she says, 'Father Coughlin is resting comfortably and he has eleven stitches,' and then she told me about the appendix nearly bursting. I see you had a couple of bullocks over against the bakery wall when I was going to the Post Office. Did you get a good price, Simon Peter?"

"I didn't do too bad at all," Simon Peter-the-secretive said.

"That Mister Thompson's a fair man to deal with," Eddie-the-curious persisted obliquely, "and he a Protestant for all of that."

"Sure, there's a whole lot of nice Protestants, Eddie," Simon Peter said. "And I hear you sold eight big bullocks in May, yourself."

Coughlin ignored Simon Peter's probing about the price he got for his own animals. He said, "There's too many Protestants, Simon Peter. They should all go back to England where they came from."

Eddie Coughlin looked around in the manner of a man who's going to impart an important secret. "At least the appendix will keep Jarlath from bothering everyone for money for his school in India. But I was just saying it wouldn't surprise me if he started after the nurses and doctors in the hospital. He has no shame when it comes to asking for money for God." Again, like a fisherman casting his net, Coughlin threw his suspicious eyes over his near surroundings. And as if he had

detected someone with big ears, he abruptly brought his runaway ver-
bosity to a halt. "I'd better get this fork welded. Bridie will have a pain
in her eye looking out for me. I'll be seeing you, Simon Peter."

Surfacing from Coughlin's verbal inundation and feeling as if a
cloud of summer midges was buzzing inside his skull, Simon Peter
restarted on his journey. He kept his eyes on the ground and avoided
anything that would cause him to slip. But before he even got to the
footpath outside Mister Morgan's shop, where the pig carts were resting on their shafts, he again bumped shoulders with someone who
demanded his attention. It was Mattie Mulhall.

"Simon Peter! Just the man I'm looking for," the thatcher said.

"Mattie! What are you doing at the fair on a day like this? The
sun shining and not a breeze to blow the straw?" Simon Peter asked.

"I've a few piglets I'm trying to sell, but all them hures of jobbers
ever do is insult you. I got tired of it, had to walk away for a few minutes. Such a crowd of hures I never saw in my life. You'd swear they're
all from Dublin. One of them offered me fifteen shillings a pig, and
they three months old and fed on milk and potatoes and scalded
bran twice a day, and a handful of pollard now and then, to say nothing of the bonemeal. The hures. I'll tell you something, Simon Peter,
this is the last litter of shagging pigs I ever want to see. I'm taking the
sow to the factory tomorrow, and they can make her into sausages. I
said to your man, the jobber, if I was to bring them home and drown
them in a boghole that's what I'd do before I'd give them to the likes of
you for fifteen shillings. The hure. And the bloody looks of him—all
dressed up in a suit and polished boots, not a speck of dung on him. I
think they're all a crowd of chancers; buy here today and sell tomorrow somewhere else for a profit. Middlemen, the whole lot of them.
Fecking gombeen men. Hanging's too good for them; a good kick up
the arse is what they deserve."

A big bullock galloped by with a young boy in pursuit shouting,
"Stop me bullock, stop me bullock."

"Remember what your Mikey told us about Doul Yank in the
bank, getting a wad of money from Hairy Gorry? The only way he

could get money out of the bank is by taking it out against the farm. Peggy found a piece of pink paper in his coupon book, right between tea and clothes. A bookmarker worth a hundred quid in his coupon book! The question is, how many times did he take out a hundred quid? You know yourself it wouldn't take too many hundred quids to put the farm in the hands of the bank. All he has himself is the old-age pension and my rent. Before that it was the dole, and that wouldn't keep an old woman in snuff. We're afraid we'll have to buy the farm back from the bank when the fecker kicks the bucket. Did Mikey say anything about seeing him up in the bank lately? God, Simon Peter, you don't know what this is doing to me, and the bloody pig jobbers coming along and doing nothing but telling me how bad the sucks look. I'd like to grab one of them by the scruff of the neck and push his nose into a pile of pig dung and ask him, 'Do you smell the bran in that, and the bonemeal and the pollard?' The fecking hures. And was Father Coughlin around yet looking for money off you for his school in India? I said to Peggy, we're hardly able to keep our heads above the water, and he looking for money for a school in India. In fecking India, for Christ's sake, thousands of miles away. And a few shillings won't do him either. He told Peggy he'd like for her to give him ten pounds. Ten pounds, and me not able to get one fecking pound for a young pig. I wanted to ask you about your drill harrow—will you be using it on Saturday? There's chickweed in the turnips, and I want to give the drills a bit of a schelp before it gets away from me. Isn't the chickweed a real hure! 'Twould scald you, the way it grows so quick after all the tilling, but there's not one bit of praiseach so far this year, thanks be to God. Did Mikey say anything lately about Doul Yank?" Mattie paused to catch his breath, and Simon Peter was finally able to answer his question.

"Sure it's the school holidays now, Mattie, and Mikey won't be going to the bank again till Sept—"

"What's Doul Yank spending the money on at all, Simon Peter? Can you think of anything?"

"I can't, Mattie. Not unless he's buying a whole lot of masses for when he dies."

Mattie Mulhall was stunned into momentary silence by Lamb's suggestion. "Masses for when he dies! Feck! Do you think so, Simon Peter?"

"Well, Annie and myself were trying to figure it out, too, Mattie. He doesn't drink, he doesn't smoke and he doesn't gamble. What else could he be spending it on?"

The thatcher rolled on over Lamb's question. He said, "Peggy thinks he has a child from when he was in America, and he's sending the money there. 'But if he had a child,' says I, 'wouldn't he have been taking out money against the farm for years, since he came home from America?' 'And who's to say he didn't?' says Peggy. The whole thing has me terrified. Here I am, after spending years ridding the place of praiseach, and the fecker could be giving the farm to the bank the whole time."

"But Mattie, if he was taking money out against the farm since he came home from America, wouldn't someone have seen him long ago? For all you know he only did it once."

"For all we know he might have done it a hundred times, too. I am always afraid the fecker will do something to diddle me out of the farm in the end, and as well as that Peggy can't talk about anything else. It's driving me mad not knowing what he's up to."

"Well, Annie and me think he's buying masses for when he dies. You might put your mind at rest if you asked Father Mooney. It's not something he wouldn't be able to tell you, especially because everyone knows the money belongs to the farm and that the farm will be yours when your uncle dies."

"That's an idea, Simon Peter. Be jakers! Couldn't I walk down the road and ask him now if he's at home? Would you mind standing beside the cart for a few minutes while I go and ask him?"

The two neighbors picked their way through the buyers and the sellers and the curious and the gawkers and the hawkers. They went down the line of carts—all with their shafts resting on the road, all with their donkeys or ponies tied to the tailboards—until they came to Mattie's load of piglets. Because of the slope of the cart, the piglets were piled on top of each other against the front creel.

"God, they're grand-looking sucks," Simon Peter said, more to bolster Mattie's deflated sense of his porcine husbandry than to compliment him. "How many's in there?"

Mattie looked around hoping that some jobber had heard Simon Peter, but none were in sight. "Twelve," he answered, "eleven and a runt. There's always a fecking runt," and he walked away toward the priest's house. The reluctant piglet protector looked at his pocket watch and decided if Mattie was back in ten minutes there would still be time to go to Morgan's shop.

Simon Peter stood with his arms resting on top of the cart's front creel, his gaze fixed on the pile of piglets, all moving in their sleep in the eternal pig-hunt for the warmest spot. His mind drifted to Eddie Coughlin, about how his brother's attempt to collect money from the neighbors was bothering the hell out of Eddie. And here was Mattie Mulhall driven to distraction by his suspicions that his own uncle was trying to rob him. It wasn't outsiders a fellow had to worry about in this life—a sharp eye had to be kept on a fellow's family members. He remembered the story of his own father's will, how some years before he died, Simon Peter's mother had asked her husband to make a will—"to put everything in order," as she had delicately worded the request. "I made a will a long time ago," his father said. "The year we got married, I went into the solicitor on my way to hospital in Marbra to get that hernia mended. I didn't want anyone trying to take the farm from you if I died." "Sure, there was no need to do that. Your family would have taken care of me," his mother said. "It was my family I was protecting you from," his father replied.

Mattie Mulhall was back in less than five minutes. Barely above a whisper, he made the report to Simon Peter. "Well, he hasn't been to Father Mooney for masses," he said. "The priest knew Doul Yank took the money out of the bank like everyone else knows, but he only heard of him doing it the once. So he's not buying masses, at least not from Father Mooney. Was there any jobber around?"

"Your man Gallagher from Clonaslee. He wanted to know did you sell yet."

"That's the hure that offered me fifteen shillings a pig." Still making sure his neighboring pig sellers could not hear him, Mattie asked, "Do you think if I went and talked to the bank manager maybe he wouldn't give the Yank any more money against the farm?"

"You could talk to him, Mattie, but all he'll tell you is that there's nothing he can do. The farm is in Doul Yank's name till he dies."

"I wish the old bastard would die," Mattie hissed, "shoot himself when he's getting out through a gap after his snipe, slip and fall into a ditch and get drownded. The fecker! He's nothing but a bastard."

A jobber in dung-splattered boots and not-so-clean clothes called from the end of the cart's shafts, "Did you sell yet, boss?" and Simon Peter used the interruption to restart his journey to Mister Morgan's shop. Bidding Mattie goodbye, he stepped over a shaft of the cart and set off before he became privy to the bargaining that was about to start.

Simon Peter knew he would not have time to buy the milk separator now—Mikey and Barlow Bracken would soon be waiting for him outside Smiley's shop. But at least he could ask Mister Morgan about it, how a machine could separate the cream and the milk, send the cream out one spout and the skim milk out the other— maybe it wouldn't be as great as the *Farmers Journal* said it was.

As Simon Peter was stepping into Mister Morgan's shop, the boys were arriving, panting and sweating, at the stall of the huckster who sold cheap tools to farmers. They had run all the way from Barlow's house in Tile Town, each elated for different reasons: Barlow, because of the disbelief, relief and pride he saw on his mother's face when he held out his palm with the two sixpences in it; Mikey, because he had been finally persuaded that he was Barlow Bracken's best friend. Mikey had heard Barlow whispering, asking his mother would it be all right if he stayed for another week at the Lambs' house, promising he would never miss bringing the film reels from the Dublin bus to the Picture House. And Missus Bracken had torn a piece of paper out of a school copybook, had written on it with a pencil, and Barlow had put the folded paper in his trousers pocket.

The huckster of cheap tools stepped up on his wooden box, a penknife held above his head. Smiling, and revealing bad teeth, he looked around at the circle of curious faces tilted toward him. Then, in his loud Dublin accent that was, to the natives, an attraction in itself, he yammered out the lies he had used for years to sell his shoddy merchandise to gullible audiences. The piece of rubbish in his upheld hand became a fire-hardened, double-bladed penknife, make in Germany before the war. "And would I ask you fine gentle-men of the land to fork out five shillings for this perfectly forged and perfectly balanced knife that would slit a turkey's throat without the turkey even knowing? No, I would not, I would not ask you for five shillings. Would I ask you four shillings for this . . . this instrument with blades made of the finest Ruhr Valley steel? No, I would not ask you to pay me four shillings. Would I ask you intelligent people of the countryside to give me three shillings for this knife with a handle made of the finest African elephant ivory? Of course not, of course not, because I would not try to make a profit off the people who make their living by the sweat of their brows. I did not come here to Gohen to make money off decent, hardworking people. I came here to bring to you the finest knives that will last a lifetime. Would I ask the salt of the earth to pay two shillings for this perfect tool, a knife that will hold its edge forever the steel is so hard? This tempered steel as tough as the bayonets of Hitler's armies; steel that was toughened in the hottest steel mills in the world; this steel that came to earth in a falling star and buried itself in the heart of Germany thousands . . . no, not thousands, millions of years ago? This steel that cannot be engraved, it is so hard? Any intelligent person knows that any steel that can be engraved is not worth the name of steel, because if steel is steel, it is so tough that not even diamonds could mark it. And am I asking you to pay two shillings for this miracle product of the modern machine? No, I am not. I am not. No, I am giving away these knives for one shilling. One shilling. I'm giving them away, and if my wife knew what I was doing she'd murder me. One shilling each. You, sir. How many will you take sir? And you sir, how many for you?"

Despite his enthrallment with the voice of the huckster, and despite his amazement at the number of eager hands reaching in over his head with shillings in them, Mikey was remembering his dismay when he and Barlow had fled Smiley's yard after the penning of the two bullocks. Barlow, without reference to Mikey and with a silver sixpence clasped in each hand, had taken shortcuts to Tile Town, had used back lanes and gaps in hedges that Mikey didn't know existed. Mikey, desperate in his fear that he was in the process of losing Barlow for ever, pleaded with him to slow down. And when he caught up with the Townie, he gasped at him, "Why have you to give her the money now, Barlow?"

"Because I've never had so much money to give her before," Barlow said. "Wait till you see her face, Mikey. Only for living at your house I wouldn't have the shilling. I wish I could live with you forever, with your mother and father and Molly and Fintan and bring my mother a shilling once a month."

But now, as the people around him responded to the oratory of the hucksterman like a flock of hungry chickens at a battered basin, Mikey's mind wandered to the piece of paper in Barlow's pocket. The whole world had changed for Mikey, and he was in love with life, he was in love with Barlow. There were colors and brightness where he had never seen them before. The voice of the huckster was music, and the reaching, buying hands were applause for a song beautifully sung. The sun was warm on his face, and everything had fallen perfectly into place for him. He had never been happier. He could easily have put his arms around Barlow and hugged him the way he used to hug the dog at home when it was a pup. Mikey could have floated away over the high roof of Horans' Bakery; he could have danced wildly, cartwheeled and somersaulted through the streets of Gohen and not once have touched a cow dung with his hands or feet.

The Angelus bell rang, and Mikey poked Barlow. "We're late," he said, and, because his father had embedded in his brain the imperativeness of being on time, he turned and squeezed his way through the wall of big men behind him.

At a gallop, twisting and spinning and dodging and leaping as if they were hares chased by baying hounds, the two boys reached the big window of Humphrey Smiley's Hardware and Farm Supply Company before Spud Murphy had finished ringing the Angelus. As they stood with their backs to the display of spades, pitch forks and mattocks, they looked to their left and saw Mikey's father coming out of Mister Morgan's shop on the far side of the street. At the same time, Eddie-the-cap Coughlin came out through Smiley's front door with the head of the newly welded four-grained fork in his hand. As Coughlin tied the fork onto his bike with a piece of binder twine, Simon Peter signaled to the boys, indicated they should follow him. At the same time he put a finger across his lips.

When the boys joined him, Mikey asked, "Who were you trying to miss?"

"Eddie Coughlin. Did you see him at his bike with the fork and that cap of his? He got me for twenty minutes already, and I don't want to hear the same stuff all over again. He'd talk the back leg off a jennet. Did you buy anything from the huckstermen?"

"No," Mikey answered, and then he prepared the ground for a future request, a preparation he felt was necessary because of his father's visceral reaction when permission was sought to be in the town outside of school time. "I'm saving the money to go to the pictures, if you will let me go with Barlow."

Simon Peter ignored the request, knew he had a carrot that could be used if Mikey was reluctant to help with the farmwork.

"What about you, Barlow?" he asked. "Did you buy anything from those crukes from Dublin?"

No, I didn't," Barlow responded. Simon Peter only discovered that the boy had brought his shilling to his mother when Mikey was preparing the ground for the request on the piece of paper in Barlow's pocket.

As they were passing the Blennerhasset Stud on the way home, a boy shuffling along on each side of the long-striding man, Mikey threw a stone at a flock of starlings in an ash tree. As the flock took off into the sky like a black bedsheet in the grasp of a playful breeze, he asked his father if it was true that a starling would sing like a gold-finch if its tongue was cut with a silver sixpence.

"Well, Mikey, let me ask you a question," the father responded. "Do you think it's true that you can catch a chicken by pouring salt on its tail?"

"I always wondered about that," Mikey said. "How could anyone catch up with a chicken to pour the salt on its tail?" Mikey said.

"And as well as that," Barlow said, "if you are close enough to pour salt on the tail, aren't you close enough to catch it without using the salt at all?"

"That's right, Barlow. And I think the story about the starling and the silver sixpence is like the story about the chicken and the salt," Simon Peter said. "First of all you'd have to catch a live starling. And supposing you do catch a starling, how would you cut its tongue with a silver sixpence? The rim of a sixpence is so wide and blunt you couldn't cut butter with it."

"You could sharpen the edge," Mikey said, "keep rubbing the edge on the side of the pump trough where mammy sharpens the knives."

"Well, *you* sharpen a sixpence on the pump trough till it can cut, and *you* get down on your hands and knees and sneak up on a starling and pour salt on its tail," Simon Peter said. "And you know, Mikey, a bird's tongue is as hard as a bone; it's not soft like ours. A starling singing like a goldfinch is every bit as quare as a cuckoo spitting."

"I didn't know that cuckoos spit," Barlow said.

"They don't," Simon Peter said. "But some people believe everything they were told as children until the day they die. Show him a cuckoo spit, Mikey."

Mikey, followed by Barlow, went to the edge of the road and looked into the roadside growth as he walked along. Within a few seconds he stepped into the grass and pulled a stalk. He held it up to Barlow and pointed to the glob of bubbly, white froth sitting in a fork of the grass. "That's the cuckoo spit," Mikey said, as his father came over to join them.

"It looks like spit," Barlow said.

"Now show him what it really is," Simon Peter said.

Mikey picked up the twig. He used its end to push the spit out of the fork until two small insects were seen moving in the remains of the froth like two swimmers in honey. Their light-green color, bordering on transparency, spoke of delicacy and vulnerability.

"The spit protects them from birds," Mikey said.

"But it's not a cuckoo that makes the spit," Simon Peter said. "The insects make it themselves."

"They're baby froghoppers," Mikey said. He handed the grass stalk to Barlow.

"But isn't it nicer to believe it *is* cuckoo spit," Barlow said. "Imagine a cuckoo with a cold with a scarf around its neck and it coughing and spitting onto the grass."

"You're a daft lad," Simon Peter said. "Throw that away and come on home. We have a lot of work to do."

Barlow pretended the stalk was a spear and he shot it into the hedge. Mikey shouted, "Last to the top of the Esker stinks." The two boys raced ahead of Simon Peter, and Mikey ran with the energy of a boy whose body is full to overflowing with pure glee.

22

Visiting the Sick

1951

In which Bridie Coughlin tells Annie Lamb a story of her brother Jarlath's cruelty, during which Bridie cries, and Annie is helpless to provide comfort.

WITH HER EARS AND HER SPARSE COCONUT HAIR concealed inside the brown French beret, Bridie Coughlin had begun milking the cow by furiously tugging the teats. The angry squirts whacking into the bucket trapped between Bridie's Wellingtoned legs was metallic, raucous and high-pitched. The cow raised her far leg in warning, told Bridie to be gentle or else. The force of the squirts eased, and eventually their sound changed and deepened until the hypnotic swoosh-swoosh soothed the jagged edges of Bridie's battered nerves.

With forehead leaning against the red-haired belly of a warm cow, her hands worked independently as they rhythmically pulled the milk out of the hairy elder. Bridie slipped into sleep for a brief second. When she surfaced, the soothing effects of the swooshing milk had been routed by the fragments of wild dreams roaring across her dream screen with the ferocity of a March hail shower. Even though the dreamy fragments dissipated before Bridie could recall any of them, they left her feeling much worse than before she had nodded off. Her fury returned.

As the cow's supply ran dry, Bridie pulled too hard on the teats again. The cow flicked her tail into the milker's face—a prelude to a kick. Bridie caressed the red flank and returned the cow into her bovine complacency. Still sitting on her three-legged stool, Bridie moved the milk bucket out of harm's way. Then, in one flowing movement she lifted the sack-cum-apron off her lap with one hand, swung the stool out from under her with the other hand and stood up—a ballet dancer ankle-deep in the straw bedding of the cowhouse.

Her mind was full of her brother Jarlath in his bed in the Mater Hospital in Dublin. She swiped at her stinging eyes with the hand holding the stinking milking sack. She would not let Eddie see her crying, did not want to hear again his unrelenting torrent of words—words intended to soothe, but which only pounded her down further into her misery. She was glad it was Sodality night, glad she had an escape from Eddie and glad it was her night to visit Annie Lamb—she could spill her heart to Annie, and Annie would sit there and listen, give succor by listening. "Our Lady of perpetual succor, pray for me."

Making sure not to turn her face toward Eddie, who was milking the cow behind her, Bridie walked out of the cowhouse and carried her bucket to the dairy. She poured the milk through the strainer into the white enamel bucket and, by the time she had rinsed her milk bucket at the pump in the yard, Eddie had untied the four cows. With a full milk bucket in hand, Eddie went in silence to the dairy, and Bridie in silence went to the pasture gate, a ritual which had wordlessly evolved over a lifetime of shared work.

The cows sniffed aimlessly around the surface of the farmyard. Some lazily lifted their tails and uncaringly relieved themselves as they continued to walk; some stood and gaped at nothing in particular with their shortsighted eyes. They all waited for Bridie to come and shoo them out into the field. One of them, hearing the distant bawl of a calf, stretched her neck and mooed unmusically until Bridie smacked her with uncharacteristic viciousness with her ashplant. "Get up ouha that."

Before Eddie had rinsed his bucket, Bridie was walking around the side of the dwelling house to the front door and wished, as she wished every time she walked around the side of the house, that there was a back door. But Eddie! "Sure, it was good enough for Daddy and Mammy wasn't it? It'll only make the house colder with the wind blowing in one door and out the other no matter what way the wind's blowing, and what's a few extra steps to take around the side of the house?" and on and on and on, till Bridie, drowning in his torrential verbiage, regretted having brought up the subject.

Standing on the new, rough-ridged sisal mat outside the front door of her freshly thatched and newly whitewashed house, Bridie heeled off her dirty Wellington boots. The remembrance of her quiet excitement when she was buying that mat, when she was watching the golden straw being thatched onto the roof, when the house gleamed under its fresh coat of whitewash—brought the scalding, secret tears back to her eyes. And as she swiped at her face with her sleeve, she had no way of knowing she was in the tube of Mikey Lamb's spyglass and only ten inches away from Barlow Bracken's right eye.

By the time Eddie finished his chores in the farmyard, Bridie had the supper ready: in the center of the table a plate piled high with buttered slices of homemade bread; two place settings with generous plates of sliced ham and tomato; the tin teapot under its Bridie-knitted tea cozy at the end of the table. When Eddie came into the kitchen, he took off his cap and said, "And to think it was for him that we bought the ham."

"We can't let it rot just because he's not here to eat it."

The bald bachelor brother and the spinster sister ate in silence, Eddie holding out his teacup when it was empty, pointing with his knife when he needed the mustard. Bridie anticipated most of his other needs, and he did not have to ask for milk or sugar or salt. Because she was anxiously expecting Eddie to start with his words of comfort at any moment, every sound of cutlery against delft, every cup dashed against saucer was like thunder in Bridie's ears. She was afraid every new noise would set Eddie off, like one cow answering when another cow bawls. However, it was the scraping of his own chair on the floor as he stood up at the end of the meal that activated Eddie's vocal cords, produced gratingly comfortless words.

"Sure, everything will be all right when he comes home again. He'll only be in the hospital for another week, and then all your worrying will be over."

As Eddie spoke, he did not see that his sister was whisking around the kitchen like a witch's broomstick. He didn't notice that for the first time in her life, Bridie simply piled the plates and cutlery into the white enamel basin and threw a tea towel over the whole thing. She didn't even wait for her brother to finish a sentence before she interrupted him.

"I'm going to get ready for the Sodality now," she said, and as she closed her bedroom door, her brother was still talking.

Two hours later Bridie was standing outside Annie Lamb's back door. Despite the lingering heat of the July day, she was dressed in her heavy winter topcoat, and her hair and ears were hidden under her black headscarf. Even though it was eight o'clock, the summer sun was still casting shadows in the pewter farmyard.

"Are you at home, Annie?" she called through the open kitchen door and was startled when she heard a noise behind her. Bridie turned around and saw Mikey and Molly and a strange boy galloping into the far end of the yard, sounding like there was a whole herd of them.

"Hello Missus Coughlin," Molly called as they passed. "Go on in. Mammy's out in the turf shed, and she'll be here in a minute. Fintan's asleep."

Not feeling that the child's greeting constituted an adequate invitation to enter, Bridie waited until Annie Lamb arrived with two brown hen eggs in each hand. In a stream of Sodality incense wafting off Bridie's heavy overcoat, Annie followed her visitor into the kitchen. Within a few minutes, the Bridie's topcoat was hanging on a peg in the wooden rack attached to the parlor door, and the women were ensconced in the straight-backed wooden chairs, one each side of the open fireplace with its summer's fire of ash-coated, smoldering turf sods. The ever-hanging cast-iron and black tea kettle was singing a very quiet tune, the lid making regular nervous tic-like jumps.

As they chatted back and forth, Missus Lamb realized that Bridie was not talking with her usual ferocity. Annie was able to add her own weather observations without interruption. She told Bridie about Barlow Bracken living with them since the beginning of the school holidays, that he had come for a week, was still here after a fortnight, and he was such a nice chap that they all hoped his parents would let him stay for the whole summer. Mikey was having the time of his life with the Bracken boy. Bridie spoke about Barlow's father, Ned, how he was such a hard worker and such a nice man, that Eddie had hired him to turn the dunghill in the spring, and how his wife was such a toil-worn woman. "Thin as a rake, gray as a badger, bent as a scythe handle."

Bridie teetered on the edge of her pool of self-pity, but each time, as if her brain had a mind of its own, something else came out. She now found herself talking about Doul Yank withdrawing a hundred pounds from the bank against his farm.

"Eddie thinks he's buying in the stock market in America, that with the war over there's going to be great money to be made in America, and Doul Yank's getting in on the ground floor. But, I was just saying, stock or no stock in America, he's doing a wrong thing by taking money out against Mattie Mulhall's farm, even if it isn't Mattie's farm yet and even if the hundred pounds does make another hundred in the stock market in America. I was just saying Doul Yank should stick to his side of the bargain, that he shouldn't be letting the bank in on the farm, and Mattie after working for years to put the place in order. There's not one yellow praiseach flower in the whole place this year. Can you imagine that? And the farm nothing but a yellow sea when he started working at it."

Then Annie told Bridie how she and Simon Peter believed Doul Yank was buying masses for his soul when he died, even if Father Mooney had told Mattie that Doul Yank hadn't bought any—Doul Yank could have sent the money to a monastery for masses.

Then Annie asked about Father Jarlath's appendix, and Bridie's dam burst. Before any words came out, she was crying, sending several large drops over her lap and splashing onto the hearth near her Peter Pan bootees. As Bridie pulled a man's handkerchief out of her sleeve, Annie stretched across and touched her shoulder.

"Is he that bad, Bridie?" she asked.

Loudly and bubbly, Bridie blew her nose. She wiped her eyes and said, "I hope the young lads don't come running in and see me crying, nor Simon Peter either."

"You don't have to worry about them, Bridie. The lads won't be in till dark, and Simon Peter's across the fields looking at the cattle. It's a bad time for the murrain. He looks at them three times a day."

Bridie blew her nose again, and while she pushed the handkerchief back into its place she took several deep breaths, sounding like a child who has lost its breath from crying. Annie encouraged her to talk. "Is Jarlath worse than you've been letting on to people, Bridie?"

"Ah, Annie," Bridie sighed. "He's worse than anyone can imagine. It's terrible, and we looking forward so long to him coming home, and now things turning out like this. I feel terrible useless, a terrible failure." She took the handkerchief out again and went through the motions of neatly folding it. She did not look up as she spoke. "When we bring him to say mass on Sundays, he makes Eddie let him out of the motor near Morgan's shop so no one will see him with us. He's ashamed of us." A sob got away from Bridie before she could cover her mouth, but she would not give in to the tears.

Annie Lamb was aghast at this revelation. Priests were supposed to be nice.

"He can't bear to be seen with us, and we after fattening eight big bullocks so we could have a motor for him when he came home, lugging buckets of mash and water all winter and then this. To say nothing of the new thatch after only three years and the new white-wash and the bluestone on the windowsills."

Annie Lamb felt a response was expected. "Maybe he likes to walk down the town to talk to people he hasn't seen for years," Annie-the-very-careful weakly offered.

"Sure he told us, Annie!" Bridie sounded like a frustrated teacher. "He told us we're dirty to look at and that we've smells off us like cows. He said he never saw an Indian dirtier than us, nor smelt a worse one either."

Believing Bridie was waiting for some verbal support against her brother's accusation, Annie Lamb desperately clawed around in her mind for the right words. She was unable to take hold of anything, and, instead, she put her hand on Bridie's shoulder again, felt the fleshless bones under the green, Bridie-knitted cardigan.

Bridie folded and unfolded the handkerchief, used it to keep her eyes away from Annie's. "We went to see him today, and when we got there he told me I was never to go to see him in the hospital again, he's so ashamed of me."

Saying out loud for the first time what had cut her to the quick that afternoon, Bridie sobbed aloud and her tears freely flowed on her crab-apple cheeks. The folds were shaken out of the handkerchief and there was loud blowing and snuffling. This time it took several minutes for recovery, and during the silence Annie Lamb prayed fervently to the Mother of God for inspiration to say something that would work magic. But the Mother of God was out of magic and at a loss for words.

Bridie fingered some loose strands of her hair and pushed them into new positions. Without warning, she began speaking again, and all the strain was gone out of her voice. From the first sentence, it seemed to Annie Lamb that the discussion about Father Jarlath had never taken place.

"Eddie and myself got up and milked and et a bit of breakfast before we went to first mass this morning so we'd get an early start. The day we brought him to the hospital, and he in the back of the motor moaning with the pain and the cold, it took us hours to get there, we got so lost, one man telling us the hospital was in one place and when we'd get there another one telling us it was in the place we came from. I was just saying that there's no one in Dublin who knows where the Mater Hospital is. And me after begging him to let us take him to the county hospital in Marbra. But he wouldn't hear of that at all. He nearly et the face off me for even saying Marbra Hospital. And today, thanks be to God, we only had to ask where the hospital was five times. Of course, the first man we asked was as deaf as a post. Doesn't it always happen? You get all ready what to say and you clear your throat to ask a body how to get to the hospital; you open the window and shout, and your man turns out to be as deaf as a stone and he wanting you to talk louder with his hand cupped behind the ear, and he saying what, what. It's always happening."

The more Bridie spoke, the stronger her verbal spate surged, and Annie Lamb remained tense on her wooden chair hoping that nothing would be expected of her in the way of sympathetic, empathetic or encouraging sounds.

"So, right after first mass was over didn't we set out, and I praying the whole way that we wouldn't get lost and that I wouldn't get sick in the motor. I hate when the motor goes over a quick bridge, and everything in your stomach gets shot up into your throat. I always bring an old towel to vomit in. We drove real slow through every town looking for a fruit shop, and the heat enough to make a body pant. It's terrible hot in a motor with the sun shining in and nothing you can do to keep it out. There were times I thought I was going to faint. I was just saying that if you weren't looking for a bit of fruit, wouldn't all the fruit shops in Ireland be falling on top of you no matter where you went. There wasn't one fruit shop from here to Dublin until we saw the one right beside the hospital, and the two of us afraid of our lives to go to see Jarlath with one hand hanging longer than the other. I nearly died of relief when we saw it. We got him three apples, three oranges and three pears; sixpence each! Sixpence each, and we feeding apples to the cows by the bucketful in the autumn. Four and sixpence for nine bits of fruit. They can charge what they like because it's the last place you can get something for a sick relation in the hospital. The government should do something with gangsters like that. Eddie said the jail is too good for them kind of cornerboys. But even so, fresh fruit is good to eat for the evacuation of the bowels."

"For the evacuation of the bowels," Annie Lamb repeated to herself. Bridie's brother, Eddie, had used the same words at the fair last

Tuesday to Simon Peter. They must have read it in "Ask the Doctor" in the paper. When Simon Peter came home from the fair that day he said, "Who the hell goes around telling other people to eat fresh fruit to make you shite regular. God! Them Coughlins are as quare as coots. Is that what they talk about sitting at the fire at night? Shiting? 'Did you have a good shite today, Eddie?' says she. 'A grand one,' says he, 'and yourself, Bridie, how was your shiting today?' 'Grand, Eddie. Grand. That fresh fruit is a great yoke for the evacuation of the bowels.' For Christ's sake!"

The outpouring of Bridie's words was picking up speed, and Annie Lamb knew that it would take a cataclysmic interruption to bring the deluge to a stop.

"You should have seen the looks we were getting when we went into the hospital; you'd think the people had never seen a big bag of fruit before. The smell of the place the minute we walked in through the door! If I was blind, I'd know the minute I stepped into a hospital from the smell, it's so mediciney and clean. The woman at the desk told us the lift was busy and that we'd have to walk up to Jarlath's room, and that's where the whole trouble began because his ward was in the fourth story. I was just saying, the last time I was up a stairs was when I was in the Convent School when I was thirteen. We went up four stairs, and I thought we were there, but Eddie says we're only halfway yet, that's four flights but only two stories, and I panting like the Horans' broken-winded jennet doing the deliveries. A stairs is the devil on your lungs, Annie, when you're not used to it. Talk about the heat—it was terrible, and I said to Eddie wouldn't you think they'd open a window or two to let in a bit of fresh air. When we got to the fourth story, I was in such a state that I had to tell Eddie to hold on a minute, and I gave him the bag of fruit to carry. I was leaning against the wall, and I had this full feeling in the chest for a minute and everyone passing by looking at me like I was going to do something terrible. Jarlath's ward was off down at the other end of the corridor, a private ward, and it hotter than Horan's Bakery when they have all the ovens going at the same time, and the minute I stepped inside the door I fainted."

"You didn't!" Annie said.

"I did. It felt like all my bones were gone, and the next thing I knew I was sitting on a chair with two nurses trying to get my topcoat off and another trying to open the knot of my headscarf under my chin. She gave up and just pulled it off from the back of my head, and all I could think of was my hair must look like the devil entirely, all pulled forward like that, and what would Jarlath say. The other two got the buttons of the coat open and pulled it down behind me off my arms. There was a terrible fuss, one of them putting a wet towel on my head, another trying to get me to drink out of a glass and another trying to get my boots off—get my boots off, mind you— and me swaying like I was going to fall off one side of the chair and then the other. I couldn't remember what socks I was wearing, but one way or the other I didn't want them nurses seeing my feet. All I could think of was Jarlath getting cross about the fuss that was being made over me, and he lying over there in the bed with his face to the wall pretending he was dead. After a while, they took me out to sit in the corridor where it wasn't so hot, but it was afraid of Jarlath I was. You'd a thought I was a patient the way they held on to me—the three of them, and then one of them telling Eddie to bring out a chair for me to sit on. There I was, sitting in the corridor with everyone going by looking at me and stepping over to the far wall like they were afraid they'd catch something. One woman even held a hankie over her mouth and nose like she'd get a disease off me. It took me a half hour to get back on my feet and one of the nurses stayed with me the whole time—she was terrible nice and kept asking me was I all right and telling me it was because of the heat and the stairs that I fainted because I wasn't used to stairs. I told her I'd like to put my topcoat and headscarf back on, and she said it'd be better to wait till we were going home. I was feeling very awkward without the coat—you know how it is yourself, Annie, when you're used to wearing something all the time and then not to have it on, and you know everyone's looking at you. 'At least give me the headscarf to cover up my few wisps,' I said to her, and then she told me that the place where the most heat leaves your body is through the top of your head and that it would be better to keep the headscarf off for a while. Did you ever hear the likes—through the top of your head! My head never gets cold in the winter, it's always my hands."

The handkerchief was dragged out into the open again as if Bridie were preparing for some unpleasantness ahead. The bony, broken-nailed fingers began to worry the damp cloth.

"In the end I sort of wobbled back into Jarlath's ward with the nurse ready to catch me with her hands out. She left me sitting beside the bed and told me to send Eddie for her if I thought I was going to faint again. She must have been gone for five minutes before anyone spoke, and me waiting for Jarlath to light into me for the fuss I'd caused. He lay there facing the wall, and while I waited to be et I kept looking at Eddie and asking him questions with my face, and all he did was turn his eyes to heaven and not make a sound. That made me think Jarlath had et him before I came back into the room. I was just going to tell Jarlath that we'd brought him apples and pears and oranges when he said real quiet, 'Is the nurse gone?' And at the same time Eddie and me said she was. Then Eddie and me looked at each other and waited for Jarlath to say something. But we waited so long, I couldn't stand it anymore and I said, 'Sure we brought you a nice bit of fruit, Jarlath. It'll help you with the evacuation of the bowels.' And then real quiet he says, 'Bridie, come here till I tell you something,' and I started to think that after all my bad thinking about him he was going to say he was sorry that I'd fainted, the soft way he was talking. I stood up and leaned in a bit over the bed because he was still facing the wall. Then he says, 'Bridie, for as long as I'm in the hospital, I don't want you to come to see me again with your fainting and the way you smell like a cow and the way you're dressed, you'd think it was the middle of winter.' The soft way he talked to me was worse than the worst shouting that was ever done at me by anyone, and a terrible feeling came into me, nearly the way you feel when someone belonging to you is dying and you can't do a thing about it. It was terrible, Annie, and I just stood there with my jaws open and my mouth getting all dry. I looked at Eddie, and he looked like someone who was hit with a swingletree, and his mouth was open a foot if it was open an inch. Then Jarlath started talking again real low like before. 'You can leave now,' says he, 'and you can take the fruit with you.' Oh, Annie, it was terrible, and all I could say was, 'Sure we bought the apples and oranges and pears for you, Jarlath, and they'll be good for your bowels,' and I don't know what else I was saying, and I was only saying anything at all to keep out of my head what Jarlath had said to me. Jarlath made his voice loud enough not to be heard outside the ward. 'Bridie,' says he, 'go home and take the blessed fruit with you. Go home this instant.' But I was still trying not to believe what I was hearing, and I said, 'But I can't go home without Eddie driving the motor.' Nobody said anything for a long time. Then, like an eegit, I started crying the way I cried when Mammy was dying, not out loud but trying to hold it in, and you know the way your throat hurts you when you do that. And I was just saying that I don't remember one thing about coming out of the hospital and getting into the motor or about putting my coat and headscarf back on. But hadn't Eddie only got the motor car as far as the hospital gates when I got as sick as a dog, and I was lucky to have the towel in my lap just in case. And Eddie says, 'It must be something you et,' and we were in the car all the way home from Dublin, one and a half hours, and neither one of us said a word till the motor car stopped outside our gate and I says, 'It was nothing I et, Eddie.'"

The handkerchief fluttered to Bridie's face, and silently she cried, her body trembling, and she rocking backward and forward like an old woman in her sadness who can't think of anything else to do with herself but rock. And once again, Annie Lamb reached out the connecting hand and placed it on the skeletal shoulder. "Aw, Bridie," was all she could muster, and she found herself fighting back the tears of empathy she felt for Bridie Coughlin, and the anger, too, that she felt toward the returned missionary.

Bridie wasn't finished yet. Twisting and torturing and strangling the handkerchief, she wrung the pain out of her soul and it dripped down onto the hearth. "The first day he came home from India, the minute he walked into the house, he said, 'You didn't get the water in! There's no lavatory, and it nineteen fifty-one! This is worse than

India.' And when we were milking the cows that night, Eddie said to me that he should have said, 'Sure, we got a motor instead to bring you around, Jarlath, and as well as that we'd have to have the electric to have a lavatory because the electric makes the pump go that puts the water in the tank for the lavatory to work.' Then Jarlath in the kitchen says, 'If I'd only known there was going to be no lavatory, I mightn't have come at all.' And Eddie said when we were in the cowhouse that he should have said, 'Sure, Jarlath, you'll just have to use the stable like Mammy and Daddy did, and it was good enough for them.' There in the kitchen the three of us stood, and Eddie and myself not able to say anything. And I thought to myself, that maybe if he'd noticed the new thatch and the new whitewashing and the new bluestone on the windowsills when he was coming in that he wouldn't be so cross. And I have a new geranium in the kitchen window, too, Annie, with the reddest flowers you ever saw and the best smell you ever smelt. But I didn't know what to say. It was like Jarlath was out of place in our kitchen, as much as I'd be out of place in a bishop's palace. It was like he was too used to nice things to have landed in our kitchen, after living in style in India with servants to do everything for him, one to do nothing but polish his shoes, and another to do the cuffs of his shirt, another to cook, another to carry his dinner to the table, another to make his bed, another to fill up his bath, another to move the fan in the ceiling with a rope, another to lay out his clothes, another to brush his shoulders when he goes outside, another to carry his umbrella to keep off the sun, another to carry his books to school, and here he is in our house and we don't even have a lavatory, and the three of us standing there and neither Eddie nor myself knowing what to do next. Jarlath was standing there with his back to us, and he looking around and I feeling there was nothing right in the house, there was something wrong with everything, and how would we be able to have Jarlath at home for four months after such a terrible start. No lavatory. I looked at Eddie and Eddie looked at me, and if you'd given us a thousand pounds apiece, neither of us could've said anything. Then after a terrible long time Jarlath said, 'Well, I suppose you can't make a silk purse out of a sow's ear—I'll just have to put up with it.' And Eddie says, 'Sure, I'll get your cases out of the motor,' and I said, 'I'll be getting the bit of dinner going.' After a few days he began to get used to the way we live, at least he stopped saying everything was worse than in India. He was a bit cagey at first about going out to the stable, but he soon got over that, especially when he saw there's always a little pile of nice soft green grass for him and he saw he wouldn't have to use straw. Of course, the first Sunday when he told us to let him out at Morgan's shop there was another terrible long silence because Eddie nor myself would never talk back to him even if we knew what to say, Jarlath being a priest and all and being away on the missions for so long. But now there's today in the Mater Hospital in Dublin. There's nothing we can do right for him, Annie. And Eddie is terrible upset the way Jarlath was going around asking everyone for money for his school in India before he had the appendix attack. Eddie says nobody has money for themselves, let alone for a school in India. And the Martyr serving him tea in the good tea set with Jacob's Biscuits—*Assorted*, no less—twice a day when Eddie and myself are out in the fields, and he all wrapped up in blankets and with his hat on sitting outside in the sun if there's any."

Bridie ran out of words, and Annie Lamb again sought inspiration of the Mother of God, but the Mother of God was still keeping her distance.

The first rule of gossip says it is socially suicidal to agree with someone who is badmouthing their own flesh and blood, and it was this rule that was keeping Annie Lamb's tongue in a state of arrest. The flesh and blood could be as blatantly unkind and cruel as Jarlath was, but to agree with his sister about his egregious behavior was a deathly trap to fall into, no matter how strong the empathetic pull. There was always the possibility of reconciliation and, if the viscosity of the blood between the family members recovered its proper glutinousness, the enemy of one became the enemy of the other.

"Maybe Father Jarlath is feeling under the weather, Bridie," Annie-the-very-careful said. "He might be in a lot of pain where he was cut open, and people with a pain sometimes say things they don't mean. I remember our old Shep the time Simon Peter backed the wheel of a cart over his paw, and when Simon Peter went to examine the paw didn't Shep bite him and he never bit anyone before that or after. It was the pain that made him bite."

But Bridie ignored Annie's weak attempt to make an excuse for the priest's behavior. "Anyway," she said, and her tone seemed dismissive of the whole topic, "after he gets out of the hospital he'll be staying at the motherhouse near Dublin for a week, and he'll have twelve lavatories there, he told us."

Annie Lamb could not determine if the "twelve lavatories" was Bridie's attempt at humor after her foul journey through the valley of rejection and hurt. And so, Annie, still keenly aware of the first rule of gossip, did not make any laughing sound. Instead, she made an effort to step back from Bridie's familial quagmire. "I'm sure when Father Jarlath comes home everything will be grand," she lied, "and will you look at how dark it got while we were talking." She stood up and took the two-wicker lamp off its nail in the whitewashed wall.

But Bridie, like a terrier remembering the biting teeth and scratching claws of the rat in its mouth, was not willing to let go of her offensive brother yet. "Eddie says Jarlath won't stay in the motherhouse for long because he'll have to come home to do his collecting. And your paraffin lamp reminds me, Annie, that's another thing he said—about the lights in his house in India are electric, and all we have is a two-wicker like yourself, Annie."

"Won't it be great when rural electrification comes this way?" Annie-the-diverter asked as she replaced the glass globe around the two weak flames of the lamp. "Men were out in our fields on Thursday with their things for measuring and for making straight lines. Won't it be great to have bright lights and a lavatory and a bath with hot and cold water?"

Bridie let go of her priestly brother, but she still spoke out of her gloomy mood. "Ah, sure them fellows measured and marked in the fields around Marbra two years ago, and there's not one pole in sight yet. It'll be years before we get it."

Then, as Annie Lamb spoke again, she realized too late that she was veering back toward the Coughlin-family quicksand. "Sure, by the next time Father Jarlath comes home you'll have a lavatory," and she rushed on to get as far away as possible from the dreadful brother, "and a sink and a bath and it all done up with nice tiles like the one in the convent in Gohen, white tiles on the floor and white tiles on the wall and an electric light over the mirror, and the whole place white and gleaming and the taps shining like they were silver, and nice dry towels hanging instead of an old rag hanging on a rusty hook—big, warm, thick towels. That's the kind of lavatory I think about when I think of rural electrification, a bath full of hot water to lie in for an hour when the children are in school and Simon Peter's in the fields." Annie poked the ashes off the smoldering turf sods with the long tongs, and the kettle began to sing. "Do you ever think of a lavatory like that when you hear them talking about rural electrification, Bridie?" she asked.

"I can't persuade Eddie to put a back door in the house, never mind a lavatory. I mentioned it to him one time, and he said what he always says about anything that's new: 'Sure wasn't the cowhouse and the stable good enough for Daddy and Mammy?' If the electric ever comes our way, Eddie doesn't want it in the house. He said the electric would set fire to the thatch."

Annie Lamb put a kitchen chair beside Bridie, and she was placing the mug of tea and the plate of curranty cake on the makeshift table when Mikey, Molly and Barlow galloped in from the farmyard in a cloud of noise. They were sweating, their faces apple-red, and bits of golden straw was tangled in their wild hair. Their loud intrusion had the immediate effect of sweeping Father Jarlath Coughlin out of the kitchen. Annie Lamb relaxed and watched with amazement while Bridie shamelessly and mercilessly grilled Barlow. Bridie learned more about the Bracken family in ten minutes than Annie had discovered during the previous two weeks.

23

In the Sunroom

In which Elsie Howard angrily tells Patrick
Bracken about the vile injustices suffered by
Bridie Coughlin at the hands of her brother
Eddie, and Sam reveals a pleasant surprise.

"PATRICK," MISSUS HOWARD SAID. "Eddie Coughlin died about
twenty years ago. Do you know that?"

"Nineteen," Sam said. "He died in 1987."

"Yes, he died six months after he told me—"

"Then you must know—" Missus Howard said.

"Else, Patrick just told you that he knows."

"How do you know what I'm going to tell him, Sam? And whether
he knows or not, it's a good story that can be repeated like a good
joke. You said so yourself."

"But it's not a good story; it's a miserable one."

"Just because it's a story about misery doesn't mean it's not good."
Elsie turned to Patrick. "Eddie Coughlin died nineteen years ago,
and his will was published in the *Irish Independent*. He had three
hundred thousand pounds in the bank."

"Three hundred and forty two thousand, nine hundred and
eighty seven pounds to be exact," Sam said, and his wife gave him a
look, told him with her eyes to stop interrupting the story.

"Over three hundred thousand pounds, and Bridie got up on her bike every morning all those years to go a mile for her bucket of well water for the kitchen. Three hundred thousand in the bank, and Bridie without the comfort of a flushing lavatory. Wasn't he the—"

"Now, Else," Sam said, "don't get up on your high horse about this again, and there's no need for every little detail."

Elsie hesitated. But when she spoke again anger was still in her voice. "It's the details that make this story so maddening and I got the details from a Protestant family who lived up the road, the Brynes."

"Protestants always tell the truth, Patrick," Sam said.

"David Samuel Howard! Will you please stop interrupting?" Elsie demanded, and she speared her husband with her eyes, too. "Every morning when the cows were milked, Bridie got out her bike and set off in her Wellingtons with the bucket. It didn't matter if it was raining cats and dogs. If there was ice on the road, she walked in the grass beside the road to keep from slipping. Eddie never went to the well, because drawing water for the kitchen was a woman's job—Eddie was a man straight out of the Old Testament or the Koran when it suited him. When she'd get to the Well Field, she'd prop the bike in the hedge. Then she'd unlatch the gate and walk for five minutes, open another gate in the fence around the well. She'd kneel down on a flagstone and dip the bucket to three-quarters full. She'd carry it back to the road and put it on a small platform of stones she had made herself. She'd bring the bike over to the bucket, put one foot on the pedal, lift the bucket up to the handlebar and wobble off. Over the years she fell several times, and when that happened she had to go back to the well again. Sometimes she didn't simply fall—she crashed on to the road, skinned her knees and hands, fell on the bike, fell on the bucket. She got water from that well every day of the week from the time she learned to ride a bike, and when her brother died he had over three hundred thousand pounds in the bank. It was his money, and he left two thousand to Bridie, and the rest, along with the farm and the house, he left to the religious order the priest-brother belonged to. Within a year, everything was sold off and Bridie was left homeless."

Sam dared to interrupt. "The order got exactly three hundred and forty thousand, nine hundred and eighty-seven pounds, the sixty-acre farm and the house."

Elsie continued, "Exactly one year to the day after Eddie died, Bridie was packing the last of her things to move into Mick Flanagan's old bungalow at the far end of the town—she was going to rent. A distant cousin came with his tractor and trailer to transport her stuff, and he found her dead on the kitchen floor. He said it was like finding a stillborn calf in the morning at the hind legs of its tethered mother. Poor Bridie! Life can be so bloody nasty at times."

Sam said, "Eddie Coughlin said at the inquest of his brother that he never gave the Martyr Madden a raise even though she worked for him for almost fifty years. He said she never asked for it." Then, without pause, Sam said matter-of-factly, "I have the transcript of Eddie Coughlin's testimony at the inquest."

Patrick Bracken felt as if he'd heard the door into Mister Howard's long-protected vault creaking on its hinges.

It took a few seconds for Sam's announcement to sink in, and when it did Else exclaimed in disbelief, "You don't, Sam!"

"I do," Sam Howard said, and he held a palm up to his wife to forestall any questions. "Don't ask, Else," he said. He fussed himself together and stood up.

"David Samuel Howard!" his wife said in a tone that was a prelude to an accusation.

"If you say another word, Elsie Howard, I will sit right down again. You are to stay here with Patrick, and I will get the transcript."

"If you have one—" Elsie began.

Sternly, her husband rebuked her, his eyes flashing, "Elsie Eloise Carter Howard!"

His wife became silent, and Sam short-stepped out of the sunroom.

"That bloody Sam! When he calls me Elsie Eloise Carter it's like he's dropping the Iron Curtain around himself. There's no way through it. You think you know someone, Patrick, and now this after all these years. He's been saving stuff and I didn't know it. He has more bloody secrets than a priest in a one-horse parish. It's so annoying. I keep telling him we'll be dead in a few years, but he still won't tell me things. I stuck the Bible in his face one day and swore I'd never tell anything he told me. 'Frivolous use of the holy book in an attempt to get privileged information,' he says. He can be so dismissive when it comes to his bloody privileged information." Else had become an agitated, brooding hen furiously using her beak to roll one egg under her feathers while at the same time pushing another one out on her far side. "If he has Eddie Coughlin's transcript, you can be sure he has all the transcripts and a lot more besides. I wonder where he hid them. And the best of it is, the transcripts of the inquest aren't privileged at all. . . . What's going on with him, Patrick? What did you say to make him do this? Sssh," she hissed, and she cocked her head to one side. "I wonder where he is. He's not upstairs, or we'd hear the floor creaking. But he went up the stairs. He hardly has a hiding place . . . but I'd have discovered . . ." She stood up and went to the door, one ear straining. "This old house," she whispered. "I've often thought there must be hiding places, but I've never found one. Maybe Sam did." She made a sudden move back to her chair and smoothed her dress, touched the cameo at her throat.

Sam came in with a thick three-ring binder. He put it on the wicker table. In silence he lowered himself, and, when his ancient muscles failed, he plopped the last four inches onto his rosy cushion.

"Sam," Elsie began, but she was immediately silenced by an uplifted hand.

"Patrick," Sam said, and his tone indicated he was about to deliver an introduction to the transcript. He put the closed binder on his knees. "My wife is a naturally curious woman. Where she believes there is a secret, she will dig. She is incorrigible. On the other hand, I am a naturally cautious man when it comes to other people's secrets."

"Naturally stubborn is what he—"

"Else, I have the floor. All our married life I have been hiding, and Else has been digging. The more insistent her digging, the more protective I became of my privileged information until, I will freely admit, I became paranoid—afraid to talk about anyone in the town just in case what I knew about them had come across my desk in the sanctity of my office."

"Sanctity, Sam?"

"Every bit as sacred as the confession box, Else, and you have always had your ear to the door, in a manner of speaking." Sam held up his silencing hand to Elsie again. "Patrick, you have been very forthcoming about yourself and your relationship with Mikey Lamb and the sorrows of your own family. It's only fair that I should be as forthcoming with you in matters which are not privileged information. Even if some of what I tell you is borderline between privileged and gossip, I know now that anything you hear in this house will remain here."

Missus Howard silently clapped her hands, and she beamed. But her husband said, "Now, Else, you are not going to find out anything you don't know already, so don't get all excited. But there is one thing you don't know. When business was slow in the office, I dabbled in writing—wrote down little things for my own amusement over the years. The dabblings are harmless, just my observations about matters in the public domain, like transcripts of inquests, wills and land sales, sales of hay and straw. I presided over only two inquests in my lifetime, Patrick. Besides Jarlath Cough-lin, there was Jack Duff who drank weed killer after several other unsuccessful attempts to shake off his bodily coil. Poor bugger! Imagine the pain as the chemicals melted his guts."

"Jesus! Sam!" Elsie exclaimed.

"I have often thought about that, Else—death by horror, terror and unspeakable agony—like Father Coughlin falling or Jack Duff's intes-tines melting—or worse, a rape victim played with like a mouse by a cat. When the victim is dead, the terror and agony are gone because they were in the victim. But the survivors continue to be terrorized vicariously when they remember their child fighting and screaming and crying and pleading and choking and bleeding and hurting and despairing and dying. It is the survivors who keep the terror alive, who keep the victim in a state of terror forever. When I think of our David, I can't help thinking of the terror of his last seconds, but his terror is over with, it went with David. David is gone, and it's only me and Else and his brother and sisters who keep his terror alive." Sam looked out into the garden, but Patrick knew the old man was not seeing anything out there.

"Remembered terror plays some part in the instinct of self-preservation," Sam mused to his own reflection. "But remembering the terror of someone we have loved seems to have no purpose at all."

"Sam," Missus Howard said, and in the word Patrick heard love. Mister Howard looked at her across the wicker table. His left arm and her right arm bent across the legs of the green teddy bear to each other, and the ancient fingers clasped while the two pairs of ancient eyes held each other in the embrace of ancient love. Elsie said, "I never think of David's terror, Sam, because I don't think he was afraid at all. I think he turned around and faced the train and embraced it because it was putting an end to his pain."

Fixed like an old couple on a Valentine card, Sam and Elsie Howard bequeathed support on each other—a pair of elderly parents talking out their memories of a lost child together.

"Remember how he used to hide my wallet in my shoe?"

"Remember how he used to hide in the dark and say 'boo' to frighten us? And his 'boo' wouldn't frighten a robin off a branch."

"He was a lovely child."

There were no tears, just sad, diaphanous smiles.

Patrick Bracken, observer and reporter of human behavior at its worst and its best, decided that this moment had to play itself out between the old couple. He leaned forward, put his elbows on his knees and enclosed his face in his long-fingered hands. For the first time he allowed himself to look at his sister, AnneMarie, sinking down into the water that would carry away her pain, carry her away from the search for her lost childhood and for her lost childish friends in a place where they could never be found. AnneMarie's hair floated up from her head and slowly swung around like the flaring skirt of a flamenco dancer in slow motion as she sank down into the nothingness that was far better than the laocoöned life that was strangling her. Thinking of his sister's choice in this way did not relieve Patrick's sadness, but for the first time he did not think of her as a suicide. Tears dropped off his chin.

Patrick used his handkerchief on his face and nose and looked at the Howards. Husband and wife were disengaging themselves.

"All right," Sam said too loudly, as if he could magically restore the atmosphere that had escaped from the sunroom on the wings of remembered deaths. "Everything's all right now," he continued, with an exaggerated show of opening the binder. He cleared his throat loudly and intoned, "A reading from the holy gospel according to Sam." But he was no Merlin, and he wasn't even quick enough to smother the sob that leaped up his throat. The old body shook from the force of the seismic pain, but he kept Elsie at bay with an outstretched hand.

Like a bird seeing its chick off on its first flight, Elsie was perched on the edge of her chair. With his eyes closed, Sam's head slowly moved up and down as if he were bundling feelings back into their respective tabernacles in his heart. Patrick watched the old man swallowing hard as he slowly gained control and finally said, "I'm sorry about that." Sam glanced at his wife, and she gave him back a smile pleated out of sadness, gladness and resignation.

Mister Howard took a deep breath. "All right!" he said. "All right. I have the transcript of the entire inquest, and I've decided I will read the whole thing, my own observations included as an introduction to each witness." He smiled and looked at Elsie. "I will abide no hissing or booing or interference from the cheap seats, so, my wife, no matter what you hear you are not to interrupt."

24

First Witness:
Mister Kevin Lalor

1951

In which the Civil Servant, a.k.a. Kevin Lalor, gives witness to finding the body, and in so doing raises the ire of Timothy, a.k.a. Spud, Murphy.

THE INQUEST WAS HELD in the Woodwork Room in the National School on the last day of September. The workbenches were pushed back against the walls; fresh sawdust lay in the cracks between the wide floorboards and old sawdust beaded the cobwebs in the windows. The previous day the summer had suddenly died, and the Great Damp had descended—it had already invaded the people's souls, and everyone was miserable. School regulations would not allow for the lighting of the fire for another two months.

Spud Murphy had made two trips between the Picture House and the school with his ass-and-cart to bring twenty chairs for the witnesses, the jury and the coroner's people. As usual, Spud was arrayed in his perennial haute couture of Wellington boots with the tops turned down, filthy and torn and belted gabardine coat, and broken-peaked cap with an explosive tear as if a shotgun had been at it from the inside.

Spud had asked Mister Morgan-of-the-shop for a long piece of twine to wrap around the chairs to keep them from sliding off each other and over the sideboards of the cart. The malodorous bell ringer told Quick Quigley-the-road-sweeper that Morgan had asked him to bring back the twine when he was finished with it. "Fecking Protestant! Bring it back—will and me hole," Murphy said.

David Samuel Howard, Esquire, Peace Commissioner, was the coroner. The first witness was Kevin Lalor, known locally as the Civil Servant. Every day Mister Lalor came in from Clunnyboe to Gohen on his bicycle. Without dismounting, he free-wheeled through the ever-open cast-iron gates of the courthouse and parked his convey-ance in the bike room. To the people of Gohen, Lalor and his bicycle were one organism—a twentieth-century centaur. So, when Mister Lalor *walked* into Gohen on the morning of the inquest, his arrival was commented on by everyone who saw him: "Is that the Civil Serv-ant off his bike?" "Will you look at the Civil Servant the way he's walking?" "He's as bandy-legged as a cowboy in the pictures." "The Hyland one must have been rough on the Civil Servant last night?" When he took his place in the witness chair, Mister Lalor had the appearance of someone who'd just banged his head on a too-low doorway. He was distracted and nervous; his eyes were on full alert, slightly bulging behind his thick glasses; he continually glanced at the door of the Woodwork Room as if he expected someone to burst in and shout at him; his hair was untidy, and his tie was slightly askew. When the inquest was over, the coroner told his wife that trying to get information out of the Civil Servant was similar to pulling a cat's teeth. Missus Elsie Howard, known in local Protestant circles as a bit of a wit, asked her husband "When was the last time you practiced dentistry on a cat?"

The inquest began at ten o'clock in the morning.

CORONER: The witness will tell his name and occupation to the jury.

WITNESS: Kevin Lalor, Civil Servant.

On the morning of August 22, 1951, did you not find a body?

I did, yes.

Mister Lalor, please tell the jury how it was that you found a body.

I was on my way to work, sir.

What road were you on?—for the recorder's sake, Mister Lalor.

Glower Road, sir.

Glower Road is the local name for the Lower Road, isn't that right?

Yes, sir.

Tell the jury about when first you saw the body.

When I went around the corner below Sally Hill, I saw the body up there on the road.

How far from Sally Hill were you when you saw the body?

About two hundred yards, sir.

And you immediately recognized it as a dead body?

No, sir. I thought it was a man lying on the road.

Tell the jury, Mister Lalor, how you thought you were looking at a man lying on the road from a distance of two hundred yards. Couldn't it have been a woman or a child or a bundle of clothes?

Sally Hill is a sudden rise in the road, sir. It's like looking at a wall in the distance.

Continue, Mister Lalor.

The person was dressed like a man.

Now tell us about going up to the body.

When I came to the bottom of Sally Hill, I got down and pushed my bike up to where the body was.

But you didn't know yet that it was a dead body.

When I got close, it became apparent the man was dead.

Did you recognize the deceased immediately?

Yes.

Tell the jury why it was apparent to you that it was a dead body you were looking at.

He looked dead, sir.

Did anything else make you suspect the man was dead?

There was no movement from the body; the chest wasn't going up and down.

Anything else, Mister Lalor?

The mouth was open.

Anything else, Mister Lalor?

One of the legs was twisted back under the body at an unnatural angle.

Anything else, Mister Lalor?

It looked like the head was lying in a shallow pothole full of black blood.

Before we go any further, Mister Lalor, can you tell us what time it was when you saw the body on Sally Hill?

When I was pushing my bike up Sally Hill, Mister Murphy started ringing the seven o'clock Angelus in Gohen.

You noticed the church bell despite the circumstances you were in?

I was looking at a dead man, and the first stroke of the bell reminded me of the dead bell.

So at exactly seven o'clock you were already on Sally Hill, if Mister Murphy was not late ringing the bell.

No, sir. He was not late that morning.

How do you know that, Mister Lalor? Is Mister Murphy ever late with the bell?

Yes, he is.

How do you know?

I always know where I should be on the road at seven o'clock.

And how do you know that, Mister Lalor?

I have a watch, sir, and I look at it every time I hear the Angelus to see if the watch is right. But I found out my watch was always right, but that the bell was sometimes wrong. Every morning, except Sundays, I push my bike up Sally Hill.

VOICE: I'd like to tell Limpin' Lalor's son—

CORONER: You must not interrupt the proceedings, Mister Murphy. If you have anything to say that will throw light on this unfortunate incident, you may give your name to Sergeant Morrissey. He will arrange for you to be heard.

MISTER MURPHY: I just wanted to say that the last time I was late with the seven o'clock—

CORONER: Mister Murphy! I must sternly warn you not to interrupt these proceedings. If there is another outburst, Sergeant Morrissey will remove you from the Woodwork Room. I have told you once how you can appear as a witness, and I will not repeat myself. Now, if the recorder will tell us where we were before the interruption?

RECORDER: Every morning except Sundays, Mister Lalor pushes his bike up Sally Hill.

CORONER: Thank you. And, Mister Murphy, I will remind you that when the inquest is in session, no one speaks unless he is spoken to by me first. Now, Mister Lalor, without any prompting from me, describe to the jury the position of the body on the road. And, I might remind you, Mister Murphy, that you should take off your cap. The same respect should be given at an inquest as is given in a courtroom. . . . Pretend, Mister Lalor, that you are writing a composition like the prizewinner you wrote years ago. Do not try to spare anyone's feelings.

WITNESS: The body was lying on its back in the middle of the road. The left leg was bent out of sight under the backside. A stranger might have thought he was looking at a one-legged man. The other leg was sticking straight out at an angle. It was sloping off to the right from where I was standing. The two arms were stretched out from the body and the palms were turned toward the road. He looked like a one-legged man trying to hold back a crowd pushing him from behind. The left eye was lying on his face near his nose. His glasses were on the ground at his left shoulder.

Thank you, Mister Lalor. Did you look around? Did you wonder how the body happened to be lying like that in the middle of the road?

WITNESS: Yes, I wondered where his bike was. He always got around on his bike.

Was his bike anywhere to be seen?

Yes, sir. Eventually, I saw it at the bottom of the hill lying in the long grass at the side of the road.

From what you saw, what did you think had happened to the deceased?

I thought he must have fallen off his bike; that he fell off and landed on the back of his head; that he hit the ground with such force that one of his eyes came out and the back of his head got flattened.

Did you touch the bike, Mister Lalor?

No, sir.

CORONER: Mister Murphy! Please strive to be normal. Roll up that piece of twine, and put it in your pocket. Missus Moore, where are we?

RECORDER: In the Woodwork Room in the—

CORONER: Missus Moore!

RECORDER: Mister Lalor said he didn't touch the bike.

CORONER: What did you do next, Mister Lalor?

I went back to ask Simon Peter Lamb to go into Gohen for Sergeant Morrissey.

Why didn't you continue on into Gohen yourself?

I thought someone should stay with the body, sir.

You are to be commended, Mister Lalor, for doing that, staying with the body. Did you tell Mister Lamb whose body it was?

No, sir.

Why not, Mister Lalor?

I didn't think it was my place to identify a dead body.

You showed remarkably good judgment in not identifying the body. A man's natural inclination would be to blurt out the name. Now, Mister Lalor, did you wait for Mister Lamb to get ready or did you go straight back to Sally Hill?

I went back to the body.

While you were waiting for the sergeant, did anyone come along the road?

Simon Peter Lamb passed by on his way for the sergeant.

Did he stop to look at the body?

No, sir. When he was pushing his bike up the hill, he kept his head turned away from the body and he didn't stop.

Did he say anything?

Yes, sir. He said, "I hate the sight of a corpse."

And you waited there until the sergeant came on his bike?

Yes, sir.

Thank you, Mister Lalor. That is all I have to ask you. Sergeant Morrissey will be the next witness.

25

In the Sunroom

In which Elsie Howard proselytizes on behalf of
skepticism.

ELSIE SAID, "I DIDN'T KNOW I was considered a bit of a wit in the
Protestant community, Sam."

"Patrick," Sam said, "my wife is fishing for a compliment. She
knows she was the most quoted wit in Protestant Gohen. She once
declared that the reason why Catholics and Protestants are reluctant
to be good friends is that each is equally afraid they might reveal the
stupidity of the stuff they're supposed to believe in."

"You are probably onto something there, Else," Patrick said. "I'm
afraid I've become a religious skeptic myself."

"Oh, don't be afraid of being a skeptic, Patrick," Elsie said. "It's
the duty of each generation to examine the 'wisdom' passed on by the
previous generation. We'd still have slavery if some brave souls had
not stood up and questioned inherited wisdom."

"May I?" Sam asked. "The floor is mine, Missus Howard."

"You may, Sam, but I think your were a bit harsh with Spud
Murphy."

"Yes, Else. Now that I read it I realize how rotten I was. I can't even take consolation from the fact that Spud Murphy was probably annoying the hell out of me."

"All is forgiven, Sam. The floor is all yours," Elsie said, and she swept the room with the back of her hand.

26

Witness:
Sergeant Morrissey

1951

In which garda sergeant Joseph Aloysius
Morrissey, using Latin when necessary, tells how
he proceeded to Sally Hill on his bike to secure
the scene of death.

SERGEANT MORRISSEY HAD a red, jowly face, and he spoke, almost
sang, in a high-pitched Cork accent that belied the mass of his
corporeality. His middle-aged belly pushed out the tunic of his blue
uniform to give him a Humpty Dumpty look. The embossed, imitation silver buttons running in a shining and straight row down
over the curvature of his gut had once prompted Pascal Lalor-the-
postman to observe that, if the sergeant had a second row of buttons
running parallel to the first, he would have the look of a standing-up
sow on her way to give suck to her sixteen newborns.

Everyone in the town was used to seeing the sergeant wearing his
peaked garda cap, and so he presented an almost indecent aspect of
himself as he sat bareheaded in the witness's chair in the Woodwork
Room. The reddish-yellow tone of his scalp was the only indication
that his few remaining gray hairs had once been flaming red.

Everything about Sergeant Morrissey was thick, his neck, his
wrists, his fingers. Many a tinker who had become obstreperous after
drinking away the Children's Allowance on the second Tuesday of

the month had felt the pincer-like force of those thick fingers—in blacks and blues had carried the painful fingerprints on his body for weeks afterward.

Sergeant Morrissey had enormous feet. His boots were so big that Pascal Lalor, who believed there was a correlation between the size of a man's feet and the size of his male organ, had once speculated, "It wouldn't surprise me at all if he has to be careful not to kneel on his whanger when he says the Rosary."

The coroner felt obliged to help the sergeant preserve what little semblance of authority he had by not cutting in and bringing the man's ambling loquacity and displays of legalese to sudden halts.

One evening not long after the inquest, Mister Howard, Esq., told his wife that the sergeant's soprano voice drove him to distraction. His witty wife asked him if she could distract him from his distraction by cranking him to expansion in the bedroom. Mister Howard accepted his wife's offer.

After leaning back to hang his peaked cap on the lever of a vise attached to one of the workbenches, Sergeant Morrissey placed his half-acre hands on his knees and nervously awaited the first question from the coroner. The sergeant hated his middle name so much that he often said it out loud out of fear of saying it, the way a man who's afraid of falling from a height will jump to end his fear of falling.

It took the coroner several moments to figure out that the sergeant was addressing him as Esk. Perhaps the officer of the law was showing the natives that he was on familiar terms with the esquire, the same as a familiar person might address a doctor as Doc. At first it seemed the man had a lisp.

CORONER: Please state your name and occupation.

WITNESS: Aloysius, I mean Joseph Aloysius Morrissey. I am the sergeant of the Gardai Siochána in Gohen, Esk the Civic Guards as they are called. Or the Guards as most people call us.

Sergeant Morrissey, can you tell the jury about the morning in question, from the time Mister Lamb met you?

As I was proceeding down Pearse Street in Gohen on my bike, Esk going, as it were, from my house to the Barracks, I pedaled around the corner at Mister Morgan's shop and observed Mister Lamb coming up the street at me. He was pedaling like a hure . . . at such a ferocious rate I knew right away that something was afoot. Before he got near me at all, I put on my back brake and swung my leg over the saddle. Just as I expected, Esk, and before my right foot touched the road, Mister Lamb applied his brake, too, and by the sound of it I knew his front wheel was out of line. He must have run into something at full force on his bike. I knew from Mister Lamb's face that he was going to tell me something. I took my bicycle clips off the cuffs of my trousers.

Sergeant Morrissey, please tell the jury what time it was.

Just as Mister Lamb's foot hit the road, Esk, I saw Quick Quigley-the-road-sweeper coming out of his gateway with his assencart. Hail, rain, frost or snow, as it were, Esk, Quick Quigley comes out through that gateway with his assencart to start sweeping the streets at half-past seven. I've never known him to be a minute late or a minute early. I don't know how he does it. I put my bicycle clips in the right hand pocket of my tunic. I always like to know exactly where everything is, bicycle clips in the right tunic pocket, handkerchief in left trousers pocket, Esk.

You may call me Mister Howard, Sergeant Morrissey.

As you like, sir.

So, it was half-past seven, exactly one half hour since the time Mister Lalor found the body. Sergeant Morrissey, please tell the jury what Mister Lamb told you.

I have it written down here, Esk, your honor. Mister Lamb informed me that Mister Kevin Lalor-the-civil-servant had found a dead body out the far side of Desker at Sally Hill on Glower Road.

That was exactly where he said the body was, on the far side of the Esker at Sally Hill on the Lower Road?

That's right, your honor, on Glower Road.

Did he tell you anything else, Sergeant Morrissey?

He said, "No morning's a good morning to find a body, but to find a body on such a morning as this is a downright shame."

What did you take him to mean by that, Sergeant?

Your honor, I took him to mean it was a grand morning; a bit misty, but grand all the same, a promise of sun but it was terrible to have a dead body in it.

Did Mister Lamb say anything else, Sergeant?

Upon questioning Mister Simon Peter Lamb, I discovered that he knew nothing more. It is my opinion that Mister Lamb's role in the whole matter could be summed up as follows: Mister Lamb was carrying a spoken message from Mister Kevin Lalor, and the message was this: I have found a body on the far side of Desker at Sally Hill on Glower Road.

In your opinion, Sergeant, Mister Lamb knew nothing else?

He didn't even know who the dead body belonged to, your honor. He didn't know whether it belonged to a man or a woman or a child. And I said to myself, I hope to God it's not a child. But then I thought to myself that it wouldn't be me but Father Mooney who'd have to tell the father and mother. That's a terrible thing to have to—

What did you do next, Sergeant Morrissey?

I took off my peaked cap and blessed myself and prayed for the souls of the faithful departed. As the catechism says, "It is a holy and a wholesome thought to pray for the souls of the dead that they may be loosed from their sins."

After you finished praying, what did you do, Sergeant?

I put my garda cap back on and straightened it. Then I asked Mister Lamb to go up to the Barracks to tell Garda Doran that I had to go out to the far side of Desker on an emergency that had nothing to do with the lavatory. I told Mister Lamb not to say anything else to Garda Doran because I didn't want word of the body to get out until I knew whose it was. That way everyone wouldn't be wondering and worrying was it a relation of theirs that was dead on the road out there at Sally Hill and come out running or on their bikes or in their assencarts and walking all over the scene in their big boots.

That was considerate thinking on your part, Sergeant. Then what did you do?

I asked Mister Lamb to go to Doctor Roberts's house as well, and to knock till he got an answer, the doctor being a bit deaf, as it were, and not to pay any attention if the doctor et the face off him. I told Mister Lamb to tell the doctor there was a corpus on the road out at Sally Hill.

Sergeant Morrissey, tell the jury what a corpus is.

It's a word we use in the law. It's the Latin for a dead body. We use a lot of Latin in the law, like corpus delicious and happiest corpus and mea culpa.

Now, tell the jury what you found when you went out to Sally Hill.

As I was proceeding on my bicycle after going over the top of Desker, Esk, I came on the Martyr Madden—Missus Biddy Madden—on her way to work for Eddie-the-cap and Bridie Coughlin. When she heard me coming behind her, she made a plunge for the hedge at the side of the road without even looking around to see who was coming, so I shouted at her that it was all right, it was only me, Aloysius the sergeant of the Civic Guards in Gohen. She's always plunging through hedges when she sees a body coming, tearing herself on briars and blackthorn bushes, covering herself with scabs that's hard to look at. And the minute I said to her that it was only me the sergeant, I heard a noise behind me. When I looked around, I saw Mister Lamb on his bike and he puffing like Mick Hourihan's steam engine at a threshing just behind me and he sweating like a pig, and the two of us overtook the Martyr at the same time, she keeping close to the bushes in case she had to get to the far side of the hedge quick, the thorns pulling her old coat and cap to bits. Mister Lamb told me he gave my message to Garda Doran and that Garda Doran said he would keep an eye on things, as it were, till I got back from the emergency I was on. Mister Lamb said Doctor Roberts must have been right inside the door, because he answered the first knock. The doctor didn't even ate the face off him and said he would go out to Sally Hill as soon as he tackled his pony and yoked it to the trap. I said, "The doctor must of had a good night's sleep to be so nice." But Mister Lamb told me he that he once shouted back at Doctor Roberts when the doctor shouted at him, and he put the doctor in his place. And that's why Doctor Roberts didn't ate the face off Mister Lamb, and it so early in the morning to be looking for a doctor in the first place.

And when you got to Sally Hill what did you see?

As I proceeded toward Sally Hill with Mister Lamb on his bike, your honor, and me on mine, I asked him was it true what they were saying about him, that he was able to hear things from far away by twisting a few bits of wire together, as it were. As we went around the last bend on Glower Road before you get to Sally Hill, Mister Lamb was telling me I had him mixed up with Kevin Lalor-the-civil-servant, that it was Kevin Lalor-the-civil-servant who could hear the prices at the Dublin Cattle Market on a piece of wire, and Dublin fifty-two miles away as the crow flies, as it were. It was at the very minute he said, "Dublin Cattle Market," that we came to the top of Sally Hill and I saw what looked like a bundle of clothes in the middle of the road and Mister Lalor standing beside it with his hands behind his back. I remember Mister Lamb said Mister Lalor's wire was forty feet long when I was asking myself who could it be at all who's lying dead in the middle of the road early in the morning and at the same time thinking, Dublin is more than forty feet from the Civil Servant's house.

You got down off your bike and leaned it against a bush, and then what did you do, Sergeant?

I got down off my bike, but there was no bush there, your honor, to lean the bike against. There was only a barbed-wire fence and that's what I laid the bike on. The sally bushes there are on the far side of the wire. I told Mister Lamb he was to stay where he was and not to approach the body, that he would only be disturbing what could be the scene of a crime, it being very important not to disturb the scene around the corpus.

Describe what you found at the scene, Sergeant.

I shook the heavy dew off my boots and took my trouser legs out of the bicycle clips and put them in the right pocket of my tunic, and I recognized the deceased right away. He was lying exactly like Mister Lalor told you; the left leg back under him, the other stretched out and off to one side a bit—to my right as I was looking at him.

The head was odd-looking, but that was because of what I found out later, that when he came off the bike he'd smashed in the back of his head like a negg. His glasses were beside his left shoulder and they weren't broke or anything. Gold frames. His hands were like the Civil Servant said, like he was pushing back, holding back a crowd of people at the gate to a football match when no one else is allowed in because there might be with too many people around; pushing and shoving, and soon enough someone takes a swing at someone else, and there you have it. One eye was out on his cheek.

Did you closely examine the immediate area, Aloysius—Sergeant Morrissey?

I did, your honor. There's a small patch of Sally Hill that's nothing but the top of a big rock that's buried, that was never dug up as it were. People say it's as big as a house. Some say it's the top of a mountain if all the earth around it was scraped away. The body was down the hill by about one foot from the top of this rock and there was a splattering of blood on it. It is my opinion that when he fell off the bike, the deceased went over backward and hit that rock with the back of his head, and then skidded along the road on his back for about a foot.

Were there any signs of a struggle, Sergeant?

None at all, your honor. The only sign of anything was the animal footprints in the dust around the head. On close inspection I came to the conclusion that a fox and a badger had sniffed at the blood around the head sometime during the night.

Were there any signs that the animals touched the body?

None at all, your honor. There were just the paw prints, and as well as that there was a very light track that the tires of the bike made before and after the deceased fell off on his head.

Were there any marks in the dust to indicate that the deceased had hit a wild animal with the front wheel of the bike that might have caused him to fall off?

None at all, your honor.

Did you search the general area, Sergeant?

Yes, your honor. I searched the grass at the side of the road at the bottom of the hill where I found the diseased's bike. The bike was new, and it didn't show any signs at all that it had been in an accident. No hairs from an animal on the tires and no bent wheels or spokes. A well-kept bike.

Did you search anywhere else, Sergeant Morrissey?

Well, your honor, as you know, Sally Hill has big, strong sally bushes growing on each side. I looked in the grass among the bushes and, on one side of the road, the right side as you're looking up the hill, the grass was pressed down like someone had walked in there.

Did you reach any conclusion because of what you saw, Sergeant Morrissey?

I came to the conclusion that a man had stood in the grass at one of the bushes to piss . . . I mean relieve himself, to go to the lav, because there was the wet mark on the trunk that you make when you relieve yourself at a tree, a man I mean, not a woman, a standing man when he does nothing but his water, not the other thing because that would mean he was squatting and he wouldn't be able to do his water on—

Did you notice anything else out of the ordinary, Sergeant?

No, your honor. I went back to where Mister Lalor was standing, and he asked me if I found anything, and I said no, just a place where a man had relieved himself, your honor. Mister Kevin Lalor-the-civil-servant said he was the one who'd pissed in the bushes . . . relieved himself in the bushes while he was waiting for me to come, standing up, of course, went to the lav. Then we heard Doctor Roberts pony in the distance, and in no time at all the trap came around the corner with the doctor in it.

Thank you, Sergeant Morrissey, for a very clear and detailed report. You may go back to your seat. There will be a five-minute break before we hear from the next witness. In the meantime, Garda Doran, will you make sure Doctor Roberts is here in five minutes?

27

In the Sunroom

In which the coroner, David Samuel Howard, notes that Sergeant Morrissey could act as God's sleeping potion.

"THAT MAN COULD RAMBLE down the highways and byways," Patrick said.

"Sergeant Morrissey would send God to sleep," Sam said.

"Sam, you must prepare me," Elsie said. "Is there going to be anything else about rummagings on the sofa?"

"Else, I wrote this stuff how many years ago? I'm as surprised as you are. If it gets bad I'll hum and haw my way over it so that Patrick isn't embarrassed."

Patrick said, "Oh, don't be embarrassed on my account." He smiled. "I am a clinical observer."

"Yes, Patrick! Just like Sam," Missus Howard said. "There's no such thing."

28

Witness:
Doctor Roberts

1951

In which Doctor George William Roberts relates
the cause of the death of Father Jarlath Coughlin
in medical terms, which he translates into
English for the incognoscenti.

BECAUSE HE DIDN'T HAVE A WIFE to tell him he looked like a slob,
George William Roberts was never recognized as a medical
professional by visitors to Gohen, even when he was carrying his
black bag. He could have been a scavenger, a picker-upper of cast-off
cigarette butts, a collector of caps of lemonade bottles.

Doctor Roberts had grown old, impatient and forgetful in Gohen
and its environs. He was so cynical it was unlikely that even a trace of
idealism had wafted near him in the misty and dim pathways of his
medical school. To him the world was utterly barren, and he didn't
care a damn what anyone in that world thought about him. He had
no bedside manner. There was no room in his practice of medicine
for words of encouragement or discouragement; his patients were
told they were going to die or continue to live indefinitely. He had no
time for anything except the bare medical facts of the current case.

"Cynic" was also a good word for a physical description of the
physician, because he looked like an ancient English bulldog that
should have been put out of its misery years ago. He was all jowls and

wattles. The rims of his bottom eyelids had turned themselves inside out, and their redness had seeped up into his ever-wet eyeballs. His bald head was vast, his ears like crinkled cabbage leaves. Tufts of hair grew out of his ears and nostrils. The nose itself was a masterpiece of architectural disproportion and misplacement, being too large and too high on his face. A copse of hairs sprouted out of its tip. A mustache covered the very long space between the bottom of his nose and the edge of his bottom lip. His mouth was not visible.

Doctor Roberts had once been four inches taller than six feet, but, with age, the body had sunk down on itself until it was thick and stooped. However, he was still tall enough to intimidate with ease.

The doctor had lost most of his hearing, and this added to his gruffness. He impatiently demanded that people speak up and stop whispering, for Christ's sake. The people of Gohen, Drumsally and Clunnyboe, many of whom had borne their pains rather than endure the blunt aggressiveness of their physician, looked forward to the day when the old man would die and make room for someone else.

After the inquest, Mister Howard told his wife that he hadn't dared ask the doctor to state his name and occupation, nor had he dared ask him too many questions; he was, he said, afraid he might get the face et off him. The Coroner's wife observed how it was a pity that Doctor Roberts wasn't a Catholic, because the only thing he did for the Protestants was give them a black eye. "And he always smells like methylated spirits," she said, thinking of the traveling clinic of her childhood when the stainless steel instruments were sterilized in gleaming stainless steel pots boiling on top of blue flames, big blunt needles inoculating screaming baby bodies against diphtheria.

CORONER: The recorder will note that George William Roberts is the name of the witness, that he is a medical doctor by profession. And now, Doctor Roberts, will you tell the jury about the morning of August 22, 1951, please?

DR. ROBERTS: When?

CORONER: Now, please.

DR. ROBERTS: What?

Please tell the jury about the morning of August 22, 1951.

What about the morning? I thought I was here about your man, the one that got killed on the hill out on Glower Road.

That's correct, Doctor Roberts. Can you tell the jury who it was that came for you that morning?

What difference does that make? It was that man from Clunnyboe, the one I stitched up in the arm a few . . . I'm not an encyclopedist, young man. I came here to give you medical facts.

Was it a Mister Lamb who came for you?

Sheep, Lamb, Ramsbottom, the fellow that cut his arm when he was sharpening the scythe and shouted at me. What difference does it make?

When you went out to Sally Hill that morning, Doctor, what did you find?

I didn't find anything. The body had been found already by the postman's son. The body was lying in the middle of the road, halfway down the hill. I have my notes here, if you'll just let me read them.

Please tell the jury about the condition of the body.

If you'd stop interrupting I'd be on my way home by now. The body was lying in the middle of the road, halfway down the hill. From the position of the limbs it was apparent the victim had not moved after he fell. His right leg was bent back and up in what was an unnatural position. If the man had been conscious after the fall he would have tried to relieve the pain this was causing. The hands were in the classic position of a person who had fallen from a height onto his back, the arms stretched out, the palms toward the ground, the instinctual position assumed to soften the fall. There was no—

Sergeant Morrissey and Mister Lalor said it was the left leg that was bent back under the deceased.

Did you ask me a question?

I was pointing out that the sergeant and Mister Lalor said it was the left leg that was bent back under the body. Is it possible you made a mistake when—?

They made the mistake. It was the left leg if you were looking at the body. It was the right leg if you were the body.

Did you recognize the deceased, Doctor Roberts?

What?

Did you recognize the deceased?

I'd seen him out and about on his bike often enough to . . . Will you let me finish what I have to say?! (Incoherent) The instinctual position . . . (Incoherent) The instinctual position assumed to soften the fall. There was no pulse and no other vital signs. There was rupture of the globus and extrusion of the right eye, which means the eyeball had burst and the contents had been ejected. These contents were on the face three inches below the socket. Various strings of tissue were still connecting the evisceration to the musculature of the eyeball, which means what came out was still attached to the eyeball itself with bits of tissue. There was little or no blood around the empty socket. Besides the ruptured eye, there were no injuries on the front of the body, except the . . . ah . . . the right leg, left leg, the bent leg which the postmortem found was broken in the thigh. The right leg. The guard and a Mister . . .(Incoherent) Lalor, Mister Kevin Lalor, helped me to turn the body over on its side so I could examine the back. There were multiple fractures of the occiput, meaning the back of the head was smashed in. The skull bone was smashed into small pieces and the brain was visible. There had been a great loss of blood through the severe lacerations of the scalp. This was evident from the amount of blood on the road. The wound was consistent with the head coming into violent contact with a solid object. In my opinion the solid object was the surface of the road. About a foot away from the top of the head, there was hair and spots of blood on the rock of the hill. The deceased met his death through misadventure; in other words he fell off his bike and landed on the back of his head. The sudden stop killed him. When I finished my notes, I went back to Gohen in my pony and trap. When I left, the guard and Mister Lalor were the only people I had seen on Sally Hill, besides the deceased and Mister Ramsbottom. That's all I have to say about the matter. Do you have any questions for me?

Thank you, Doctor Roberts. Please tell the jury what was the time of death in your estimation.

I said that at the start. But let me go back to the beginning of my notes. (Long silence) Like I said, it's here at the beginning. I wish people would listen. I'll tell you again. From the state of rigor mortis, I estimated that the man had died from six to eight hours before I saw him, and I saw him at twenty-seven minutes past eight o'clock.

Do you have anything else to add, Doctor Roberts?

No, I do not.

Thank you, Doctor Roberts, for your time.

What?

I said, thank you for your time, Doctor.

All right. You don't have to make a song and dance about it.

The next witness will be Mister Edward Coughlin.

29

In the Sunroom

In which Elsie Howard reveals she never did approve of Doctor George William Roberts as an obstetrician, even if he was a Protestant.

"NO WOMAN EVER WENT to Doctor Roberts when she was going to have a baby. We all dealt with the Jubilee Nurse. Can you imagine that man in the room with a woman? 'Will you push the bloody thing out and stop wasting my time, for Christ's sake!'"

"Stop interrupting, Else."

"I can't help it when I remember that man. And for your information, Sam, I wouldn't even wish him on the Catholics."

"Quiet, Missus."

30

Witness:
Mister Coughlin

1951

In which Eddie-the-cap Coughlin makes a
late-night visit to the coroner, David Samuel
Howard, Esq., to take preemptive precautions
hours before his appearance as a witness.

WHEN EDDIE-THE-CAP COUGHLIN took his seat on the witness chair,
the people in the Woodwork Room held their breath. Spud
Murphy, that weak-minded-resident-at-large and public-stroker-
of-his-in-house-organ, became visibly excited. The sergeant, Joseph
Aloysius Morrissey, who had already been a witness, had unhatted
himself while he was giving evidence. So had Doctor Roberts. Spud
Murphy, like all the people in the room, was obviously in suspense
awaiting the removal of Eddie Coughlin's cap. Nobody there had seen
Coughlin uncapped since he was a youngster. Even at Sunday mass,
when he knelt on one knee in the church porch, Eddie managed to
inflame curiosity by keeping his too-large cap on. Occasionally, in the
pubs in Gohen, men deep into their pints dared each other to knock
Coughlin's cap off to see what was underneath. And from the pubs
came speculations, which quickly mutated into rumors and more
speedily into facts: Coughlin had a hole in the top of his head shaped
like the tip of a cow's horn; he had a hairy growth the size of a hen's egg
on his forehead; he had a third ear, not fully developed, growing on the

back of his head; he had a line of white hair running across his head from one ear to the other—the result of a wound received when, as a child, he lay down and fell asleep in the barley field where his uncle, Tuppence Tom, was wielding a scythe; that it wasn't his cap that was too large for his head—it was Coughlin's head that was too small for the cap.

And now, in the Woodwork Room the rim of Coughlin's fawn, peaked cap was resting on his stuck-out ears and the peak was half-way down his forehead, hiding the eyebrows that were not there. He was the only one not holding his breath on account of his headdress. He had taken preemptive steps to ensure the cap would not be an issue when he appeared as a witness at the inquest.

Two nights before the inquest, Eddie-the-cap had boldly knocked at Mister Howard's door in Gohen in the dark. Because he had never thought that anyone besides Mister Howard would answer, Coughlin was thrown into a panic of uncertainty when the door, with more brass on it than he had ever seen in one place, swung open so silently that it seemed to vanish before his eyes. And a woman was standing there, tall, comely, posed like one of those women in the posters out-side the Picture House. In the brightness of the electric light over her head, she put her fingers to her lips as if trying to suppress a scream, while Coughlin, as if in the presence of Venus naked on her seashell, covered his eyes against the bright light with one hand and declared, "I was looking for Squire Howard!"

"I beg your pardon," the vision said in a Protestant voice.

Lowering the hand to cover his nose, Coughlin said, "What?" It sounded like "Haw?" The woman was wearing clean shoes, the light over her head glistening in their polished toes. Coughlin noticed very little about the inside of the house, but on his way home he must have recalled the gleaming brass, a white door and a floor of reflect-ing brown. There hadn't been a bit of animal dung or muck in sight.

The woman turned to call back into the house, while at the same time keeping Coughlin in the corner of her eye. "Mister Howard!" she called, in a voice as excited as any woman's reacting to the sudden appearance of a mouse.

Mister Howard appeared in front of that white door before you could say Jack Robinson, and Coughlin did not notice the bedroom slippers, the cardigan, the open shirt collar, or the rumpled hair. Mister Howard recognized the farmer immediately because Coughlin, two years earlier, had paid the solicitor five pounds to write a letter to that fecker, Douling, about keeping his fences repaired and his cattle in his own fields. The solicitor assured his wife that the man was not a threat, and when he invited Coughlin to come in, he received a poke in the back. However, the becapped one was of the same mind as Missus Howard and said he would rather talk outside in the dark where they would not be seen.

Missus Howard, more curious than anxious for the welfare of her husband, positioned herself inside a darkened window in her parlor and watched through the lace curtain. After two minutes her husband patted the departing visitor on the shoulder, and the peeping wife skipped back to the front door, believing that the mysterious man was connected with the upcoming inquest. Things had been happening at a furious pace since the missionary was killed on Sally Hill, and since that other Catholic had the accident with his shotgun two days later. The last two weeks had been a time of exciting and breathy gossip, and everything was coming to a head with the inquest. Her husband's name would be in the national newspapers again, no matter what the outcome of the inquest. As far as Missus Howard was concerned, this slinking visit in the dark by the man in the cap was straight out of Conan Doyle. All that was needed was a swirling fog and a scraping fiddle.

But Mister Howard, who liked teasing his wife and who also wished to reestablish the atmosphere which had been rapidly developing when Coughlin had knocked on the door, refused to tell her anything about the visitor until both were back, thigh to thigh, on the sofa in the parlor. After explaining who Eddie-the-cap Coughlin was, Mister Howard said, "Besides suffering from diarrhea of the lips, he suffers from alopecia, and he wants to keep his cap on during the inquest so that—"

"What has he? Not the diarrhea, the other thing."

"Alopecia, fox mange. Mister Coughlin is as bald as an egg. In fact he has no hair anyplace on his body. He's embarrassed that—"

"No hair at all?"

"He can't grow hair."

"Under his arms, on his chest?"

"None at all."

"At his private parts?"

"Nowhere. He doesn't even have eyebrows."

"He told you he has no belly hair?"

"Of course he did. Didn't you see him through the window dropping his drawers to show me his bald hanging gardens?"

Howard's wife smacked him on the knee and told him not to be sarcastic.

"He didn't even use the word 'alopecia,' but from what he said, that's what he has."

"What did you tell him about his cap?"

"That he could keep it on, of course. Why embarrass him?"

"I wonder what it's like to look at a man with no hair on his body."

"You'd certainly see everything at first glance, like when you look at a baby."

"Did you ever think of shaving your belly hair?"

"No, the thought never crossed my mind."

In the Woodwork Room, Mister Howard cleared his mind of what he and his wife did after Eddie Coughlin's visit to his house. He cleared his throat, and there was instant silence because Mister Howard's recent blistering reprimand of Spud Murphy was still shaking the cobwebs in the windows.

To the disappointment of all present, Mister Howard seemed to be unaware of Coughlin's cap when he said, "The witness will please state his name and occupation."

WITNESS: Edward Coughlin's my name, Squire, and I'm a small farmer, mixed farming—a few cows, sugar beet, a bit of oats and barley and wheat and spuds—

CORONER: Excuse me, Mister Murphy, are you ill?

MISTER MURPHY: His cap is on.

CORONER: Mister Murphy, I am telling you for the last time not to disrupt—

MISTER MURPHY: I thought you mightn't a saw his cap, sir, and if Sergeant—

CORONER: Mister Murphy, please stop talking. Sergeant Morrissey, remove Mister Murphy from the Woodwork Room, and if he speaks on the way out put your hand over his mouth. Missus Moore, please indicate in the minutes that the Coroner suspended proceedings while the obstreperous Mister Murphy was being removed forcibly from the inquest. Thank you, Sergeant Morrissey. Now, Mister Coughlin, please state your relationship with the deceased priest, Father Jarlath Coughlin.

WITNESS: I'm his brother, Squire. He was my brother and was always Mick until the order changed his name. He was Bridie's and mine—brother, that is. Jarlath is the oldest, then—

The minutes of this inquest will show that the Coroner and all the people of Gohen extend their sympathy to the Coughlin family on the tragic death of their brother. Your brother was home on holidays, Mister Coughlin. Is that right?

Yes, Squire, he was an order priest, a missionary in India for the last thirty years, and I was just saying to Bridie—

For the minutes of the inquest, will you please explain the difference between an order priest and a priest like Father Mooney here in Gohen?

An order priest belongs to an order, and a priest like Father Mooney doesn't. But to look at them, you wouldn't know if a priest was an order man or not. It's like a bus driver and a postman and a guard—you can never tell one from the other the way they dress, navy blue uniforms, silver buttons and peaked caps. Some order priests run schools, and that's what Jarlath—

When did Father Coughlin come home?

He came home from India in June, Squire, on a White Star ship, two big suitcases, and we met him at the bus the same day as Annie Lamb's day-old chicks came. They must be laying hens by—

There's no need to call me Squire, Mister Coughlin. When was the last time he was home before that?

Before the war. When he was going back that last time the war was just after starting, and he had to go around by the bottom of Africa and he threw up all the way into Dindian—

You and your sister must have been looking forward to seeing him after such a long time.

We were, Squire. We got Mattie Mulhall to thatch the house even though he only thatched it for us three years ago, and we got the Martyr to whitewash the house, and bought him a new Raleigh in Jimmy Ryan's because I was riding his old one since he went back the last time and it's rattling a bit, and we fattened eight bullocks last winter to buy a motor to drive him around in, a black Morris Minor, a secondhand one, we got it in Ferguson's. We had to deal with that black Protestant because Jimmy Ryan only had Mortimer's second-hand hearse to sell, and we couldn't be seen driving Jarlath around in a hearse. We tried to have for him what he was used to in India, and we made sure the Martyr Madden would be at the house the whole time to take care of him and not come to the fields with Bridie and me. But we hadn't the running water for him, because I was just saying to Bridie the rural electrification—

Mister Coughlin, please tell the jury when was the last time you saw your brother alive.

That was the night before he got killed, Squire. That Tuesday night in August when he was setting—

There's no need to call me Squire, Mister Coughlin. What time was it—that Tuesday night in August?

About a minute before I saw him over the hedge, Squire, I heard the chapel clock striking eight, and I says to Bridie, he's a bit late tonight, and at that minute didn't—

What was your brother doing when you saw him for the last time?

Myself and Bridie were out in our Long Field stooking the oats, and we saw the top half of Jarlath sailing by on top of the hedge on his bike all dressed up in his black suit, and he had his topcoat on because after the heat in India he was always cold in Clunnyboe. That's one thing about living—

Why wasn't he in the motor you'd bought for him, Mister Coughlin?

He can't drive, couldn't drive. He has his own motor driver in India. He was just home from the hospital after the appendix, and that night I told him I'd drive him to the Martyr's house and—

And that's where he was going, to Missus Madden's house? Did he say anything to you or your sister while he was riding by?

He said, "God bless the work," Squire, and the two of us stopped stooking and said, "And you, too." As I was just saying, we could just see his shoulders and his head and his black hat going along the top of the hedge, and Bridie says to me, I hate him going to the Martyr's to—

And when was the next time you saw your brother, Mister Coughlin?

The next morning, Squire, Wednesday morning, but he was dead on Sally Hill and the new Raleigh in the grass at the bottom of the hill. The sergeant wants to buy the bike for his son—two bob off the buying price, so there'll be little—

What time did you get to Sally Hill on Wednesday morning?

About a quarter past eight, because the chapel clock struck eight just as Simon Peter rode his bike into our yard, and I says to myself, what in the name of God is Simon—

Mister Coughlin, your brother left your house on Tuesday night at eight o'clock to go to Missus Madden's house. Did he return to your house on Tuesday night after visiting Missus Madden?

No, because the next day his bed . . . the day he was found dead, Bridie went to make his bed and empty the water basin and the poepot, but he hadn't slept in it—the bed.

So you and your sister did not know till Wednesday morning that your brother never came home from Missus Madden's on Tuesday night?

No, Squire. I was just saying to Bridie that only for that—

Describe your house to the jury, Mister Coughlin.

It has a new thatched roof with a grand comb across the peak that Mattie Mulhall spent a day doing at two pounds a day. There's four windows with a fresh coat of bluestone on the sills and a—

Excuse me, Mister Coughlin. I did not make myself clear. Explain to the jury the layout of your house. Imagine you are standing inside your front door looking in and then tell us where the rooms are.

There's only one door, Squire, and that's the kitchen door at the front of the house with two windows on one side and two windows on the other. When you go in through the kitchen door, you're in the kitchen. The fireplace is over to your left, and behind the wall that the fireplace is in there's a room that's Bridie's because any bit of heat that goes through the wall into the room makes it a bit cozy in there for her. Behind the wall that's ferninst the wall with the fireplace is the parlor, and beyant the parlor is the room where I sleep, except that when Jarlath is home he sleeps in the room that I sleep in and I sleep in the settle bed in the parlor. That settle bed is the best—

Your brother had to go through your room to get into his room. Is that right, Mister Coughlin?

Yes, Squire, the parlor, and before Jarlath came home from India I put a drop of oil on the hinges, because you know yourself that a squeaky hinge in the middle of the night could waken the—

So when you went to bed on the Tuesday night, you knew your brother had not returned from Missus Madden's—is that right?

Yes, Squire. I knew he wasn't home.

Were you worried that your brother was not home?

No, Squire, I wasn't. I was asleep in the settle bed nearly every night before Jarlath came home, and I was used to not seeing him once we et the supper. I'd go back out to the yard or the fields, and he'd go into his room to get ready to—

And whenever he came home after you were in bed, did you ever wake up when he was going to bed?

No, Squire, he never wakened me once. He knew I had to get up early in the morning, and as well as that the oil on the hinges of the door was a great idea because I was just saying a squeaky—

When he did not get up on that Wednesday morning, did you not wonder that maybe he was sick or that he wasn't even in his room?

No, Squire, because there were a few times when he did not go to say mass in Gohen. And as well as that—

So you never looked in on your brother when he did not get up at his usual time?

No, Squire. Once Jarlath came home from India, that room was his and the only other one who could go into that room was Bridie to make the bed and sweep the floor and take out his poepot and the water in the basin he washed himself in. The Martyr Madden couldn't go in there either, no more than myself. "I like my privacy," is the way he—

How about his bike, Mister Coughlin? Did you not notice it wasn't there at your house?

No, Squire, because we keep the three bikes, Jarlath's, Bridie's and mine in the turf shed, and the only time we go there is to get deggs out of the hen nest in the barrel and the turf at nighttime or to get our bikes. Bridie hadn't gone to the well for the water yet, so she hadn't gone there to get her bike out and neither did I go there, and I was just saying, that if only Bridie had gone to the well early for the water that morning we'd a noticed Jarlath's bike not there. Even if the Martyr had heard a hen cackling in the shed she might have gone in for—

Missus Madden was the last person that we know of who saw Father Coughlin alive. As a matter of interest, Mister Coughlin, how long has Missus Madden worked for you and your sister?

I remember the Martyr tying sheaves at our house during the Boer War when she was a girl because her father got kilt in Africa one day when I was tying with her at the far end of the Long Field. She'd bundle, and I'd tie because she was so small. The old Mister Gorman, Doul Yank's oul lad was going by in his assencart and he shouted in over the hedge to the Martyr that her father got blew up in the siege of Mafeking. Then when her husband Mick got kilt in the first war she started working full time for us. That was in 1916, and what is it now? 1951. So 1916 from 1951 is what? Thirty-five years, Squire, the Martyr has worked at our house, and she never once asked for a raise and—

Was your brother a good man on a bike—was he in the habit of falling off his bike?

Jarlath was only five when he learned to ride my father's bike with one leg under the bar and the bike at an angle for balance, and he was a great biker as far—

So, were you surprised to see that your brother had fallen off his bike on Sally Hill?

Well, Squire, I never thought about that, but sure anyone could fall off their bike even if they never fell off it before, and especially in the dark on Sally Hill if you're not used to it. The hill drops down so sudden you could think in the dark that the bike was going out from under you, and do you know the way you think something is going to fall and you reach out real quick to stop it but you only hit it and make it fall, and it might not have been going to fall in the first place? Well, maybe that's what happened with Jarlath—maybe he thought the bike was going out from under him when it started down the steep hill and he tried to save himself instead of leaning forward and just holding onto the handlebars, but he didn't need saving at all if he'd left well enough alone—

Mister Coughlin, you have been an excellent witness, and again I would like to express my sympathy to you and your sister for the loss of your brother. Sergeant Morrissey, Missus Madden will be the next witness.

31

In the Sunroom

In which Elsie Howard appears as Venus on the half shell, and Sam comments on the weaknesses of verbal sphincters.

IT WAS PATRICK WHO SPOKE first, and he quoted Mister Howard: "'A woman stood there, tall, comely, posed like one of those women in the posters outside the Picture House, Venus naked on her half shell.'"

Missus Howard clapped her hands. "Oh, Patrick. Sam was such an old romantic—still is. Venus naked on her half shell, indeed! He was a man of many names for me, romantic and otherwise. Tall, comely and posed! I think he fell into idealizing in the loneliness of his office. When he'd come home, he was as likely to call me Old Hen as Wandering Voice like the cuckoo."

Mister Howard said, "I can remember being so annoyed at Coughlin with his Squire-this and Squire-that that I felt like choking him. Squire! It's a hundred years since anyone was called Squire, and then it was the landlord. Maybe Coughlin thought he had to call me Squire because I'm a Protestant. Did you notice he called Cyril Ferguson a black Protestant? I've never met a man with a worse case of diarrhea of the lips."

"What about Sergeant Morrissey?" his wife asked.

"He had better control over his verbal sphincter," Sam said.

32

Witness:
Missus Madden

1951

In which the Martyr Madden tells the coroner
that the priest, Jarlath Coughlin, took the prize
she won in the Protestant horse race and tried to
take something more precious.

Miss Biddy (Brigid) Swierski married Mister Michael Madden
on a Tuesday in 1913 after the 7:30 a.m. mass in the Catholic
Church in Gohen. Biddy's married sister and Michael's brother were
the witnesses. After the brief ceremony, the priest brought the four
people through the gleaming, filigreed gate in the altar rails and led
them to the sacristy. On the vesting bench, the priest opened the
large marriage register and produced an ink bottle and a pen with a
wooden handle. He held the nib up to the light to make sure there
wasn't a hair or a tiny piece of blotting paper stuck in it. As he elic-
ited information from the wedding party, he wrote their responses
in the big book. He pointed out to the best man where he should sign
his name, and warned him not to make blots. Then the bridesmaid
wrote her name in a slow and careful hand, the tip of her tongue
showing through her tight lips, anxious and fearful that she wouldn't
do it according to the rules of penmanship she had learned with
great difficulty in school; she had practiced signing her name eighty-
five times during the previous week. The best man gave the priest

half a crown, which the priest, unthankfully, quickly dropped into his trouser pocket as if he were embarrassed by the introduction of Caesar into God's house. Then the priest showed the wedding party out through the back door of the sacristy.

As the Madden brothers led the way along the side of the church to the street, Biddy said to her bridesmaid, "Wasn't it grand when he brought us through the little gate and we had to walk on that beautiful floor with the picture of Jesus in it? I stepped on one of his eyes and nearly died."

At the iron gate in the churchyard wall, the brothers and sisters parted to go back to their respective homes to change into their work clothes.

"I'll see you tonight, Missus Madden," Mick called to his new wife, and they all laughed.

"All right, Mister Madden," Biddy called, and they laughed again. And as she walked away with her sister, Biddy said, "Thank God I'll never be called Swierski again in my life. There's Murphys and Coughlins and Ryans and Traceys, there's Horans and Gormans and Gorrys, and we, of all the people in the whole world, had to be Swierski. Mammy's the only one left now."

The story of how a family bearing the name Swierski ended up living in Gohen has two versions. The Protestant story says the original Swierski had been a Polish bishop who impregnated an entire conventful of nuns, or maybe a dioceseful of nuns, and had to go on the run. His run had ended in Ireland in the eighteen hundreds, and after years of wandering the country the defrocked one had settled down in Gohen, leaving a trail of pregnant women across the continent, each one a day's journey from the next and some within a half-day's walk of each other; two of the women lived fifty yards apart. The Catholic explanation for the Swierskis in their midst was that a Polish pilgrim to Lourdes looking for a cure for forgetfulness, but he took a wrong turn when it was time to get dipped in the frigid baths and kept walking till he ended up in Gohen.

In 1915, the recently married Mick Madden, in desperate need of a job, joined the British army. In 1916, he became part of the soup of Passchendaele, nothing left except his name carved in the Menin Gate in Ypres. For the last thirty-five years, the widow had lived by herself, getting steadily madder as the days slipped by. The childless Biddy had subsisted on her British army pension and the ten shillings a week she earned at the Coughlins' house—according to Eddie-the-cap Biddy didn't get a raise in thirty-five years because she never asked for one.

Biddy Madden was the first to arrive at the Boys' School for the inquest, had stood with her back to the pebble-dashed schoolhouse wall looking at her feet, dressed in her ancient green topcoat and red French beret with its one-inch node erect as always, her socks falling down her thin scabbed shins onto her battered leather boots.

When Spud Murphy arrived with his ass-and-cart full of chairs, he took advantage of the absence of anyone else. "Any chance of an oul ride, Biddy?" he asked, and he pushed aside the flaps of his gabardine topcoat, thrust out his pelvis and rubbed his crotch. "Would you like to see what I have in here, Biddy?" he asked. "Big as a Protestant carrot in October."

Biddy ignored Murphy, pretended he didn't exist, just like she pretended no other people existed either, except in cases of extreme necessity.

Murphy had his hand in his pocket now, stroking himself toward an in-trouser delight. "Come on, Biddy. Give me a look at what you have there," he asked, and at that moment, Missus Moore, the recorder for the inquest, came around the corner with papers in her hands. Tall, straight-standing and big of bust and body, the recorder took in the scene immediately. Like a hen defending her chicks against a rat, she flew into Spud Murphy's face and reduced him to a quailing coward with a verbal barrage fierce enough to stop a whole herd of rats. When Murphy withdrew to the other side of his cart, Missus Moore went over to Biddy. "Did that smelly old goat touch you, Missus Madden?"

Biddy, as if unaware of the drama raging around her, continued to look at her shoes and ignored Missus Moore.

"If that dirt says one more word to you, Missus Madden," Missus Moore said while looking at Murphy, "call me and *I'll* scrape his carrot for him."

One night not long after the inquest, Mister Howard told his wife that Biddy Madden reminded him of a vole in one of his childhood books, a vole who always wore a French beret and very thick glasses, except that the vole did not have as many whiskers as Biddy Madden. His witty wife asked Mister Howard if he would like her to grow whiskers so she could tickle his fancy as she made her way south in the bed. The solicitor told his wife she was depraved. He knocked her on her back on the sofa and pantomimed a rough sexual encounter, which very soon led to the real thing, but without the removal of one piece of clothing by either party. Missus Howard, who loved unexpected sexual surprises, had to squeal through clenched lips lest anyone passing their house should think her husband was beating her to death, to say nothing about terrifying the sleeping children upstairs. Afterwards, while still *in coitus*, Mister Howard wondered aloud about the perpetual erectness of the node on Missus Madden's beret. Missus Howard wondered aloud about the brains of men.

As the vole-like, bereted Biddy Madden was shepherded to the witness chair by Missus Moore, the solicitor felt a sudden surge of pity for the loony, lonely old woman.

CORONER: Please tell us your name, address and occupation, Missus Madden.

WITNESS: (Unintelligible.)

Missus Madden, you will have to speak louder so everyone in the room can hear you.

Brigid Madden, Father, I have my bag and my handkerchief; I have my bag and my handkerchief. It's Mick's pension, I told him.

And your address and occupation, Missus Madden?

Relict of Michael Madden, Father. Relict of Michael. Of Mick. Mick. My Mick in the muck and my father blew up at Mafeking.

Who do you work for, Missus Madden?

Bridie Coughlin, wash the clothes on Monday mornings. Work in the fields and the yard. Look at my hands. Look at my red hands, Mick.

Missus Madden, could you lift up your head so we can all hear what you're saying. Now, the only reason we have asked you to come here is because, as far as we know, you are the last person to have seen Father Coughlin alive. Do you understand that?

All he wanted was my winnings, Father.

Who wanted your winnings, Missus Madden?

Bridie's brother, Father. The soft hands, clean like a nun's fingers, and that's clean, says I to Bridie. What's so funny, what's so funny? Menin Gate.

Keep your head lifted up, Missus Madden. The winnings he wanted, Missus Madden! Tell us what the winnings were.

His name's in a rock at Menin Gate—Michael Madden, Irish Furzaleers. Never found. But he was my Mick, and that's his and no one can take it. It's Mick's. Mick's. Mick's.

The minutes of this inquest will show that the witness appears to be agitated, and that the coroner is doubtful concerning the ability of this witness to remember the events in question. However, in the hope that the witness will settle down, the coroner will continue to question her. Missus Madden, would you please look over here at me?

Everyone will know now, Father, but no differ, the money's all gone, and it can never be took again. He took it—the winnings on the Protestant horse race, and I didn't tell anyone, because everyone . . . Mister Morgan-of-the-shop told Eddie, and Eddie told Bridie, and Bridie told Father Coughlin. But Father Coughlin took the winnings, and now it's all gone. I knew someone would take it. But not Mick's pension. Not Mick's.

How much were the winnings, Missus Madden?

He wanted me to give him a bit of Mick's pension every month, too, Father, but I said, that's Mick's. That's Mick's, I had to shout at him. That's Mick's. Nobody's getting Mick's, not even God. It's Mick's.

Missus Madden, can you remember the last time you saw Father Coughlin?

He kept after me at Bridie's for the winnings with the tea and biscuits. Good teapot. Asking and asking and asking and never stopping, but I stopped him at Mick's pension. That's Mick's I told him, and not even God can have that.

Did Father Coughlin go to your house one night in August, Missus Madden?

He wouldn't go home till I gave him the winnings, Father, and then he wanted a bit of Mick's pension. That's Mick's. That's Mick's. My name would be carved into a rock in India, and Mick's name carved in Menin Gate. They never found him.

How much did you give him, Missus Madden?

The winnings, Father. One blue tenner and a brown fiver, and another tenner I had under a statue of Saint Anthony so there'd always be money in the house, so he'd stop about Mick's pension, and he stuck it in his pocket like it was a bit of a rag. I have my bag, and my handkerchief, I have Mafeking.

Missus Madden, can you remember what time it was when Father Coughlin left your house?

I gave him the winnings and the tenner. The winnings and the tenner. The clock is fast so I'm not late for getting to Bridie's. I said that's Mick's and he wouldn't listen. It's Mick's, I had to shout. It's Mick's.

Please lift up your head, Missus Madden, so we can all hear you. Can you tell us what time it was when he left your house?

He wouldn't do but take Mick away from me, Father, asking me to give him a bit of the pension Mick died getting. I'd get my name carved in a rock in India, and Mick's name in a rock in the Menin Gate.

Did Father Coughlin leave your house before your clock struck twelve?

That day Mick died, I never wound the striker, just the part that makes the hands go by. My Mick and never again was my name Swers—... I won't say it. I won't. I won't. It was terrible the way they laughed in the convent yard.

After Father Coughlin left your house, when was the next time you saw him?

He fell and broke his head, Father, and God got him for trying to take Mick's pension. He's dead. I'm glad he's dead. I'm glad, and I don't care if that's bad. My Mick. He was my Mick. My Mick and no one else's. He was mine.

Did you ever see Father Coughlin again after he left your house with the winnings?

I did, Father.

Where did you see him, Missus Madden?

In the settle bed in the parlor, Father.

Was Father Coughlin alive when you saw him in the settle bed in the parlor?

He was dead with a patch on his eye, Father. He was not a holy priest like they're supposed to be. Blew up in Mafeking.

When was the last time you saw Father Coughlin when he was alive?

I went to bed when it struck twelve in Gohen. He was in the settle bed when I saw him, Father. The Protestants. The Protestants. I have my purse and my handkerchief. What's so funny? What's so funny?

Thank you, Missus Madden for coming here today. Missus Moore you may now return the twenty-five pounds to Missus Madden. I am sorry Missus Madden that we had to keep the money as evidence for a while.

WITNESS: God bless you, Father, God bless you. Mick will God bless you too.

Now, Missus Moore, please show Missus Madden out of the Woodwork Room. The next witness will be Mister Timothy Murphy.

33

In the Sunroom

In which the Howards and Patrick Bracken agree
that obsessiveness is a positive human trait.

"THE MADNESSES THAT CAN take over our lives!" David Samuel
Howard said. "Gathering money from the poor of Gohen
to support a school in India! What was the man thinking? There
must be a weakness in our brains that allows one idea to become
all consuming, that dominates us, enslaves us. Yes, that's the word:
enslaves us."

"But maybe that's an important weakness," Patrick said. "Maybe
obsessiveness is like a spearhead that benefits the entire herd. Take
one obsessed person—say James Watt with steam, and the Industrial
Revolution follows for the rest of us."

"Or your man with hydrophobia, Louis Pasteur," Elsie said, "or
the German with aspirin; or Galileo and his telescope. Imagine all
the people who stood around telling them they were mad, equating
obsessiveness with a mental illness."

Mister Howard said, "I suppose it has good and bad sides,
creative and destructive or just plain nonsensical. I think Father

Coughlin was well-intentioned but unable to see that the poor of Gohen couldn't support his obsession."

"He was blind to the poverty of the people he was begging from."

"I know someone who is obsessive about privileged information," Elsie said.

"I know someone who is obsessed with cracking secrets," Sam said.

"I know someone who, when he was a child, wondered why all the adults were obsessed with telling lies about how Coughlin and Gorman died," Patrick said.

"Patrick! What—?"

"I have the floor, Else, if you please," Sam said. "You will have to rein in your impatience. And I, too, will patiently wait for Patrick to explain himself. There's only one more witness, and he had nothing to add at all. He just wanted to defend his job performance. And by the way, Patrick, Father Jarlath Coughlin's religious order wrote to me and demanded the return of the Martyr's money to their coffers because it was in the possession of Coughlin when he died."

"And?" Patrick asked.

"In thinly disguised polite language I told them to fuck off."

34

Witness:
Mister Murphy

1951

In which Mister Murphy avows that he who
performs the most menial tasks in society has
pride in his work.

SPUD MURPHY, ANXIOUS for the spotlight as much as to defend
his reputation as the punctual ringer of the church bell, strode
toward the witness stand. Every step taken was accompanied by
the sound of water in his Wellingtons squelching from heel to toe
and back again. It appeared he was already in the act of shaping his
body to the contours of the witness chair when he suddenly turned
and went directly to the Coroner's table. He leaned across to Mister
Howard, and the people in the room heard his sibilations, but no one
heard what he said. All the straining ears were suddenly ambushed
by the stern and commanding voice of the Coroner: "Either sit in
the witness chair, Mister Murphy, or go back to your seat. This is
not the place for whispers."

"I've often wondered why it is that the village idiot is always in the
wrong places at all the wrong times," Mister Howard said that night
in response to his wife's enquiry about Spud Murphy's whispering.

"That's what makes them village idiots," Missus Howard said.
"But Spud Murphy isn't a total idiot. . . ." She trailed off because she

realized her husband wasn't looking for answers; he was cogitating aloud. She would have to wait impatiently to find out what Spud had whispered in her husband's ear.

After a long discourse on the community's obligation toward an idiot in its midst, the Coroner stretched out along the sofa and rested his head in his wife's lap. "He wanted to know if he could leave his cap on like the Coughlin man. And the breath of him! It was like I was suddenly swamped in a raging river of rotten eggs."

"Suddenly swamped in a raging river of rotten eggs!" his wife repeated, and she stroked his hair.

"Suddenly swamped," Mister Howard said, and he pushed the back of his head down into his wife's lap.

"And did he make any more of a fuss about the cap?"

"No. I think in his own idiotic way he was trying to make a point, like a greedy child ever vigilant in case a sibling gets more than he gets."

"Ever vigilant," Missus Howard said, and she ran a finger around the outer rim of her husband's ear.

"Why are you mocking me?"

"I'm not. The blood must seep into some remote part of your brain when you lie down. You always sound a little poetic when you're on your back."

"A little poetic?"

"Aye, just like yer man Shakespeare."

"Me and Billy," Mister Howard said. "The bell ringer didn't take off his cap by taking it by the peak and lifting it off. His hand went up one side of his face and suddenly the cap disappeared. It must have been a trick he had practiced. His pate as white as something you'd find under a rock with his couple of clinging wisps stuck on with sweat."

"Clinging wisps!"

"Do you want to know how *you* sound when you're lying on your back?" Mister Howard asked his wife.

CORONER: Please state your name, occupation and address.

WITNESS: Me name is Timotty Murphy. I ring de bell in de church an' draw horseshite fram de Blennerhasset stud to de convent in me assencart. I live in Tile Town, Gohen, an' I want everwan to know—

Mister Murphy, only answer the questions I ask.

Dat hure, de Son of Limpen Lalor, said I'm always late—

Mister Murphy! Please look at me, and remain looking at me until I have finished speaking to—

I haven't bin late wid de seven clock Angelus since dat day me ass started foalen just as I was getten up on me bike to—

Mister Murphy!

Dat's all I have ta say, an dat was de last foal me ass had, an' dat was six years ago.

Mister Murphy!

An ya can stick dat up yer arse, Son of Limpen Lalor, an' smoke it, ya hure. Yer up aten daltar rails ever Sunday an' yer tellen lies about me at de same time. Ya hure.

35

In the Sunroom

In which Sam Howard claims he is being cross-examined by Patrick Bracken and Elsie.

"YOU LOST CONTROL of the Woodwork Room to Murphy," Elsie said. "I did," Sam agreed, "and I lost it until Murphy gave it back to me."

Patrick asked, "As Coroner you ruled that Father Coughlin's death was the result of an accident—you accepted the findings of the jury. But, as a private resident of Gohen did you believe what you heard in the Woodwork Room?"

"Patrick," Sam said, and he paused to choose the proper clothing for his thoughts. "In the matter of Father Coughlin's death, there is only one conclusion—the official one. What I, as an individual, or anyone else believes concerning the matter is not germane. And as the coroner in the case, it would be unconscionable of me to indicate in any way that I did not believe the jury's finding was correct."

Silence dropped into the sunroom and lingered. Patrick looked over at Elsie, and she answered him by raising her eyebrows. She inclined her head to her husband and slowly lowered the lid of her right eye.

"Sam, did you know Deirdre Hyland?" Patrick asked.

"Patrick," Mister Howard said, "you are treading into the area of client-solicitor privilege where you have no right to—"

Missus Howard impatiently snatched the conversation away from her husband. "Deirdre Hyland was the Catholic with the accent," she said. "And yes, *I* knew Deirdre Hyland, Patrick. What did you want to know?"

"Now, Else," Sam said.

"*Now* yourself, Sam," Elsie said. "You just sit there and listen. As they say in American pictures, Patrick, 'Shoot!' Ask me anything."

"Did you know that Deirdre Hyland was a friend of Kevin Lalor's for a while?" Patrick asked.

"Of course we did. Everyone in Gohen, Catholic and Protestant, were holding their breaths waiting for the banns to be read."

"Did you ever hear what happened, why they didn't get married?"

"Yes. As a matter of fact, I believe Sam and I were the first to know she had dumped the Civil Servant."

"Now, Else."

"*Now* yourself, Sam. *You* take care of *your* conscience, and I'll take care of mine. Deirdre Hyland came to this house on the day before the Coughlin inquest and demanded that she be allowed to take the witness stand."

"Else!" Sam said, as if he were telling a cat to get off the furniture—had told it a thousand times before, and knew the cat would ignore him.

Elsie continued, "Deirdre Hyland said in my presence in this house that Father Coughlin's death had not been an accident at all. That's why she wanted to be a witness. She said that Eddie-the-cap had killed his brother-the-priest by knocking him off his bike with a rope tied across the road."

Mister Howard creaked his chair urgently. "No, Else!" he sternly said. "No, Else. Let me answer Patrick's questions. He didn't come to hear you clucking in your gossipy way."

"Clucking! Well, excuse me, mister-who-loves-his-bit-of-gossip-like-anyone-else! Patrick, my husband loves to listen to gossip, but he never repeats it. Sometimes he knows stuff I've been dying to hear for weeks."

Sam rolled on over his wife's sarcasm. "Deirdre Hyland never said that anyone killed anyone. I cut her off and told her I didn't want to hear what she had to say."

"I know you cut her off, Sam," Elsie said, "but not before she said, Eddie Coughlin killed his brother—"

"That's not what she said, Else, and you know it. I shut her up the second she said '*Eddie Coughlin killed his—*.'"

"But she was going to say—"

"It doesn't matter what she was going to say, Else. The thing—"

"Even though she didn't say it, Sam, you know and I know that she was going to say that Eddie Coughlin killed his—"

"I never heard her saying that Eddie Coughlin killed his brother, and neither did you."

"For Christ's sake, Sam! Look at the context. She was talking about Father Coughlin's death, and her next sentence was, 'Eddie Coughlin killed his . . .' She wasn't going to say Eddie Coughlin killed his chickens, because she wasn't talking about chickens; she was talking about Father Coughlin." Elsie slapped her thighs in exasperation.

Sam Howard sighed and sat back in his chair. "I am not conceding the point to you, Else. We did not hear what she didn't say. And she certainly never mentioned anything in this house about a rope across Sally Hill. That was something you heard in the town later on."

Missus Howard seemed to have tired of the point, waved her husband's legalistic brain away with the back of her hand. She turned to Patrick. "Imagine, the only way Eddie-the-cap believed he could get the Martyr's money back was to ambush his brother in the dark. He could not approach Jarlath-the-priest on the subject, because of Jarlath's haughty and dismissive ways, and in his isolated way of thinking, Eddie was unable to come up with a strategy other than the rope in the dark."

"It would appear that Jarlath was beyond hearing anything his siblings had to offer," Patrick said.

As if his attention had been absent from this brief conversation between Elsie and Patrick, Sam said, "Deirdre Hyland! She was a self-righteous woman. Do you know what D. H. Lawrence said about self-righteous women, Patrick?"

Missus Howard did not give her husband time to quote his quote. She quoted it herself in the tired voice a prisoner uses to tell his interrogator his story for the fortieth time.

"'The self-righteous woman in her martyrdom is a terrible thing to behold, but every self-righteous woman ought to be martyred.' Sam says that to me every time he thinks I'm being self-righteous."

"That's why she knows it by heart," Mister Howard said.

"He says it when he knows I'm right and he's wrong and won't admit it. There's nothing as self-righteous and as sure of his place in the universe as a man in a uniform, be he judge or a coroner," Missus Howard said dismissively.

Mister Howard would not be dismissed. "Self-righteousness in anyone else is objectivity in a coroner," he said without any trace of irony. "Deirdre Hyland was so self-righteous that she never met the man who was perfect enough for her. She remained unmarried all her life and was found dead in her own bed after not being missed for a week." Sam leaned forward in his chair. "Since Else is inclined to color the facts, I will tell you about Deirdre Hyland coming to see me. She wouldn't come in when I asked her. She wanted to speak to me outside."

"No, Sam. I told you this before," Else said as if addressing a refractive child. "That was Eddie Coughlin-with-the-cap and the mange. Deirdre Hyland came into the house, and I gave her tea. And that accent! She sounded like she was enduring an itch in a place she couldn't scratch in company. She held her little finger out when she lifted her cup."

"You're right, Else," the husband conceded. "I remember the little finger too. And it was the only time you ever used that tea set—your grandmother's wedding present, with all those fat Japanese men in their bathrobes in red and gold and black."

"No one could drink out of those cups without spilling the tea. They have six sides."

"Hexagons, and that's the only reason why Else gave her tea in the first place, Patrick."

Missus Howard looked over at Patrick and smiled. "As the man said, Fury finds its own weapons."

"But what had *you* to be furious about, Else?"

"Oh, Sam! You're getting to be such an old fogey. I told you all this before, and you must have heard me telling it a hundred times to others." She turned to Patrick. "That one was so prim and proper it was only a matter of time before someone spilled something on her. Every woman in the town was furious at her, not just me. It just happened that I was in the right place at the right time. You can never get rid of a tea stain. The Civil Servant was lucky he never married her. Better a life of loneliness and mild insanity than married to a yoke like that. 'Yoke' is a Catholic word. In looks, Deirdre Hyland could have competed with our minister's wife—what was her name?—Libby Metcalf. But Libby was down to earth; no need for an accent there."

Patrick turned to Sam. "Knowing what you knew from Deirdre Hyland must have made you doubtful about what you heard in the Woodwork Room, Sam?"

"As the Coroner, the only thing I knew about the death of Father Coughlin was what I heard at the inquest. I could not bring anything else into the room with me. The jury heard the evidence. The jury reached a decision of accidental death. I was a glorified referee making sure that the legalities were observed."

"But you were the one who asked the questions."

"Meaning?"

"You had control of the answers."

"Of course not."

"The witnesses could not answer the questions you didn't ask," Elsie said.

"Did you believe what Deirdre Hyland told you, Sam?"

"I'm being cross-examined. That is a moot question, Patrick. When I realized she was passing on secondhand information, I stopped her, wouldn't let her talk about the case at all. Besides saying the death was not accidental, all I heard her saying was, 'Eddie Coughlin killed *his*.'"

"You still heard her saying, 'Eddie Coughlin killed his,' and, as Elsie said, she wasn't talking about chickens at the time—she was talking about the Coughlins."

"Patrick, I have always maintained a wall between my professional and personal self."

"If you don't mind, Sam," Patrick said, "during the inquest you asked Kevin Lalor if anyone came along while he was waiting by the corpse on Sally Hill. Kevin said that Simon Peter Lamb passed by on his way to get the sergeant. He didn't answer your question fully, and you didn't ask him again."

"And," Elsie said, "it was obvious at the inquest that Eddie-the-cap was very upset about his brother's strong-armed begging, and it was obvious that Father Coughlin all but stole the money from Missus Madden."

"Hold on a minute, now," Mister Howard said, and there was a flash in his old eyes.

"But isn't it possible that Deirdre Hyland's gossip did manage to seep through the barrier you maintained between your personal and professional life? Perhaps you did not press Kevin Lalor when he didn't answer your question because your sympathies—"

Mister Howard sat forward onto the edge of his chair, his hands on the arms of the wicker chair as if he was ready to propel himself forward. "Patrick," he said, "I never let other people's stories—"

Patrick interrupted. "Sam, it was other people's stories . . ."

36

Lies the Mushroom Pickers Told

1951

In which Mikey Lamb and his best friend, Barlow
Bracken, learn from experience and observation
that adults do not always tell the truth.

I T WAS OTHER PEOPLE'S STORIES that motivated Mikey Lamb and
Barlow Bracken to get out of their shared bed at five o'clock
every morning during the mushroom season, to gallop through the
misty, hauntingly quiet morning fields, swinging their one-gallon
once-upon-a-time sweet-cans by their wire handles. But on this, the
twenty-fourth day of August, with two mushrooms in each can,
the boys' hopes of ever finding the fungal El Dorado were fading.
Not once had they found a trace of the manna-like harvests which
other people claimed to have reaped in the past. The boys had even
heard stories of mushrooms growing in such profusion on August
nights that at first glance it appeared snow had fallen.

But now there were signs that the enthusiasm which had propelled them out of bed during the first half of August was waning.
No longer did they line their cans with soft hay before leaving the
farmyard to keep the mushrooms from bruising; no longer did they
excite each other with imaginings of such harvests to be reaped that
they would have extras to sell and Barlow would have more money

for his mother. There had been a time when they had galloped out of the farmyard, chased each other through the damp grass to distant fields, vaulted over gates on the run and urgently helped each other through fences of barbed wire as they raced to get to the fields with fantastic mushroom reputations.

Now, downcast under the weight of the accumulating disappointments, the boys trudged through the grass, leaving two weaving trails in the fresh dew behind them as they aimlessly and unexpectedly veered back and forth in their search. In silent frustration, Mikey swung his can at a tall thistle and sent pieces of purple spikes into the sky. While the battered flowers were still in the air, the sound of the seven o'clock Angelus came whispering across the fields from Gohen. In more enthusiastic times, Mikey had believed he could see the soft gongs vibrating in mild waves across the grass, while imagining Spud Murphy swinging up off the floor in the belfry on the heavy bell rope, his Wellingtons beginning to slip off by the time he landed again. But the music had faded and the Angelus bell was merely a signal that the boys should begin heading homeward.

Barlow stopped walking and looked at Mikey for direction.

"Will we give Doul Yank's Back Batens a try on the way home?" Mikey suggested.

He waited for Barlow to join him before heading for the hedge of whitethorn bushes on the far side of the field. The last stroke of the Angelus was still trembling in the clean morning air, and Mikey knew that Spud Murphy would be tying the bell rope into its iron ring on the wall out of the reach of children. The bell-ringer had told Mikey that one morning he had found so many mushrooms in Doul Yank's fields he had to take off his topcoat to make it into a sack; that he dropped so many mushrooms from the bulging sack on the way home, he had to go back and pick them up to keep anyone else from following the trail to the secret place where they had grown; and that the dropped mushrooms alone had filled two big buckets. When the wide-eyed Mikey repeated the story to his father, Simon Peter said, "Spud Murphy! That eegit doesn't know the difference between brussels sprouts and mushrooms." But despite his father's observation,

Mikey had led Barlow through all Doul Yank's fields every morning in hopes of finding Murphy's manna.

Now, they reached the whitethorn hedge, and the boys used a moldering, ivy-covered tree stump as a stile and the three rows of barbed wire stapled to its side as steps. When they jumped down into the Back Batens, they stood there, Barlow again waiting for directions. Barlow's hesitancy only made Mikey feel more despondent. In the corner of his eye he saw Barlow shifting his feet in the grass as if he were bored.

In the end, Mikey swung his can at the yellow head of a chest-high ragwort and said, "Come on. We'll just walk straight across to Sally Hill." He indicated the direction with a swing of his can. "We'll get out on Glower Road and go home that way. I'm hungry, and I'm tired of looking for mushrooms."

Side by side and in silence they started across the wide field. There was an unspoken understanding between the boys that they would not stray far from each other in the early morning stillness. Even though they tried not to believe them, the stories they had heard about strange goings-on in morning fields kept their anxiety on a low simmer.

Without even looking up, Mikey swung his can at the tall weeds in his path. Barlow kept his eyes on his boots gliding through the dew-wet grass; saw with every step taken how the seeds of weeds and grasses were moved from one spot to another on the dripping toes of his borrowed Wellingtons. He was startled when he heard Mikey loudly declaring, "Why would he have to go and tell lies about it?"

"Who told lies?" Barlow asked, just above a whisper.

"Spud Murphy, telling me he had to make a sack out of his topcoat, there were so many mushrooms." In his effort not to give away their presence to lurking unknowns, the fierceness in Mikey's whisper exaggerated his whistling esses.

"Paul Butler, too," Barlow offered. "He said he found buckets of them, and so did Mister Gorman."

"Doul Yank!" Mikey hissed in derision. "They *all* tell mushroom lies—Paul Butler, Spud Murphy and Doul Yank. Mushroom lies are worse than fish lies." Even though Kevin Lalor had told colorful mushroom stories too, he was excluded from Mikey's angry list of liars. "We're the first people out in the fields every morning, and we've never found what they say they found."

"And as well as that," Barlow said, "we never see anyone else out looking, so how can they find all those mushrooms when they're at home in bed?"

"So many mushrooms it looked like it snowed in the night!" Mikey said with as much grown-up indignation as he could muster. "That's what Spud Murphy said. I think my father was right—Spud Murphy *is* a bit of an eegit."

"Spud Murphy's my father's first cousin," Barlow said. There was no defensiveness in his voice. "Daddy said Spud's always telling stories about doing things that can't be done, like going to Marbra and back in his assencart in an hour because the wind was in his back coming and going."

"The wind wouldn't make any ass go quicker!" Mikey said. "I hope they're not all codding us—Doul Yank and Paul Butler and Spud Murphy. I hope they're not, because I'd hate them for doing that, getting us up at five to have a laugh. Some old people think it's funny to tell tall stories and swear they're true."

The boys came to one of the narrow drains dissecting the field at regular intervals and, like a pair of dancers performing an old routine, they leaped across without breaking their stride.

"And the stories about bushes moving around when they think no one's looking—the ones out in the fields by themselves. How do you think they get there, he asked me, Spud did, and I said they grow there, and he looked at me like I was a thick. He said they move out of the hedges the minute the sun comes up, and if you see them moving they'll run after you and squeeze you into themselves with their branches and suck the life out of you with their thorns, and what's left of you blows away like a piece of old newspaper in the wind."

"People tell him real daft things because he believes them," Barlow said. "Spud thinks people find babies under the rhubarb in the convent garden. He said he catches goldfinches by just holding out his hand and saying chuck-chuck."

During his first days living at the Lambs' house, Barlow had learned the most important rule of the open countryside: when near a thick hedge, don't talk loudly because someone might be on the other side. As the boys approached the sally bushes at the edge of the Back Batens, they stopped talking. Mikey pushed aside the thin, big-leafed branches and led the way to the barbed-wire fence on the other side of the bushes. When he emerged he stood to one side, grabbed the top strand on the smooth place between two barbs and lifted. Barlow pushed down the middle wire and climbed out through the hole they had made. But as Barlow turned back to lift the top strand for Mikey, he whispered, "There's someone on Sally Hill."

"Who?" Mikey whispered back.

"I don't know. There's two of them, and one's lying on the road."

"Quick, get back in the bushes," Mikey said as if warning of an imminent tiger pounce.

Standing side by side in the bushes, Mikey asked, "What's the man lying down for?"

"I don't know. The other one was looking down at him."

"Maybe there was a terrible fight." This speculation raised the boys' fear another notch.

"Come on, we'll sneak back through the bushes," Barlow said, and he grabbed Mikey by the arm.

"No, don't stir. They'll hear the bushes and find us and be terrible cross with us for seeing them."

It took a while for Mikey to work up the courage to bend down, place the mushroom can on the ground and make a peephole in the leaves in front of his face. And there the Civil Servant was with his hands behind his back and his face bent toward a one-legged man lying on the ground. "It's Kevin. But it can't be. Kevin's on his way to Gohen on his bike. And the other lad has only one leg."

Barlow shook Mikey's arm. "There's a bike coming the other way," he warned. And Mikey heard familiar rattles and the sound of a misaligned wheel rhythmically rubbing against a front brake. "That's Daddy's bike," Mikey whispered. "But it can't be Daddy! He's doing the milking." When the two of them turned and made another peephole, there was Simon Peter Lamb pedaling so hard he could have been on his way to get the fire brigade in Gohen to come and put out his burning hayrick.

They followed the bike through the leaves, and when Mister Lamb ran out of steam halfway up Sally Hill, he hopped off his bike. He didn't look at Kevin Lalor and the cripple on the road—but kept his face turned away. With as much speed as was left in his leg muscles, he pushed the bike to the top of the hill, remounted and pedaled off toward Gohen. But, clearly and distinctly, the boys had heard what Simon Peter Lamb said as he passed Kevin Lalor and the other man: "I hate the sight of a corpse."

Mikey and Barlow looked at each other, eyes enlarged. "A corpse," Mikey whispered, using hardly any air to shape the words. "A corpse is a dead man."

The boys stared unblinking at each other for a long time. Then Barlow indicated he wanted to whisper in Mikey's ear. "Come on back to the Back Batens." Gently but firmly, he put pressure on Mikey's arm.

Mikey put his mouth to Barlow's ear. "This is old people stuff we're not supposed to see. If Kevin finds us, he'll have to kill us."

This piece of puerile reasoning glued the boys firmly to the ground. After a long time, Barlow opened up the peephole again. Cheek to jowl, the boys looked out and saw Kevin Lalor still in the same position, still holding his hands behind his back like a pig jobber at the fair trying to look like a businessman.

"I thought a corpse would be all terrible and rotting," Mikey hissed.

"Look," Barlow excitedly said, too loudly, "there's someone moving in the bushes on the far side of the road near Kevin. Will I shout to warn him?"

"No, Kevin will know we're here."

As they watched, a man emerged from the trembling bushes, the peak of his cap low on his forehead.

"That's Eddie Coughlin." Mikey's whisper was still on his lips when Coughlin spoke. Clearly and distinctly, the two boys heard what he said.

"Was there a rope, Kevin?" Coughlin called, and Kevin Lalor jerked around as if he'd been startled.

"Jesus Christ, Eddie. What are you doing here? You frightened the shite out of me."

"Bridie's in a terrible state. Was there a rope?" Coughlin persisted.

"Jesus, you shouldn't creep up on a fellow like that, especially when there's a corpse around."

"Did you see a rope?" Coughlin asked again.

"Of course I saw a rope. How could I miss it? I took it off and pissed against the tree to make an excuse for the grass you flattened when you were tying it. The rope's under a furze out there in Lamb's field. Go on home, Eddie."

"Did you know it was mine?"

"I thought it was, but I was hoping it wasn't."

"How did you know?"

"It was a matter of deduction, Eddie."

Silent behind a bush on Sally Hill, Mikey muttered, "Sherlock Holmes," and he remembered a fox's tail sticking out from under a bush. He farted loudly, and Barlow poked him with his elbow. "They'll hear you," he whispered.

Eddie Coughlin said, "I only wanted to get the Martyr's money back, but I didn't want him to know who took it. I thought he'd fall off the bike in the dark and that he wouldn't know it was me who was robbing him. But he must've fell wrong when he ran into the rope. Come here for a minute, Kevin." Coughlin gestured with his right hand, something clutched in his fingers. "I nearly died when I was getting the money out of his pocket, and I couldn't feel him breathing. I got such a fright I ran away and forgot the rope."

"Eddie Coughlin hung the corpse," Mikey deducted aloud, neither his lips nor his tongue moving. Barlow Bracken heard only the sound of a sigh.

"You'd better go home, Eddie," Kevin Lalor said, as he walked toward Coughlin. "Simon Peter's gone to Gohen for the sergeant, and besides that, someone might see you."

"There's no one to see me on Glower Road at this hour of the morning."

"Mikey Lamb and Barlow Bracken are out looking for mushrooms every morning at five o'clock since the first day of August."

At the sound of their names, the boys looked at each other as if they had caught their first glimpse of their personal gallows, two nooses swaying in the breeze.

Coughlin, reacting to Lalor's warning, stepped back out of sight, but he wasn't finished talking. "Bridie got a terrible brain wave in the middle of the night and said if I gave the money back to the Martyr everyone would know where I got it. She woke me up to tell me, and her teeth chatting like a dying dog's."

Kevin Lalor walked into the roadside grass and stood at the bushes where Eddie Coughlin had disappeared into the leaves.

"Here, put this in his pocket—the breast pocket in his short coat." Coughlin's hand and arm came out of the bushes. "What et his leg?"

Lalor took the money and looked at the body on the road. "Nothing ate his leg, Eddie," he said. "It's bent back under him."

"Bridie's in a terrible state," Coughlin said. "But to tell you the truth, I can't feel sorry for Jarlath. He wasn't nice at all to Bridie, nor me for that matter. Do you think they'll know I did it, even though I didn't mean to kill him?"

"Without the rope it looks like he just fell off the bike," Lalor offered reassuringly. "You'd better get on home, Eddie, and get the cows milked before the sergeant comes looking to tell you the bad news."

"Bridie's in a terrible state," Coughlin said again, "but I don't think it's because he's dead. She was terrible upset about him going after the Martyr's money, not to mention the way he talked to her in the hospital when he had the appendix. She begged him not to ask the Martyr for her winnings, but nothing would do but for him to go. He changed terrible since he was home the last time, got terrible mean, and nothing we did was good enough for him. He wouldn't be seen in the motor with us; we were too smelly and dirty for him."

Kevin Lalor walked back to the corpse and bent down to put the Martyr's money in the pocket of the suit jacket.

"Kevin's touching the corpse," Barlow said in alarm, and Mikey poked him into silence with his elbow.

When the Civil Servant straightened up, he said, "You'd better go on home, Eddie, or the two of us will get in trouble. Mikey and the Bracken chap could show up any minute and see you, and then the cat's out of the bag."

"Jeepers," Mikey whispered.

"Bridie's afraid they'll find out I did it and think I did it on—"

Kevin Lalor strode back to Coughlin's hiding place while Coughlin was talking. With a fierceness that sent a shiver up and down Mikey's spine, the Civil Servant said, "Eddie, fuck off. Go home. I might risk going to jail for you because you're unlucky, but sure as hell, I'm not going to jail for you for being stupid. If you're not gone in one second, I'm going to get the rope and tie it back where I found it."

"It's only Bridie—"

"Fuck off home, Eddie. Now!" the Civil Servant said in a voice that Mikey did not know he had.

The boys saw the bushes moving in front of Lalor, and then there was silence. With a flushed face, Kevin returned to the corpse and stood there looking down, his hands behind his back again.

In Mikey's ear, Barlow Bracken whispered, "Come on, Mikey. I'm afraid."

"I'm too afraid to move."

"If we go now, he won't hear us."

"All right," Mikey whispered. While he was bent down picking up his can, Kevin Lalor called out, "Hello," and Mikey drew in his breath sharply, catastrophic expectations flooding his face wetly. He *knew* Kevin Lalor was about to lunge through the bushes to rip them apart before they could swear never to tell anyone what they had seen.

But the expected did not happen, and when Mikey straightened up without his can, he peeped through the new hole Barlow had made in the sally leaves. On the crest of Sally Hill, each standing beside his bike, were Mikey's father and Sergeant Morrissey. Clearly and distinctly, the boys heard what was said.

"Now, boy, you stay here with your bike, and don't be ruining the scene of the crime, if there was a crime," the sergeant said, his long-suppressed Cork accent leaking into his phrases. "I don't want any smart bollicks from Dublin coming in his motor car with his little suitcase and telling me I didn't perserve the scene."

The sergeant, stepping high through the long grass beside the road, pushed his bike over to the fence and propped it against the wire. He shook the bike twice to make sure it wouldn't fall and sent vibrations down the wire, causing Mikey and Barlow to clutch each other in terror as the strands of wire beside them danced in their staples.

The sergeant, trouser legs pulled up and exposing his white shins above the tops of his black boots, stepped back through the grass onto the road. Like a duck stretching after a long sit-down, he stuck each foot out behind and shook the dew off his boots. Then he leaned down and brushed at the trouser legs with his hand.

"I have the cows to milk, and I hate the sight of a corpse," Mister Lamb said.

"Hold your horses for a few minutes, Mister Lamb," the sergeant commanded magisterially, "the Law might be needing you." Without looking at the corpse, but circling widely around it, Sergeant Morrissey stepped down Sally Hill and confronted Kevin Lalor.

As if he had practiced the move in front of a mirror until he had developed it into a tone-setting gesture, Morrissey unbuttoned the breast pocket of his uniform and extracted his notebook. He opened it to the first page, took a pencil from the same pocket, looked at its point and pressed it against his tongue. He rebuttoned the pocket flap, pushed the stiff, shiny peak of his hat one inch up his forehead, looked over the top of his notebook and said, "Tell me your name, Mister Lalor."

"Joan of Arc, Joe. Who the hell do you think I am?"

"For the sake of the Law, Mister Lalor, tell me your name."

"Kevin Lalor, for Christ's sake." Mikey had never seen Kevin so impatient before. Maybe he was still cross at Eddie Coughlin.

The sergeant wrote, then asked, "Were you the first person on the scene, Mister Lalor?"

"I don't know, but there was no one else around when I got here."

"At what time was that boy, Mister Lalor?" The Cork idiom and singsong cadences had been ridiculed so loudly by amused schoolchildren that the sergeant had tried to bury what was natural to his speech patterns within his first weeks of coming to Gohen.

"Spud Murphy was ringing the seven o'clock Angelus," Kevin Lalor said.

"Did you recognize the body, Mister Lalor?"

"Yes, I did."

"And whose body do you think it is, Mister Lalor?"

"Josef Stalin. Can't you look at the body yourself, Joe, and see it's Father Coughlin?"

"Father Coughlin!" the boys in the bushes echoed in unison, but neither heard the other.

"Everything in its own good time, Mister Lalor. Everything in its own good time. In the Law we have procedures to follow." The sergeant wrote, the tip of his tongue sticking through his lips. "Mister Lalor, since you discovered the body have you seen any other person in the vicinity?"

"Simon Peter went up the hill on his way to get you."

"And how would Mister Lamb have known to come for me unless he had been in the vicinity in the first place?" The sergeant lowered his head until his eyes were peering at Lalor from just below the rim of the peak of the cap. He was a cat tensed to spring.

"When I came across the body, I went back to Simon Peter's house and asked him to go for you."

The tension fell out of the sergeant's poise. "So, Mister Lalor, you left the body by itself for the time it took you to ride your bike to Mister Sheep's house and back again?"

Kevin Lalor did not respond to this question, and the sergeant tried to make himself clearer. "Did you leave the body by itself while you went for Mister Sheep, Mister Lalor?"

In the bushes, Mikey whispered, "Sheep?" and did not know he whispered.

"Oh, for God's sake, Joe," Kevin Lalor burst out, "will you stop your old shite! How the hell could I go for Simon Peter and stay here with the body at the same time. Do you think I'm Padre Pio? Or maybe you think I brought the body on the bike with me."

"He called him Joe again," Mikey said inside his head.

"You are speaking to the Law, Mister Lalor," the sergeant said sternly. "So I'll take it the answer is yes, you left the body by itself while you went for Mister Lamb."

Simon Peter Lamb said from the top of the hill, "Can I go on home now, Joe, to do the milking?"

"Mister Lamb, the Law will be needing you," the sergeant snapped. "Now, Mister Lalor, did you touch any of the devidence?"

"What evidence, Joe?"

"Did you touch the body?"

"Why would I touch the body, Joe?" Lalor asked.

Lalor's irritating informality in the very formal atmosphere which the sergeant was trying to establish caused the lawman to completely lose his suppressive grip on the singsongedness of his accent. "I don't know why you'd touch the body boy. All I know is I have to have answers for the bollickses from Dublin when they come to examine the scene."

In the bushes, Barlow nudged Mikey. "We saw Kevin touching the corpse."

"Why will anyone have to come from Dublin to examine the scene?" Lalor asked.

"The Law says the superintendent's the one who says there'll be an inquest or not, and when he gets here he's going to ask me what I'm asking you, and he'll ate the face off me if I can't tell him the answers."

"When the superintendent comes, he's going to say this man fell off his bike and broke his head and that'll be the end of it. Any eegit could see—"

"Wait now, Mister Lalor. Hold your horses there boy. What bike, and how do you know the man broke his head and you after saying you never touched the body."

"Oh, Jesus Christ, Joe. The man's bike is at the foot of the hill in the grass, and if you look at the head you can see it's as flat as a pancake unless it's lying in a hole, and there is no hole there because I've walked up this hill every morning of my life and I know where there's no holes."

"Kevin cursed at the sergeant," Mikey said, without moving his tongue and without bringing his open lips together. But not even Barlow, whose ear was inches from Mikey's ear, heard him.

"Keep your shirt on, mister. I'll remind you that you're assisting the Law with its enquiries. And now, Mister Lalor, you will point out to the Law the injuries on the victim's head, but be very careful; don't touch devidence."

For the first time since his arrival on Sally Hill, the sergeant looked directly at the body. "I didn't know he'd only one leg," he exclaimed, his control over his accent in total shambles. "And I've seen him often on his bike. Like your own oul lad. Isn't that a curious thing?"

"The leg's under him," Lalor said. He looked up at Mister Lamb, almost imperceptibly shook his head slowly and turned his eyes to the sky. Simon Peter waved and did a tiny dance in the dust.

"How do you know that, Mister Lalor?"

"Any eegit . . . Look at it, Joe, up there at the crotch"—Lalor pointed—"you can see the leg is bent back, and the foot is under his arse."

"So it is boy. That must have hurt like hell." For several moments the sergeant contemplated the pain caused by such twisting of the limb, his hand slowly moving on his face as if feeling for missed stubble. "And will you look at that yoke on his face! In the name of Jesus Christ, what is it? It looks like a big bird shite."

"It's his eye," Lalor said.

"How would you know that?"

"If you look higher up his face, you will see there is no eye in one socket. Therefore, it is reasonable to deduce that the mess on his cheek is the remains of the missing eye."

Mikey breathed, "Holmes."

Lalor's sarcasm was lost on the sergeant. "Were the crows at him when you got here, Mister Lalor?"

"No, Joe, there were no crows."

"Then how did the eye get out of its socket if there was no crows?"

"Maybe he hit his head so hard on the ground that the eye came shooting out."

"In the name of the Sacred Heart of Jesus!" the sergeant exclaimed.

In the bushes, Barlow felt his two eyes with his fingertips.

"I never saw the likes of this before. Will you look at his empty eye-hole? And what did you say about the head, Mister ah . . . Lalor?" The two men moved to the top of the corpse. "Just make sure, boy, you don't touch anything," the sergeant warned.

Lalor went down on his hunkers and the sergeant was forced to follow, his knees loudly creaking. Lalor pointed. "Look how flat the back of the head is, and look at all the blood that seeped down under the neck."

"But you said there's a hole there in the road, Mister Lalor, and the head's lying in it."

"No, Joe, I said there's *no* hole there, that the back of the head got smashed in when the man fell, and that's why it *looks* like it's lying in a hole."

"But look!" The sergeant pointed. "Look at them footprints at this side of the head, and you said there were no crows around to pick out his eye. There's devidence!"

"Those are paw prints, Joe, not birds' claw prints."

"How do you know about footprints, Mister Lalor?"

"Any eegit will tell you a dog or a fox or a badger made those prints, not a bird."

"I'm not so sure about that." The sergeant looked up the hill at Simon Peter Lamb. "Mister Lamb," he called, "come down here for a minute and help the Law, and I don't want to hear another word about the way you hate a corpse."

"Aw, Joe, you know I hate having to look at a fecking corpse," Mister Lamb said.

"My father cursed," Mikey said, but only he heard himself.

"Mister Lamb, the Law demands that you come down here to examine these footprints and tell the Law what they are before

Doctor Roberts gets here and ploughs around through devidence in his big boots."

Sighing loudly in protest, Simon Peter gently laid his bike down on the road. Holding his hand in front of his face, as if warding off a blinding sun, he came down the hill. Even as he went down on his hunkers, he kept the hand between his eyes and the corpse.

The sergeant pointed toward the paw prints. "In your opinion, Mister Lamb, what made them footprints?"

"A badger, Joe," Simon Peter said. He stood up and headed back up the hill.

"How can you be so sure of that and you only gave them a quick look?" the sergeant called after him. "Maybe they're crows' footprints."

Kevin Lalor answered for Simon Peter. "For someone who's lived in the country all his life, Joe, knowing paw prints from claw prints is as simple as knowing your arse from your elbow, that is if you *do* know your arse from your elbow in the first place." Lalor stood up.

The sergeant tried to imitate Kevin's no-hands ascent out of his hunkered position, but his knees were not able for the pressure and he toppled forward. His hands landed on the chest of the corpse, and the corpse made a sound like the sound an old man shamelessly makes while delivering himself of a cubic foot of gas.

"Jesus Christ," the sergeant said, and as he pushed himself up he exerted more pressure on the body. The corpse made a verbal sound of relief. "Aaaah."

"Did you hear that?" Mikey asked, but his voice was only heard within his own skull.

"Be careful not to disturb devidence there, Joe," Simon Peter Lamb called down from the hill.

"Now, men, no matter who asks you, be it the superintendent himself or anyone else, don't tell him I touched devidence."

"Can I go home to milk the cows now, Joe?" Simon Peter had retrieved his bicycle and was pointedly poised to take off, his foot on the pedal.

"While this investigation is still going on, Mister Lamb, the Law might have to call on you for assistance. Your missus will know what to do with the cows. Now, Mister Lalor, what were you saying about the bike?"

Lalor pointed. "The bike's down there in the grass on the right, Joe."

To the boys in the bushes, it seemed that the Civil Servant was pointing directly at them. Quietly, as silently as a great-grandfather rat slipping into black water, the boys withdrew their hands and let their peephole fill up with leaves. They held their breaths against imminent exposure, but once again they had not been discovered.

"Show me exactly where you found the bike, Mister Lalor. This is very important to the case," the sergeant said, and he waited for Lalor to accompany him. Shoulder to shoulder they came down the hill, and stood opposite the spot where Mikey and Barlow were trying to be silent in the sallies. Mikey made a sound like a hen sighing in her sleep.

"There it is. . . there," Kevin said.

Through the tiny spaces in the leaves the boys saw the two men outlined, shaped like standing-up bears, one thin, one stout, ten feet away. With mouths like the mouths of dead fish, with eyes hooded like the eyes of a hunting cat trying to make itself invisible, with chests rising and falling silently, the boys struggled to contain their expanding terror.

"That's a new Raleigh bike," Sergeant Morrissey said. "I wonder did it get damaged when it crashed?"

There was silence.

"Did you touch the bike, Mister Lalor?"

"No, Joe, I did not touch the bike."

The sergeant pulled up the legs of his trousers and stepped through the wet grass, putting his feet down as carefully as a gleaning turkey in wheaten stubble. He moved to within five feet of the boys and bent down to examine the bike. "Brand new bike," he said. "Not a scratch on it, nor any muck or cow dung either. It's a peculiar man that keeps his bike in this condition, always worrying it with a rag. It doesn't look like it's damaged at all. I'm on the lookout for a second-hand bike for one of my lads. I'll have to ask Eddie the brother about that. He must have come straight off onto his head, and then the bike kept on coming and it never got a scratch. Would you think that, Mister Lalor?" But he was not asking a question, only demonstrating his own powers of deduction.

The sergeant stood up and stepped closer to the boys and said, "The first mug of tea in the morning always runs through me like a dose of jollop." The fumbling silhouette of the stout bear moved between the spaces in the leaves in front of the boys' faces. Then they heard water hissing, smelled the odor of fresh man urine. The hissing stopped, and the silhouette shook its shoulders, fumbled again and the two shadowy figures went away, moved back up the hill and out of sight.

The boys reopened their leafy peephole.

As Kevin Lalor walked back to the corpse behind the sergeant, he waved in the air to get Mister Lamb's attention. "Did I just hear a cuckoo, Simon Peter?" he called. He pointed to his temples with his index fingers and imitated the action of tightening loose screws.

"Ah, sure I've been hearing a cuckoo all morning since I went in to get Joe there," Simon Peter called back.

In the bushes, Barlow nudged Mikey with his elbow and said, "If the sergeant catches them, he'll—"

"The doctor should be here any minute," the sergeant said, and, as if Sergeant Morrissey were a puppeteer, Doctor Roberts's black pony came trotting around the corner. The doctor, as usual, was sitting too close to the back of the trap, causing the bellyband to snap against the pony's belly just behind her front legs. Over the years, the continuous snapping had caused the pony to develop a personality every bit as abrasive as her master's.

With angry ears laid back, the pony came to a stop on top of the hill beside Mister Lamb. It promptly nipped him painfully on the upper arm. Acting on an instinct developed over years of dealing with willful animals, Mister Lamb, equally as promptly, smacked the pony in the nose with the back of his hand and said, "You impudent get!" The pony threw her head up in the air in pain and surprise and, like any defeated bully, immediately became docile.

The doctor, unaware of the mild altercation between his pony and the farmer, got out through the back door of the trap, and as he walked past Mister Lamb he absentmindedly handed him the reins.

With obsequiousness in his tone and body language Sergeant Morrissey greeted the doctor. "Good morning, Doctor Roberts."

And from the top of the hill, Mister Lamb held up the pony's reins. "I always knew if I lived long enough I'd get to do something terrible important before I died," he declared.

Ignoring Sergeant Morrissey's greeting, Doctor Roberts went down on one knee on Sally Hill. He put his hand on the victim's chest, glanced at the mess on the face, moved it about with a curious finger, wiped the finger on the seat of his trousers.

"Would you like any help, Doctor?" the sergeant asked, but he was ignored again.

The doctor rheumatically stood up and rested for a moment with his hands on his knees before going to the head of the corpse. He bent down and peered, the right knee of his trousers floured with the dust of the road. Without looking at the sergeant or Kevin Lalor, he held out his right hand, made a weak click with his thumb and middle finger, twirled his hand in a circle and said, "Turn him over."

In the bushes, Barlow said, "I can't look," but Mikey did not hear him.

Kevin and the sergeant pulled and lifted until the head moved. What was left of the ejected eye unstuck itself from the cheek, swung off the face, and became swingingly suspended in midair on stringy bits of tissue. The doctor got down on his knee again and poked at the back of the head with the pointed end of his pencil. Satisfied with his examination, he gradually stood up again, wiped the end of the pencil on the leg of his trousers and said, "That'll do."

Sergeant Morrissey and the Civil Servant lowered the body back to its original position. As they rubbed their hands together to cleanse them of contact with the dead, the doctor bent down and put the misplaced eye back on the cheek. He cleaned his fingers on the corpse's coat. Then he searched in several of his own pockets before pulling out a used envelope that looked as if it had been torn open by a hungry monkey looking for a peanut. The doctor vaguely indicated the Civil Servant with his penciled hand: "You're Lalor, Kevin Lalor." He stuck the lead of the pencil in his mouth before he wrote, used the palm of his left hand as a resting place for the envelope. He made a slight gesture in the direction of his pony and trap. "Your man on the hill, he's Lamb. Matthew? Mark? Luke?"

"Simon Peter," Kevin Lalor said.

"I knew it was a quare one," the doctor said, the recent medical probe flashing to his lips before he wrote. Then, with a glancing gesture at the sergeant, he asked, "Your name?"

Morrissey straightened himself against this indignity. "I'm the sergeant in Gohen," he said.

"I know that. What's your name?" The doctor did not look at the sergeant as he spoke.

"Sergeant Morrissey."

"Christian name?"

"Joseph."

The doctor wrote again and then pointed the end of his pencil at the corpse. "Do you recognize the corpse, guard?"

Morrissey reddened at this instant demotion through the ranks, and he could not allow the insult to pass. "Sergeant!" he said, and paused for effect.

"The corpse's name, not yours," the doctor snapped.

"Jarlath Coughlin, priest," the cowed lawman replied.

The doctor wrote and put the envelope back in his pocket. "I'm finished," he said, and he started back up to his pony and trap.

"Is he dead or what, Doctor Roberts?" the sergeant called angrily.

The doctor did not turn around as he raised a hand in the air and swept the sergeant into oblivion with a dismissive gesture. "'Course he's dead," he muttered. He continued on past Mister Lamb, taking the reins from the outstretched hand, and stepped into the trap through the door in the back. The bellyband whipped up into the pony's stomach and she angrily laid her ears back along her skull. Mister Lamb raised his hand in warning.

"You ought to put a muzzle on that pony of yours," he said. But Doctor Roberts did not hear him as he jerked the pony's head around and started back toward Gohen. The three men and the two boys watched, and the moment the trap disappeared around the corner, the sergeant began the task of recovering his authority. "Of course, any eegit can see your man is dead, but a doctor has to say a body is dead before it can be moved. Only for that I wouldn't ask him at all. Fecking contrary Protestant!"

"The sergeant cursed the doctor," the whisper in Mikey's head said.

"I'm going home to milk my cows," Mister Lamb declared, and he emphasized his intention by putting his foot on the pedal of his bike.

"No, Mister Lamb, you are *not* going home." Sergeant Morrissey grasped at his ruined authority with his angry voice. "You are going into Gohen on that bike of yours, and you're going to tell Guard Doran to call Dublin and tell them we want the superintendent because we have a corpse."

"Aw, Joe. Have a heart. I'm starting on the headland of the barley today, and I'll never get going with this carry-on. Can't you go into Gohen yourself?"

"Remember you're assisting the Law, Mister Lamb, and—"

"Will the fecking law help me with me barley, Joe, or—?"

"Mister Lamb, the Law says I have to guard the body. Go to Gohen and tell Guard Doran to come out here to relieve me so I can go home to polish my boots before the super gets here. Don't tell Guard Doran who 'tis that's dead. The Coughlins have to know the news before anyone else, and Mister Lalor here is going to go to the Coughlins to tell them."

"Joe, I'm late for work as it is," Kevin Lalor objected.

"You're assisting the Law, Mister Lalor."

"Well, if *I* have to assist the fecking Law," Simon Peter Lamb said, "I'm going to do it right now or the fecking day will be over before I get to sharpen the fecking scythe." He turned his bike toward Gohen and put his foot on the pedal.

"Wait, Simon Peter," the Civil Servant called. "Joe here is doing this all arseways. I have to go to Gohen one way or the other, so I can tell Doran when I pass the barracks. You're only a mile from the Coughlins, and you can tell them and then go home to milk."

"Now you're talking," Mister Lamb said, and he turned his bike back down the hill.

Kevin Lalor walked into the roadside grass to retrieve his bike from the barbed-wire fence.

"Now, hold on there a minute," the sergeant barked. "I'm the one in charge here, and youse must do as I say."

But Simon Peter was already on his bike, and, while avoiding eye contact with the corpse, he swept down the hill past the sergeant. "Kevin makes more sense than you do, Joe," he called out.

"Mister Lalor—" the sergeant began, but Lalor cut him off.

"I know what to tell Doran," he said, and he pushed his bike up the hill, threw his leg over the saddle and rode off.

Sergeant Morrissey slowly climbed the hill and stood looking at the empty road leading to Gohen.

"Now," Barlow said, and he poked Mikey. "Come on."

"The cans," Mikey said, and they took their mushroom cans out of the grass. Mikey led the way back through the sallies into the Back Batens. When he emerged into the sunlight, he turned, put his finger across his lips. Doubled over like osteoporotic old men, the two shuffled along the hedge until they knew the Lower Road had bent away from Sally Hill.

When Barlow caught up, the two boys collapsed into the long cool grass. They stretched their arms straight out and made vees with their extended legs. For a long time neither spoke. In the distance, a magpie sharply chattered, and a crow passing over their heads on lazy wings cawed tunelessly. Faintly, the summer hum of insects started to build up, and the sun shone warmly on the boys' faces. The tension seeped out of their bodies into the absorbing earth.

"I peed in my trousers," Mikey said.

"So did I, a little bit."

Mikey stared directly at the sun, imagining it was a hole in the sky letting in light from the outside. When he looked away, he could still see the silver disk even when he closed his eyes.

"I think Eddie Coughlin hung his own brother."

"No, he didn't."

"Didn't you hear Kevin talking about the rope in the tree?"

"The rope was to knock his brother off the bike. He tied one end to a tree and held the other end."

"Oh. I thought he hung him."

Silence.

A woodquest rocketed across the high sky on furious and squeaking wings.

"Why did he knock his brother off the bike?" Mikey asked.

"He stole money from Missus Madden, and Eddie wanted to take it and give it back."

"A priest would never steal money."

"That's what Eddie Coughlin said in the bushes, that his brother took it."

Silence.

Barlow plucked the flower off a buttercup and, close-up, examined the golden petals.

"Did you hear the noise Father Coughlin made?"

"That was the worst."

"No. The worst was when Kevin and the sergeant were standing ferninst us and the sergeant nearly peed on us."

"Gold dust rubs off the insides of buttercups," Barlow said.

"I know. Sometimes when you run through a field of buttercups you'd think you had golden boots."

"Big people all tell lies."

"Kevin said he never touched the corpse."

"The sergeant said they were to tell lies when he fell on the corpse. The catechism says it's a sin to tell lies."

"If the gold dust in buttercups was real gold—"

"We can't let on to anyone what we saw," Mikey interrupted.

"We'd be in terrible trouble."

"They're going to ask us why we're so late getting home, but we'll have to tell lies."

"What will we say?"

"Say we never heard the Angelus."

"But everyone hears the Angelus."

Silence.

"I thought when there was a corpse that everyone standing around would be crying."

"So did I."

"Maybe something happens to you when you go away for a long time."

Silence.

The hum of the insects grew louder. The chattering magpie was answered by another.

"One for sorrow," Mikey said.

"Two for joy," Barlow said.

"Three for a wedding."

"Four to die."

Mikey looked into the sun again, imagined what it would be like to fly through the hole in the sky, zoom through it as quick as a woodquest into the brightness on the other side of the blue.

"We'll just say we went looking farther today, because we only found two each. We'll say we went off into the Protestant fields to see if we'd find any, because we said we wouldn't get up early anymore unless we found a whole lot today."

"That's a good one," Barlow said. "And after what we saw in the bushes, I don't want to look for any more mushrooms."

"Neither do I."

The warm sun raised the summer hum another few decibels.

"Everyone who told us about the mushrooms they found was telling lies."

Their exhaustion, the sun and the hum of the insects sent them into a semiconscious state. When the first bong of the clock in Gohen began to announce the time, Mikey forced himself to count.

Ten!

He jumped up and called to Barlow. They examined their fronts for wetness and ran all the way home, the cans swinging wildly, two battered mushrooms rattling around in each one.

37

In the Sunroom

In which Patrick Bracken startles the Howards
by announcing that he knows who shot Doul
Yank.

PATRICK BRACKEN LOOKED at Sam Howard. Sam Howard looked at
Patrick Bracken. Elsie Howard said, "Well, well, well."

"Well, well, what?" Sam said.

"It's not gossip or rumor any longer. There were witnesses and,
for sure, the verdict was wrong."

"Bullscutter!" Sam said.

"Oh, oh," Elsie said.

"Oh, oh what?" Sam demanded.

"Patrick, when my husband says 'bullscutter' he is not referring
to that which is propelled from rear end of bull. It is a Protestant
expletive which Sam reserves for special occasions, like when he sees
he's trapped in chess."

Sam said, "Based on the evidence presented at the inquest for
Father Coughlin, the jury decided his death was accidental. As the
coroner supervising the inquiry into Father Coughlin's death, I insist
that the verdict rendered was the correct one."

"Sam, let's leave the Father Coughlin thing alone for the moment and talk about the Yank Gorman matter."

"But I want to clear up—"

"If I may, Sam?" Patrick interrupted. "I'd like to tell you something else that I discovered and which you may not know about the death of Lawrence Gorman. Remember Gorman was letting the bank get in on the ownership of the farm. When Mattie Mulhall asked you what could be done to stop Doul Yank from giving the farm away, you told him there were no legal maneuvers available to stop him."

"And that was a privileged conversation—"

"Oh, Sam!" Elsie said. "It was privileged for about one half minute. Mattie Mulhall had told everyone he was going to talk to you about the money being drawn against the farm, and no sooner was he out your door than he was telling everyone that you said nothing could be—"

"But you know how I am, Else, about stuff like that."

"We went through all this before, Sam. I was the one who heard it all back in gossip the next day. Mattie was saying that people had been murdered for less than for what Doul Yank was doing. You asked me not to get involved in the gossip in case anyone would *think* I was using privileged information that I'd heard from you."

"Well, then I concede it's outside the bounds of privileged information," Sam allowed.

"Patrick," Elsie said, "right after Mattie Mulhall's visit to Sam about the bank and Doul Yank and the farm, Sam told me *how* Doul Yank would get killed. Everyone knew Gorman hunted snipes for the sick nuns and anything else he could shoot, and Sam said he would have an accident with the shotgun. Just like that: he's going to have an accident with the shotgun, and two days later, just after Father Coughlin was killed, Doul Yank was dead too, shot, like Sam said, by his own nephew."

"Else," Sam said sternly, "I never said that his nephew would shoot him, and I have never said that it was the nephew who shot him. It was rumored so long that the nephew killed the Yank that it has become a fact in people's minds. But it was never proved that he did kill his uncle."

"Sam, you are the only one in the whole world who believes it was an accident."

"What else can I believe? The Dublin inspector said the death was an accident—that there would not be an inquest."

"The inspector was very cross that he had to come down here to Gohen for a second time in a week, Patrick," Elsie said. "He'd just been down for Father Coughlin, and, two days later, here was another violent death to be ruled on. He shouted something very funny at the sergeant, the one with the Cork accent. Do you remember what it was, Sam?"

Mister Howard chuckled as he spoke. "'Why couldn't he have been dead when I was down last Tuesday all the way from Dublin in the motor looking at your man?' meaning Father Coughlin."

Elsie could not contain herself. "And the sergeant says in that dreadful Cork accent of his, 'Sure, Inspector boy, he wasn't the kind of man who was given to conveniencing other people.'" Missus Howard laughed at her imitation of the high-pitched Cork accent, and Mister Howard laughed with her. "Oh, Else!" he said.

Patrick asked, "Why did the Dublin inspector recommend an inquest for Coughlin and not for Gorman?"

"Without casting aspersions," Sam said, "I would say it all came down to a matter of gray cells. Being a member of the Garda Siochána in those days should not in any way be equated with having brains. Brawn would have been the main ingredient looked for in a young country trying to get on its feet after the departure of the English. But even so, that Inspector Larkin was particularly lacking, Patrick. It was generally known in the legal community that Larkin believed all parts of the country should have a fair shot at having an inquest— that no one county should have more than another. He decided there should be an inquest for Coughlin because there hadn't been an inquest in our county for eight years. He decided against an inquest for Gorman because it would have meant a second inquest for us too soon after the other."

Elsie joined in. "Most of the guards only had minimal education. In those days most boys left school after sixth class, when they were fourteen. When they were recruited later on, they spent six months training in Dublin. Every guard in the country opened his court statements with the same words, whether they applied to the particular case or not, because that's what they learned by rote: 'Your honor, as I was proceeding . . .' Every week in the local paper guards announced they had been proceeding somewhere or other." Then Elsie used a mimicking voice. "Your honor, as I was proceeding up the road, I saw the suspect with no light on the front of his bike. On closer inspection, I discovered he hadn't a light on his rear end either."

As the humor seeped out of the room, Patrick said, "I know who killed Lawrence Gorman, and it was not his nephew."

The Howards glanced at each other and then looked at Patrick expectantly. Elsie asked, "You're not going to say it was an accident after all these years, Patrick?"

"No, I'm not," Patrick replied, and before he could finish, Elsie eagerly asked, "Then who shot him if it wasn't the nephew?"

"The nephew's wife, Peggy."

"No!" the two Howards said in unison. Then Elsie said, "Sam, oh Sam, we've been wrong all this time."

Sam was glaring at the preposterous thing Patrick had suggested. But then his face changed, and he looked out into the garden as if trying to force Peggy Mulhall into the jigsawed landscape of those long-ago years.

Elsie sat at her side of the table staring at the floor, her face reflective of the workings of her brain as it tried to adjust itself to the new information.

Sam returned from his thoughts first. "We have to be very careful here, Patrick. We *are* talking about murder *and* a reputation."

Elsie said, "But how could *you* know this, Patrick? You've been away all this time and we have been—"

"I was with Mikey and Fintan Lamb the day Lawrence Gorman was killed, and Fintan saw Peggy Mulhall in the vicinity of the shot."

"But Fintan was what . . . three or four, not much more than a baby?"

"I also saw her at the stile when we heard the shot. And Peggy Mulhall told me herself that she'd killed Gorman."

"Well, I'll be!" Missus Howard said again. "The wife! The woman! The nurturer! I wonder how she felt about it later on. Does that kind of thing bother a person till they die, especially a woman?"

"It didn't seem to bother Peggy Mulhall," Patrick said. "As a matter of fact, she was very devout in her belief that she did a good thing."

38

The Reluctant Good Neighbor

1951

In which Barlow Bracken and Fintan and
Mikey Lamb see what no one was supposed to
see, and Barlow and Mikey almost get killed by
a shotgun blast.

DEVOUT IN HER BELIEFS and envious of saintly ecstasy portrayed
in holy pictures, Annie Lamb was always mindful or hopeful
that someday she might see her own heavenly apparition. Often, in
her solitary moments, she fantasized that she might be a Bernadette
of Lourdes, a Jacinta of Fatima or a Juan Diego of Guadalupe. She
imagined a book with her own picture on the cover, eyes turned up
to God in the sky, hands joined in supplication and adoration, a nice
Italian scarf carelessly but artistically placed around her face. She
had always been sensitive about the size of her ears.

Annie Lamb would have been satisfied with a visitor less majes-
tic than God, would have been delighted to be like that woman
in Knock in County Mayo who saw John the Baptist on a wall—
recognized him, she told ecclesiastical investigators, from his picture
in the stained-glass window in the parish church, the one with the
Baptist's head on a plate and that woman's hairpins in his tongue.

Several times, Annie had thought her heavenly moment had
come, only to realize there was nothing otherworldly about what her

senses had picked up. Her most promising heavenly connection had lasted for three days, until a distant and indistinct voice turned out to be coming from a newly installed amplification speaker in Humphrey Smiley's Hardware and Farm Supply yard almost three miles away. It was only a casual comment by Mikey which had revealed the truth to her, and in silent prayer, Annie thanked heaven she had not made an enormous arse of herself by running to Father Mooney to tell him she had been chosen to be God's messenger.

At two minutes past ten on the morning of the discovery of Father Coughlin's body on Sally Hill, Annie Lamb was in her haggard reaching into a hole in the remains of last year's hayrick, cautiously feeling for hens' eggs. With the side of her face pressed into the hay as she stretched in her fingertips, Annie's mind was full of the scene on Sally Hill which Simon Peter had painted when he finally came home to milk the cows. She was thinking about how, for the rest of her life, she would be afraid of the hill in the dark because Father Coughlin's ghost would be in the vicinity.

As she thought about the ejected eye on the priestly cheek, sharp, needle-like pieces of dry hay pressed into her face, and in the far distance of Doul Yank's Back Batens, Annie saw flashes of light as bright as sunshine. Her heart quickened, and through her mind fled a herd of stampeding fears and hopes: God's chosen one, Father Jarlath Coughlin, not yet cold in death, was coming to her; she was going to receive a message from heaven, and maybe she would be granted the power to heal. People would come from all over Ireland to be cured, and Simon Peter would have to make a place for all the motors like that bone-setter down in Carlow had to do, and one way or another, her husband would have to install running water in the house for a flushing lav for the pilgrims, holy pictures all over the place. No longer conscious of the hay sticking into the side of her face, and unaware that her exploring fingers were annoying the hell out of a hen in the act of laying her egg in the dark nest, Annie watched open-mouthed as the glints of sunshine danced over the top of the green grass in Doul Yank's field. There was no doubt that the glints were moving toward her, and as she slowly withdrew her hand she was not aware that the angry hen had pecked her several times on the back of the hand and had drawn blood.

During her past pious fantasies, Annie had often wondered if she should kneel in the presence of a heavenly apparition. Now, as she stared at the approaching bits of glinting sun, as bright as a soul in the state of sanctifying grace, her knees felt weak, and she was afraid she was going to totter to the ground whether she wanted to or not. She grasped at the hay for support and saw a drop of bright blood on the back of her hand exactly in the place where a nail would have come through if she had been crucified. Her brain was full of words—asterisk, asthma, astigma—but she knew none of these was right. She tried to feel the pain Saint Teresa felt when her wounds bled, but there was nothing, except that strange feeling on one side of her head as if a crown of thorns had been lately removed. And then Annie saw that the soul of Father Coughlin was dancing around two boys running for their lives. Then she saw that the two boys were Mikey and Barlow—that the sun was glittering off their swinging mushroom cans, and she knew the soul of Father Coughlin was in some place other than Doul Yank's Back Batens.

Annie Lamb sighed a mixture of disappointment and relief.

As she walked into the farmyard with sixteen brown eggs in her praskeen and still wondering how blood had got on the back of her hand, the mushroom pickers arrived at the gate, bursting to tell their concocted story to explain their late homecoming. Before they could launch the lies from their lips, Annie, still breathing hard after her escape from sainthood, said, "I have something to tell you, boys. I told Molly when she got up, and she's gone into Quigleys on her bike for the day."

Mikey and Barlow flung cautionary glances at each other.

"Your father's inside, Mikey, putting on his good suit and Sunday boots to go over to the Coughlins' house for a while. Now, I don't want the two of you getting all upset, but there was a terrible accident, and Father Coughlin got killed last night."

The boys looked at each other and, after a split-second pause, Mikey asked, "What happened to him?"

"He fell off his bike on Sally Hill."

"Sally Hill!" Barlow echoed.

"Your father's putting on his good boots to bring stuff to the Coughlins to feed all the people who'll be calling to see them, and when he comes back I'll go to stay with Bridie. Your father is so cross it would be better to keep out of his way. Take Fintan out to the haggard, and you can eat your breakfast when your father's gone."

The boys did not get to tell their lies.

Two days later at half-past twelve, Mikey and Barlow were sitting at the kitchen table eating fried bread and fried eggs, when a freshly shaved Simon Peter, looking for assistance with the back stud of his shirt collar, came into the kitchen from the room behind the fireplace. He stumbled over Fintan on the floor, playing with an empty thread spool. "For God's sake, Fintan," Simon Peter muttered, "will you get up out of that and stop sitting in the dark where a man could trip over you and break his neck. Here, Annie," he said, and he held out the stud to his wife. His wife, all dressed in her best clothes, stopped adjusting her hat in the shaving mirror on the kitchen table to help her impatient husband. She gently slapped his fidgeting fingers out of the way.

Simon Peter said, "We'll never get the barley cut, and the sun splitting the trees for the last three days. It's a terrible time of the year for a funeral." Then, using the tone which bode no contradiction, Simon Peter commanded Mikey and Barlow to be available to work in the barley field the minute he got home. In the meantime, the two boys were to keep Fintan from falling into drains and stepping in cow dung; keep him away from nettles, and if he did get stung to rub him with a dock leaf; hold up the leg of his trousers when he had to do his pooley and make sure it didn't run down his legs into Molly's First Communion shoes.

"We should have been at that barley three days ago, the morning he got killed," Simon Peter concluded, "and only for that Sergeant Morrissey, him and his—"

Annie Lamb hit her husband in the back, stopped him from saying in front of the children what he had said during the telling of the terrible news about Father Coughlin; how the sergeant was an eegit of a man who thought he could tell everyone what to do just because he wore a uniform—"him and his Cork accent, singing like a bloody woman." In a moment of insightful and poetic inspiration, Simon Peter had declared, "The uniform may have helped Joe Morrissey with his authority, but it didn't do anything for his brains, because he's every bit as thick as he was before he put on his suit of silver buttons."

Annie moved around her husband to put in the front stud, too, and spared the household the sounds of huffing and puffing that went with the lunging and plunging of Simon Peter's impatient fingers. As she lined up the two holes of the shirt with the two holes of the collar, her hand pressed against her husband's Adam's apple and cut off his air supply. Simon Peter's face darkened until at last the stud was in place and his air flowed again. Everyone in the kitchen expelled their breath in unison.

"And don't be going near Sally Hill," Simon Peter continued with his list of instructions. "There might be guards from Dublin still there measuring and stepping around like dunghill cocks trying to look as important as new priests. You can go across the fields to Tinnakill Castle, and the minute you hear three o'clock striking you're to start heading home. And if you run into Doul—Mister Gorman, don't be telling him anything. Just keep saying you don't know, no matter what he asks you." Simon Peter put his knotted tie over his head and pushed the knot up to his throat. "Even if he wants to know your name, tell him you don't know. It's better he thinks you're stupid than to tell him anything."

"And make sure he doesn't think you're a rabbit or a partridge," Annie Lamb added.

"We'd have to be flying to be partridges," Mikey said.

"Mister Gorman's the kind who'd shoot a sitting partridge," Simon Peter declared, and his wife by way of another poke, reminded him that children repeat what adults say.

"That collar is too tight for you," Annie said trying to distract the children from her husband's indiscretion, and she tugged at the knot of the tie until it was lined up properly.

"All dressed up in the middle of the week and the sun splitting the trees!" Simon Peter said, as he raised a foot to the edge of the chair Barlow was sitting on. He laced his shining, soft Sunday boot. "And I don't want you climbing up to that magpie's nest in the Sandpit Field, either."

"One for sorrow," Fintan sputtered through untrained tongue and undisciplined lips. *An for sorry.*

"And Fintan, you're to do everything Mikey and Barlow tell you, and you're not to swing on anyone's gates."

Simon Peter changed feet on the chair and laced up his other boot. "We'll never get another day like this, and the barley bucking to be cut. Of all the days he had to . . . The middle of the week, for God's sake . . . Wait till you see! It'll be pouring tomorrow. Are you ready, Annie?"

Annie Lamb went back to the mirror and inserted a six-inch pin into her hat, the one with the black swan. She hated black, so the black swan would have to be enough to show her respect for the dead.

"Make sure to keep an eye on Fintan the whole time. That lad's always getting into trouble, and don't teach him anything wrong."

Mikey wished his father and mother would leave so that he and Barlow and Fintan could have the whole world to themselves—every big person in Clunnyboe gone to the funeral.

When the hasp on the wicker gate clicked into its catch behind the big people and their bikes, the three boys, all holding hands, left the farmyard by way of the haggard gate, Fintan in the middle.

The haggard, empty of everything except for the last bench of last year's hay, was strangely empty, a track of lush green grass out-lining the bare patch where the rick had sat all winter and a hundred winters before that, too. When they approached the ten-foot-wide wooden gate that led out into the fields, Fintan freed himself from the others. He ran ahead and slipped the short chain off the nail in the gatepost. He grabbed the third bar with his hands, stepped up on the bottom bar and said, "Push me, Mikey."

"Daddy will kill us," Mikey said, as he pushed the gate and sent Fintan swinging in a wide arc.

"Barlow, Barlow, push me back," the child called, when the gate came to a stop against the hedge.

Mikey and Barlow swung Fintan back and forth to each other in the long semi-circle, all making wheeing sounds to create the illusion of speed. Abruptly, Fintan grew tired of the game, and when he stepped off the moving gate, he fell on his face in the grass. He emerged laughing, his blond curls bedraggled with bits of straw and hay.

When they came to the roofless remains of Dan Deegan's house, the boys ran up the low pile of whitewash-speckled rubble that had once been the front wall. They looked down into the ruined kitchen, its gabled wall streaked with blackness where once there had been a fireplace and its chimney.

"The dandelions are back since we pulled them when the chickens were young," Barlow said.

"And there's the hole in the back wall with a blue tit's nest," Mikey said and pointed.

When Fintan demanded that he be shown the tit's nest, Mikey bent down, put his head between his brother's legs and lifted him up on his shoulders. A shotgun banged in the distance. In unison, the boys turned to the sound and two voices said, "Doul Yank!" while one voice said, "Owl Ank!"

As Mikey took a step down the pile of rubble, Fintan said, "Missus Mulhall on the stile."

"Where?" Mikey asked, but Fintan didn't have the words and he pointed, his arm showing one direction, the pointing finger another.

Barlow took Mikey's spyglass out of his pocket, pulled the ends apart and brought it to his eye like an explorer in a Tarzan picture. He looked along the top of the barrel until he saw someone in Doul Yank's Back Batens where the field begins to slope up the Esker. Then he peered into the narrow end. "It's Missus Mulhall, all right. She's looking around and she's pulling up her dress and she's . . . " Barlow took the spyglass from his face. He looked at Mikey. "I think she's doing her pooley," he said. Barlow and Mikey looked at each other. "Let me look," Mikey said urgently, and he took the spyglass from Barlow. "Hold on to my head, Fintan."

"Let me look," Fintan said. Et me uck.

"I missed her," Mikey said. "She's standing up and looking down at what she did. I hope she kicks something over it if she did her jow. Now she's going away. Why do girls sit down to do their pooley?"

"Et me uck," Fintan demanded and held out his hand for the spyglass, but Mikey gave it back to Barlow.

"She's gone, Fintan," Mikey said, and he carefully picked his steps down the pile of rubble to the blue tit's nest in the hole in the wall.

"You can only see a little bit of the moss," Mikey said, but Fintan had already reached into the wall and pulled the nest out, sending a shower of fine sand and pebbles down on Mikey's head.

Recriminations followed the vandalism.

In the Sandpit Field, Mikey and Barlow threw two token stones each at the forbidden magpie's nest before moving on to the Sandpit. Standing at a safe distance, they threw big stones and caused small collapses of fine sand on the sheer, vertical wall. Fintan wandered over to one of the lower side walls, drawn by the small, dark entrances of the sand martens' burrows. Fearlessly, he plunged his hand into the darkness and when he found nothing, he moved on to the next hole. When Mikey saw what his brother was doing, he stood there holding an unflung stone in his right hand. "You'll get bit," he called, speaking off his own fear of poking his hand into a dark hole where there might be an angry bird with a sharp beak or a rat with sharp teeth on an egg hunt.

As Mikey looked on, Fintan pulled his hand out of the burrow with the feet of a fluttering sand marten trapped in his fingers. Mikey and Barlow ran to him. Fintan covered the bird with his left hand and calmed the terrified wings. "Bud," he said. He uncovered the marten's head and held it out to the others. The tiny eyes were like two drops of black ink, the short beak as sharp as the thorn of a sloe bush.

"Can I pat it?" Barlow asked, and when he stretched out his finger to touch the top of the head the bird pecked at him. Barlow jumped back, and Fintan, laughing, launched the bird into the sky.

"Aw, Fintan!" Mikey said angrily. "Why did you let it get away? We wanted to touch it too."

Under the bottom strand of barbed wire, they crawled into Doul Yank's Hollow Field, and the moment he stood up, Mikey said, "Last one to the stile stinks!"

Across the late August field of barley stubbles he fled, his boots swishing in the short golden stalks. A flock of woodquests zoomed into the sky on frightened wings. From far behind him, Mikey heard Barlow's cries, calling for him to come back and begin the race on the count of three. The demands for fair play did not slow Mikey, and when he reached the far hedge he hopped up on the stile. With arms raised in victory, he proclaimed himself king of all Ireland.

But the royal reign was short-lived. Barlow and Fintan came puffing up and pushed him off his throne. On the seat of his pants in the stubble, Mikey watched as Barlow lifted Fintan onto the stile. Fintan tottered precariously on the narrow board, but Mikey wasn't worried. If the boy fell, he would land in the thick grass of the headland. Barlow plonked down in the stubbles beside Mikey, and drew up his knees to keep the sharp stubbles from hurting the backs of his legs.

Fintan stopped in the act of raising his hands above his head, and without thought he jumped off the stile. He bent over into the long grass and grunted as he came back up with a shotgun in his hands. He could only lift the gun to the height of his knees, but he managed to shuffle his feet until it was pointing in the direction of the other two boys. Before Mikey or Barlow could call out, the grinning Fintan said, "Bang, bang," and the gun slipped out of his hands.

As if controlled by the nimble fingers of a master puppeteer, Barlow and Mikey twisted away from each other, and Fintan moved his foot out of the way of the falling gun. The spread palms of the rolling boys came down flat onto the tops of the stubbles, and their bare knees were stabbed before the cropped straw gave way under their weight. But they were not aware of the sharp straw, they were not aware they were moving in the unison of long-practiced ballet dancers.

As they twisted away from the imminent danger the gun exploded with the noise of a hundred thunderclaps, and both saw the passage of the shot as it ripped a narrow track through the clay and the stubbles between them. A small cloud of dry soil and shattered straw spewed into the air like coal smoke shooting from the chimney of a speeding, miniature, puffing train.

At the far end of the field another flock of woodquests sprang into the air and disappeared over the hedge.

Wide-eyed, the three boys remained motionless in the deafness created by the gunshot. Their pale faces reflected their fright, the two older ones frightened all the more because they had felt the passage of the shredding discharge, had fine clay on their faces and bits of straw in their hair.

At the same time they all heard a cow lowing, and the familiar, soothing sound seeped into their ringing eardrums, releasing them from their terror. But, still, they spoke in whispers as if afraid the gun might be agitated into going off again.

"Don't stir, Fintan!" Mikey commanded. "Wait till we move away."

Slowly, the two boys stood up and silently high-stepped in a semicircle until they were standing behind the gun. "Now, come away from there, Fintan," Mikey whispered.

Shoulder to shoulder they stood looking down. When the gun had writhed on the ground after the blast, it had sprung itself open and the brass casings at the end of each cartridge glistened brighter than the wheaten straw in which they lay.

"Well, it can't go off anymore," Mikey said.

"Bad gun," Fintan said. And then in a croaking voice, and in sounds only a brother could understand, he told how the noise had frightened him. Finally, his words were drowned in his bawling. Mikey knelt to him in the strip of cool grass between the stubbles and the wire fence, and Fintan put his arms around his brother's neck, buried his face in his shoulder.

After a while, Mikey said, "That's Doul Yank's gun—the two hammers, and he's always showing off the ivy on the barrels. 'My etchings,' he says."

Fintan loosened his grip and slithered down into the grass between Mikey's knees. He was still trembling.

"I wonder why he left it there in the grass," Barlow said.

"Janey!" Mikey hissed. "Maybe he's doing his jow on the other side of the hedge."

This surmise caused them to gape at the stile as if Doul Yank was already coming to punish them for touching his gun. Then Barlow whispered, "If he's on the other side of the hedge, he would have heard us and started shouting."

Despite that bit of reasoning, they kept their eyes on the stile. They waited for a movement in the bushes on the far side of the barbed wire that would announce the approach of a very angry man dressed in feathered hat and knickerbockers.

Mikey whispered, "Maybe he fell off the stile and the gun landed on one side and he landed on the other."

Barlow looked in alarm at Mikey. "He'd have to be knocked out, or he'd be shouting about the gun."

Before the two boys could paralyze each other any further with fear, Fintan jumped up and trotted over to the stile. He was already climbing up onto the step before Mikey hissed at him to come back.

Fintan grasped the top strand of wire between the sharp barbs and looked out into the bushes beyond. He lifted one hand off the wire and pointed. "There!" he said.

"What's there, Fintan?" Mikey asked.

Fintan half turned on the stile and looked back. "Doul Yank," he said.

Barlow and Mikey came to their feet. "Where is he?" Barlow asked, but Fintan had turned away and was pointing again.

"Fintan!" Mikey demanded his younger brother's attention. "Look at me. Where is he?"

"There," Fintan said, and he pointed up in the sky as he turned around to look at Mikey. "On the ground."

With hesitation and trepidation, Mikey and Barlow went over to the stile and stood on each side of Fintan. There, on his back in the long grass and the dwarfy bushes, was Doul Yank with no hat on, his upper false teeth halfway out of his mouth and a very big hole his chest. It wasn't the empty space in his chest that frightened them—that immediately signified to them Doul Yank was dead. It wasn't the dull eyes or the grotesque way he was lying twisted in the nettles and grass on the other side of the stile; it wasn't the utter immobility of the body and its parts; it was his yellow false teeth, so out of place, hanging over his bottom lip. The sight of those fiendish fangs set atonal bells to clanging in the boys' heads.

Quietly, Mikey said, "Fintan, turn around and catch our hands." The two bigger boys yanked Fintan off the stile and dragged him through the stubbles. They were halfway across the field before Fintan finally got his feet under himself, and he got no answer from the fleeing boys when he asked them repeatedly, "What's wrong?" Hots ong?

39

In the Sunroom

In which Sam Howard is not convinced by what
three young boys saw, but Patrick Bracken then
tells what Peggy Mulhall told him.

Sam said, "Patrick, you haven't told us anything that proves it was
Peggy who shot the uncle."

"Fintan Lamb saw Peggy Mulhall when he looked to the sound
of the shot," Patrick said. "I saw Peggy in the spyglass squatting over
Lawrence Gorman, even if I didn't know at the time that Gorman
was on the ground under her."

"Come, now, Patrick, that's stretching it too far altogether," Sam
said. "It's almost impossible to pinpoint the source of a shot in the
countryside."

"Sam, Peggy Mulhall never even hesitated when I brought up the
subject of Lawrence Gorman three years ago. She was sitting in the corner
of her room, surrounded with pillows and blankets to keep her upright
and warm. She was an old woman who knew that nothing and nobody
in this world could touch her anymore. She died six weeks after I saw
her for the last time. After I had delicately suggested that everyone had
been whispering the wrong thing since nineteen fifty-one—saying it was
her husband who had shot Doul Yank, she said, 'Oh, it was me who . . .'"

40

What Peggy Mulhall
Said She Did

1951

How Peggy Mulhall became an outside servant,
served death up on a stile with a shotgun and
then washed the body.

"OH, IT WAS ME shot the old bollicks all right, so I did," is how she put it. "Mattie couldn't shoot the bastard because he hadn't the nerve, even though he told everyone he felt like shooting duncle. But Mattie never said anything to contradict what he knew everyone believed. He enjoyed it—everyone thinking it was him, so he did. He told me he was protecting me, the woman murderer. You know yourself, mister, like everything else about men and women, a woman murderer is worse than a man murderer. Maybe he didn't want people to know he was married to a murderess. Murderess is so opposite of giving birth, what a woman is supposed to do." Missus Mulhall paused and stared at the wall for a few moments. Then she shuddered. "I'll tell you something else, mister: not only did I shoot Doul Yank, I enjoyed shooting the bollicks. I'd do it again if I had the chance, and again and again, so I would."

A sparkle flashed across Peggy Mulhall's eyes as bright as a falling star in a January sky. "The look on his face when he knew!" She paused to enjoy what she was seeing in her memory. "I love remembering that look, and he knowing. The pity was that it all happened too quick. I wish the stuff had come out of the gun real slow, that he'd seen it coming for a couple of hours. If I had a meat grinder big enough, I would have stuffed him down into it feet first, so I would, while I turned the handle as slow as I could, maybe one turn an hour. That's what I would have done. He was nothing but pure bollicks." Another meteorite flashed across the wintry sky, and she drifted away, her dreamy face wrapped in the long, thick strands of her own gray hair. "I remember the exact minute the notion to kill the bollicks came into my head, so I do. I was in Estelle Butler's pony and trap going to Gohen and she was talking dirty. She loved talking dirty, that one. I think there was something wrong with her between the legs. Mattie had gone to your man, Mister Esquire Howard, to see if anything could be done to stop Doul Yank taking money out of the bank against the farm. And Mister Esquire told Mattie that the only thing that would stop Doul Yank was death, so he did. In Estelle's trap I suddenly discovered how the bollicks and death were going to meet. In the weeks it took me to get around to doing it, I felt strange, so I did, like strong or something, looking at the bollicks and knowing what he didn't know, that he was soon going to be a rotten corpse instead of a rotten bollicks. It was like I was playing with him like a cat with a mouse, and I liked it, I wanted to keep putting it off, it was so nice to know what was coming. And then when Eddie-the-cap killed his brother on Sally Hill, it was like the first drill in a potato field had been opened and all I had to do was keep the horse in the furrow to keep the rest of the drills straight. And it was so nice when I did do it, so it was—shoot the bollicks. Besides having a newborn babby on my chest, the best feeling I ever had was executing that mangy hure. It was the look of him that made it so good. It was like he saw himself in a mirror for the first time when he looked at me, saw for the first time in his life how other people saw him, saw what a terrible old bollicks he was. He saw in my face the pleasure I was taking out of scooping him up and throwing him out of our lives, like I'd shovel over the hedge a dung left by a dog in a wrong place. I enjoyed killing him, so I did, for being such a smelly bit of dung.

God, I felt so good about that, pulling the trigger of his own gun. But I didn't know what the gun would do to him. It lifted him right off the stile and into the air and bits of his chest went flying out behind him. I never knew till after, when I was home again, that the gun broke one of my fingers, this one."

Peggy's right hand moved on her lap and she moved a crooked index finger that looked like a long-ago broken toe on a crow's foot.

"It hit me in the chest, too, so it did, and I was sore for a month, the end of the gun, the wooden part, right on the breast. And it was because he was such a bollicks that he gave me the gun in the first place. He always thought he should have an outside servant to carry his gun for him like the English in India, besides one to serve him in the house. Bloody breakfast every morning with ketchup and the fish on Friday with the ketchup. Ketchup! I hate that fecking word: ketchup. Him and his fucking ketchup! That's why he called me over when he saw me in the field on the far side of the hedge. I was just the inside servant who happened to be outside, so I was. He was so full of himself that it never crossed his mind that I'd been waiting for him, that I'd waited at the stile every morning since Father Coughlin got killed, knowing he'd come that way sooner or later. I only had to wait two times. It was all so easy, so it was. My plan was to offer to carry the gun to the other end of the field for him and shoot him down there in the ditch like you'd shoot an old animal that's never going to come to anything after digging its grave and walking it into the hole so you wouldn't have to be dragging it all over the place dead. But here he was handing me the gun across the stile as if to say, sure, go on and do it here. When he stopped to get his breath on the step of the stile and saw me with the barrels three foot away from his chest, he said, 'Never point a gun at anyone, it could go off.' And the look on his face when he saw the hate on my face! If I could paint like them lads on the calendars, I'd paint that look on his face and hang it over the fireplace, so I would. I might be sorry to God that I killed someone, but there's some people God puts on this earth to be killed, they're such bollickses, and Lawrence Gorman was one of them; took money out against our farm so he could have his name carved on the frigging wall of a fecking school in fucking India. It was written down in Father Coughlin's little book, so it was: "Lawrence Gorman, one hundred pounds," as clear as daylight. Coughlin and that bollocks.

"I could never remember what happened to the gun, whether it fell out of my hands or whether I put it down somewhere. But I do remember hopping up on the stile and stepping over the barbed wire and hopping down on the other side where he was lying, dead before he hit the ground. He was staring up and the yellow teeth hanging out of him, making him look worse than when he was alive. I yanked off my knickers, so I did, without even getting it caught on the heels of my boots. I put a foot each side of his face, pulled up my dress and went into a sort of a half squat and did my pooley all over his face and into his eyes and into his mouth. The rotten bollocks. I hope he's burning in hell, stuck on the end of the devil's fork like a bit of bread against the grate on a frosty morning to toast it. I took off like a greyhound, so I did, and I got into Coughlin's funeral in Gohen before the mass was over and nobody knew a thing."

41

In the Sunroom

In which Sam cogitates in the garden after being reminded it was he who told Mattie Mulhall that only death would stop Doul Yank from giving the farm to the bank.

"GOD ALMIGHTY," ELSIE SAID. "What terrible anger—to do that after shooting him. She must have gone over the edge thinking about Gorman selling the farm out from under them."

Patrick said, "It wasn't just the money and the farm. It was the way he treated Peggy, spoke to her as if he was the liege lord and she the serf."

"And is that what she said I said?" Sam interrupted. "That death was the only thing would stop Gorman from taking the money?"

"The exact words were, 'Mister Esquire told Mattie that the only thing that would stop Doul Yank was death."

Sam sat back in his chair. His eyes drifted.

Elsie was too taken up with Peggy Mulhall's behavior after Doul Yank was dead to involve herself with Sam's withdrawal. She asked, "What do you think, Patrick? Was she mad to do that, desecrate the corpse?"

"I think if she were put on trial today, Else, the defense would claim her crime was one of passion, that she was temporarily insane."

Elsie pondered for a moment. "Is a crime of passion committed when we lose our humanness, when our animalness takes control? Was Peggy reduced to her animal state fighting for her life against a predator?" Elsie was musing more than talking to anyone. Then she saw that her husband was in a reverie, that only his body was in the sunroom. She signaled to Patrick with a finger. Patrick nodded.

"Sam," Elsie said. "Sam," she said again, and waited for her husband to turn to her. "You've been orbiting Mars, Sam."

"You're right, Else. And I'm going to blast off again now into the garden for a minute." He began to move forward in the chair, to propel himself slowly into a standing position. When he stepped out into the garden, he closed the door gently.

"I know what he's going to cogitate about, and I hope his cogitation helps him to come clean with himself after all these years." Elsie said. "But I can't get Peggy Mulhall out of my head, Patrick—what she did to the body. It's such a desecration but at the same time it speaks to Peggy's frame of mind. I knew her and she was always full of good spirits. She never behaved like someone who had murdered."

"I would think it was her delight with herself for having rid the world of Doul Yank that put her in a happy state of mind for the rest of her life," Patrick said.

"I could feel Peggy Mulhall's anger when she was remembering, but I can't feel sorry for him—Doul Yank."

"And I could feel her delight, too," Patrick said.

Patrick watched Sam through the sunroom wall; saw him scanning the seat of the bench before he sat down at the fishpond.

Elsie came back from gazing at the pieta she had conjured up in her mind—woman giving water to wounded warrior. "I'm sorry for laughing, Patrick. Sometimes I laugh when I should be horrified or weeping," Elsie said, "While Sam is out there, can you tell me what happened between Kevin Lalor-the-civil-servant and Deirdre Hyland?"

"Women love the romantic," Patrick said.

"Even the breakup of romance," Elsie said. "I wonder, are we always looking for clues to help us maintain our own relationships by examining the failures of others? Or is it simply that we love gossiping, need to chatter like magpies in the long grass of loneliness to keep in touch with each other, to give courage to each other?"

Patrick said, "Beneath her glamorous exterior Deirdre Hyland was as dreary as a late November day . . ."

42

The Day Before the Inquest

1951

In which the Great Damp of autumn descends
on Ireland, and Mikey Lamb and Kevin Lalor
pass each other like two abandoned, silent and
leaking ships on a dark afternoon.

IT WAS A LATE NOVEMBER DAY in late September, and like anything
out of season, everything was wrong with it. That morning the
country had awakened to an unexpected damp autumnal day, and
when dampness descends on Ireland it is as ubiquitous and as
cloying as God in the Short Catechism.

The Damp was in the bedrooms and on the top bedcovers,
whether they were old coats or embroidered eiderdowns. The Damp
was in the clothes the people put on after hesitating in their beds like
swimmers contemplating the chilling waters of a mountain river. It
was in the kitchens even after the fires were set to blazing; it was in
the boots and overcoats and caps the people and children put on
before venturing out into the cold, liquid morning.

The Damp extinguished everyone's summer mood with the same
swift and brutal finality as a brass snuffer smothering a candle flame—
nothing left but the darkness and the insidious stink of the smok-
ing wick. The Damp was here with the same disturbing presence as
the family drunk; in one night it had descended like the precursor of

the final fungus. It might be eight months before next year's late spring sun would kill it.

The hot breath of farm animals came whitely out of their nostrils and briefly hung its shape on the cold droplets in the air. Dogs stood on tippy toes shivering, drops on their noses like those on aged men too old to care anymore about social niceties. Cats queuing up for warm milk in cowhouses angrily eyed each other. Birds ruffled their feathers on bare branches, moved their scaly feet like the fidgety hands of old women in church pews at a loss without their knitting needles.

People went to work on their bicycles wrapped in their dismal thoughts and their heaviest topcoats, ungloved hands turning red and raw on the handlebars. Depressed schoolchildren dragged themselves to cold classrooms, where everything was harder to understand and learn, the language in the catechism even stranger and more meaningless than usual. Throughout the day the dampness tightened its grip, and by evening it had penetrated the souls of the people, sending their spirits spiraling downward as efficiently as the first warm summer sun had sent them soaring.

With peaked cap resting on his eyebrows, overcoat collar tied under his chin with a huge safety pin, overcoat hem covering the tops of his cold Wellingtons, Mikey Lamb stood with his back to the gable end of his father's barn, hands buried in his pockets. His chin was on his chest, his heart in his boots. This had been, still was, the worst day of his life, the saddest, the most depressing, the dampest. His insides were aching worse than his battered face. He was crying on the outside, the salty tears flowing across his split lip and making it burn—Barlow Bracken had disappeared into England with his family last night, and the whole world was in the grip of a darkness and a dampness that would last forever.

Mikey was waiting to talk to Kevin Lalor.

Two miles away, on his way home from Gohen, Kevin Lalor was straining to keep his wobbling bike in motion as he neared the top of the Esker. The rawness of the day had found its way inside his socks, and his feet were cold. From his shoulder blades to his waist he was as cold as if he were wearing a wet blanket. His nose was cold. He hadn't eaten since breakfast. He was aching on the inside as if a frozen hand was squeezing his heart. His soul was weeping. Not even when his father and mother died had he known the feeling now residing in his chest. If he had been able to talk about it, he would have said it was the antithesis of the feeling which had inflated him after he had been introduced to Deirdre Hyland in July.

This morning Deirdre had leaned over his desk in the Courthouse. In a strong whisper she told him he was no different from any other man in Gohen. Before she said another word, the Civil Servant knew that by this equation he was no longer the apple of Deirdre's eye—that he had been consigned to membership in her vast void where resided the men of the world who had disappointed the women of the world because they had expressed behavior which defined them as males.

Mikey Lamb looked up Glower Road toward Gohen, and even before he had confirmed that Kevin Lalor was not approaching, he was lifting his right foot and planting the sole of his boot against the wall behind him in anticipation of a long wait. Like a one-legged miniature remnant of the First World War, he stood motionless, the pain in his guts twisting the flesh of his face into knots. His sadness was underpinned on a deep foundation of anger; Barlow Bracken could at least have told him, could have warned him. Not once during the long summer, not once during the days since school had resumed, had Barlow even given a hint about disappearing. He hadn't even left a message, written a note. It wasn't fair; it just wasn't fair.

This miserable morning, Mikey hadn't even had the time to miss Barlow at school before he heard that the Bracken family had gone away during the night. The schoolboys were huddled in groups whispering about it, as if a dire supernatural power had been involved in the disappearance. Some children were frightening themselves and their listeners with the breathless news that the front door and the windows of the Brackens' house were gone, and the doors of the rooms inside, too. The house was so clean that the fairies must have come and cleaned the house after the occupants had been spirited away.

Kevin Lalor crested the Esker and the moment he put pressure on the pedals to get the momentum going, a swooshing sound startled him. Then, in the handlebars, he felt the flatness of his front tire.

"What else could I expect?" he muttered as he dismounted. He lifted the bike and spun the front wheel slowly until he saw the rusty staple, one leg buried to the hilt in the rubber. "Scuttering farmers and their scuttering barbed wire and scuttering staples," he said aloud. Grasping the staple between his thumb and forefinger he pulled it out and put it in his pocket. "Nothing's any good outside the place it's supposed to be," he grumbled. With gloved hand on one handlebar, he started walking.

"Scutter!" he said to himself, and his mind filled up again with thoughts of Deirdre Hyland.

He knew now, too late, that he should never have confided in her about tomorrow's inquest. He had made a conscious decision not to confide in *anyone*, but he had fallen into the trap of showing off. If only he'd listened to the advice he'd given to Mikey Lamb many times: never show off, you'll only fall on your face.

During lunchtime yesterday, Kevin had tried to impress Deirdre Hyland in the stupidest way; he had tried to show her how clever he was by talking about how thick Sergeant Morrissey was. In so doing, he had told her what he was *not* about to reveal at the upcoming inquest.

Yesterday, on his way home after work, he'd had an uneasy feeling in his guts. Deirdre had not only failed to applaud his cleverness, but she had voiced dismay that the Civil Servant was more interested in preserving social harmony than he was in telling the whole truth. He had slapped the handlebar several times in anger at himself.

This morning, not only had the unexpected dampness depressed him the moment he felt it beside his face on the pillow, but the memory of yesterday's stupidity came galloping into his head, filling him with trepidation. And then, he was just sitting down at his desk in the Courthouse when his worst imaginings began to take on the shape of reality. There was Deirdre bearing down on him, and before he was even equated with every other male failure in Gohen and environs, he knew his dreams of a future with this woman were now as real as the mirage of a puddle of water on a tarred road in summertime.

"Feck!"

In the schoolyard some of the Tilers were pretending to know more than everyone else, scoffing at the talk of fairies, jeering at the stories about the windows and the doors. The Tilers said they knew all along that the Brackens were getting ready to go to England, that Mister Bracken had brought tea chests home from Janey Delahunty's, and this was a sure sign they were going to move.

Mikey, too proud to ask a question that would reveal his ignorance about his friend's disappearance, listened with growing anger at Barlow for not telling him.

The Tilers said that Joe Coss had come in his car in the middle of the night, and before anyone could say Jack Robinson, all the Brackens were gone. The toughest Tiler, Elbows Kelly, said the Brackens had run away to England because they were crooks.

"They were not," Mikey said.

"They were so, Sheepy-Shipey, Wammy-Lammy."

"They're not crukes," Mikey persisted, even though he was very afraid of Elbows Kelly's fists.

"Crukes, crukes!" Kelly jeered, and gleaned encouragement from the laughs of his Tiler entourage. "He can't even say the word because he never goes to the pictures. Crukes! And the Brackens were *crooks*. They owed a whole lot of money in Janey Delahunty's shop."

"No, they didn't."

"No, they didn't!" Kelly jeeringly whined back at Mikey. "Sheepy-Shipey Ba Ba, Wammy-Lammy Ma Ma." As Kelly glanced around for more encouraging smiles, Mikey ran forward and, winding up a haymaker, tried to hit his tormentor in the face. Before Mikey's fist had completed half its arc, Kelly had already beaten the snot out of him with four lightning jabs to the face. But Mikey was too angry at Barlow Bracken to give up. He wanted to land a punch no matter what the cost, and it didn't really matter what that punch landed on.

Kelly put his foot behind Mikey's feet and pushed him in the chest. Mikey didn't know he had fallen until the ground jumped up and whacked him in the rump.

Since the moment he'd been introduced to her, Kevin Lalor had been besotted by Deirdre Hyland. Lalor was not only in love with a person, he was enthralled by all her individual parts; he was blinded by the perfection of her eyes, her hair, accent, ears, nose, eyelashes, the shape of her nostrils, her lips, teeth, eyebrows, chin, neck. Her hands were masterpieces. Her skin was as flawless as the surface of a lake that hasn't known a breeze in a billion years. The underlying form her body gave to her clothing bespoke a female perfection surpassing any of the women in the pictures. Her mind was sharp. Her speech was direct. She was very clear about her likes, dislikes, prejudices, fears, hopes and expectations. She spoke correctly.

In the four months he had known her, Lalor had heroically curtailed the impulses which had been carved into his being since the time his one-celled ancestor tried to mate with a passing speck in the swamp. Not once had he even held her hand, even though he had fantasized wildly about kissing her fingers, sucking them one at a time into his mouth. In his daydreams he had been incapable of removing her last layer of clothing.

"Even if you *do* go to Germany for the operas, even though you read literature, even though you are a *civil servant* and have a *crystal set* and a *stamp collection*, you're still like the rest of them," she had said across his desk, he sitting there with his mouth open and in his guts the cold, bitter, rusting, cast-iron claw of rejection.

After she had walked away, he just sat there with his mouth open, his intestines all knotted. Across his frozen brain, vague, snowy eddies of thought wafted. He could never unsay what he'd said yesterday about the inquest. If he told her now that he'd reform himself and throw Eddie Coughlin bare-arsed onto the scales of justice she would not have him. He was simply another man. In Deirdre Hyland's mind he was just one of a zillion tadpoles wiggling around in the cold, brown water of an early spring ditch.

And all because he had wanted to show off how superior he was to that big, fat, thick galoot of a gobshite from Cork in his silver-buttoned uniform.

"I am *thoroughly* disappointed in you, and I have no desire to ever speak to you again."

To fall from grace because he had made himself superior to Sergeant Morrissey!

"Oh, good fuck!" he groaned aloud, and in a deeply visceral reaction to his own stupidity Kevin Lalor propelled his bike across Glower Road toward the ditch on the far side. Then, disembodied and dismayed at what he'd just done, he watched as his precious Raleigh lost its uprightness and, with a rattling of the bicycle chain inside the chain cover, fell out of sight.

From the gable end of his father's barn wall, Mikey Lamb lowered his foot in an unconscious reaction to what he was thinking. From the surface of the schoolyard that morning, despite his blindness, despite the blood coming out of his nose, despite not knowing how he had suddenly landed on the ground, he had propelled himself forward and thrown his arms around Elbows Kelly's leg.

Then he buried his teeth into the flesh on the side of his nemesis' knee.

He had *bitten* Kelly.

Like an ill-bred dog, he had bitten Kelly on the knee; he had sunk lower than the most miserable person in the school. Biting a person was worse than spitting on someone. There was something wrong with people who bit other people.

The shame of what he had done was pushing Mikey down into the tall weeds at the edge of the Lower Road. He didn't know he had sunk, had disappeared from view until he heard Molly calling him to come to help her with her sums. Molly even came out and stood on the road in front of him, but she didn't see him in the weeds, and he was too far gone into his own darkness to respond.

Elbows Kelly had clutched Mikey by the hair and yanked him off his flesh. Holding him as if he were the head of a guillotined king,

Kelly showed the bloody teeth marks on his knee to the circle of onlookers that had quickly gathered at the cry of "Fight, fight."

"He bit me!" Kelly shouted. "The dog bit me! He's nothing but a biting dog that should be put in a sack with a rock and drownded." Kelly began to bark and was immediately joined by twenty other howlers.

It was Mister Tracey's bell that had interrupted the humiliation. But at lunchtime, and again when school was let out at the end of the day, Mikey was greeted everywhere he went with the sounds of barking dogs. And beneath all this torture was the bottomless feeling of loss. Barlow Bracken was gone.

In the dying weeds of summer, Mikey put his forehead on his knees and cried, not caring, not even aware that the cold dampness was seeping into the seat of his pants.

The Civil Servant looked down at the spinning rear wheel of his bike, the axle mechanism clicking in his ears with the belligerent rancor of an early-morning alarm clock.

For a long time Lalor stood there, his mind a block of black ice, no thoughts zipping about, just the same lumpness of skull that is felt after walking into a phone pole in the dark. He wasn't angry, sorry, or sad. He was nothing. He was as unfeeling as the Damp. He was his own Damp.

As if reaching across from one world into another, he bent down and stretched his hand toward the rim of the back wheel of his bike. He slipped his fingers between the spokes and heaved until the bike was lying on its side at the edge of the roadside ditch. He picked it up by the handlebars and set off again toward home, guided only by instinct like an old horse.

He didn't feel the cold. He didn't feel the shocks that his airless wheel was sending up through the frame of the bike. He didn't hear the rhythmic scraping that the bent front wheel made every time it completed a revolution. He didn't know when he came within sight of the Lambs' house. He didn't know, as he passed the end of the barn, that Mikey had peeped out at the approaching noise; had decided that no matter what the Civil Servant could say, there was nothing that would alleviate the pain he was feeling.

As Kevin Lalor passed, the opening in the weeds closed in front of Mikey's eyes, and he lowered his forehead onto his knees.

43

In the Sunroom

In which Sam Howard makes a confession, even though he's a Protestant.

"POOR MIKEY," ELSIE SAID. "Poor Kevin. Even poor Deirdre; she was her own only and worst friend. I wonder how it was for them for the rest of their lives—Deirdre and Kevin—working in the same building."

"Seemingly not bad," Patrick said. "Kevin told me that Deirdre was able to make certain people invisible in her world. Kevin became invisible to her, and after his emotions regained their equilibrium, the magic began to work both ways. She became invisible to him even in narrow hallways and doorways."

"Deirdre must have lived in a sparsely populated world. She did not deign to lower herself to those beneath her, and she had few equals."

Patrick said, "Here's Sam coming back to tell us the conclusion he has reached."

"What?" Sam asked as he stepped into the sunroom.

"There you go again, walking into a conversation and saying what. My answer to that question in future will be which what are you whatting about because while you were away a lot of whats were whatted about. You will just have to be more specific with your whats."

"I'm sorry I asked," Sam said, and he plonked down into the creaky chair.

"Well, did you arrive at a conclusion?" his wife asked.

"What conclusion?"

"The conclusion you reached—what other conclusion would I be talking about?"

"There are times I don't know what you're talking about, Else."

"There are times you pretend you don't know what I'm talking about so you won't have to talk."

"Now you're in my brain, Else, misreading my snapping synapses," Sam said. "Patrick, my wife talks in enigmas sometimes."

"Sam says I talk in enigmas when he wants to avoid talking—it's a man thing, avoiding talk."

"Any man is reluctant to talk when he knows he is going to be pestered with questions while he *is* talking, all of which questions would be answered by the time he would have finished talking if he hadn't been ambushed and quizzed in the first place with every sentence spoken, or half sentence, for that matter. It's a woman thing—the interrupting. Talking to a woman can be as exhausting as running with a horse on your back in the Grand National with Becher's Brooks popping up all over the place without warning."

"He's getting poetic, Patrick," Elsie said, "and Sam . . . you're making it sound as if you can only sparkle and effervesce if courtroom or inquest-room rules are in effect, when you would have absolute control of the floor."

"Yes, I am more likely to talk at length if inquest-room or courtroom rules are in effect, where I can eject an interrupter with the flick of a finger like I did with Spud Murphy."

Elsie turned to Patrick. "Sam's introduction of playfulness into a serious conversation is the equivalent of a cerebral guilt-grimace trying to be suppressed." And turning to her husband, she said, "I believe I can observe inquest-room protocol if that's what's needed for you to make your public confession."

"Public confession?" Sam asked.

"Semi-public, Sam. Else and I are hardly the public," Patrick said. "And, a little bit of public confession never hurt anyone—makes us feel that we're no worse than most of our fellows."

"I smell a conspiracy," Sam said.

"There's no conspiracy, Sam," Patrick said. "But I do think that Else and I have independently reached an expectation."

"An expectation, no less!"

Elsie said, "Patrick and I are only assuming we arrived at the same expectation. We have not discussed the matter. And Patrick may have only reached his expectation since he arrived today, while I reached mine a long time ago."

"Actually, I reached mine several years ago," Patrick said, "not long after I began talking to the old players in the Coughlin and Gorman saga."

"You go first, Else," Sam said. "What expectation did you arrive at a long time ago?"

Without hesitation, Elsie said, "That you, David Samuel Howard, Esquire, would confess that, because of your position in Gohen, you are the cork in the bottle in which the killings of Coughlin and Gorman are sealed—the bottle being the people of Gohen and its surrounds."

"That's a terrible thing to say, Else," Sam said, but the edgy, defensive tone which he invariably used within the confines of his cerebral legal castle was not there.

Elsie wasn't finished. "Count one, Sam: you have pretended since nineteen fifty-one that the wool was pulled over your eyes at the inquest for Father Coughlin. Count two: for all these years you have hidden behind the findings pronounced by that oracle from Dublin about Lawrence Gorman's death being an accident, so that his murderer wouldn't be prosecuted. Otherwise, as a servant of the law, as a citizen, you would have been obligated to initiate charges against Doul Yank's killer."

"Anything else, Else?"

"Everyone in Gohen with half a brain knows that you know as much as everyone else about what happened in both cases."

"This is serious stuff, Else."

"Not really, Sam. The only difference this public confession of yours is going to make is that you will be acknowledging you are the one flame that the Catholics and Protestants comfortably flutter around in Gohen."

"I am an ecumenical center!" Sam exclaimed. "Like Simon Peter Lamb said when Roberts, M.D., gave him the reins of his pony, 'I always knew if I lived long enough I'd get to do something terrible important before I died.' And here I am with the power to convene an ecumenical council around myself in the village of Gohen."

"He's at it again, Patrick," Elsie said, "introducing nervous humor onto the floor while losing control of the guilt-grimace that's twitching around inside his brain."

Sam leaned toward his wife and assumed a defiant posture. "Tell me, Else, what led you to this expectation—this expectation that I'd make a public confession, and I not even a Catholic?"

"All these years I've listened to the people of Gohen talking about Coughlin and Gorman. And don't sit there and pretend that you don't know what was said, because I brought it all home to you. You always tried to dismiss it as gossip, but you knew damn well you were hearing the truth. And the truth is that you were more complicit than anyone else in covering up what really happened to the returned natives, and I knew that someday you would tell me."

"Jesus, Else!"

"Jesus yourself, Sam! And now I want to hear what Patrick has to say on the matter, what led him to his expectation."

Patrick hesitated as if waiting for permission from Sam. The old man waved a hand and cleared the floor, resigned himself to receiving the contents of the second barrel of a double-barreled shotgun.

"Mister Howard—Sam . . ."

"Jesus! I'm glad I'm not David Samuel Howard, Esquire, to you, too, Patrick. I thought for a minute Else was reading out a charge against me in a courtroom."

"The guilt-grimace is winning," Elsie said.

Patrick started again. "Sam, your grandfather and father spent their lives in Gohen. You did the same, and your son is following you. Your family belongs to Gohen, the place of Gohen—your family lives with the people of Gohen, the saints and the sinners, the Catholics and the Protestants, the one Jewish family, the Quakers and the Methodists, the foolish and the wise and the entire cross-section that is to be found in a spot of Gohen. I would even say that your family loves Gohen. From your grandfather to your son, the Howards were and are respected, are seen as the longest standing, the most solid and the most reliable pillars in the village. Your family is the safe repository of every legal secret in Gohen. You can't help but know that the people of Gohen are as protective of the Howards as much as the Howards are of the people of Gohen."

Sam asked, "Else, why aren't you telling Patrick that he's getting poetic? What are you getting at, Patrick? Spit it out. And why do I feel that an avalanche is thundering down the mountain?"

"You said that the occurrence of new people in any group might give rise to a general anxiety—remember *The Valley of*—"

Sam interrupted, "The occurrence of Coughlin and Gorman did give rise to anxiety in some people, but I never met Coughlin, and I only had a nodding acquaintance with Gorman. They didn't make me anxious."

"But you knew the effect both were having on the community of Gohen," Patrick said, and he paused for a moment before he continued. "I think that subconsciously—"

"Patrick, don't bring Freud into this," Sam said.

"Especially," Elsie said to Patrick, "if you are holding Sam's Freudian feet to the fire." She turned to her husband. "Sam, you wield Freud when it suits you. So just relax and listen and stop being so defensive."

"Jesus!" Sam said. "Go ahead, Patrick. What subconscious thing—whatever that means—did I do?"

"You told Mattie Mulhall to kill his uncle when you—"

"Mister Bracken!" The wicker chair creaked in loud protest.

"And you felt so guilty about putting the idea into his head that you confessed it to your wife in your kitchen under cover of foretelling how Lawrence Gorman would die."

"Bullscutter! I never told Mulhall any such thing."

"Not in so many words, but you *did* tell him that death was the only thing that would stop Doul Yank from taking the money out of the bank. That was like applying a not-too-subtle spark to Mattie Mulhall's smoldering mind."

"Freud again, Patrick?" Sam waved his hand dismissively. "You're accusing me of—"

"Oh, Sam," Elsie said. "You're being accused of nothing, unless it's a crime to be human."

"Mister Howard . . . Sam," Patrick said, "I don't believe that anyone could accuse you of ever having been anything but scrupulous in your professional and private life. I would never suggest—"

"What's another word for suggest? Insinuate? Accuse?"

"Oh, for God's sake, Sam, will you just shut up and listen to the man?"

"Is there more?"

Patrick said, "Simon Peter Lamb's wife, Annie—my mother-in-law—was the first person I spoke to about Father Coughlin and Lawrence Gorman-the-Yank. What she said, and what everyone else said after her, revealed there had been a cover-up and, of course, it became obvious that the cover-up could only have been possible with your assistance. Father Coughlin and Lawrence Gorman belonged to Catholic Gohen, and the Catholics all covered for you by pretending the wool had been pulled over your Protestant eyes—that the Catholics had outwitted the cleverest Protestant of them all, and you, Sam, went along with the pretense."

"Cleverest?" Elsie asked.

Patrick continued, "You yourself said some revealing things here today. And I suspect you said them, maybe subconsciously, to make way for your public confession."

"Bullscutter. More Freud."

"You said, 'We all knew that Mattie Mulhall killed Gorman, and we were all relieved when the Dublin inspector said the death was an accident.'"

"And?"

"Were you not the one who was most relieved, Sam, because of what you had said to Mattie?"

"God! You're in there in my head along with Else, misinterpreting the cracklings in my brain. What else, Patrick?"

"Several items in the minutes of the inquest show how you controlled the answers given by the witnesses."

"Oh! For Christ's sake, Patrick. You're ascribing talents to me I do not have."

Patrick continued. "Two instances stuck out; you allowed the sergeant to wander all over the place with his irrelevant observations. At the same time you seemed to do all in your power to keep the talkative Eddie Coughlin from confessing. At one point Eddie was going to say why his brother was going to the Martyr Madden's house, but you cut him off. The second instance was when you asked the Civil Servant if anyone had come to Sally Hill while he was standing watch over the body. The Civil Servant said yes, that Simon Peter Lamb had passed by on his way to Gohen for the sergeant. You let it go at that—didn't ask him if anyone else had been there because you thought that Eddie Coughlin might have been there, too, and you didn't want the Civil Servant to perjure himself."

"Is that it, Patrick? Is that what led you to think I would make a public confession?"

"No, Sam. When you decided to get the inquest papers out of their hiding place, I believe you were consciously preparing the way for the confession."

"We're out of the subconscious and into the conscious. Freud again! How did you know about the paneling on—?"

"Deduction, Sam," Patrick said. "Deduction, as the Civil Servant would have said to Mikey Lamb. And I suspect, too, that when you heard years ago that I was snooping around you asked your colleague, Mister Harrigan in Portlaoise—"

"Alphonsus A., Esquire!" Elsie almost shouted. "Oh! Sam, you didn't?"

"Didn't what, Else?"

Patrick answered, "Ask him to keep the minutes of the inquest safe from prying eyes."

"Oh! Sam," Elsie said, with reproof in her voice. "You always said Harrigan, Alphonsus A., Esquire, was an eegit."

"That's exactly why I asked him," Sam said, and Elsie clapped her hands together.

"At last, at last," she cried out. "Sam, you are finally admitting that—"

"Now, Else," Sam said, "don't start. Don't tell me what I am admitting. If I am going to admit anything, let me be the one to admit it."

"Oh, Sam," Elsie said, "I am going to sit back and observe the formalities of the inquest room. I won't say one word till you're finished."

"Have you made a quick trip to Lourdes?" Sam asked.

Elsie looked over at Patrick. Almost imperceptibly, she nodded. She folded her hands on her lap, pushed her shoulders into the cushion at the back of her chair.

Sam asked, "Did you come here today, Patrick, to expose me? To steer me to the point where you could force me to make a confession?"

"Not at all, Sam. If you had stuck to the village myth about you and Coughlin and Gorman, I would have gone away quietly. But when you began giving signs that you were ready to talk—"

"—make a public confession," Elsie lobbed in.

"—I do admit that I tried to grease the way by telling you personal details about my own family, especially AnneMarie and my father and Mikey. I tried to obligate you to reciprocate. And when you told me about your David dying in Canada, I suspected you would eventually talk about yourself and Coughlin and Gorman. There was never any intention to expose you, because there's nothing to expose. You and your family enjoy an enviable reputation in Gohen, and as far as I am concerned, that reputation is intact and well deserved."

"Maybe the reputation is not as well deserved as you want to believe, Patrick. In the cases of Coughlin-the-priest and Gorman-the-Yank, I flinched, turned a blind eye legally. I could be accused of aiding and abetting in the cover-up of two murders."

"Jesus, Sam, don't put it that way," Elsie said.

"There's no other way to put it, Else."

"You could be accused of taking care of the people of Gohen, protecting them from two predators," Patrick said.

There was silence in the sunroom. Elsie steered her eyes out into the garden, and she watched her pest-controlling thrush whacking another garden snail on the stone near the pond. Patrick turned and looked at a black and white magpie hopping across the short grass—a midget nun on a pogo stick. The snail shell broke, and the thrush tore the snail to shreds. Elsie could see the gobbled pieces swelling the gullet as they were forced down into the craw. For a moment the thrush seemed stunned or else was waiting for its body to adjust aerodynamically to the new load it had taken on board. Then, in a blur of wings it was up in the laburnum. The magpie went into a reflex crouch, sank down into the grass and scanned the sky with one eye in response to the thrush's sudden movement, but it soon resumed its searching.

"Of course, everything, or nearly everything, you have said—the two of you—is true," Sam finally said. "And I agree with Else, I have been throwing roadblocks down across your way to slow down the arrival of this moment. The simple truth is that I failed the law."

"Sam," Elsie said, "How can—?"

"Else, the rules of the inquest room are in effect." Mister Howard smiled faintly at his wife—smoothed the sharp edges she might have heard in his tone of voice.

"First of all, Father Coughlin! I did go out of my way to elicit answers from the witnesses that would lead the jury to conclude the man's death was accidental. I cut into every one of Eddie Coughlin's answers to stop him hanging himself. Of course, what Deirdre Hyland almost said here in this house about Eddie killing his brother did influence me. Second, Lawrence-the-Doul Yank Gorman. For many years I was unable to decide whether I had purposefully told

Mattie Mulhall how to solve his problem with his uncle. The fact that I couldn't decide eventually persuaded me that I was simply avoiding accepting responsibility for what I had done. So, yes, I admit that I consciously—not *sub*consciously, Patrick—planted the idea in Mattie's head that his uncle might have a hunting accident."

Mister Howard paused and narrowed his eyes as if ordering the points of an argument.

"A day has not gone by since August nineteen fifty-one when I haven't been tormented by my role in denying justice to Coughlin and Gorman. Of course, I have a rationale that I use to give myself some ease." Another pause. "In a small community where everyone knows everyone else, more than the facts immediately surrounding a case influence the application of the law. In the larger, anonymous society of the big city, prosecutors concentrate on a couple of moments of unsociable behavior in the accused's life. In the small community, the prosecutor, whether he likes it or not, and the coroner, whether he likes it or not, know the background of the accused and the backgrounds of the people close to sudden and violent death. In the case of Father Coughlin, most people saw him as a greedy spider. He was also unconscionably cruel to his own sister and brother. He even tried to get his hands on the Widow Madden's tiny World War I pension. He had such an inflated opinion of his status that he never even made his own bed. He was critical that our way of life hadn't changed much since he had left it—judging it by standards that no one except himself was familiar with. He was the classic case of the returned emigrant with the enlightened attitude. To put it bluntly and crudely, the community collectively said to Father Coughlin, 'To hell with you, Jack!' When he died, there was no one to stand up for him, not even the servants of the law—because they too, by association with the village of Gohen, had been included in his scorn. If the coroner-as-resident knew more than the coroner-at-law, if he knew that to recommend further inquiries by the guards would allow an insufferable man to further disturb the community from his grave, then I believe the coroner-as-resident was wise and humane in this case. No members of the community ever approached the coroner to thank him for being wise and humane; as Else said, they all pretend that the wool was pulled over his eyes by witnesses who didn't tell everything they knew. In this instance, the coroner is pleased to be perceived as a man with bushy eyebrows made all the more bushy with strands of sheep's wool." Sam smiled. "Doul Yank's death was just a variation on the same theme, but he was a bigger fool than Jarlath Coughlin. He tried to impress on the natives that he was a gentleman farmer—thinking a gentleman was someone who gets up late, gives unasked-for advice, dresses up to shoot birds and has tomato ketchup with every meal. Lawrence Gorman had an overblown sense of his personal importance."

Mister Howard rested his hand on the book with the brass bookmarker beside him. "Not only had Doul Yank got the best part of the bargain when he promised to will the farm to the nephew, he was willing to put Mattie and Peggy Mulhall into debt so he could play the role of the great white benefactor. Instead of being anyone's benefactor, he was one big pain in the arse and I don't know anyone who wasn't glad to be rid of him." Sam stopped talking and looked at his wife. "That's all, Else. You can now unloose your tongue."

"Sam," Elsie said, "why didn't you tell me this during all these years when our heads were on the same pillow in the dark?" She went to her husband and pulled the side of his face into her chest.

Patrick began to stand up—to remove himself from an intimate situation. Sam stopped him. "It's all right, Patrick. Sit down. I couldn't tell you, Else, because I am ashamed of myself and still feel guilty about what I did." He silenced his wife with an outstretched hand when he heard her pulling in her breath. "It's no use trying to rationalize for me, Else. There's nothing you can say that will relieve me of my guilt. I have lived with it a long time and I'll manage for whatever is left."

"But let me say, Sam," Elsie insisted. "Guilt feelings or not, you did right by the people of Gohen by protecting them from the ones who'd returned bearing nothing but misery. And as far as the people believing they pulled sheep's wool over his eyes, Patrick, I can tell you that underneath the wool he has always been a lively ram."

"Aw shucks, Else," Sam said. "We watched *The Wizard of Oz* for the ten millionth time last Sunday, Patrick. And Patrick, are you satisfied now? Is this the end of the story for you?"

"I am satisfied, Sam."

"I am satisfied, too, Sam," Elsie said. She bent down and kissed him on the lips. He rubbed her back.

"I am very glad you came to see us, Patrick," Sam said. "Very happy you did." Elsie kissed the top of Sam's head. Then she fluttered over to Patrick and took his face between her hands. She pulled him down and kissed him on the forehead. She said, "Patrick, I am delighted that you came today, so delighted. I can't tell you how delighted I am. Sam will soon feel the relief that Catholics feel when they confess their sins."

"All right, Else! Don't push it too far," Sam said.

Elsie said, "In a few days, Sam, you're going to say, 'Why didn't I tell Else all about this years ago?' And now I'm going to put the dinner on. Can you call your wife, Patrick, and ask her to come into town? We'd love to meet her." Elsie went back to her husband's chair and rubbed the top of Sam's head. "You're such a big galoot sometimes, Sam," she said in the same tone she would use to tell a grandchild he is a fuzzy wuzzy teddy bear.

Patrick said, "Wait, Else. Molly and I have plans to go out to dinner. I told her if Sam and you didn't throw me out, I would ask both of you to come with us. And Molly would love to get a tour of your house."

"That is very generous of you, Patrick," Sam said, "and before Else says another word, we accept your invitation. Where are you taking us?"

"I was hoping you'd have a suggestion."

Acknowledgments

THANKS TO my brother Mike Phelan for his thatching knowledge and to Jerome Ditkoff, M.D., for medical information.

I am grateful to the Heinrich Böll Association on Achill Island in County Mayo, the Tyrone Guthrie Centre in County Monaghan, Cill Rialaig in County Kerry, and the Ireland Fund of Monaco and the Princess Grace Irish Library for residencies that were a great help to me while writing *Lies the Mushroom Pickers Told* and other novels.

Thank you, staff of the Freeport Memorial Library, for your unfailing and enthusiastic assistance.

My gratitude to Cal Barksdale, executive editor, and his colleagues at Arcade Publishing and to my agent, Tracy Brennan of Trace Literary Agency, for their hard work on my behalf.

Thank you, family: the Hourigans and Phelans for their detailed information about farming life; my sons Joseph and Mica for their support ("Keep at it, Dad. Maybe you'll be a best seller when you're dead and we'll get the loot.")

I am especially grateful to Belfast/Mayo artist Keith Wilson.

Patricia Mansfield Phelan—my wife—has been my great encourager, she has been of wonderful and patient editorial assistance, and her suggestions, despite my occasional resistance, are always on target.

Glossary

1014: the year Brian Boru defeated the Danes at the Battle of Clontarf, near Dublin

an oul: an old; has a negative connotation: *He's an oul bollicks.*

Abel Magwitch: character in Charles Dickens's *Great Expectations* who becomes Pip's secret benefactor

alopecia: fox mange; in humans, a disease causing hair loss

Angelus: prayer honoring the announcement of the Angel Gabriel to the Virgin Mary that she was to become the mother of Jesus

ashplant: ash sapling cut to length for use as a walking stick or as a reminder to misbehaving animals

assencart: ass (donkey) and cart

aten daltar rails: eating the altar rails; receiving communion very often; showing deep religious devotion or hypocrisy

Autry, Gene: American actor (1907–1998) known as the Singing Cowboy

babby: baby

backband: chain attached to each shaft of a cart; the chain fits onto the bridge of the straddle to keep the shafts in place. See *straddle.*

Batens: name of a field, probably corruption of "beatings," meaning a place where beaters walked to raise game for shooters

Bay of Fundy: bay between New Brunswick and Nova Scotia; has the highest tidal range in the world

Bayreuth: German town where Richard Wagner's operas are performed at an annual festival

bed of straw: pile of straw neatly shaped into the size of a double-bed mattress and about five feet high

Becher's Brook: a notorious hedge-and-water jump in Aintree Racecourse in Liverpool, England. Many steeplechasers fall here.

billhook: a machete-type heavy knife on a long handle; used for cutting bushes

biro: ballpoint pen, named for the Hungarian Biro brothers, who invented it

Boadicea: queen of a Celtic tribe in Britain, she rebelled against the Romans c. 60 A.D. She lost.

bob: a shilling. There were twenty shillings in a pound, which was about $3.50.

Bogger: a person who lives in or near Ireland's Bog of Allen, which covers much of Counties Laois and Offaly. Sometimes used derogatorily by outsiders to describe an uneducated country bumpkin who speaks unintelligibly through half-closed lips

bollicks: testicles; a curmudgeon; an annoying person; one who is a pain in the arse

Brehons: judges in early medieval Ireland who dealt with civil laws, commonly called the Brehon laws. They made decisions concerning ownership of property, contracts, compensation for injury, and inheritance.

bridge (in a horse's tacklings): shaped like a Japanese-garden bridge, with three-inch "parapets" and attached to the straddle; it accepts the backband, which in turn bears the weight of the cart and its cargo on the horse's back. See *straddle*.

calfshare: rich mixture of boiled cereals fed to young calves

chester cake: made from a mixture of molasses and stale confections returned to the bakery by shops. A thin layer of pastry was applied to the top and bottom of the mixture; it was then baked and sold in small squares.

Children's Allowance: government payment to mothers to assist with the cost of rearing children

cod: a prankster; a fake. Also a verb

codding: kidding; pulling a leg

colcannon: peeled boiled potatoes mashed with butter, milk, and chopped scallions

continental money: euros from the European Union

cornerboys: out-of-work men standing at street corners and waiting for Godot

council cottage: cottage built by the local County Council and rented out

cruke: crook

dant: the aunt

dead bell: when there was a death, the parish was alerted by the ringing of the church bell at spaced intervals after the Angelus had been rung at 7 a.m., noon, and 6 p.m. Same as the bell in John Donne's "Ask not for whom the bell tolls."

deal: pine wood that has been preserved in a bog; when dry, it burns furiously; usually called *bog deal*

Desker: the Esker

Dinglish: the English

dock leaf: leaf of a dock plant, containing tannins and oxalic acid. When rubbed on skin stung by nettles, it gives immediate relief.

Doul Yank: the old Yank

eat the face off: scold viciously

eegit: idiot; fool

elevenses: in Ireland, farmworkers were given tea and food at 11 a.m. as part of their pay

elder: udder

et: ate

fair day: day the local farmers drove their livestock into the heart of the town to sell

feck, fecking: mild form of *fuck, fucking*

ferninst: opposite to; also *fernent*

First Babies: first year of kindergarten

First Fridays: pious belief that attendance at mass on the first Fridays of nine consecutive months would guarantee the ministrations of a priest at hour of death

fixed-wheel bike: bike with a drive train that keeps the pedals in motion and thus allows a person to propel the bike with one leg

frig: mild form of *feck*

Garda Siochána: literally, the civic guards; Ireland's national police force; pronounced "GAR-dah shee-a-CAW-na"

garda, newly minted: The Garda Siochána was established in 1925, so in 1951 the institution had only been in existence for twenty-six years.

get: literally, the offspring of an animal; a son-of-a-bitch, a bastard, a shithead, a cheat, a sneak, an oul shite, an old bollicks, an arsehole, an oul fecker, and possibly a real fucker

gobshite: nasal mucus; a bollicks; an underhanded person

gombeen: pejorative: merchant who takes advantage of the misfortunes of others to enrich himself

Good Companions, The: 1929 novel by J. B. Priestley

haggard: small (quarter acre), roofless, enclosed area for storing straw, hay, turnips, potatoes and other winter food for housed animals

ha'penny: halfpenny: pronounced "HAPE-ney"

hure: whore. Not necessarily a woman; often applied to a man who is a real bollicks

Indian torture: the tight grabbing of the enemy's wrist with two hands and twisting each in the opposite direction, thus inflicting pain

jobber: person who buys farm animals and sells them off quickly for a profit

jow: excrement

knickers: women's underpants

lamb's-quarters: a weed that can grow to five feet tall. It is an invasive enemy of farmers

laocoöned: to be suffocatingly entwined in woes. Laocoön was a Trojan priest who, with his two sons, was strangled by sea serpents

le vessie vieux: the old bladder

lorry: truck

Mafeking: town in South Africa where, during the Second Boer War, the British were besieged by the Boers for eight months until relieved

Marbra: corruption of Maryborough, a town in County Laois; now renamed Portlaoise ("port-leash")

mass, buying a: When a Catholic asks for a mass to be offered for a special intention, a donation is given to the priest. Masses for the souls of the dead were often requested. People could arrange to have masses said for their own souls long before they died.

me hole: my asshole; akin to saying "My ass!"

Messenger of the Sacred Heart: monthly pamphlet promoting devotion to the Sacred Heart of Jesus

motor: automobile

murrain: disease of cattle, noticeable by blood in the urine

nettles, stinging: plant with tiny hairs on leaves that sting by delivering histamine, acetylcholine and serotonin into the skin

noul, a: an old

odor: repute. Saints were often said to have died in the odor, or reputation, of sanctity

ouha: out of; depending on the speaker's tone, "Get up ouha that" can mean "You're kidding me" or "Move your fecking arse."

oul: old; considered disparaging

oul lad: old man; my old man (my father)

Our Lady of Mount Carmel: patroness of Christian hermits who lived on Mount Carmel (Israel) in the twelfth and thirteenth centuries; the present-day Carmelites are the spiritual descendants of those early hermits.

paddy bollicks: Irishman who dispenses unasked-for, useless advice under the misconception that he is exhibiting wisdom, knowledge and experience

Padre Pio: Italian catholic saint reputed to have the gift of multilocation, the power to be in more than one place at the same time

Passchendaele: town in Belgium located five and a half miles from Ypres. The Third Battle of Ypres, fought during the First World War, is also called the Battle of Passchendaele. During the war more than 88,000 soldiers disappeared into the mud between the two towns.

Pat: There was a time when English people believed every man with an Irish accent was named Pat.

Plain, the: large stretch of level terrain between Dublin and Gohen

poepot: chamber pot

pollard: the part of grain beneath the bran; used in cattle feed

pooley: urine

Portarlington: town straddling the river Barrow, one half in County Laois, the other in County Offaly. Sometimes pronounced "por-TAR-le-ten"

praiseach: Irish word for charlock or wild mustard; a vicious, invasive, yellow-flowered weed much feared by farmers.

praskeen: Irish for "apron." Usually made with a burlap sack. One end of the sack is tied around the waist and the two hanging corners are brought together in the grasp of one hand. The grasping hand is pulled up to the belly and a bag is formed. Praskeens were used to carry apples, potatoes, hens, cats, rhubarb, eggs, feed grain, dead rabbits, suckling pigs, a goose, ducks, one large turkey, artificial fertilizer for spreading by hand, and anything of medium size on a farm in need of carrying in a bag.

Princess Elizabeth of York: the future Elizabeth II of Great Britain

pull the straw: straw for thatching was straightened by pulling it in small handfuls out of the bed of straw

quare: queer, meaning odd; eccentric

R.I.C.: Royal Irish Constabulary; police force founded in 1822 and disbanded in 1922

right y'are: you are right; I agree with you; you're a good man; can also mean goodbye

rise the pump: prime the pump by pouring water down its dry throat

sally: the sallow tree; pussy willow

scall crow: carrion-eating grey crow that also eats small animals and young birds

scapular: two postage-stamp-sized pieces of cloth, made of the same material as the Franciscan religious habit and worn on a string around the neck

schelp: a blow, as in *I gave him a schelp on the side of his head*

scollops: thin, pliable saplings used in thatching roofs

seal of confession: Catholic priests may never repeat what they hear in the confession box

settle bed: piece of wooden furniture about six feet long and shaped like a wooden box. The lid could be opened for the storage of bedclothes. During the day it was used to sit on.

shag, shagging, shagger: a mild expletive on the same level as frig; the word had no sexual connotations

shebeen: an illicit Irish drinking house—illicit because no excise tax was paid

Sloper: person who lives on the slopes of the Esker

sloping: slyly sidling

snug: separate small room in a pub away from the "public" drinkers; usually occupied by single women or married couples

Somme, First Battle of the: major battle of the First World War that took place on July 1, 1916; there were 57,470 British casualties within the first four hours, of whom 19,240 died. Many Irishmen, especially from Ulster, died that day.

stag: rough game of tag

Stations of the Cross: a Catholic devotion of contemplation before fourteen images from the passion of Christ, beginning with the death sentence and ending with the entombment

stone: unit of weight equal to fourteen pounds

stooking: four sheaves of cereal straw were placed standing against each other, the end containing the grain at the top. The stook was erected to keep the grain dry until the sheaves were brought into the farmyard for threshing

straddle: similar to a horse's saddle, but with a wooden bridge for the backband

suck: piglet

sweets: candy

swingletree: corruption of *singletree*; a thirty-inch piece of stout wood with a hook on each end; attachment for horse-drawn, fieldwork machinery

thin (sugar beet): to thin out sugar beet seedlings so they do not smother each other. Seedlings were left nine inches apart.

thruppence: three pence, or pennies

tinker: (now considered pejorative) a person who worked with tin; an itinerant mender of kitchen utensils. The word evolved to mean a person of low character with no fixed above.

townland: for identification purposes, all of Ireland is divided into small areas called townlands. There are 61,402 townlands in the country, most of them not signposted. Most of the names come from ancient times.

tractor me hole: tractor my hole; tractor be damned. The "arse" part of arsehole is often omitted in Ireland.

tuppence: two pence, or pennies; twelve pennies in a shilling; twenty shillings in a pound sterling. In 1950 one pound was valued between three and four American dollars.

turf, turn the: after some weeks of drying in the sun and wind, sods of turf must be turned over to help the drying process

Valley of the Squinting Windows, The: 1918 novel by Brinsley MacNamara. The book, about the happenings in a fictitious Irish village, came too close to the truth and was easily recognized as the author's hometown of Delvin in County Westmeath. After publication, MacNamara never went home again, and his schoolmaster father had to emigrate.

whitewash: mixture of lime and water used to waterproof the outside walls of houses, and often used on inside walls, too, for waterproofing and decorative purposes

Wolfe Tone, Theobald: one of the leaders of the United Irishmen rebellion of 1798. He was captured and died in a British prison under suspicious circumstances.

Women's Sodality: a pious association for women organized under the patronage of a heavenly personage

woodquest: large pigeon; also called *wood pigeon* and *ring dove*

yoke: thing; something whose name the speaker momentarily forgets

yoking: placing the tacklings on an animal

Ypres: ancient walled town in Belgium, site of major battles of the First World War